BARBARA BOEHM MILLER

WHEN YOU SEE HER

When You See Her
Red Adept Publishing, LLC
104 Bugenfield Court
Garner, NC 27529
https://RedAdeptPublishing.com/

---

1.   http://StreetlightGraphics.com

For Bill

To be yourself in a world that is constantly trying to make you something else is the greatest accomplishment.
—Ralph Waldo Emerson

That Night

Autumn Valley, Wisconsin
1976

The small cast-iron frying pan felt heavy in my hand, like a stone about to drop in the sudden silence of the kitchen. Only the sound of cicadas sawing their wings together, calling out for companionship, could be heard through the open screen door. The kitchen where I stood was the most familiar place in the world to me. Indeed, I could have described, in great detail, every notch and bump of the peeling linoleum, every surface and angle of the gas-burning stove, and every line and swirl of the wood-grain table.

Time seemed to have stopped. In the normal course of events, I would have been washing the dinner dishes. The smell of fried chicken and the fainter, homey scent of cookies baked hours ago lingered in the air. It was still light outside because days went on forever in summer. I had to leave. I knew that. I pretended for another moment, though, as if nothing had happened.

I placed the skillet in the sink of dirty dishes. For a long time, I had wanted to leave the claustrophobic confines of home. However, weighing as much as I did—probably about five hundred pounds, by my estimate—the idea of going to college, having a job, or getting married had seemed impossible without losing an exorbitant, outrageous amount of weight. Every diet had failed, making any other plans beside the point. Those past efforts had been nothing more than an unnecessary waste of time. Now, I was going to simply walk out the door and not come back. How had it never occurred to me, before it was too late, that such an act had always been in my power?

First, though, I had to find the phone number Mr.—I couldn't even remember what he called himself—had given me. The other man, the bald one, was named Jim. The two of them had visited the house only three days ago to get a look at me and ask me about working as the fat lady in the carnival sideshow. Decent people didn't run away with the carnival, so I had told them "no," of course. Still, the idea of escaping my house and leaving behind my brother, Jared, and the encased drudgery of my life had been appealing enough to prevent me from crumpling the scrap of paper on which Mr. Whoever had written a telephone number to call if I changed my mind before the show left town.

Such a tiny piece of paper—easy to lose, impossible to replace—and there it was, folded in tight squares under the silverware tray. "Thank God," I said, pulling open the utility drawer, mashing my hands over the tools to find a pencil to dial the phone, since my fingers couldn't fit in the holes of the rotary dial. The sight of my reflection in the window, the whole breadth of my bulk, so wide that the glass wasn't large enough to fit my entire image, caught my eye. Leaving would mean navigating a new world, one that had not been outfitted with a strong bench and reinforced furniture and a bed to accommodate my size. The pulsing twitch of my eye appeared as a red smear that spread across my field of vision. Picking up the receiver, I couldn't remember the last time I had called someone other than Mrs. Schendel. Possibly, in my seventeen years, I had never used the telephone to contact anyone else. My mouth felt dry and creaky, like it would after eating an entire sleeve of salty crackers with no water. I had to slap my own face hard.

The paper shook in my hand as I inserted the pencil into the rotary dial, moving with care and deliberation from number to number. The line rang. Rang again and again. Each peal sounded longer, more extravagant than the one before it. Sweat, hot and itchy, beaded on my lip and dripped down from under my arms. I should have pushed the table bench closer to the telephone so I could have sat to relieve the ache spreading through my hips and knees, but maybe if any part of my body were allowed to relax, then some creeping inertia would conspire to keep me trapped in the house. Stuffing the phone between my neck and shoulder to grip my hands together, I prayed—not to God precisely but to whomever it was who had created me and given me my life. Something had to happen. Someone had to save me.

"Hello." The sound of a woman's voice on the other end of the line startled me so much that I nearly dropped the telephone. The impossible, having the exact thing that I wished to occur, had taken place. "Hello?" she repeated, annoyed impatience edging the word.

"Hello! Hello," I said. "I'm, um... I'm sorry. I didn't think you were going to answer." I wiped my wet hands on the front of my skirt.

"Yeah, well, it kept ringing and ringing, and I thought, you know, no sense running to get it, because whoever it is will hang up by the time I get there. I mean, normally, I'm up and around and doing stuff, but there's this program I wanted to watch on TV, and—"

This woman's story might go on forever. "Okay. I see. Well, I actually called to talk to... the carny man. I mean the person who runs the carnival." For a merciful instant, an exact recollection of the two men standing on the porch sprang to my mind, and I could hear the one who seemed to be in charge introduce himself. "I'd like to speak to Mr. Hinkle Musgrave," I said.

"Hinkle? Sure. I'll pass a message on to him. Let me just write it down." I could hear the woman tap the edges of a stack of paper on some hard surface.

"The thing is, actually, this is an emergency. I need to talk to him right away."

The woman's busy rustling sounds ceased. "Well, okay," she said at last. She must have cupped her hand over the receiver because her words became indistinct, part of a murmured conversation with someone else in the room.

"Hinkle here." The man's tone was a little sharp, a little annoyed, a little confused. "And who's this, and what seems to be the emergency that you think I should help you with?"

"It's me, Sarah." I coughed. "You might not remember me, but you came to my house a few days ago with that man, Jim. You said I could come work for you as the... um..." I swallowed hard to say the words. "In the sideshow, you know, as the..."

"Yes, yes, as the sideshow fat lady. So you've changed your mind, then? That's great. Not exactly what I'd call an emergency, though."

I stayed silent while Mr. Musgrave talked about meeting at his trailer the next morning to sign a contract and make arrangements of some sort. The truth was I lost track of what he was saying as soon as I understood that he meant for me to stay the night in this house.

"No, it has to be now. You see, my brother is very against my doing all of this. He cares about me. He really does. But I think it would just be better for everyone if I left before he got home." The stillness of the house, the smallness of the rooms, the prospect of an endless night alone filled me with fear, like water pouring into an overflowing pitcher.

There was a pause on the other end of the line while Mr. Musgrave apparently weighed my argument, considering the best course of action. Then I heard him swallow and take a drink. "Sorry about that, honey. I was just finishing up my dinner." He hadn't been thinking it through, after all. He had been chewing. "I'll send Jim over in a bit."

"Hurry, please."

There was no way to know or calculate how much time was available for the various correct before-leaving chores. Even so, my first move was toward the row of low bookshelves lining the back wall of the living room. After I had to leave school in the fourth grade, my father taught me himself from those texts. He would hold me next to him in the soft recliner, both of us squeezed into that tight, breathless space, while Jared watched from the dining table, bored and uninterested in the public-school homework spread out in front of him. I selected the big volume of Emerson's collected essays and poems, cumbersome and impractical though it was, because it had been my father's favorite. My father had been dead less than a year, and the thought of compounding that sad misery with having no memento of him seemed worse than failing to pack items that were actually practical and necessary.

Next, I rolled my nicer clothes around the book and tied the whole thing up in the top sheet of my bed before going to the pantry. I knew, the way a person could know obvious things, that it would be a long night, with no idea where or when my next meal would be. After lining the cleaning bucket with two cloth napkins, I filled it with a loaf of sandwich bread, the peanut butter cookies that Jared had never even tasted, and a pound of deli ham from the ice box. I hadn't eaten one bite of dinner with Jared, and the sight of so much untouched food on the counter filled me with a sudden righteous hunger. All the pieces of fried chicken from the platter didn't fit in my travel bucket anyway. They were still warm, and... I took a bite, or maybe it was two, possibly more.

The sink was a mess. Mrs. Schendel would be disappointed in me. I pushed the dirty dishes to one side of the basin to rinse the small skillet under the tap, taking care to turn my head away so that I wouldn't gag or get sick. Most of all, I wanted to be done with the tasks of packing my belongings, folding up my vital documents, and stuffing the cash I'd scoured out of the house up into the high crevasse where my left breast fell into my stomach. I longed to be outside, breathing good, clean air.

The house felt haunted already, in obvious ways but also by me, by my never-ending presence inside those walls. I turned out all the lights except for the one over the kitchen sink. "I left the light on for you, Jared." I paused for no good reason. "And... I want you to know that I did not mean for this to happen. I'm sorry. I'm just so sorry." Tears stung my eyes and rolled down my cheeks as I closed the door behind me.

A thunderstorm threatened on the purple horizon as I pressed my back into the front porch rails, waiting. After some time, a set of lights appeared in the distance and came closer, passing by the Schendels' barn, while I played a game where if I held my breath long enough, then the truck would turn up our driveway. The effort made me dizzy and, with a quick stab of longing, want to rest in my bed, to close my eyes and sleep—the siren song of certain insanity. Still, I wouldn't breathe until the lights grew bigger and brighter then switched direction toward the house, making me laugh with relief as I sucked air into my lungs. The thumping diesel of the truck's motor reminded me of my heart.

Jim cut the engine and walked toward me. "There you are," he said.

The lighthearted tone of his words relieved me, erasing my fear that he would be as sharp and annoyed as Mr. Musgrave had sounded on the phone. Looking at Jim, I realized he was quite a bit taller than I remembered. He was also older, probably around the same age my father would have been. Jim's baldness struck me as unique, too, and different from the ordinary type with an exposed pate on top and a ring of hair around the sides. He didn't have a single strand, while the skin covering his skull was nearly shiny, as if he polished his head in the mornings. A scar started near his right eye and extended down the side of his face, giving him a squinty look on one side.

"Are these all your things?" Jim pointed to my hobo's bindle and the beat-up cleaning bucket draped with a frayed dish towel.

"Yes," I whispered with quiet shame because I had so little.

Jim appeared not to notice as he picked up the bucket and hoisted my sheet bundle over his shoulder. "Don't worry," he said when he opened the passenger door of his pickup truck for me. "The 250 is good and roomy on the inside."

I could plant my foot on the running board and grab the doorframe but didn't have strength enough to pull myself up onto the seat. My arms and legs shook with the effort. Panic fluttered across my heart that I would be left behind, that I had only dreamed this escape, and that I was still back in the kitchen hours earlier, frying a pan of chicken.

Jim put both hands on the back of my skirt and squeezed my bottom. "You pull, and I'll push."

His touch, unexpected and unflinching, surprised me. *He's just trying to help,* I told myself. We drove away, the light above the kitchen sink glowing against the cloudy gray sky.

"So, Hinkle said you were in a hurry." Thunder cracked in the distance. A flash of lightning and the sudden darkness that followed made the small space of the truck cabin feel even more confined. "It's a lot of work, going from town to town and doing one show after the next," Jim continued, "but it's a good time too. You'll see."

We drove past the Schendel house, all the windows dark. Mr. Schendel was probably already asleep. Maybe Mrs. Schendel was on the mattress next to him, staring up at the shadowy ceiling, or in the kitchen, smoking a cigarette at the table.

There were a thousand questions I should ask Jim, but instead I just looked out the windshield, watching the road. Having finished the chicken in the yard, I reached my hand under the cloth napkin on top of the bucket, secretly fiddling the lacy edge of one of the peanut butter cookies.

"We can stop by my place first, so you can rest up a bit." Jim took his eyes off the road to stare at me for a moment. "What do you think of that?"

"Okay," I said. His voice sounded disjointed, a bit strange perhaps, as if he wanted me to understand more than what he was saying. There was no productive reason, though, for me to try to figure out what he meant. I was going where I was going. Every mile we traveled into the night was a stretch of distance farther away from what I needed to leave behind.

We drove out toward the fairgrounds, the Ferris wheel lights visible from some distance. Passing by the crowded parking lot and entrance, I pressed my forehead against the window for a better look, getting only a jumbled impression of light bulbs, the skeletal frames of rides, the talking and laughing of people, and the loud rushing and receding screams from the roller coaster that sped down a hill of track and turned away around the curve. A banner hung over the main entrance: 1976 Summer of Independence, it read in high white letters atop a swirling red-and-blue background.

Jim turned the truck to take us away from the thick bunches of people walking here and there so that we were moving past the backs of the booths lining that part of the midway. He veered again until we were driving over the bumpy ruts of a grass field.

The trailers where the carnival people must have lived were parked together in a group, looking like a small settlement all its own. Jim pulled up to a good-sized one compared to the others. "So," he said, fumbling for the keys as we stood in front of the door. "What made you change your mind?"

I shrugged, an exaggerated gesture. "I thought about how you said that the sideshow performers liked doing what they do and how some people can't just do regular jobs or get married and have families like everyone else."

Jim nodded. "Home, sweet home," he said, unlocking the trailer.

I had to crab walk through the narrow door sideways, scared that at any minute, laughter at the sight of me would come floating from an open window in another trailer. I felt safer and more protected once we were inside. The living room had an orange-and-brown plaid couch and chair and a small table wedged against the back wall. A kitchen with a sized-to-scale stove and refrigerator was visible over a type of half-wall partition with a countertop and leatherette swivel stools pushed up against it. I reached in to touch one of the cookies again. There was even a television.

"It's nice." That seemed like a normal sort of thing for me to say.

"I'm glad you like it. Have a seat."

My father had used mending plates to reinforce our couch and had shored up my bed with boards and cinder blocks. Jim would probably make me leave if I broke his furniture. "Oh. That's okay. I'll just stand." My feet began to ache in anticipation of being upright for an extended period of time while I pretended like nothing hurt and hoped I wouldn't have to use the bathroom. I leaned against the countertop to find a position that would both look and be comfortable.

Jim laughed. "You need to relax a little bit. It's your first night with the carnival. You'll be busy soon enough." He pulled the cushions from the couch and arranged them on the floor. "This way we can stretch out." He went down the short hallway, where I could see a bed through a half-open door. "Here. I brought a few more pillows, so we'll be more comfortable."

I eased myself down among the cushions. It wasn't exactly comfortable, but it was at least better than trying to brace myself against the counter.

"Are you hungry?" Jim took a plastic-wrapped package of meat from the refrigerator. "How about I fry us up some pork chops?" Lightning cracked the sky, illuminating the entire room. "Looks like we're going to get a doozy," Jim said just as the rain began to pound outside.

He made us a good dinner, lighting a nearly continuous chain of cigarettes while he did so. The air felt dense with fried meat and smoke, reminding me of home and Mrs. Schendel and being inside a familiar place that was knowable and understandable, even if I had wanted to leave it. An image of Jared flashed in my mind, making me squeeze my eyes closed for a second. *Don't think about it,* I said to myself because something was pounding behind my eyes, threatening to take over my body and mind and not give them back.

We sat together at the table to have dinner. Jim had stirred up a good, salty gravy from the pork fat to be sopped up with the bread and margarine he set out on the counter. "Eat up, Sarah. You don't have to be so shy," he said when he noticed me cutting a small, neat triangle of meat and raising the fork to my mouth, careful not to touch my teeth to the tines when I took a bite. Jim didn't even use silverware. He just held the chop by the bone and tore into it. "We can't have a good show if you don't eat enough." He laughed.

I did, too, because what he was saying was hilarious. "Do you have any ketchup?" I ate in front of him like I had never dared at home, dragging pork chops and bread with margarine through a slurry of thick ketchup and white gravy flecked with black pepper. Jim opened a bottle of Coca-Cola for me then a second one before asking if I wanted to try a little of the whiskey he was drinking. The sharp smell of the alcohol reminded me of Jared.

It tasted awful, like whiskey did. Jim had some half-stale Entenmann's donuts for dessert, probably left over from his breakfast. Then he flopped down on one of the cushions, his back resting against the couch frame, glass in hand, with the whiskey bottle wedged upright between two pillows. His legs were stretched out in front of him. My face flamed red with self-conscious embarrassment because he was watching me. I rubbed a finger over the nubby sugar and cinnamon left on the counter.

"Come here," he said. There didn't seem to be enough room for the both of us. Standing or sitting by Jim was one thing, but given how he had positioned himself, he would be practically lying alongside me no matter how I arranged myself on the floor.

"I'm okay," I said.

Jim motioned me over with his hand. "Sit by me. There're a lot of things we need to talk about to get you ready to be in the show. Have another drink."

I lowered myself down next to him and accepted the refilled glass. I had almost forgotten that people were going to pay money to look at me. The whiskey, now that I had grown somewhat accustomed to the taste, wasn't so terrible.

"We'll have to get some costumes made for you." Jim grazed his knuckle down my arm. "Something sleeveless with a short skirt." He rubbed the flat of his hand down my thigh and squeezed my leg a few inches above the knee. "With the hem right about here."

Jim's willingness to touch me, something I had never experienced, felt warm and satisfying. I grabbed one of the pillows he had brought from the bedroom and held it on my lap. It was the heavy feather kind, the stained ticking covered in a thin blue case that smelled vaguely unwashed, like the intimacy of a human body—Jim's body.

Jim brushed away the bangs from my forehead. The skin of his fingertips had the same texture as coarse sugar, his touch light. "Did anyone ever tell you what a pretty face you have?"

"Okay." I couldn't think of any other response to this shocking flattery. My sense of unreality formed a hard, unmovable ball in my gut. I shifted my torso to alleviate the uncomfortable fullness of my stomach, made worse by the closeness of the room, the burning sensation in my cheeks. I coughed into my hand, closing my fingers around the small bits of ketchup-red pork that had come up from my throat. Maybe there was some way to wipe them on the floor underneath the sofa. The trailer was hot. The small electric fan whirring in front of the cranked-open Florida windows didn't provide much relief. My stomach seized again. I covered my mouth, afraid to speak or move.

"Are you okay? Are you sick?" Jim held the upper part of my arm and leaned down to try to look into my face.

I kept my head lowered, pressing my hand tighter over my mouth. Tears leaked from my eyes from the strain of holding back the vomit filling my throat. I tried to think of some way out of this situation, even as I knew that it wouldn't and couldn't last forever. My coughing came out as a series of truncated little snorts that would have been retching if my hand unclutched, so I clung tighter.

"Ah, shit," Jim said, jumping up from the floor. I heard him digging around in the kitchenette, then he quick stepped back through the maze of cushions with a green plastic dishpan in his hands that he slid on the floor in front of me. I leaned forward and vomited with such ecstatic relief that the red, pushing force of it even blacked out the repeating reel of scenes playing in my mind. Jim placed his palm on my forehead to push back my hair. He rubbed my back with his other hand, alternating between small pats and gentle circles. "All right. Get it all out, and you'll feel better," he said.

After my stomach emptied, I coughed and pulled long runners of spit from my lips, snapping them from my fingers into that dishpan mess of chicken and pork and clotted gravy, squeezing my eyes closed to blot out my shame and horror. What if I had to leave? Where would I go? How would I even get there?

Jim's hand continued to move in its same soft pattern as he murmured a sibilant stream of comforting sounds. "Shhh... sssss... shhh... sut, sut, sut..."

"Let's get this mess out of here then." Jim picked up the full dish-pan, the dreadful contents of which slogged back and forth with the movement. "Shit," he said, half coughing and gagging at the awful smell. He walked out of the trailer, leaving the door open a few inch-es. As soon as he was out of sight, I struggled to my feet and went into the kitchenette, where I splashed water on my face, washed my eyes and nose, and rinsed the inside of my mouth. Muscles between my ribs and through my abdomen that I didn't know I had or had forgotten existed felt stretched with the trembling pain of exertion.

The open door was my last chance to leave. If I could make it up to the midway, maybe I would see someone I recognized who could give me a ride to Mrs. Schendel's house, or maybe I could call Mrs. Schendel, and she would come running again like she did the day my father died in the bathroom with no one there but me to figure out what to do. I would think of something to tell her. My head pounded with exhaustion, and I wished it was yesterday.

Jim stepped back inside the trailer, shaking water from the dish-pan that he must have rinsed out somewhere. "How are you feeling?" he asked.

I opened my mouth to answer, but nothing came out. I turned back toward the sink and crossed my arms in front of my face to hide my bitter helplessness.

Jim walked up behind me and put both hands on my shoulders. He was standing so close that the front of his body pressed into the back of mine. My arms dropped at the sensation of his pelvis pushed up against my backside, shocked at his hardness down there jumbled up with our clothes and other soft body pieces.

"It's nothing to cry about," Jim said, kissing the top of my head. The sensation was unexpected and tingly. No man other than my fa-ther had ever put his lips on me. I wanted to say something or make some kind of movement or do anything, but I was nailed to the floor by my sudden understanding that Jim, who up until then had been a means—a ride, a meal, an escape from a horrible string of repercussions—was more than just some supporting actor in my life's drama. He had his own ideas about what would happen next.

His talk about costumes and carnival business and rules were only props, bits of conversation, to move the evening forward to some point where the kiss on my head would be the next logical step. He provided the meat and the whiskey, the comfort and the lull, wanting something else as well, and no matter how I might try to convince myself otherwise, there was no going back to my old life. I had been right enough on one front. It was going to be a long night.

Jim handed me another Coke from the refrigerator to help settle my stomach and clean out my mouth. It tasted cold and sweet, so I drank it in three long swallows while Jim watched.

"Let's get comfortable again." Jim stretched back out on the couch cushions. I would have to walk right by the door to join him. Would he try to stop me if I left, or would he just let me turn sideways and wiggle my way out into the night? That last detail, the thought of wedging back through the narrow space and stepping down to the ground and the grotesque ungainliness of such an exit, even in the face of all the awkward, shame-inducing moments preceding it, closed off my last real thought of leaving. I sat down on the cushions, my body falling the last few inches, tinkling the glasses on the coffee table against each other. I grunted a little with the effort. "Like a piggy," Jared would have said.

Jim rubbed my arm, as if he wanted me to lie next to him. "Here, come relax with me."

I studied his face, only inches from mine, to take my mind off the burden of my body and the uncomfortable stress of navigating it through a new situation after years of being accustomed to its own, same routine played out in familiar surroundings. As close together as we were, Jim's eyes, the soft color of sky on a clear day, were beautiful to me. I touched his scar without thinking, drawn by the imperfection, unmindful for a moment of the strangeness of putting my hands on a man I barely knew.

"How old are you?" I asked.

Jim moved my hand from the side of his face to press his lips against my fingers. "Old enough."

He began unbuttoning my blouse. Never had it occurred to me that a man would have a sexual interest in me at my current weight. Every fantasy of mine—the romantic ones with a handsome husband and the more prosaic ones with the Schendels' hired hand, whose bulging forearms flexed and relaxed in a complicated way when he tossed hay bales—had been set at some point in the future when I had a trim, perfect body.

Jim pushed my shirt off my shoulders to put one hand up under the straining wire cage of my bra and closed his fingers around a nipple while he reached around and laboriously opened the line of hook-and-eye closures extending down the back of the garment. I shifted slightly to keep my tucked-away cash out of his reach. He took a breast in each hand as if determining their texture and heft.

"You're a nice big girl," he said and stood to peel off his own clothes.

Hugging my shirt and bra to my chest, I watched as he pulled his T-shirt over his head, hopped on first one foot and then the other to take off his boots and socks. I closed my eyes shut when he unbuttoned his jeans. A light heat radiated from his body as he knelt in front of me, making me turn away, not wanting to see his nakedness.

Jim laughed under his breath. He tucked his hand under my chin to pull my face away from my chest. "Hey there," he said.

When Jim had visited my house, he had looked me up and down and told me that a pretty girl like me would have a lot of admirers. Now, I chanced a glance at his body, a look so quick that it gave me little more than the impression of white skin broken up by patches of hair.

Jim pressed his face against mine so that our noses and foreheads touched, then he put his lips on my mouth. My first kiss. Never, even in my wildest imaginings, could I have conceived of or invented the circumstances under which it would take place. The gesture was soft and hard at the same time, better and more enjoyable than anything else that had happened so far. "Here, let's get the rest of these clothes off you," Jim said, sliding two fingers inside my skirt waistband.

"But... I can't. I have to..."

He would see how my skin and fat fell in long sheets and folds, with my belly hanging down to the middle of my thighs, a flesh-toned apron hiding everything underneath it.

"Just lean back then. I'll help you."

I rested my head against the couch frame while Jim took off my shoes and stockings. Willing myself not to look or move, I concentrated only on the dark nothingness behind my closed eyes. He pulled off my skirt and slip and slid my panties down my legs while I tried not to notice how they snagged on the ridge of my stomach and then snapped back. At one point, the hard, cylindrical warmth of what must have been his penis brushed against me. Jim took the shirt and bra I still held bunched up against my chest from my hands and pushed my legs apart so that he was kneeling between them.

"Come on, now. Open your eyes, Sarah."

I did for a split second, seeing what Jim saw—the avalanche of fat, spread wide and flat on the low cushions. "Oh God," I said, turning my face to the side.

Jim stroked my hair. "Hmmm," he said. "How about we move this here?" He slid both hands up under my belly overhang to push it back and to the sides. "There we go." When he moved closer to me, I could feel his hardness push the softness of my thigh. "Why don't we put this here?" He stacked one of the couch cushions on top of a bed pillow before sliding them both under my backside. "There. That's good."

He repositioned my abdominal rolls, then he put himself inside me. It hurt. I seemed to have forgotten in the midst of everything else going on that there would be pain involved. Combined with that sensation, though, was a profound sense of relief. The fear of never knowing what it felt like to have someone do this to me, to have someone want to do this to me, dissolved. I patted Jim's rib cage. He braced his body weight on his arms, his eyes shut, as if he were lost in a separate world.

"That's good. That's nice," he said.

He moved himself in and out until it was over with a warm rush I could feel inside of me. Jim brought two hand towels from the bathroom, draping one of them over my lap, while he used the other to clean himself. When I pushed it down between my legs, bloodstains bloomed on the white fabric, causing me even more embarrassment and panic at the thought that there was no way for me to wash out the stain, the evidence of my body. I pawed through the cushions to gather up my clothes to cover myself.

Jim put his arms around me to quell my frantic movements. "Don't be so worried, sweet Sarah." He held each of my hands in one of his own and stretched our arms open to look at me. "You're a beautiful woman," he said. "Don't forget that people are going to pay good money just to stare at you."

And then I smiled. Seeing Jim see me, I took the first step from being a huge invisible girl with two dead parents, who hadn't even been allowed to go to school, to becoming prancing and visible, an abundant sideshow attraction who could put on a crackerjack show night after night and who understood how fine, how thin, the line was between desire and revulsion.

Night and Day

Jim slept stretched out on the floor among the cushions and pillows, wearing only his underwear. Everything was jumbled up, ratcheting up my unease. I had an itching compulsion to reorder the couch, to return everything to its rightful place, and to wash my body. The bathroom door looked miniature and had a dreamy Alice in Wonderland quality that complicated the all-too-real problem of having to empty my bladder and being unable to pull my balled-up skirt and blouse out from under Jim. My bra was stuffed under the couch.

The small fluorescent bulb over the range top, the only light in the dark trailer, cast a slight, sickly glow over Jim's bare skin, making him look gray, a man made of ash. He didn't move and could have been dead except for the rise and fall of his chest. His right hand was tucked into the waistband of his undershorts. They were yellowed and sagged a little bit between his legs like a polishing rag.

I had to wedge myself sideways to get through the bathroom door and then press on my fat to squish and mold it piece by piece until my whole body was in the bathroom. My skin beaded with sweat from the effort and from the dread of being seen, of having someone witness the rituals I had devised for moving myself around or of having anyone even know about the need for them.

When I was finished, I went into the bedroom. There was a full-size mattress and box spring on the floor with a fitted sheet pulled free from one corner. I took the untucked top sheet from the center of the bed and wrapped it around me, glad to be able at last to cover myself. The bed looked inviting and called me to rest and sleep in forgetfulness, but I knew better than to close my eyes in this unfamiliar place. I was Wonderland Alice through the bathroom door, and now I became Goldilocks. These childish fairy tales of lost girls with streaming blond hair. I looked nothing like them. Yet they stayed with me, all of us sharing the experience of sudden entry into a world of dark enchantment. I lay down on Jim's mattress and waited. There was a drinking glass stuck fast to the surface of his night table.

A little while later, Jim started moving around in the other room. I could hear him putting the cushions back into place. I pretended to sleep while he stood in the bedroom doorway to postpone, for a little while longer, at least, what waited for me outside my bed cocoon and the four walls holding me tight inside. I couldn't say that I felt safe there or protected by Jim, but he had come to my rescue, had given me food like my father used to, and I had seen and felt him in an entirety that I had never had with any other person. I was shrouded now in a thin, worn sheet so long unwashed that its meager softness and sweet-and-sour odor might have been the same as having Jim's arms around me.

Jim padded into the bathroom. I pressed my face down into the mattress at the splashing sound of his urine hitting the water in the toilet. He walked back to the living room, and through a slit of eye, I could see him pulling on his undershirt then buttoning up his blue chambray shirt, all the while humming some monotonous melody I couldn't recognize. The repetitive rise and fall of the sound rocked me like a lullaby.

I needed to think about what was happening back at my house, to figure out how to manage the falling-domino chain of events that would require only the lightest touch to begin. The thought of Mrs. Schendel calling the house the next morning, of how her annoyance at my continued silence would change to concern and then to fear, made it hard to breathe. She would purse her lips then hang her apron on the kitchen hook where it belonged before going out the back door, with a wave to Mr. Schendel up at the barn. She would walk to my house, determined to check on me, to talk to me, to do something for me.

Jim came into the bedroom. "Hey, Sarah," he said in a loud tone. He clapped his hands together. The sharp cracking of his palms made me open my eyes even when I wanted to keep them closed. "Up and at 'em. We need to head on over to the sideshow tent. Monty's probably got a pretty good-sized tip built up by now." Jim dumped my clothes onto the foot of the bed.

"Huh? What's a tip?"

"That's the crowd the outside talker attracts. Monty's not bad at building a decent-size one. Then he gets them into the tent to see the show."

"Oh."

"Get dressed so we can head on up there." Jim walked out of the bedroom. It felt good to put on my clothes again, to be covered, to seem more normal and like myself. I felt better able to consider and analyze my situation. The idea of walking somewhere sounded exhausting.

When I came out of the bedroom, Jim was stacking dishes in the kitchen sink, a cigarette dangling from his lip. "You about ready?" he asked over his shoulder.

"I was actually thinking that..." My voice, scratchy and soft, didn't carry far enough for Jim to hear. I coughed. "You know, it would probably be a good idea for me to stay here maybe. It's not that I don't want to see the sideshow," I amended.

Jim laughed. "See it? You're going to be in it, sweetheart."

"Wait. What? You mean now? Tonight?" I fumbled at the arm of the couch, afraid of the spinning sensation that Jim's words generated. I managed to sit before I fell down, not caring how my body crashed into the furniture frame. The couch must have been sturdier than it looked, though, because it didn't break or even crack under my extreme weight. I had known, of course, that I would have to do some sort of performance or display, but I had assumed there would be a transitional period or perhaps a time of training, never considering the dangerous possibility that I would have to stand out in plain sight where anyone could recognize me.

"No time like the present," Jim said. He studied me for a moment. "Did you bring something else you could change into? I mean, you're not really giving people much to see with that outfit you've got on."

I was wearing a bark-brown skirt with a blue wave pattern embroidered along the hemline and a long-sleeve beige blouse that buttoned at the cuffs and under my chin. "All of my clothes look like this." Everything Mrs. Schendel had ever sewn or made with me provided the same degree of full coverage, the appropriate camouflage.

"Shit. I can't remember now where Fat Fanny got her stage outfits from. I know she took them with her when she left." Jim must have noticed the stunned expression of terror and confusion on my face. "She was the fat-lady act before you," he provided by way of helpful explanation.

"If I had the material, I could make my own dress. I mean, it might take me a couple of days or so, but then I'd be ready to go, I suppose."

Jim didn't respond in the instant to agree with my plan, so I kept talking to fill in the blank silence. "I always make my own clothes anyhow. My, um..." The words stalled in my mouth as I struggled to assign a descriptive role to Mrs. Schendel. "My stepmother showed me how."

"Is that right? We could use that around here." Jim smiled, generating an expected jolt of embarrassed pleasure that heated my entire body. No one had ever, in my life, suggested that I was useful, that my presence or actions could somehow improve a situation. "Ah, well.

We can figure that out later," he said. "Right now, we can make do by cutting a piece off the bottom." As he spoke, Jim rummaged through one of the kitchen drawers, looking for a pair of shears, no doubt.

"This is good broadcloth cotton with hand stitching." My tone was sharper than I wanted, but the thought of slicing up Mrs. Schendel's careful work, especially the wavy blue decorative border, made me react before I had time to think. "I mean, I could probably tuck it up and under somehow."

By unbuttoning the waistband of the skirt then reclosing it with a rubber band that Jim gave me, I had enough room to pull up the bottom edge of the skirt and have it lap back over so that the pretty embroidery showed. My legs were exposed a good five inches above my knee tops so that I had to remove my slip from underneath to keep my makeshift outfit from looking even more ridiculous. Jim also thought it would be a good idea for me to unbutton my blouse and tie the tails together to show off my stomach and cleavage.

He rubbed one of my braids, which was how I wore my plain brown hair every day, between his fingers and thumb. "You'll need to lose these. It's good to look young, but you don't want to overdo it," he said.

After untwining my hair, I gathered the whole wavy mass into one big, high ponytail. Jim told me it looked nice but that I would need some makeup to keep my face from appearing too pale and washed out in the glare of the footlights.

"Besides which, it looks like you've got a shiner coming up there." Jim tapped softly at the corner of my left eye but didn't ask how I'd gotten that bruise. When I told him I didn't own any makeup, he gave me some Vaseline from his medicine chest and had me smear a coat of it on my lips and eyelids, claiming it would give me some reflective shimmer at least.

"Good enough," Jim said, squeezing my shoulder. He dropped a pack of cigarettes into his shirt pocket, the last-minute movement of a person ready to walk out the door.

"Wait," I said. By following Jim's sequential suggestions and getting drawn into a discussion about clothes and hairstyles, I had somehow lost the bigger point of what we were talking about, of what I was advancing toward. "I don't understand what I'm supposed to do."

Jim stopped moving. "Well," he said. "The sideshow's a way for people to get a look at stuff they don't normally see. You're the fat lady act, so you do something that draws people's attention to the fat. You could dance or shimmy or have a funny song..."

"But I don't know how to do any of those things." I cut myself off before I voiced out loud my even bigger concern, my fear that someone might recognize me or connect me with that same fat girl who lived in the little house at the edge of the Schendel farm or who once in a while sat in the back at First Lutheran, taking up enough pew space for three people.

Jim seemed oblivious to my fear. "Well then," he said, "you can just talk to the people in the audience or flirt with the men. You can tell them how you eat twenty pancakes for breakfast every day and put one hundred teaspoons of sugar in your coffee."

Despite my concerted desire to convince Jim that I shouldn't be in the sideshow that night, I found myself getting caught up again in the details of what he was saying. "One hundred teaspoons of sugar wouldn't fit in a coffee cup," I protested. "And you know, I don't actually eat twenty pancakes a day. No one does." My voice had risen a notch at the notion that Jim would have these outlandish ideas about my fatness. "For your information, I drink my coffee black."

Jim shrugged. "That's not the point. The more outrageous, the better. People want things like that to be true. So you give them what they're looking for. Ready, set, let's go." Jim opened the trailer door.

In that moment, I saw that, unless I followed Jim, there was nowhere else for me to go.

Maybe no one would recognize me. It was late at night now. The good folks who saw me in church once in a while would surely be asleep at this hour. Perhaps it didn't matter anyway. The people I had encountered until this point in my life, fewer and fewer in the growing number of years since I had to leave school, considered me nothing more than a shocking, repellent visual oddity. My fatness was my entire identity to them. They wouldn't think me competent enough, sentient enough, or even human enough to have a broken heart and execute actions I would regret. Even at five hundred pounds, I was invisible. Performing in front of a crowd probably wouldn't make me any less so.

The sideshow tent was only a short walk from Jim's trailer, which was very fortunate indeed, since I wasn't sure I could have gone much farther. My pace was a great deal slower than Jim's. Every six feet or so, he would stop when he realized I had fallen behind again until at last, he wrapped my arm around his as best he could, his opposite hand covering the one I had rested in the crook of his elbow. There weren't as many people around outside as there had been when we first arrived. Jim seemed to read my thoughts.

"It's not too busy now," he said. "The rain must have cleared people out."

The late-night air smelled damp and fresh, like it had been washed, and over that scent, I detected the thick aroma of deep-fried food and the unmistakable smell of newly made popcorn. Jim lifted a piece of canvas so we could enter the tent from the back. We were in a sort of dressing room with a single fold-up metal chair and a mirror nailed to a wooden post. There was some piping and a spigot in the corner with a wash basin and an outflow underneath it.

"Huh," Jim said. "I thought Gigi would be in here. No matter. I'll find her. I'm going to go signal Monty." Jim turned to leave then glanced back at me standing there. "You're going to do fine, kid. I'll put you on first, then it's over and done, okay? When you hear me introduce you, just walk right out through here then up the couple of stairs onto the stage. There's not much of a crowd left, so this will probably be the last show of the night anyway."

Jim kissed my cheek. The gesture sparkled all the way down my spine, surprising me with its electric pleasantness. After Jim left, I thought again about the day he had come with Hinkle Musgrave to the house to ask if I wanted to join the sideshow. As they were about to leave, he drank the last of the cold, milky coffee I had served, thumping the cup so that the sugar at the bottom could fall into his mouth. The sound of him crunching the crystals between his teeth had been so distinct that I could almost taste the sweetness myself.

My hips and knees began to hurt. The chair in the dressing room probably wouldn't hold my weight, leaving me to brace myself against its back. The mirror reflected my bare skin and hunched-forward body, causing me to turn my head away from the rolling parts of myself uncovered for display, my clothes rearranged as if I were a stupid child playing dress-up and trying to look like a sexy grown-up woman. What would Jared do if he could see me now? He would turn and walk away without a word or maybe cough or gag into his fist, taking care to make the gesture loud and obvious enough for me to notice. Mrs. Schendel would tell me to cover up or remind me not to carry on so. I could hardly bear to think what my father would say. Jared's fiancée, Missy, would surely find the spectacle entertaining, at least. She would laugh until her sides hurt, until she couldn't stand the pain of laughing at me anymore.

The sound of clapping and whistling floated in from the other side of the canvas, followed by Jim's amplified voice. The show was starting. Jim was welcoming everyone, telling them they were going to see oddities of nature and feats that defied the imagination. "First up," he said, "I've got a nice young lady here with a great big heart and an even bigger backside. Folks, Sweet Sarah, who you're about to meet, weighs six hundred thirty-two pounds. And I'll have you know that's an exact figure because we had the chance to weigh her on a truck scale last week. She just finished up her dinner of eight pork chops and ten big buttermilk biscuits. I'll tell you she likes the whole thing slathered with gravy."

Jim's words caused me such embarrassment that I nearly lost my grip on the chair and fell to the ground. The thought of falling, the damage I could do to my body, terrified me. Was that how I had looked when I ate dinner in front of him?

"To tell you the truth, they say this girl likes everything she puts in her mouth to be covered in gravy." Jim waited for the laughter to die out, to give the men in the crowd a chance to whistle through their teeth at that remark, which I only half understood. As instructed, I walked toward the stage and waited on the bottom step. Jim winked at me over his shoulder. "And now, it is my distinct pleasure to present to you, appearing on stage for the first time anywhere—Sweet Sarah."

I took his outstretched hand and climbed the four steps up to the stage. He passed the microphone to me with a smile, likely meant to encourage me, then stepped off into the wing. I walked to the front of the stage.

"Hello," I said, my mouth too close to the microphone, causing an alarming audio feedback screech. People in the audience groaned and covered their ears. The footlights were bright, just like Jim had said they would be, making it hard to discern individual faces in the crowd. As my eyes adjusted, I could see people having side conversations, looking at the stage, waiting for me to do or say something. I scanned the room to see if I recognized anyone. Everyone looked like a stranger. The audience was growing restless. Jim was making some gesture off to the side, holding his fist under his chin and then pointing outward. He wanted me to use the microphone to talk to the crowd. I nodded toward him.

"Hello," I said again, with no clear idea of what to do next. These people had paid to look at a fat lady. I had poundage enough not to disappoint. "Here's the fat," I said, drawing in a whistling, amplified breath. I raised both arms above my head, eyes squeezed shut, my mouth open and teeth showing. The first burst of laughter erupted somewhere in the third row.

An old man close to the stage cupped his hand around his mouth to yell toward me. "Hey there, look at the jiggle girl." His comment drew more laughter from the people around him.

The woman sitting next to him, his wife maybe, fanned her red, fleshy face. "My God," she said. "How could anyone let themselves get like that?" The fat along her upper arm swayed with even that slight movement of her hand.

Their comments and the unexamined hypocrisy of her words in particular caused a familiar anger, as deep almost as the rage Jared used to incite, to rise up in me. They didn't know, as I did, what it meant to be a target for ridicule. They hadn't grown up in extreme isolation with a father who never wanted or would never have permitted me to leave home and have a separate life. In that thin, barren existence, only food, vast quantities of it, had brought me any solace or joy, stronger even than the shame and self-hatred eating it inspired.

A person toward the back called out to me. "Come on and do something. Don't just stand there, fatty."

The crowd laughed again, bigger and wider, feeling both surprising and familiar at the same time. My assumption that maybe people would express more interest than derision since they had paid money to see me had been wrong. I wanted to walk off the stage to hide myself, just like at home, but Jim was making a frantic gesture off to the side. Whatever literal message he was trying to convey, the meaning was the same. Do better. Be better.

"Hello there," I said. Some man near the entrance yelled that I had already said that three times, but I ignored him. "My name is..." Even though Jim had referred to me as "Sweet Sarah," there was no sense in repeating it, in making myself more memorable or identifiable. What did these people want to hear me say? "So, you're probably wondering how I got so fat like this, and, well, it's because I just never feel full." Studying the room again, I did recognize someone near the back—Hinkle Musgrave, the owner of Midstate Traveling Amusements Carnival. His arms were folded across his chest, holding that posture so tightly it looked as if he were hugging himself.

"Anyway, thanks for coming." Reasoning it was the appropriate and usual thing to do, I took my bow, both arms raised straight up with my hands toward the top of the tent and out to the sides and then flung them down and back while I leaned forward, as deeply as possible.

Passing the microphone back to Jim, I walked off the stage to the sound of some half-hearted, confused applause, passed through the dressing room, and was already standing outside before realizing that I had no idea what to do next. Jim had locked the trailer when we left, so I couldn't go there. There were lights on in some of the other trailers. Out on the midway, some places were still open, some rides still running. As I was trying to decide where to go, I pulled my skirt back into its correct position, fumbling to rebutton it.

"Hey, Sarah."

The sound of Jim's voice startled me, making me scream a bit.

Jim placed his hand on my wrist where I was trying to pull apart the jumbled mess of my hair. "You doing all right? You're shaking an awful lot."

I realized he was right. My entire body was trembling, so much so that I was afraid to answer him for fear I might bite off my tongue. I stopped messing with my hair to stare at him.

"Ah, Jesus," Jim said. He looked down at the ground with his hands on his hips. "The sideshow's great. It gives work to people who otherwise maybe couldn't get a job, you know? The thing is, though, it's not for everybody. And there's nothing wrong with that." Jim reached over to smooth my hair. "I got Monty to finish up in there because the crowd's shit anyway. We can pick up your stuff from my trailer, then I can give you a ride home. How does that sound?"

It sounded like, improbable and absurd though it was, that I had failed as a fat lady. "No," I said in a quiet voice, clasping my hands together to minimize the shaking of my body. "There's nothing at home for me. I can't go back."

Jim half smiled. "Come on. You could be in your bed in less than an hour, and things might look a lot different in the morning."

I thought about what I would see at my house in tomorrow's day-light. "I. Can't. Go. Back," I repeated, spacing the words for empha-sis, enunciating each one with force to make sure Jim understood me.

He didn't ask what I meant. Maybe as old as he was and running a sideshow like he did, Jim took it as a matter of course that every person must have some trouble somewhere, some kind of compul-sion, a backstory.

"I can do better the next time. I think it's just because before this, I didn't get out of my house too much. It's a kind of, you know, stage fright."

Even though I didn't sound very convincing, Jim said he would walk me back to his trailer. His face registered a familiar emotion, easy for me to recognize—pity. His expression reminded me of Mrs. Schendel, of how she used to tell me I could have a husband and chil-dren if I lost weight.

I thought Jim would stay with me. Instead, he disappeared out into the night again after he told me to get some rest. Even as I stretched out on Jim's mattress, thankful for an end to what had been the longest day of my life, I knew I would never sleep, fearing the sights that awaited me in the realm of the unconscious.

"Get up, Sarah." The firm persistence of Jim's words and the vigor of his shaking my shoulder made it apparent that he had been trying for some time to awaken me, giving me a dim recollection of the sound of his voice and the touch of his hand in my dreams.

Morning really had arrived. A chink of pale light crisscrossed the room, a line from the outside world streaking across the floor and bed, bisecting my face. My dreams, half-remembered fears and illusions, were like knotted ribbons, suggesting a jumble of characters who only now in the light of day were packing their bags, rolling their sharp instruments into cloth kits, and retiring to wherever it was they rested during waking hours.

My heart banged in my chest. I shouldn't have slept for so long, wasted time when Mrs. Schendel would already be up working before anybody, even Missy, would have been inside my house yet.

"Okay," I said. "What I'd really like to do, though, is find a telephone. I need to make a call first thing."

I hoped I hadn't used up Jim's good grace and indulgence the night before by sleeping in his bed. It never occurred to me that I could have left a sliver of space, regardless of how slight, for him to join me. Neither did I question my assumption that it would have been acceptable, preferable even, for me to sleep on the floor. Jim seemed different this morning, less solicitous and less interested than he had been the night before.

"Later. I've got some stuff to care of. You can go outside and take a look around, say hi to some people maybe." Jim radiated a sort of intense alertness that made me wonder if he ever slept.

When I came out of the bedroom, Jim was leaning back against the bar separating the kitchenette from the living room, holding a yellow coffee cup in one hand and a lit cigarette in the other, tapping his boot toe in obvious impatience. "All right, then," he said.

I stood in front of him like I was presenting myself for inspection and waiting for some pronouncement on my suitability. Seeing Jim standing there like any other man on the street or in this world reminded me of what he looked like without his clothes and how he had seen me and what we had done the night before. Shame and empathy for the disgust Jim must have felt, like the revulsion I experienced when I touched my own flesh, flared inside me, highlighting the uncomfortable burning sensation in my crotch. Despite that, I wanted to smash my face against his chest and to feel him grip my back—as close as I could come to being wrapped in a man's arms, of being enveloped and sheltered in a way that only a thin, beautiful woman could be.

"I've got some business to take care of. You'll need to talk to Hinkle at some point today about your contract." Jim stubbed out his cigarette. "Just so you know, he saw you up on stage last night, and he'll probably try to use that against you, so make sure you stand up for yourself."

"Okay," I said, mostly to get him to stop talking about these other things that didn't particularly interest me. "I really do need to make a telephone call right away, though, because, you see, I left without telling my stepmother what I was doing, and I would hate to have her worry."

"Later, like I said." Jim opened the door, pushing on my shoulder to get me moving. Even though there was no resemblance at all between the men, I felt a flash of Jared in the impatient stiffness of Jim's hand, heard a familiar frustration in his sigh.

I had to do what Jim said. I needed his help. Wanting to take matters into my own hands didn't make me able to do so. My father might have taught me far more than your average high-school student, but I didn't know enough about how things worked to be able to cover my own tracks.

Outside, the sun was only a dull orange shimmer on the horizon. A white haze hovered over the ground, like a dreamscape. I thought Jim might kiss me goodbye, but instead he gave me a simple pat on the back before walking away with the easy, distance-eating strides of an unencumbered person.

The surface under my feet was piebald grass in some parts, while other areas had gravel spread over patches of dirt. Last night's rain-water had filled in the deep ruts, leaving wide puddles between and behind a lot of the trailers, which when the wind stirred, gave off a vaguely unpleasant odor like sewage. Tripping and falling on such uneven ground were easy likelihoods.

I had been to the carnival exactly one other time in my life, when I was about eight years old, but it was hard to imagine that experience being any help to me. Riding the Ferris wheel then had been a terrifying experience, certain as I was that my weight, which had already made the basket feel unbalanced, would cause it to flip backward and Jared and me to fall to the ground.

"And it'll be your fault if we die, piggy," Jared said. The two of us were alone together in that tight space, with me terrified, hating every minute of it and despising, too, the ride operator, who was smoking a cigarette and talking to two teenage girls in shorts instead of paying attention.

My father did buy me a nice caramel apple afterward. The sweet creaminess of the caramel against the tart crunch of apple felt good and right in my mouth. I was taking small bites when we ran into

Mr. and Mrs. Schendel. She smiled at us, while Mr. Schendel glanced away, pretending not to notice how my father had reached out to shake hands with him.

"Really, Abraham," Mrs. Schendel told my father, "you have to be more careful about what you feed this child." She reached over to pull the apple from my hand, but I wouldn't let go of the stick and took a giant bite while there was still a chance to eat it. She wrenched it from my grasp. "Sarah, stop it," she said. "You're behaving like an animal."

I lowered my head, noticing the different shoes of men and women. My tears made soft divots on the dusty ground. My father's feet shifted from side to side.

"If Sarah can't eat her apple, then I can take care of it for her," Jared said, and then, incredibly and horribly, Mrs. Schendel handed it to him and even smiled.

"No!" I screamed. "That's not fair."

My father pressed his hand against my shoulder. "Enough now, Sarah. People are staring."

The world was an unjust place in which even then I knew I had fewer rights. It was only a caramel apple, yet it was a lesson in the sin of wanting, the pain of enjoyment, and the horrible knowledge that everyone was always looking at but never seeing me.

Later that night, Jared pulled back the quilt that divided our bedroom. "Hey, Sarah," he said, the half-eaten caramel apple in his hand. He must have hidden it somewhere when I wasn't paying attention. He took a big bite and waved the apple near my face. "I bet you wish you had some of this." The lithe outline of his body could be seen through his cotton pajamas, his wrist a network of bumps and bones. I rolled over to hide the hot, salty tears stinging my face, which was red from too much sun.

"Yum, yum, yum. Here's the scraps, piggy."

The apple core and stick hit the wall near my head, stuck for a moment, then landed on my mattress, leaving an icky brown stain on the wall. Jared laughed, letting the quilt fall back into place. I could hear him climb into his bed. The caramel along the top and bottom fringes of the apple core still tasted sweet and good. When I was certain that Jared was asleep, I ate the remnants, even the seeds, and tucked the stick up my nightgown sleeve so I would remember to drop it into the burn barrel the next morning.

Thinking about Jared was an unhelpful distraction from the situation at hand. Smoke or steam rose from a trailer near the edge of the parking area farthest from the carnival. The smell of coffee and frying bacon wafted from that direction, or maybe it was my imagination. If there were food and drink at that trailer, there might also be a telephone. I was afraid of doing the wrong thing, though. I wouldn't know any of the people who were there to eat or have Jim with me to do introductions.

There was a vacant weedy field behind the trailers and, in front of me, to my left, the quiet, empty carnival. The unmoving rides and the booths closed over with plastic sheeting or squares of plywood exuded an eerie, almost haunted feeling of abandonment. My best bet, not to mention the easiest course of action, would be to walk around to try to find someone who could maybe help me look for a telephone or to keep moving until, at the very least, I found a safe place to sit and think of a plan.

"All right, then." I walked in the opposite direction that Jim had gone, partly from fear of running into him and having to watch him extricate himself from me again but mostly because I had to pick some way to go, and it seemed as good as any. The drumming pull in my knees was still bearable, but I knew it would soon become painful. I would need to find a place other than the ground to sit because getting back up on my feet was a tricky maneuver all its own.

The muted stillness of the scene made me think everyone must still be asleep, then a voice called out to me.

"Hey there," a woman said. "Yeah, you. Come over here, will you?"

She was sitting on a lawn chair on the hard-packed dirt outside a small white travel trailer. The seat and back of the chair were made of interwoven green and white nylon strips. It would never have supported me, even if I could have managed to squeeze myself between the aluminum armrests.

She gave a low whistle. "By shit, will you look at you? You must be the new fat lady."

That word "fat" had been a wounding weapon, a destructive device plaguing me through my brief school years, in my own house and in my own mind. It made me look away from my reflection or sometimes grab handfuls of my lapping, avalanching body and twist and pull until it hurt, until it felt closer to the punishment I deserved for being blobbish and repellent. After the previous night's onstage debacle, however, the pain and memory wrapped up in that small word stayed curiously dormant. I saw that identity was simply its axiomatic self. A fat lady had to be fat.

"Come on over and have a seat." She gestured to a log someone must have rolled over to sit on alongside the trailer. Empty beer bottles and clusters of cigarette butts littered the ground, with a few starbursts of broken glass near the log, very close to the woman's bare feet. She seemed not to notice or care. The log, though, looked as sturdy as the tree it had once been, even down to the network of hairy roots attached to its bottom. Someone had looped a black brassiere over one of the roots, and a few pairs of white underpants had been arranged in a line over the top of the log.

"You can just move that stuff out of the way," she said. "I brought it out here to dry because there's just no goddamn room in the trailer."

I rolled the underwear in a straight line so that all the clothes were twirled together in a single cylinder and left the brassiere to dangle from the roots. Sitting down on that log was no easy task, and possibly, I looked like a giant squatting bullfrog, but the goodness of finding a reprieve from the strain on my body prevented me from caring.

The woman dug around in the sides of her chair to find her pouch of loose tobacco. She shook some into a rolling paper and cracked a wooden match to light her cigarette. The woman was wonderfully thin and wore a cotton housecoat pushed up above her knees. The garment looked old and flimsy, worn out in patches, a little shiny across the chest. Her feet were covered in dried dirt, her knees and elbows red, a little scaly maybe, with flaking white skin. Her hair, a cascade of color from the thick ridge of dark brown along the top to the hot, deep red at the tips, was like nothing I'd ever seen before. I wondered what unusual beauty made it grow that way.

The woman rubbed the dark smudges around her eyes. "My name's Gigi, by the way," she said.

I remembered Jim mentioning her the night before. "I'm Sarah... just Sarah," I said, not wanting to tell her my last name.

"Nice to meet you. I don't know about the 'Sarah,' though. You need something better than that," Gigi said. She took a long drag on her cigarette.

"Excuse me?"

"You need something jazzier for the show. The last fat lady was Fat Fanny—and man, she really did have an ass the size of Ohio. You're bigger, though." Gigi nodded in appreciation.

"Well, thanks," I said. "I don't suppose you know where I could find a telephone?" I looked down at the ground so Gigi couldn't see how much I wanted her to answer yes.

"Huh? Oh well, I guess your best bet would be to head into town for that."

"Oh." I wished I could think of something else to say or do to help myself.

"I don't suppose you have any aspirin, do you?" Gigi asked.

"No."

"Aw, that's too bad. This fucking hangover might kill me. The worst part is I can't even sleep it off. Every time I put my head down on the pillow, my eyes pop wide open." Gigi tipped her head back and exhaled a long plume of blue smoke. "So, how'd Jim find you, then?"

My face immediately reddened at the sound of Jim's name, at the casualness of Gigi's reference to him. "Oh well, he and Mr. Musgrave came to my house to visit, and—"

Gigi burst out laughing. "Mr. Musgrave? Jesus, I don't think I've ever heard anyone call Hinkle that. Exactly how old are you, kid?"

"Seventeen."

"Don't let on to Hinkle that you're underage." Her tone had shifted, her words harder, urgent, making me pay attention. "He'll get to thinking you're easy pickings."

And he would be right, I thought.

It occurred to me then that I didn't even know Jim's last name. I was a thousand times worse than my brother's fiancée, Missy, ever thought to be. What kind of woman would do what I had done with a man she barely knew? I tried to picture Jim's face, but aside from the memory of his scar, I couldn't do it, couldn't paint a vivid recollection in my mind. I recalled only bits and pieces of his person—the horizon of his shoulders and head with the wall, the windows rising behind him, and the otherworldly image of his closed eyes, making him look fetal and pre-human in the half light.

"Well sir," Gigi continued, "Fat Fanny left about two—no, three—years ago. She's living somewhere out in Washington State. Or maybe it's Oregon. Anyway, I hear she married some short little Portuguese fisherman who goes out on these trips for weeks at a time

and that his skin's so dark he looks like an Injun. But there's no ac-
counting for taste, I guess."

This knowledge of following in someone else's footsteps, of feeling an improbable competitive edge to be the better fat lady, to be
better liked, was unexpected. So, too, was the realization that, having
focused nearly every moment of my existence on becoming smaller
and pinning every shred of future happiness on the thin body that
I thought I would someday have, I could take such pleasure in the
plain knowledge that I was fatter than some other woman.

"So, Fat Fanny then. Did she leave because she got married, or
did she get fired or something like that because she couldn't get along
with Jim..." I could feel my face heat at the mention of Jim Last-
Name-Unknown. At the very least, I knew that Jim must like me,
or he wouldn't have done such intimate things with me. I missed
him with a sudden intensity and wanted to feel his hand stroking my
hair—an action that had never taken place but that would have been
soft and sublime—and to have him kiss my lips. This time I would
caress the side of his face.

Gigi laughed. "No, she didn't get fired. Fat Fanny was no Dolly
Dimples or anything, but she got along with Jim all right. But that's
nothing. I mean, he gets along with all the girls. Short, tall, skinny,
fat, black, white, whatever."

It slowly dawned on me that Gigi meant to say that Jim slept
with different women all the time. I hadn't known a person could be
that way, could put his body in one situation after another like that
with no thought for the consequences. The thing he had put inside
me had been in many women, meaning he could compare my naked
body against his memory of any of them. I looked down at my hands,
at the nubby nails that didn't even reach the tops of my fingertips.

"Hey, kid." Gigi leaned toward me. "Did I tell you that I'm
a sword swallower? There aren't too many lady sword swallowers
around. In fact, I might be the only one. I used to be in the cootch

show. Hinkle wasn't too crazy at first about me working the sideshow, but the men in the audience love it. I have this bit where I get down on my knees, and I get a lot of inside money for that."

I wiped my nose on my sleeve. "But you don't really swallow a sword, right? I mean it's some kind of trick."

Gigi smiled. "No, it's real, all right. No trick. You could do it yourself. You just tip your head back and open your throat, and you get used to it. The cootch show, now that was a crazy gig."

"The what?" I asked this time.

Gigi laughed. "The cootch show," she repeated. "A girl show. It's sort of like the sideshow, except only men go in. The talker comes out and gives his bally, and the girls walk around in their costumes while he talks them up. And then you get up on stage and dance and take off your clothes." Gigi narrowed her eyes and flicked the ashes from her cigarette. "You see these men out on the street or sitting in church. They're so nice and polite, but you get them inside that tent, then they're nothing but a bunch of disgusting, snorting pigs."

"Oh." My mouth felt so parched that it was difficult to speak. I tried not to picture Gigi naked, dancing in front of a crowd filled with these dirty animal men who might have been identical to the ones I saw in church or the grocery store or to Mr. Schendel or Jared or even to my father.

"Well, you can see why nobody in their right mind would want to keep doing it. Before I thought to learn the sword swallowing, Jim and me did this act for a while with me in the blade box. The sword swallowing, though, that's a real skill." Gigi shook the two fingers holding her cigarette at me. "You're lucky you got something special like being so fat. It's a hell of a lot easier than being a working act. Anyway, if you're looking for a phone, somebody will probably take a ride into town today. Although I do know that some people around here are probably going to want to lie low for the next few days until we blow out of here. The cops were around here last night, so there must have been some beef with a townie."

"The police were here?" A crow called overhead. "Is that normal?"

Gigi stared at me, smoking, considering maybe the expression on my face, how my hands clutched the fabric of my skirt. I relaxed my grip and looked away—just an easy, expected question from a new girl trying to figure out how everything worked. A warm breeze stirred my hair. *It's only the wind,* I thought to myself.

"I don't know that it's normal," Gigi said, "but it happens often enough. We're always getting hassled for some shit or other."

I had combed my hair into its usual braids before leaving the trailer, and I pulled one of the plaits over the front of my shoulder, twirling the unbound fringe of hair at the end of the rubber band, trying to think. No matter how I probed the parts of my brain responsible for imagination and conniving, no ideas were coming to me. Meanwhile, Gigi talked on about her life before the carnival, about growing up in the flat, open land of central Kansas, about the terrifying storms that would roll across the sky—the unexpected tornadoes. Gigi told the story, too, of how one day her restless, unhappy mother decided she had had enough—at least that was what she had told Gigi, who at the time has been called Jenny.

"Jenny, I want you to know that I won't be here when you get home from school. You'll stay on with your father." Gigi repeated her mother's words, adding that she, Gigi, had worried each minute of the school day, wondering what exact moment her mother would pick to leave.

I pictured Gigi with simple brown hair and no black makeup staining her eyes and wondered how a mother could leave like that. Or how one like mine would rather be dead than with her children.

"I never saw her again," Gigi finished. "She went away and never looked back. No letters, no 'I'm sorry.' And then five or six years later,

I left my father too. We didn't have much to say to each other, and if I had stayed around, I would probably have married some other dirt farmer and ended up doing the same thing my mother did. So I got out while the getting was good and ran off with the carnival.

"Anyway," Gigi said, batting her fingers in front of her face to tear through the spiderwebs of bad memory. "Here I am. And now I'm a blade glommer."

The sun made its way up the sky. The heat started to swell, seeping into the back of my shirt. I wanted to drink a tall glass of wonderful cold water, with delectable drops of condensation on the glass that I would smear on my face and neck. Gigi shifted in her lawn chair, yanking on the waistband of her underpants beneath her nightgown. Did she want me to leave? Was I acting like the tedious Mrs. Person, one of the neighbor ladies who used to sit in our kitchen and talk until she had drunk three cups of coffee? Mrs. Schendel had hated that and hated her too. Was Gigi thinking that about me? I didn't know. Maybe. Probably. I tried to come up with something else to say.

"I didn't do too well on stage last night," I confessed.

"Yeah, Jim and me talked about that a little bit after the show. It's nothing to worry about, all right? You just need a few pointers is all. For starters, them people watching ain't nothing but a bunch of goddamn marks. They don't matter. Also, you gotta be the one in charge of them. Not the other way around."

"That's a good way to look at it, I suppose." This approach made me consider the sideshow might be more like a good source of employment, the way it had been pitched to me, than something that presented me as an object of disdain.

We sat in companionable silence until my thirst got the better of me. I was about to ask Gigi for a glass of water despite my strong suspicion that if she went into her trailer to get it, she simply wouldn't come back out and would fall asleep in her bed, when I saw Jim walking down the grade from the midway, making his way toward the trailer lot.

"Hey, Jimmy," Gigi called out to him.

"So this is where you got off to," he said, sitting on the log beside me. Jim reached over to grab Gigi's bare knee and moved her leg from side to side. "Gigi here can tell you everything you need to know."

Gigi stood up and laughed. She stretched her arms over her head. "I guess I'll take a couple of pills and get some sleep then. I tell you, Jim, this drinking will kill us all one day." Gigi arched her back, held her hands up to the sky, and rotated her wrists in small circles. "Nice to meet you, Just Sarah. You need any help getting a good act together, you come to me, all right? Jim here don't know shit about what gets a crowd, especially a bunch of men, going."

Jim laced his fingers behind his head and leaned back, at ease and relaxed, an endless smooth operator. "You get me going, Gigi girl," he said, reaching over to swat the back of her housecoat. They were like friends, but the brush of Jim's fingertips, almost skimming Gigi's backside through her ratty night clothes, was unusual, unexpected—familiar.

I needed more air and wished that I could draw enough of it into my lungs. "I really have to find a telephone to use," I told Jim as soon as the trailer door closed behind Gigi. My voice wobbled in opposition to the casual nonchalance I hoped to feign. "Please," I added, touching the top part of Jim's leg.

"Huh? Oh well, the gal down to the county office is pretty good about letting us use the telephone." Jim seemed unsure whether this unnamed county worker would be as helpful to a sideshow performer waddling up alongside her desk, while I was terrified the woman would recognize me. Would she see me as just the carnival fat lady or connect me with that girl Sarah, the one people talked about and spotted at the grocery store or at Woolworth's once in a while?

I couldn't afford to press my luck again. "No! Please... I mean, isn't there some type of pay phone or something? Somewhere, you know, where no one will see us?" I squeezed Jim's hand. My voice was too loud. Jim's annoyance that my simple request was changing into this time-consuming undertaking was apparent, but what choice did I have but to convince him?

"Please," I whispered while I silently prayed, *Let him do this for me. Help me, Jesus.* I wouldn't let go of Jim's hand until he said yes, until my prayers were answered.

"All right, fine. Okay. Okay," he repeated but with less irritation in his voice. Maybe he could feel my desperation. Maybe Jesus really had interceded on my behalf. "We'll take care of it." Jim stroked my arm and kissed the top of my head.

Maybe every man wanted to be a hero, especially when so little was required to achieve that status.

Just the Sound of Her Voice

Jim drove me in his pickup truck for some twenty miles or so. The ride lasted long enough that I began to wonder if he had forgotten the original point of my request. Each mile we traveled caused a new doubt to rise in my mind that he was even taking me to a telephone. At last, we pulled into the small gravel parking lot behind a yellow building with a paint-peeling sign hanging out front. Some of the words were missing. It was the Something-or-Other Bar. I couldn't tell whether it was closed because of the early hour or because it was no longer in business. The place was surrounded by pasture and farmland, with bulky Holsteins on one side of the road and endless rows of knee-high corn on the other.

"We come out here once in a while to let off steam," Jim explained. "I bet I've driven every inch of Wisconsin, traveling around with Hinkle."

A glass phone booth was behind the building, next to a big propane tank. Crushed cigarettes dotted the ground nearby, dropped, I guessed, by earnest drinkers needing to make sudden calls. I pictured a person wearing wide-legged jeans and a satin shirt, looking much like Jared, with terrible wispy facial hair, leaning down to light a match off the tip of his boot, smoking, and telling someone his story into the mouthpiece.

My relief at finally being delivered to a telephone and my elation at being able at last to provide my account of the night before was short-lived, however. I couldn't fit into the phone booth. Jim had left me to make my call and was leaning against the passenger's-side door, looking out into the endless landscape, his back to me. He couldn't see my predicament and had no way of knowing how difficult simple interactions could be when everything was so small, so clearly designed for someone else. I pushed open the door and fumbled with the handset. Maybe my arm could reach far enough to dial Mrs. Schendel's number because, if it couldn't, then I would have no choice but to ask Jim for his help.

"Jim," I called, wishing again that I knew his last name so that I could address him as Mr. Something because, regardless of what had taken place between us, I couldn't shake the impertinent weirdness of calling a man so many years my senior by his first name. "Hey, excuse me."

"I'm sorry," I said to Jim when he walked around the front of the truck, the cigarette stuck to his lip. "We probably should have used that phone in the office because I'm having trouble dialing the number here. And you know, I guess I didn't think to bring any money."

"Jesus Christ," muttered Jim. He pulled a handful of change from his front pocket then shook it on his open palm so he could fish out a dime. "All right," he said. "I'll put in the dime and dial the phone, and you can stand out here. The cord probably stretches far enough that you can wedge in your top half and talk real loud." Jim went into the booth and lifted the handset. The phone dinged. "What's the number?"

I stayed rooted to the spot, afraid to tell him the number or to have him hear my conversation.

"Sarah, the dime already dropped. Tell me the number." He could just drive away and leave me because he didn't want to waste any more time on me. I told him the number.

And then Jim got out of the phone booth and passed me the handset. By standing sideways and bending a bit at the waist, I was able to almost cradle it against my face. I hoped Jim would walk back to the other side of the truck to smoke another cigarette, but now he seemed intent on standing right in front of me to listen to my conversation. We could both hear Mrs. Schendel's line ring. I could picture her in the kitchen, wiping her hands on the dish towel slung over her shoulder before she reached out to touch the receiver on the wall.

"Hello," she said. Her voice was loud and breathy, as if she had had to run to answer the phone. "Hello?"

I tried to say something, but all that came out was some stupid, mangled choking sound. The intensity of Jim's gaze scared me, making my mouth dry and useless. My indrawn breath sounded like a wheezing harmonica.

"Sarah, is that you?" Mrs. Schendel's voice was scared, panicked, shocked. She must already know what had happened with Jared. "My God, where are you? Oh, honey, Missy found Jared dead at the house. You weren't there. And..."

"Wait," I said. "Don't tell me anything yet." The wind blew up some dust around my feet while Jim leaned forward to try to peer into my face. I should hang up the phone. I should have just written a letter. The plan I had perfected in the quiet places of my mind wasn't unfolding the right way out here in the real world, in the wide-open space with no walls to keep me safe or hold me back or to stop my imagination from running wild.

"I have exciting news."

"Sarah—"

"No! You—please, be quiet and listen. I'm in New York City. I mean, I'm going there. I'm on my way there." I stopped, realizing too late that the compulsion to provide huge amounts of information was the mark of a liar. "Just hang on, please. Okay?" I made my voice calmer. "I'm going to go live with my grandmother." I struggled to push more of my upper body into the telephone booth to ease away from Jim because I wished I could whisper the words I wanted to say.

"How on earth would you get to New York City? Sarah, I need you to listen to me now." Mrs. Schendel was steady and calm, but there was an undertone to her words, a snappy briskness meant to stop me from talking so much. "Honey, Jared is—"

I raised my voice to talk over her so that her words wouldn't be left hanging in the air for Jim to hear—for me to hear. "No! Stop. That's not what happened. I'm in New York. I mean I'm at the train station, at a place."

"Be quiet. I need you to stop talking for just a minute. Missy went to the house this morning. She found Jared on the kitchen floor. I ran over there, too, when I saw the rescue squad and the police in the driveway."

At this point, Jim angled himself so he could stare directly into my face and watch me, gauging my reaction to the words he heard loud and clear.

Mrs. Schendel paused. "What's going on, Sarah?"

I squeezed my eyes shut, scrunching the fat of my face into pleats. "Nothing. I don't know what you're talking about." I lowered my head, struggling to stand, to breathe, to find the right words. "I'm here. Jared is fine. I know he's okay."

"Honey, you have to come home right now. My God, I didn't even know where you were or what had happened. I thought you might be dead too." She was crying, and Mrs. Schendel never cried.

"Just listen to me, then. I'm fine. Everything is fine. New York is wonderful. My grandmother is actually a really nice person." I cleared my throat and opened my eyes. "You know I hate to say it"—here I managed to insert the merest sliver of an unsteady laugh—"but you were really wrong about her. She said she didn't even mind about my being so fat and that she knows now that Dad was a good man. Okay?

"And don't worry about Jared, all right? I made him his dinner last night. He ate it all up, then I just came right out with it and told him I was going to New York City. He couldn't understand it at all because you know how he is, but in the end, he told me to just go.

And he didn't even say it in a mean way." My hand left a humid smear on the handset.

"Okay, okay, Sarah," Mrs. Schendel said in a quiet, calming voice as if she were soothing a nervous horse, the tone she had used when my father died, when she had held the full weight of my head on her lap, her fingers brushing my bangs from my forehead again and again. "I don't quite know what to make of all this. Everyone is really confused and sad, too, I suppose, about Jared, but we can figure all that out when you get here. Sarah, you're going to need to sign some papers and take care of arrangements. I'll help you get back home..."

Was it because she loved me that she didn't understand or wouldn't believe what had happened between Jared and me? Or was it because she couldn't imagine something so horrible? Or just because, like everyone else, she didn't believe I was relevant enough, angry enough to fight back?

"I'm very sad about Jared. I mean, I really do feel horrible about this." I bit my lower lip hard so I wouldn't cry. "But I'm not coming back."

Mrs. Schendel tried again to tell me something or other, but this conversation had already lasted too long.

"Just remember, when I left, Jared was alive. He was in a good mood, even though he had been drinking. I don't know what happened after that." Finally, I had managed to tell her what I needed to say. "That's what you need to tell people."

I wished I could slam down the receiver, but instead, I pushed it into Jim's hands, sending away the rising tide of Mrs. Schendel's voice, which was sharp and high-pitched with confusion and urgency. Walking away, I pretended I was home in the backyard, pulling a clean sheet off the clothesline, breathing in the sunshine that had it baked it dry. Only that sensation of freshness—of newness—existed. My thoughts twined in the soft cotton.

Jim dug his fingers into my forearm. He probably wanted to whip me around to face him, but no man—not even my father or Jared—was strong enough for that. "Turn around, and look at me, Sarah," he barked. He held my arm too tightly, his hand sinking deeper and farther down, wanting to grab the hidden bone. A small, hot splash of urine trickled out of me.

He held both arms now and shook me, but I was no rag doll and barely moved. It was his body that rocked back and forth, which only made him more angry. "Goddamn you, girl. What the fuck are you mixed up in?" Jim stopped trying to flop me around and eased his grip a small fraction. He, at least, appeared to think me capable of anything.

My skin under his hands burned, so much so that I worried he might really break my arms if only to relieve the mounting pressure of his anger. His face was red. There was no way skin could burn that brightly and not explode. I wanted to say something, to provide some sort of explanation, but my mind was a sheet snapping in the wind. My mouth hung half open, my words stunned, my face frozen with shock, dazzled by his anger and the unending cascade of events, the forever-falling domino chain of the last twenty-four hours.

"Goddamn, fuck, fuck, motherfucker." Jim let me go and walked away while I pressed my back against the truck, both hands wrapped over my head, as if that gesture could block out Jim's rage. Jim circled back and stood in front of me.

"Fuck," he said, his voice still angry but cooler. "Do you know what it means to bring heat like that on the carnival, Sarah? The goddamn police are always looking at us for one thing or another. How fast do you think they would shut us down if they thought we were hiding a fugitive—a killer?"

"It's not like that. Not like that at all." I cleared my throat to be sure that Jim could hear me. "I'm not a fugitive. No one is after me.

And certainly... I'm no killer." I said the last words with a quiet intensity, staring straight into Jim's face, willing him to believe me.

"Jesus Christ, I don't need this." Jim looked up at the sky, hands on his hips. "I should just leave your fat ass here and save myself the trouble."

His statement was so matter-of-fact that a dark-purple panic, like the blooming spots behind my eyes, threatened to stop my breathing. What would become of me if he left me out on this lonely road? When would the Something-or-Other Bar open? Would anyone find me sweating and reeking, stained with pee and dirt, having to explain why I couldn't call for help as I cringed on the ground next to a public telephone booth?

"You can't leave me. Please. I beg of you." The sun burned into my scalp as the salt of my tears dripped onto my lips. I tried to imagine snow. Quiet, cold flakes, falling like secrets on my flaming skin.

"Motherfucker," Jim said again but with less conviction this time.

As he looked down at me, Jim's expression wavered, his anger mixing with pity, apparently, at the sight of my desperate tears. I leaned harder against the side of the truck, waiting because I needed Jim to tell me in so many words that he wasn't going to leave me to fend for myself.

He reached behind my head to massage my neck roll. "It's just that this is a big deal, you know?" His fingers were dry and rough, shiver making.

Now that Jim appeared calmer, more like the easygoing man of the night before, I had to appeal to his sense of reason, to convince him that I was worth the trouble. "I know it's a big deal. I understand that, but I can still be a good fat lady. Gigi gave me some tips, and it's not like you can find a five-hundred-pound woman around every corner." That final assertion was irrefutable fact, at least.

To my complete surprise, Jim laughed softly at that last comment. "You're unique, all right." He took the truck keys from the pocket of his jeans and jangled them in his hand. "Let's head back, then," he said.

My body sagged with relief that Jim wasn't going to drive away without me. I represented a risk for him and the carnival, certainly, but Jim apparently lacked the detached cruelty, the calculated heartlessness required to leave someone as endangered and needy as me to suffer an unknown fate in an empty landscape. Somehow, the high heat of our emotions, underscored as they were by the mention of death, the possibility of abandonment, and the danger of discovery, had created a greater intimacy between us, a closeness that made me feel seen.

Jim must have experienced something similar because he kissed the top of my head, holding his lips in place for several moments. "How about I treat you to lunch?" he murmured into my hair. "We'll go back to the carnival, and you can hide out in my trailer and get cleaned up, and I'll bring whatever you want to eat. There's everything you can think of. Hamburgers, corn dogs, funnel cake, cotton candy, caramel corn." The remorse he felt was apparent in his voice, as if he loathed his own rage. Where only moments before he had seemed monstrous and uncaring, now he appeared soft and contrite.

"Whatever you want," he said. "As much as you want."

Carnies

Carnival food was wonderful and amazing in its density. The intoxicating combination of fat, sugar, and salt was more satisfying than most of what I used to cook at home, especially since my father died, and Mrs. Schendel stopped working as our housekeeper. I devoured the thick-cut French fries splashed with malt vinegar, a dripping cheeseburger, a fatty sausage buried in peppers and onions, and even a bag of blue cotton candy that Jim had brought me. I ate with my back to him, embarrassed that he might be repulsed by my rapt pleasure, at my ability to consume so much food at once.

The completeness of my satiety, hard to achieve and short-lived, as it tended to be, brought me a sense of peace, which Jim apparently did not share as he walked the trailer from one end to the other. He stopped directly in front of me.

"Sarah." The abrupt seriousness of his voice made me cringe. "You can't ever, and I mean never, tell anyone that you offed someone." Jim held up his hand to shut off my protests and denials before I could even voice them. "And don't tell me nothing either. What you need to do now is lie low, and what we damn sure have to do is make certain you don't get back up on stage here where somebody might recognize you."

"But it's not like how you think," I said. Jim had snagged a plastic ketchup bottle, probably from the grab joint where he'd gotten the food. I squirted a red hieroglyph over the top of the fries. "It doesn't matter. That's the funny part. People wouldn't imagine I was capable of something like that because they think I'm too fat to think or feel anything. So they just..." I paused to suck grease and salt from my fingertips, hearing the truth or at least a rising conviction in my theory, as I spoke.

"There's no way to be sure of something that like, Sarah. Secrets don't stay buried forever. Something always happens. Someone always figures it out."

No one would find me, I reassured myself. What if Jim were right, though? It would only take one person, someone whose life was tied up with Jared's continued existence, someone accustomed to getting her own way. She would need to be determined and to hate me.

"Missy," I said, my voice too soft for Jim to hear over his footfalls.

At night when Missy would visit Jared at the house, I often heard her talking about their proposed wedding, sometimes waxing about the most original color for bridesmaid dresses, other times voicing breathless options for proposed honeymoon locations, like Chicago, a particularly coveted spot of urban allure for a hog farmer's daughter. I got to listen to every word she said while I stayed hidden behind my bedroom door, with all of us, it seemed, hoping to forget that I existed.

The problem with Missy's designs and plans had been that, regardless of her fashion choices or where she spent her vacation, she and Jared would have no place to live after they got married. They couldn't actually make me leave the house because I had owned half of it since our father died. Missy often ranted about wanting to live a normal life with a husband and children without having to step around what she referred to at alternate intervals as a fat cow, a smelly slob, or my personal favorite, a disgusting waste of life. The house was small, with no basement or second story and only two bedrooms. My father had had it built from some sort of kit, pasted together at low cost, and hung with cheap pine interior doors that did nothing to block out sound.

Nothing had worked out in any way that Missy, Jared, or I would have ever imagined. I pulled a long billow of cotton candy from its plastic bag, letting the sugar cloud melt in my mouth. Jim still appeared agitated, but there was nothing I could do about that either. It was a relief when he finally left me alone to go do whatever it was he did. I was happy to obey his edict to stay out of sight for the time being, glad to be alone to eat in privacy and wash my body and hair with no one to see me do it.

The long-handled scrub brush was one of the items I had brought from home, impossible to forget really, because there was no way for me to clean myself without it. The warm, sudsy water on my skin revived me. Much like dinner the night before and sleeping in Jim's bed, washing myself was one more ordinary activity accomplished outside my home, serving as a place marker, another step moving me farther from my point of origin.

Jim called out my name as he entered the trailer. Given how strange it would have been for him to knock on the door of his own home, I supposed that was his way of not wanting to startle me.

"Hello," I answered from my spot on the couch. At intervals, I would hold up one section of my damp hair to the window fan and then another, trying to dry it.

Jim sat next to me and patted my thigh. "All cleaned up then? What do you say we go get something to eat at the cook trailer? You can meet some of the other performers there."

The hour or two that Jim had been absent had provided enough time for me to view and review my situation in detail. No matter how I looked at it, being secluded in Jim's trailer was the best alternative. No one would find or even know to search for me there. "You don't think maybe it would be better for me to hide out here some more?"

"Nah. Hinkle is probably already pissed that you haven't been to see him. It will only look more suspicious if you don't show up now." He squeezed the ends of my hair, wetting his fingertips. "This is nice. You should talk to Gigi. She can do a pretty good haircut if you want."

He continued to stroke my hair from scalp to tips—a strange, gentle gesture—and then nudged his hand under my elbow to help me up from the couch. "Listen, you're going do fine," Jim said. "Just don't tell anybody where you're from exactly or your last name or anything like that. Fuck, there are so many of these little shit-box towns around here, you could just make up some Indian-sounding name, and no one would ever know the difference."

"Pat-a-lot-of-me Falls," I said.

"How's that?"

"A tribe only slightly less known than the Potawatomi."

Jim laughed but only a bit, making me wonder if he knew that the Potawatomi were the actual tribe who had once lived in that part of Wisconsin.

"See, it's funny because—"

"Stop it, Sarah." He had been about to the open the door, but now he turned back to me with such suddenness that I had to put my hand on the arm of the couch to steady myself. "You need to pay attention and remember what I told you."

"Okay."

Jim grabbed my chin, swiveling my head so that our faces were almost close enough to touch. "You can never, and I mean ever, ever, tell anyone what you did or that the fuzz might be looking for you. Look, I'll take care of you, but you better know that if Hinkle finds out about this or if he knows that I knew and let you stay here, then we'll both be screwed."

"Okay. I mean, yes." Would Hinkle call the police? The more I thought about it, the less sense it made. "But why would he call the police? I mean, wouldn't that just be trouble for him?"

Jim lowered his voice. "That's not the problem. Hinkle isn't the kind of man you want knowing something about you. He would have this thing he could hold over you. I've worked with Hinkle for a lot of years, and he cut me in when I needed a break, but he's not the kind of guy you want to turn your back on."

"Right." When Jim and Hinkle had visited my house, Hinkle had clearly been the one in charge, the one who had knocked on the door. He had looked to be about ten years older than Jim, wearing gabardine dress pants and a short-sleeve collared shirt, a packet of reading glasses and a pen in the chest pocket. His hair had been pomaded and full, a dark sheen slicked straight back from his shiny forehead. The literal brilliance of his grooming had suggested time in front of a mirror, his gold jewelry an indicator of his status.

"Don't get taken in just because he's nice and friendly to you." Jim's voice went up a notch.

I looked at his face. There was so much skin to it, an unbroken sheet from the top of his head to the vee of his shirt buttons where a few tufts of brown and white chest hair were visible. "All right, I hear you."

"Well, good then. And I'll stick with you when you go see Hinkle to make sure he don't talk you into getting on stage here where someone might recognize you." Jim opened the trailer door. The early-evening air, though not much cooler, felt refreshing compared to the trailer. "Just so you know, Hinkle will probably want to meet with you alone because he likes to give people whatever deal he can get them to take."

"So how do you know who got a good deal?"

Jim laughed. "The ones who take the shitty deals don't stick around that long. You see somebody that's been here for a while, and they have half a fucking brain, then they must have gotten a pretty good deal."

I thought of Gigi, of her story of the different jobs she had done with the sideshow, of the number of years she had been on her own, taking care of herself. "So Gigi must have a pretty good deal then, I guess."

Jim kissed my cheek. The unexpected gesture made me draw back a little bit. "Don't worry about Gigi," he said. "She can take care of herself."

Five or six picnic tables were arranged next to a propane stove wedged alongside a prep table in an L shape. The cook trailer was on the far side of the back lot, not far from a converted semitrailer, which Jim explained was the bunkhouse where the grunt workers paid to sleep in a three-by-five confinement. These were the men who broke down the structures and packed them up or who went on ahead as the lead team, traveling to the next town in the dark of night.

According to Jim, they had to stay cranked up on amphetamines pretty much all the time to keep the carnival moving. Some only managed to last for one season, but others returned year after year, driven back by a steady stream of domestic outrages. Jim warned me against walking near the bunkhouse after dark, where these stinking workers loitered around, shirtless, smoking cigarettes, and peeing freely in the open air. Some of the ride jockeys stayed in the bunkhouse, too, but a lot of them camped out under their rides to save money. A carnival in the early morning, I learned, was an eerie sight, with men rising like unholy corpses to sit up straight in the mist and curse the dew soaking their clothes.

One of the setup men whistled as we approached. "Goddamn, Jim, man, you be careful that woman doesn't eat you." His shirt was unbuttoned almost to the waist, showing a wild mat of black chest and dangling armpit hair. He stood up to take a closer look, stroking the sides of his thick mustache.

"Finish your fucking supper, Weedy," said Jim with easy nonchalance.

"All right, all right," Weedy said, sitting down. "I'm just saying she looks like she could gobble you up and suck your bones." Weedy scratched the side of his face, grinding his other elbow into the man sitting next to him.

"You can suck my bone, if you want." His companion laughed.

Jim put up his middle finger and stuck his arm straight out, pointing at Weedy and the friend. There was more laughter, like an ice rain of slicing knives from which there was no shelter, no help, no umbrella. Gigi appeared by my side and latched on to my forearm. Her hands were small and cool even in the dense heat.

"Just ignore those assholes," she said loudly enough for them to hear. "They give everyone a hard time."

I turned toward Gigi, smiling in relief at seeing someone familiar. She looked much better than she had that morning. She must have washed her face and then applied a fresh coat of makeup. Her long hair, a mess of multicolored tangles before, had been brushed and sprayed and stacked up in a mysterious swirl rising above her head like tawdry pie topping. She had somehow flattened her bangs into a seamless sheet that ended just above the ridge of her plucked brows. Her eyelashes were thick and black with the barest shimmer of visible adhesive holding them in place. The ghostly white of her face was offset by her vibrant-red bow mouth and pink-circle cheeks. She reminded me of a doll I had once held—one that closed her eyes when placed on her back and that opened them wide when she was put on her feet. So strong was the impression that I had to resist the urge to stroke the silky sheen of hair along her forehead and kiss the sides of her face.

"Hey," she said, "they don't mean anything by it, really." Gigi grazed the skin near my eye with the knuckle of her forefinger, almost touching the bruise that had darkened in color since the day before. "You could use some makeup there."

Unable to meet her gaze, I remained still, unsure whether to sit or stand or what permission or payment was needed to get a plate of food.

Jim steered me over to the cook table to get some dinner. "A meal will cost you a dollar," he explained. "A lot of people eat from the food stands, but that can take up a big piece of your money. Some of these guys, especially the rookies, get pretty hungry by the end of the week."

Hot tears pricked my eyes. "I didn't bring any money. I..." My voice petered off, weighed down by the exhaustion of getting everything wrong and having to have everything explained to me, never knowing how to maneuver myself, where to put my hands, or how to talk to these people, many of whom looked too dirty—filthy in the way of long-unwashed people who slept in their clothes—to eat dinner at a table with other people.

"Don't worry. I'll get us something." Jim flattened his hand against my back to steer me toward the food. "Now that I think of it," he said with amusement in his voice, "Fat Fanny used to complain all the time about how she spent half her pay getting enough to eat so she could keep earning money."

"This is Marva." Jim gestured toward the thickset woman at the cook table.

The woman glanced in my direction as she pulled a plate from the top of the stack. Her broad red face had a flat, almost beaten-in look, as if she had been smacked with a shovel. Her hair was pulled back into a single braid with a halo of escaped strands stuck to her skin or floating in the humid air. She wore blue polyester shorts, in-expertly-hemmed, and a flowered tank top.

"Marva, this is Sarah. She's going to be doing the sideshow with us."

Marva crossed her arms and rested them below her breasts, heaving them higher. "You must be the fat lady act." She shifted around so that her chest rested on one arm. With her free hand she reached up her tank top and scratched the underside of her breasts.

"Nice to meet you, ma'am."

"Ma'am. How do you like that? Like this is the goddamn tea room. Kid, you can just call me Marva," she said, sniffing her fingers.

"Marva, sweetheart," Jim said. "Give us two plates, and double it up for my pretty friend here." Jim winked at me. "We've got to keep her in shape."

"If you say so, Jim." Marva filled up a heaping plate with hamburger meat and gravy and rice and string beans, with a piece of white bread slathered in orange margarine on the side. The food looked good if not as delicious as what I could have made at home.

Jim and I walked over to the table where Gigi was sitting next to a man with a child-sized body and another man plastered with tattoos in every bright color imaginable. I lowered myself in the center of the empty bench to distribute my weight evenly. Jim sat on the end, one long leg on each side, and shoveled rice and meat into his mouth. I started eating, too, keeping my eyes down on my plate, forcing myself not to stare at the tattooed man and the dwarf sitting at the table, at the freaky oddness of their bodies.

"I'm Ike," the tattooed man said.

I raised my eyes, taking his introduction as permission to stare at him. I had never seen anything like him, hadn't even known that such a person could exist in the world. The drawings on Ike's skin were so complex and intertwined I wondered how long it would take to see and understand each image. "Hello."

"See this one here? The long red heart with the teardrop on the end? That's the heart that bends but never breaks." When Ike traced the contour of the design with his dirty fingernail, I could feel the tattoo heartbeat in my throat.

"It's pretty," I said and noticed Jim watching me.

The dwarf stood up on the bench to lean across the table and shake my hand. "I'm Freddy," he said. He had the body of a misshapen doll with the bullish head of a full-grown man—a shrunken minotaur that I feared seeing in my dreams that night. "Daisy and Spanky was here before."

Gigi rolled her eyes while Ike, Freddy, and Jim all laughed. "You ain't missing much there. I used to dance the cootch show with them, and they been pissed off ever since I left," Gigi said as she pulled a dark-red lipstick from the beaded drawstring bag at her side, using the back of the spoon as a mirror to apply a fresh coat. She kissed the palm of her hand to blot the color. "Mwah." Gigi made a kissing motion at Freddy, who had been watching her gestures in open fascination.

"You and me can get a drink over at the G-top later tonight, and I'll introduce you to the fortune teller, Ora Ann," Gigi said. "Only she likes it when you call her Oracle."

"So long as you don't believe anything she tells you," Freddy said.

Gigi stood up to slap Freddy's arm. "You'd be amazed," Gigi said to me, "at the things she can predict."

"Bullshit," Ike said.

Jim laughed again, leaving me to wonder if I could indeed go out later with Gigi. And after that? Would I make my way back to Jim's trailer alone? Was that even where I was going to sleep? And would we do the same thing we had done last night? I picked up my fork and ate faster, wanting the feel of the food in my mouth, inside me, filling me, more than I cared about how I looked. I didn't hear the footsteps behind my back, didn't notice anyone approaching until I felt a hand fall on my shoulder. My body started in surprise, making me drop my fork in the meat and gravy.

"Well, hello there," Hinkle said.

"Oh," I said. I started licking the handle of my fork to clean it then stopped.

Freddy took a toothpick from behind his ear and cleaned his teeth with it. "Hinkle's a sneaky one, for sure." Freddy sucked his tongue along his gums then slid the toothpick back behind his ear. "I'll see you all later." I couldn't help but stare as he hoisted himself down from the picnic bench, mesmerized by the impossible size of his form, his hitching gait and swinging hips.

"Well, well." Hinkle sat down next to me, straddling the bench. "Are you enjoying your dinner,—Sarah, isn't it?"

"It's very good." I should have been looking Hinkle in the face, but Jim's warnings had made me wary of him, afraid that he might be able to read my thoughts.

Hinkle smiled, the sunlight glinting off the shiny gold chain and medallion he wore around his neck. "I thought you would have come to see me by now to talk about your flop onstage last night and to see if we could still come up with a contract instead of having Jim drive you all over creation and socializing with people."

Jim slapped the wooden tabletop to draw Hinkle's attention away from me. "I took Sarah for a little ride so she could use the telephone."

"Is that right?" Hinkle asked. "Were you calling your family, then? You have a brother, if I'm not mistaken."

His oblique mention of Jared startled me. For the sake of my own well-being, I had taken for granted that no one in the carnival knew anything about me or my life and that I could make up whatever story I wanted. I had ignored the fact that Hinkle and Jim could only have learned of my existence when Jared visited the carnival a few days earlier with Missy. They must have asked Jared about his very fat sister who might be interested in joining the carnival. Missy, glued to Jared's side, would have turned her face from Hinkle, from his shellacked toilette and unctuous charm, annoyed at the embarrassment she had to suffer because of me.

"His name was Jeremy? No, no, it was Jared. Is that right?" Hinkle's eyes scanned my face, calculating my reaction, probing, as if he had an apple, to find the soft spot, the center of the bruise to insert a finger.

"Yes, Jared." I paused to consider the best way to answer. All around me, people were talking and eating. Weedy and his companion were moving the dial on a transistor radio over at their table before settling on a Rex Farish song. "But no, I wasn't calling my brother." Believable stories contained as much truth as possible. "Honestly, he and I were never very close. I called my stepmother to... to tell her goodbye because... I didn't really get the chance because... I didn't have time, I guess."

"Yep." Hinkle nodded. "You were pretty anxious to get here last night. Couldn't even wait until morning."

I turned back to my plate and shoveled up some rice and meat, forcing my mind to picture an endless blank white space so that there was nothing to read in my face or gestures.

By my side, Gigi sang along with the radio, her voice soft and quiet, words I could barely discern. "Let it roll, let it roll. Now she's seen the bright lights, bless her soul..."

"So, you wanted to get here right away then," Hinkle said.

I wiped the corners of my mouth with my thumb and index finger and took a sip of water. "That's right." I had to treat this as a casual conversation, to roll along with whatever was being said, as if Hinkle and I were simply two people getting to know each other. "To tell the truth," I paused, "and no offense, but my stepmother wouldn't really approve of my coming here. In fact, she probably would have talked me out of it, so I figured I would just leave and then call and explain it to her later."

Hinkle had his back to Jim, so he didn't see Jim's slight nod, his tacit approval of my tone, of how I let a single kernel of truth expand to fill an entire story. "Maybe she'll come around," Hinkle said, patting my hand. He reached across the table to latch on to Gigi's wrist. "How are you doing tonight? Ready to give them a good show?"

"Yes," she answered, looking away from him.

Hinkle turned back to me. "It looks like you're just about finished here. Why don't we go now and straighten out the details, Sarah?" Hinkle stood and dusted off the back of his pants. "We'll have to see about getting some makeup to put on that eye."

"I'll come with you," Jim said while I shoved the last forkfuls of food into my mouth.

"I'm sure you have better things to do, Jim. Sarah here can take care of herself." Hinkle smiled down at me as I struggled to get my leg over the bench to stand.

"It's no problem," Jim said.

"All right, then," Hinkle said. "Jim, if I didn't know better, I'd say this big girl was making a little pet of you." Hinkle laughed, his mouth so wide the silver fillings in his molars were visible.

Jim pulled his lips in tight, a fault line on his face. I started to say something to defend Jim, to ease his displeasure at being called a "pet," but then I changed my mind, feeling and liking the warmth of my face, the blush of wondering that maybe I did have some control over Jim.

Hinkle's space was two single-wide trailers hitched together, one of which he lived in and the other he used as an office. The office area was neater than I'd expected, with a series of wooden boxes lining the side of the desk with precisely stacked papers in each one.

"Marva helps keep me organized here," Hinkle said with a sweep of this hand. He sat in the swivel chair behind the desk while I took a seat in the good, solid wooden chair across from him. Jim pulled the metal chair out from under the small typing desk against the wall and turned it around backward to sit down.

Hinkle picked up a stack of typewritten papers and tapped them on the desk. "So then, Sarah, like I mentioned when we came to your house, I'm the proprietor of Midstate Traveling Amusements Carnival. Jim here runs the sideshow, but I've got a financial stake there too. Now, assuming you can get it together to provide folks with some decent entertainment, I'd be willing to pay you seventy dollars a week cash every Friday."

For a moment, my imagination was flooded with the idea of having money all my own that had never passed through my brother's or my father's hands, but then I started running the figures in my head. "But... if the minimum wage is $2.30 an hour, I should be getting at least around 90 dollars a week." Hinkle and Jim both watched me, saying nothing. "I mean, assuming you calculate it at a forty-hour week."

"Sarah, now, there's a lot there you're not taking into account," Hinkle said. "For one thing, the tax man would take a big bite out of that money, and you'd be paying social security besides. Here I'm offering you cash money free and clear."

"Even so, I'd say we can do a little bit better than seventy," Jim said.

Hinkle looked annoyed at the interruption. "This offer is more than fair, Jim."

The two of them were discussing my future as if I weren't even there. "Jim just wants to help me," I interjected. They both turned to me at once, seeming surprised at the sound of my voice.

Hinkle coughed. "Sarah dear, what Jim here knows and you likely don't understand, is that fat ladies aren't worth quite as much as other performers. So they get paid less."

I swallowed hard and pictured Little Freddy and Ike and Gigi. There was a magic to their bodies and movements, a straight-up visual enticement that I lacked.

"That's only the half of it," Hinkle continued. "We're a small business here, Sarah. We don't have money to spread around like some of the big operations. I have to decide all the time what's a good investment and what's not. The fact of the matter is that the sideshow doesn't bring in money like it used to. It seems that a bunch of upstanding citizens have decided that there's something bad or wrong about displaying freaks for money. Now, what these shit-for-brains do-gooders think freaks should do instead or where they should work is a complete mystery. We try to stay on the good side of public opinion by having our freaks put on a show because there ain't nothing illegal about hiring a handicapped entertainer. In fact, that's the sort of thing that would get you a civic award. Then I see you with no finesse or ability to give a good performance, and you want more money for that?"

Hinkle had relied on flattery and unspecified monetary promises when he had come to my house to try to entice me to join the sideshow. Now, he was using disdain to achieve his ends, giving me my first inkling of what Little Freddy had meant when he said Hinkle was sneaky. Hinkle thought I was easy pickings, and worse still, he was probably right.

I opened my mouth to say something, but Jim talked over me. "Come on, man. Sarah here just had a little stage fright. Besides which, she isn't your average fat lady. She's a dressmaker and a... What do you call it? A seamstress. God knows we could use that kind of help around here."

"Is that right?" Hinkle asked. He stood up from his chair and began unbuttoning his shirt, pulling the tails from his pants. "The second button is loose." He took off the shirt and tossed it to me over-hand. "You can go ahead, then, and fix it for me."

I caught the shirt before it hit my face, hating the smell of it, the fruity sweetness of his cologne, and the tacky feel of dried perspiration. Jim shook his head at me in warning. I drew a long, slow breath, resisting the urge to throw the shirt back at Hinkle. "I could do it for about one hundred," I said. "And I want my food free from the cook trailer. Being this fat doesn't come cheap, you know."

The air in the room stagnated in an instant. All movement and sound were suspended except for Jim's very quiet appreciative laugh, which maybe I only imagined. Hinkle hunched forward over the desk, ready now, it seemed, to negotiate in earnest.

In the end, we settled on eighty-five and free food and extra cash for materials and ribbons and sewing tools. I had already managed to stand up from my chair, with the full intention of going back to Jim's trailer to eat the rest of the food he had brought me earlier that afternoon, when Hinkle, still shirtless, said, "You'd better give us a good show on stage tonight. Don't make me think I put my money down on a bad bet."

Jim and I both stopped moving. "Sarah here needs some time to put her act together and get her costume done," Jim said. "She can get started again when we get to Beloit."

"Is that right?" Hinkle asked. "I can't remember anyone else taking time like that. Sarah, honey, if you think I'm about to pay you for doing nothing, you're sore mistaken."

"Well, the thing is…" I began, bracing myself against the back of the folding chair, but Jim answered for me. His intercession should have been welcome, since I didn't actually know how to finish that sentence, but instead I found myself irritated that he was speaking for me again.

"It'll all get done, Hinkle. Don't worry about it," Jim said.

"Sarah, sweetheart," Hinkle said to me, leaning in close, like a good friend, a trusted confidante. "One thing you should know about me is that I don't abide freeloaders. You need to earn money for us. It looks to me like you've settled in, being chummy and eating dinner with the others. So, now that you've made yourself at home, I expect to see you on stage tonight. You're either with it, or you're not." Hinkle rubbed his nose back and forth with his hand, leaving behind an unpleasant dampness, a just-perceptible ugly sheen. I assumed that being "with it" meant you were a part of the carnival but figured now wasn't the time to ask for clarification.

"Time enough for that when we move on," Jim said.

I held my breath, waiting for Hinkle to insist again. Instead, he straightened and adjusted the hem of his sleeveless undershirt. "No work, no money. It's that simple. Until you start performing, you buy all your food and all your supplies."

I didn't want to dip into my stash of money from home, didn't even want Jim to know of its existence—and who knew how long it would last? "But—" I stopped myself there at the edge of saying that I couldn't do that, that Hinkle couldn't take such a hard line when I very clearly needed a break.

"Fair enough," Jim said. "Take it out of her first pay."

I turned my head to look at him, shocked that he would take Hinkle's side now.

"With interest," Hinkle said, and Jim nodded while I stared down at the floor, afraid my outrage at their dealing with me, as if I were somehow invisible, could be too easily read.

"Well, Sarah," Hinkle said. "That's a hard hit right out of the gate, especially for a girl with no money of her own. Maybe there's more than meets the eye here. Is there something I should know about?"

Jim stood up from his chair and turned it back around. "Jesus Christ, Sam Spade, don't be so goddamn suspicious all the time." Jim laughed, easy and smooth. "Sarah just doesn't know jack about how anything works. She's used to the quiet life, staying inside, reading books, and sewing dresses. She needs to learn and get used to things. No big mystery." My God, but Jim sounded just like Jared.

"Is that right, Sarah?" Hinkle smiled.

"Call me Lola," I said as I placed Hinkle's shirt back on the desk. "Lola Rolls. That's what I want to be called from here on out."

The name had occurred to me while eating dinner with the other performers. The vowels were wide, a full-sounding combination of sounds that bounced on the tongue. "Rolls" were my soft shelves of fat, but the word was a verb as well as a noun, containing a new truth about me. I was on the move, hiding, part fugitive like Jim said, but with a bounding resilience too.

"It has a certain ring to it," Hinkle conceded.

What I Had Really Wanted

Gigi visited me the next afternoon at Jim's trailer. For all I knew, he might have asked her to check up on me to make sure I was lying low, like he had told me to do. Then again, maybe she had just got it into her mind that she wanted to stop by and chat, like Mrs. Person and the other farm wives who used to bring my father—the lonely widower raising two children by himself—baked goods and peach pies in the summer and brown bread in the winter.

Gigi didn't stand on ceremony like those ladies, though. She walked right in and sat down on the couch. "You doing okay?" she asked. She got up to take a cigarette from Jim's pack of Pall Malls on the kitchen counter and lit it from the gas burner of the stove.

I stood in the middle of the living room, awkward and a little ill at ease. "Yeah. No. I guess."

Gigi nodded, as if what I had said made perfect sense. She was wearing green satin shorts with a sleeveless cotton blouse and long knee socks. Her hair was tied up in a pale-blue chiffon scarf secured to the sides of her head with silver beauty parlor clips.

"So, we're going to Beloit tomorrow. You ever been there?" She concentrated on blowing smoke rings in the air.

"I've never been anywhere." I stopped talking because I was tee-tering on the edge of telling Gigi my story, maybe even my whole story, the unedited one that could get me into unimaginable amounts of trouble.

Gigi hopped onto the kitchen counter and fumbled around in the cabinet above her until she latched on to the half-empty bottle of Four Roses whiskey that Jim and I had drunk my first night with him.

"Let's have some," she said.

"No. No, thanks," I said, unsure whether either of us should be handling or consuming things in the trailer without Jim's permission. "What I could really use is some help with my act. Hinkle will be pissed for sure if it doesn't get better in a hurry." It no longer occurred to me to refer to Hinkle as Mr. Musgrave. I was surprised, too, to hear myself say a swear word out loud, mild though it was. It fit the context. On some level, Hinkle and profanity had become linked in my mind.

"Well, here's mud in your eye." Gigi raised her glass and drank half of it down in one swallow. "Don't worry too much about Hinkle." She coughed. "He's always sniffing around for something. You know what I mean?"

Her description of Hinkle made him seem animalistic, predatory. I had noticed how he liked to watch Gigi whenever she was near him. "I suppose," I said. "Jim helped me get some stuff so I could I start working on my outfit, but other than that, I can't think of what else to do."

My dress would be beautiful, yards and yards of magenta with a top layer of chiffon cut to move with the wearer, and scores of sequins attached one by one with painstaking care along the straps and hem. The monotonous precision of the task would be certain to keep my imagination from wandering.

"Well," Gigi said, "it's all about the inside money. People pay to get in, and then you can sell them extra stuff like a pitch card or a bible."

"But why would people want to buy Bibles at a carnival?"

"No, not the real Bible, but like a thing, something you sell that has to do with you or your act. See, you don't have to share the inside money with the house, so you have a chance to really cash in if you got a good sell. And then at the end, you can do an extra bit, and people pay more money, men especially, if they think they might get to see some tit."

My mouth dropped open so wide I could feel my chin pressing far down into the collar of fat around my neck. The world tilted a slight bit to the side, causing me to grab the arm of the couch to steady myself. As it was, I could hardly stand to imagine any part of the show besides the flashy sequins of my getup. Now, Gigi was hinting that I might have to show naked parts of my body.

"Goddamn." Gigi laughed. "If you think that's bad, you got to go on over to take a look at the dancers in the cootch show one of these days. They play it strong over there." She topped off her glass. "Don't take it to heart, all right? Nobody's saying you have to take your clothes off. Like, when I was in the blade box, Jim used to have me hand out my dress. He'd talk it up real good, so the men would line up to look. Most times I had on a full slip. We made some decent money with that one."

"But what is it, then, exactly that I'm supposed to do?"

Gigi rubbed the corner of her mouth with her finger and stared at the ceiling. "You could probably get people to pay extra to have you lift your dress and bend over. That's the thing with all the girl acts."

"No!" I grabbed Gigi by the shoulders, moving her toward me so that she was mere inches from my face. "You said—"

"Careful. You're going to spill my drink." Gigi pulled away from me. "Don't get so damned worked up about it. You'll have on those ruffled underpants, so that's all they'll see. And then you can just give a little twitch or whatever." She sat down on the couch, took a sip from her glass and a drag from her cigarette. "Honestly, that's how people are," she said. "They want to know what little Freddy's dick looks like. And Ike. Jesus, he spreads his ass cheeks, and he's got an eye tattooed around the hole that he makes wink at people. He thinks it's the funniest damn thing, having all these uptight jerks pay money to look at his asshole."

"I think I might be sick," I whispered, sitting down next to Gigi.

"Yeah, well, don't do that. You sure you don't want a drink? It might help calm your nerves."

I shook my head.

Gigi walked over to the window, glass and cigarette in hand. "I think you'll be okay, kid. Jim said how you never got out much before this." She turned to face me. "Maybe you're just a little homesick, you know?"

The thought of missing my house made me want to laugh. Following on the heels of that dismissal, however, came an instant longing to be back home, not as I had left it but the way it had been before Jared fired Mrs. Schendel as our housekeeper and before my father died. Back then, my father and I used to sit at the table and drink tea. Sometimes Mrs. Schendel could be persuaded to sit and have a cup of coffee with us while Jared was somewhere outside of the house, absent and silent but alive nonetheless.

"I just... I guess I didn't expect any of this to happen."

Gig spat on the end of her cigarette to douse it and flicked the butt toward the door. "Believe me, I know," she said, sitting on the couch next to me and pulling her knees up to her chest. "I mean, I thought I was going to get married and have a bunch of kids." Gigi pulled one of the silver clips from her hair and rubbed it back and forth between her thumb and index finger. "I was going to marry someone rich, you know, so I wouldn't have to work so hard like my mother and wouldn't end up sad like her. She cried all the time." Gigi pressed her eyes against her knees. "And then she left us." She wiped her face with the palms of her hands then sprang to her feet to go to the kitchen for another drink.

"Hey, you know, I don't usually drink like this so early in the morning." Gigi took another cigarette from Jim's pack. It dangled between her lips, tilting up and down as she talked. "So, what did you think you'd be doing instead?" Jim had left a dirty pair of jeans draped over the coffee table. Gigi fished through the pockets until she came up with a match booklet.

"Umm... well," I said, watching her constant movements, overwhelmed by her familiarity with everything in the trailer, with Jim's clothes even. Gigi took a half-full ashtray from the counter and sat back down next to me.

"I wanted to get married, too, you know. Afterward, I mean. First, I was going to lose a ton of weight and be really thin so I could tell every single person who made fun of me to go straight to hell. Then I was going to find some guy who was rich but really smart, too, like a doctor or lawyer or something. I was going to leave town and maybe go live in New York City because that's where my mother's family is. I was going to be a famous writer too."

"A writer, huh? Well, that's something. Like books and stuff like that?"

"I don't know. I guess I thought I would have some kind of newspaper column or something. Maybe I would write a book."

Gigi smiled and leaned back against the couch, her hands interlaced behind her head. "Like about what?" She closed her eyes.

I twirled my hair, looping it over and through my fingers. "Let's see... There's this girl, right? She's the main character, and she lives with her father and her brother, let's say, in a tiny little house."

"Where's the mother?" Gigi asked, not opening her eyes.

"The father told the girl that her mother died from sepsis when the girl was just a baby, but really—" I stopped myself, wondering if I should continue to tell the lie my father had invented or the truth Mrs. Schendel had told me. "She killed herself, the mother did, when the girl was only a baby. The father never said anything, I guess because he was ashamed."

Gigi turned her head, opening her eyes to look at me. "He thought he could save her?"

"Maybe," I said.

My father had always been reluctant to talk about my mother, never wanting to share any memories of her. One night, though, not long after my fourteenth birthday, I overheard my father, who had been drinking a great deal or at least more than usual, muttering in low, angry half tones while he sat in the recliner. He said my mother's name—Emma. It was late at night with just the two of us at home. Jared, like usual, was away from the house, so I seized the opportunity, pressing my father with questions, asking him to speak louder. In response, he walked over to where I sat eating slices of bread at the table. He dropped to his knees and ground his face against my shin, making an animalistic noise not instantly recognizable as human sobbing. When he glanced up at me at last—his glassy red eyes making him look like a demon who grabbed at the feet and ankles of careless children while they slept—he whispered that his relationship with Emma hadn't been shameful, not like people said.

Beside me, Gigi waited for me to continue, her body soft and relaxed as she let herself rest against my arm. "Anyway," I said, "everyone in the town made fun of this girl. Her brother was the worst of all. He said awful things to her. He used to poke her and pinch her. He even made fun of the way she walked. The father..." I swallowed hard. "He never tried to stop the brother. He would say something once in a while, but he was just too tired or sad to really do anything about it, so the brother could be as mean as he wanted. The girl had a stepmother too."

"An evil one?"

"No, a nice one. You know, she harped on the girl a lot about her weight, but... she really did want her to be happy." My voice was quiet, barely audible over the turning fan blades. In my mind, in the version of the truth I told myself, Jared played the role of tormentor, a fantastical meanie, who loved to laugh at me and be cruel to me in all the ways available to his limited imagination. Mrs. Schendel was in the middle. She loved me and wanted the best for me, but she couldn't resist the compulsion of being stern with me, of forever searching for the right formula to make me snap out of it and behave like a normal person. My father was the hero, the one I loved in that diminished emotional life of only three people and no friends. Hearing myself tell the story to Gigi, though, made him seem less than what I had thought him to be. He could have stood up for me or could have made Jared hate me less or could have engendered a feeling of family within us, of being a cohesive group, instead of keeping me stuffed in the house like an overfed pet and resenting Jared for not needing him. My father had never wanted me to leave him. He had always been there pulling at my hands, tweaking the fingers, wrapping his arms around my neck.

Gigi turned her head without lifting it from the edge of the couch. Her eyes were less focused from drinking. Her lit cigarette held a long column of ash. She clapped her hand on my leg. "Well, it's no wonder, then, why she left home. Who'd want to stick around for that shit?"

"Nobody, I guess." I paused. "She wasn't really my stepmother," I confessed. "She was our housekeeper. We weren't rich or anything, but my father had to have someone help him. She lived at the farm next door and came over every day." Mrs. Schendel had always seemed like one of the family. It felt like a cruel oversight to give her the same label as some domestic employee who hadn't taken on the additional tasks of telling me the truth about my parents' marriage and my mother's death or of forcing me to leave the house when I wanted to stay inside and hide. "I don't know why I said she was my stepmother."

"Was it because she was sleeping with your father?" Gigi asked.

"What? No!" My voice got louder at Gigi's suggestion. "She was a married woman who went to church every Sunday!"

Gigi just shrugged. "Well, that doesn't necessarily mean anything."

I opened my mouth to express more outrage then said nothing. My father had confided everything in Mrs. Schendel, even the fact that he had met and impregnated my mother when my mother was only a fifteen-year-old student in the high school English class he taught. Mrs. Schendel had been his only confidante and the person to whom I had turned, without stopping to wonder why, when I wanted the truth about anything involving my own family.

"You didn't know her, though," I said in a calmer voice. "She thought I could go to college even. My father said I needed to stay home with him, but she was pretty sure I could figure things out on my own."

"Yeah?" Gigi asked.

"Yes. I got really good grades when I was still in school. I had to leave in the fourth grade because I got too big to fit in the desks. Then my father taught me at home after that."

"Is that right? I never got any further than the sixth grade."

I shook my head. "Right, but my father was a real university professor someplace famous back East, and he tutored me, so... I mean, I would have done great in college."

Gigi flicked her ash toward the ashtray and missed. "That's right. You asked me right away for a newspaper when you got here, so you must be good at reading."

How could I explain the ocean between what Gigi thought of as schooling and the world of ideas my father and I had shared? A surge of loneliness washed over me at the thought that I would never again have discussions like the ones I had had with my father.

"Yeah, but it probably wouldn't have happened anyway." Gigi stood up and stretched her arms over her head. "Like with me, where the fuck was I going to find a rich man anyway in that shit town?" She bent down and touched her toes, holding the pose, until her balance gave out and she fell onto the couch. "Goddamn, I guess I had more to drink than I realized. I think I'll lie down for a little while." She walked into the bedroom and flopped face first onto the bed.

I followed her, astonished again at her level of comfort in the trailer, but she was already asleep, snoring, her indrawn breath a high-pitched wail, her exhale a whooshing rush of air. So I left her where she was, deciding to use the time to reread some of Emerson's collected works and better my mind to feel closer to my father. He often used to recite the essays and poems aloud, his voicing rising and falling with perfection, like rain clattering down through the leaves.

I started to read, trying to recapture that happiness. Instead, my mind kept returning to Mrs. Schendel. I had always wanted my mother, like all motherless children do, but I had only had Mrs. Schendel—homely Mrs. Schendel with her beak nose and big, competent chapped hands. She had scrubbed our house clean, had cooked enormous pots of chicken pieces and gravy, and had demonstrated an uncharacteristic dislike for the farm wives who had visited our house, charmed and half in love, as they were, with my father's flat stomach and strong body with hands softer than their own. How, in all that time, had I never realized that he and Mrs. Schendel were lovers?

Returning to the here and now, I snapped Mr. Emerson shut. Maybe it had been foolish to bring that bulky book with its cracked and splintering spine with me from home. It weighed a ton.

I was tired and wished Gigi would leave. I thought about waking her and asking her to go, but if Jim had sent her over to the trailer, he might be angry if I did that. Gigi had one of the pillows in a tight grip, as if she were holding hands with it, as if it were a good friend.

I took off my shoes and sat on the edge of the bed. Gigi was sprawled in the very middle of the mattress, so I put one hand under her stomach and the other under her thigh to roll her over to the edge. I must have been too forceful or been too effective as a human spatula because she turned twice and hit her head against the wall.

"Oh God," I said. "I'm sorry."

Gigi sat up and rubbed her head. "The fuck, you say." She flopped back down and resumed her sleep.

I burst out laughing, but Gigi didn't even open her eyes. Easing myself down onto the other side of the bed, I felt suddenly exhausted and glad, too, that I hadn't asked Gigi to leave. I drifted off, savoring the experience of being next to someone who could be so comfortable by my side—someone who didn't require watching, who didn't have any plans for my fat body. I didn't have to worry about her coming up behind me.

That was how Jim found us a few hours later—both of us fast asleep on the bed. "Well, will you look at this?" he said. I struggled to sit up at the sound of his voice while Gigi only murmured something and kept on sleeping. "And here I thought you might be lonely and want some lunch," he said, showing me a clear plastic trash bag filled with buttered popcorn in one hand and a brown paper sack stained with grease in the other.

When I came out of the bedroom, Jim was standing in the middle of the kitchenette, holding the opened Four Roses, waiting, it seemed, for me to see him staring at the less-full bottle. "I see Gigi made herself at home here," he said. "Or was it you?"

"No, no," I said. "Drinking's not my thing. You know that."

As I waited for Jim's next words, for his reaction, I thought about picking up the full ashtray from the floor, worried that it might be a magnet for his anger. In the other room, Gigi shifted on the bed, rolling and noisy, making me forget about the ashtray.

"Anyway," I said, "Gigi came by to keep me company, and, you know, it didn't occur to me to tell her 'no,' that she couldn't have a drink or make herself comfortable. I mean, at home, we always had coffee and something to eat when people came over." I closed my eyes for a second, savoring the darkness, the internal quiet impossible in strong light. "Or at least that's how it sounded."

Jim stared at me for a minute then screwed the cap back on the whiskey bottle. "What do you mean, 'That's how it sounded'?"

"I always stayed in the room I had to share with my brother when people came to visit my father." I coughed. "And I would hear them out in the kitchen, drinking coffee and tea and eating pies or bread or whatever."

Jim sat down on the couch, elbows resting on his knees. "How come you didn't just go out and join them?"

"Because I wouldn't give them the satisfaction of being able to make fun of me, of watching me eat, so they would have a hilarious story to tell their friends or families." There was a metallic taste in my mouth. "Also, I think my father wanted me to stay away. He didn't want people looking at me either." That last part, something I had never voiced aloud, was terrible to admit but a relief to finally say.

Jim reached over and ran two fingers down my forearm, raising my flesh. "You won't have to worry about that here. Everybody is going to want to get a look at you." Jim motioned to the bags of food on the table. "Come on and eat. Fergs dumped out the fry bins, and these are the leftovers. I've got some funnel cake and sausages too."

"It looks good." I smiled. "Do you think Gigi wants some?"

"Ah, let her sleep," Jim said. He picked up a handful of French fries and started eating them one by one. "Gigi's got a good heart, but she drinks too goddamn much." Jim shook his head and kept eating. "Almost thirty years old and still crying for her mother."

Jared Comes to Call

Working on my beautiful, outlandish dress helped to fill the long, monotonous hours until the carnival left town. The loneliness and boredom, familiar and unpleasant, provided me an unwanted reminder of home. The silence in that house had had such freedom and space that it could expand and warp back around until it stopped being itself and became the sound of murmured conversation in the whirring of the refrigerator or maybe high-pitched singing as the water squealed out from the bathroom tap. Jim and Gigi were both over at the sideshow tent. Once the carnival closed for the night, they would go to the G-top, which I had learned was the tent housing a sort of after-hours club for the carnival workers where they could drink, socialize, and gamble.

We were scheduled to leave town the next day. No matter how my mind whirred with anxiety about what the future held, anything had to be better than continued confinement. The trailer was hot, like always. Maybe I could put a chair outside to sit where there was some breeze, at least. The kitchenette stools would be easy to lift, but balancing on them would be too much work, with too much risk of falling, so I decided to bring out the wooden chair wedged in the corner of the bedroom. A pile of dirty clothes covered it. Moving them to the bed and clearing out the chair legs tired me. Pulling the chair out of the corner and getting it to the doorway entailed a lot of sweaty, noisy scraping and maneuvering. I paused bent over the chair, gripping the wooden arms. My heart pounded with such intensity I could hear it banging outside my body. The idea terrified me. I clutched my chest.

There was a tapping on the window, the tink tink of something touching glass that sounded like my heartbeats but was not.

"Jesus, Lola, open the door and let me in." Gigi's voice, low and intense, startled me. For a moment, I thought she was tapping on the wrong window until I remembered that my new name was Lola. Gigi was standing outside the trailer with a long stick in her hand.

"Gigi?"

"For God's sake"—she banged the bottom of the stick on the ground—"douse the lights, and let me in."

The ferocious urgency of her tone and the unexpectedness of her presence terrified me to immobility. Gigi dropped the stick and ran to the front of the trailer. I snapped back to action when I heard her rattling the knob. I pushed my way to the door as quickly as possible to let her in.

Gigi squeezed past me with surprising strength and scrambled to the bedroom. "Get the kitchen lights," she whispered. "And lock the door."

"Oh my God, what's going on?" I asked, doing like she said. We sat down together on the mattress in the bedroom. Gigi held my arm, straining to hear some sound. When there was nothing but silence, she released me from her grasp. "Okay, good," she said in a quiet voice. "Whooo..." She exhaled.

"Gigi, what is it?"

"Oh Christ. The fuzz showed up here looking for you, so Jim had me run over to tell you to turn out the lights and hide."

My stomach dropped to the floor. "The fuzz? You mean the police? They were here looking for me? I mean, why were they here?" I clarified.

"I don't know," Gigi said. "I seen Jim talking to them, then he sorta motioned to me on the sly. So I go over, and I hear him tell the fuzz, 'Now, gentlemen, I'm happy to escort you anywhere, if you'd like to see for yourself that, unfortunately, we don't have any fat-lady act at present.' And then, he turns to me and says, 'Gigi, honey, I'm going to be tied up with these officers for a bit, so would you be a dear and stop by my trailer to pick up the props and make sure everything is locked up when you leave.' So I come running over here, and then I almost had a heart attack when you didn't answer right away." Gigi patted my hand. "Don't you worry, though. Jim's the best patch there is."

"Patch?"

"The person who fixes things, especially when stuff needs to get smoothed over with the police." Gigi shifted her position. As my eyes adjusted to the dark, I could make out the shape of her on the mattress, see the muted shimmer of her neckline. Her expression was invisible, though. "Basically, he makes sure that people have what they need so there's no trouble. Like he gets speed for the workers so they can get their shit done then gets them bennies to bring them back down. He hustles some business on the side with the marks, but that's just for the cash."

I knew "mark" was the name for people outside the carnival, the ones who paid money for the games and shows and rides, but I didn't fully understand the rest of what Gigi had said. I just replied, "Oh," because I was picturing Jim, red-faced and enraged, threatening to leave me alongside the road, then his annoyance again when I couldn't keep my mouth shut with Hinkle. Now, he had to run interference for me with the police while I holed up in his trailer, taking up all the space.

"Maybe I should go out there and talk to the police myself. All this is probably more trouble than it's worth for Jim."

"No, no, no." Gigi dug her pretty fingernails into my shoulder. "Jim wanted me to keep you here, so that's what I'm aiming to do."

"Ouch," I said, pulling Gigi's hand off me.

"Oh, sorry about that," she said. "Just don't worry, okay? Jim's good at handling stuff like this. Besides which, he would never turn anyone over to the police, not when his daddy died in jail, and he's done hard time himself."

I stared at Gigi in the dark. "What was Jim in prison for?"

"Some shit or other. Jimmy never told me. He doesn't like to talk about it, but I guess I can't blame him there." Gigi fanned her face with her open hand. "It's hot in here. I think I'm going to sneak out to the kitchen to get myself a drink. You want me to bring you something?"

"Huh? Yeah, there's a big bag of popcorn on the counter. I might as well eat some of that."

Gigi and I sat there side by side in the dark. She sipped her glass of whiskey, gasping after each swallow. I listened to her sip and gasp, sip and gasp, and to the sound of the popcorn, covered with congealed butter flavor and salt, squeaking against my teeth. As the initial wave of anxiety abated a bit, my eating slowed.

"So how come the fuzz are looking for you?" Gigi asked.

I made a big show, which Gigi could probably only half see anyway, of prying stuck popcorn from my back molars. "Well..." I began. "Um... I'm not really sure. It might have something to do with my brother, Jared."

As I began my story, a bumbling weave of fact and fiction, I had the feeling that Jared was listening to me, maybe even watching me from the floor, waiting to see what I would say. "So, he and I didn't get along at all. That's a big part of the reason I left." The sensation of Jared staring at me with cloudy, unblinking eyes made me so uneasy that I hugged a pillow to my chest. He seemed to become more present and active with every word I spoke. "Anyway, when I called my stepmother... You know, the one I told you about who was our housekeeper but like a mother too. She told me that Jared was dead, that he had some kind of problem with his head." In the uncertain light, it nearly seemed that a pale-gray hand, drawn in white outline, may have reached out to touch one of my feet. I shuffled back farther on the mattress, too terrified to continue any version of my story.

"A problem with his head?" Gigi asked. "You mean like he was crazy or something like that?"

"No, like it was bashed in." I stuffed another double handful of popcorn into my mouth, chewing as hard as I could.

"And so what? The fuzz think you know something about that?"

"I don't know what they think," I answered truthfully. Gigi and I lapsed into silence, her drinking and me eating in our dark, quiet little world. I don't how long we stayed like that.

"Anyway, I should probably get back out there," Gigi finally said.

"What? No. Can't you wait here with me?" Jared still felt present in the room. I had the impression of him stretched out on the floor, waiting in patient silence for Gigi to leave.

"Yeah, I wish, but if Hinkle don't see me around, he'll start asking questions, and then I'll have to hear all about it later on." Gigi's voice sounded flat, dead.

"How do you mean? Does he come over and yell at you at the end of the night?"

Gigi sputtered her lips. "I wish that was all he came around for."

The thought of Hinkle slinking over to Gigi's trailer, sidling up to her door, and then spending the night in her bed disgusted me. Judging by her offhand disdain, I knew she didn't relish the thought either.

"Hey, you know what?" Gigi asked with such suddenness that it startled me. "Don't worry, though, all right? I mean, even if you did do something wrong, because there's always a reason." Gigi got up from the bed and stood on her tiptoes to stretch the backs of her legs.

"I was thinking about my father before," she continued. "Yeah, he used to tell me all kinds of stories. His favorite was about Judge Roy Bean, who was some hanging judge down in Texas from when they still did that kind of thing. Anyway, Judge Roy Bean used to hold court right in his saloon. So one day, he orders this horse thief to be hanged. And then the next case was this man who killed this other guy. After Judge Roy Bean hears his story, he lets the man go with no punishment at all. And everyone is shocked, and they ask Judge Roy Bean how he could let a murderer go free after he sent a horse thief to hang. And he says, 'Well, I've met plenty a men that needed a-killing, but I never met a horse that needed a-stealing.' God, that used to make my father laugh, but you know, that's how it works sometimes. I think about it once in a while, especially for Hinkle."

After Gigi left, the air in the trailer felt blacker and took on a persistent meaty smell, like ground beef left too long on the kitchen counter. The sensory overload had to be my imagination, and the un-shakeable sensation of Jared's presence was only illusion. I told myself these things. I knew these things to be true. Jared, bolder now that we were alone, stood and started moving around the room.

The Worst Night of Jared's Life

Jared had gotten home from the paper mill that night around six and poured some bourbon into a coffee mug almost as soon as he came through the door. Earlier that afternoon, I had washed all the dishes in the kitchen but was too dizzy from not eating to scrub the floors in our house. He didn't mention the improved appearance of the place, but I could tell he noticed the new tidiness by the way he scanned the whole room. Jared sat down in our father's recliner, shielding his face and upper body with an open newspaper.

"I'm frying up that chicken for dinner."

"Good." Jared lowered the newspaper to look at me. "That's good," he said and took a sip from his cup.

"And I made some peanut butter cookies."

"Good. I really like those cookies." He started reading then lowered the paper again. "Thank you," he said. It was the first civil snippet of conversation we had had in days. A hard lump formed in my throat because there had always been so little kindness between us. He refilled his cup.

Jared drank through dinner, his head bent over his plate to concentrate on tearing the greasy meat from the drumstick. "Aren't you going to eat something?"

"No, I'm not hungry." In truth, I was starving, but if there was any hope of meeting and reuniting with my mother's family in New York City, then I would need to lose as much weight as I could, as quickly as I could.

"Well, will wonders never cease?" he said.

I ignored him, told myself it didn't matter what he said because one day, sooner than he realized, I wouldn't have to hear his voice ever again. "I went to see Mrs. Schendel today."

Jared wiped his mouth on one of the paper napkins. "So? What's new about that? Aren't you over there all the time anyway?"

I forced myself to think about Mrs. Schendel's advice about using honey to catch flies. With my dry mouth and empty stomach, though, it was hard to swallow anything. "She was telling me about our mother's parents. She said you knew about them and never told me."

"Yeah, well, you're not missing much there." Jared raised the coffee mug to his face and drained the last drops.

I couldn't tell if he refused to betray any reaction to annoy me or if he really was utterly unmoved by my sudden mention of grandparents he had never discussed. I tried again to jump-start a degree of interest or involvement on his part. "Mrs. Schendel also told me about how our mother really died. I guess—"

"I remember how she died." His voice was cold, angry.

I saw again the portrait Mrs. Schendel had painted. Me, sound asleep in a baby bassinet while a sweet, soft-faced child Jared clung in disbelief and despair to the cooling body of our beautiful mother, who had forced herself to drink drain cleaner because she didn't believe that things would ever be better. She had taken her own life when my father had stepped out to buy a newspaper. He should have returned soon, except he had been delayed, had decided to take advantage of a fine spring day to run more errands. Ever since Mrs. Schendel had told me what had happened, knowledge my father had always denied me, I found myself wondering if maybe my mother's untimely, tragic death had been but nothing more than a misguided, poorly executed attempt to make my father see her and save her. Had her own desire to be visible killed her?

Jared now looked as if the wires holding his face in position had been cut, leaving his whole countenance to droop, hung low in sadness. Some instinct, deep and unaffected by our history together, made me reach out my hand to touch Jared and comfort him. I stopped myself, remembering in the nick of time how contact with me would only repulse him. I moved the bowl of mashed potatoes from the table to the counter and stood looking out the window with my back to him.

"Well," I said without turning around, "I've been thinking. I'd like to get in touch with them, our mother's parents, our grandmother especially."

Jared tipped back in his chair to study the ceiling tiles. "Why bother? Bring back the potatoes, would you? They're really good. Did you put sour cream in them?"

I moved the potato dish back from the counter to the table. "What do you mean, 'Why bother?'" There were so many other things any normal person, anyone besides him, would have said, that I hardly knew where to begin with my reply, so instead I said the first thing that came to mind. "For one thing, our mother's family has money. How do you think Dad paid for this house?"

Jared's reaction to this statement was to keep eating and take another drink from his cup before remembering that it was already empty. "I know how Dad paid for this house. I know all about the checks they sent him every month. You know that was payoff money, right? They gave it to him so he would stay away from them and keep us away from them." He stood up and dropped his half-full plate into the sink. "They don't want to know me, and I don't want to know them."

"Well, fine, then. That's fine. You just give me their names and addresses and a telephone number, too, I guess, if you have one, and I'll take care of the whole thing myself."

Jared flopped down into the recliner. "Really? What precisely do you think our long-lost family will have to say when they get a look at you? You won't get a goddamn dime out of them."

I opened my mouth to tell him it wasn't all about the money, to say that I only wanted a family to love me, people who could tell me something about our mother. It was all true but a tenuous truth covering a lie. What I really wanted was to escape that house and that life to be free of a loneliness so crushing it could make me long for death, if only to break up the monotony.

"What do you care anyway? I thought you'd be ecstatic at the idea of me getting some money so maybe I could live somewhere else."

"Trust me, Sarah, if I thought any of this had even half a chance of working, I'd jump up and down for fucking joy. But it won't."

"What am I supposed to do, then? Stay here with you forever?" I pulled the dish towel from the stove handle and rubbed it across my face. It smelled like mildew. I thought about the visit from the two carnival men only a few days before. "I can't just get a job or get married like a regular person."

Jared jumped out of the chair and took the bourbon bottle out of the cabinet then slammed the door. "You know what, Sarah? I don't care."

I played my trump, the needle I had been saving to show Jared how cruel he was, how wrong he had been to treat me like an inhuman burden this last year we had lived alone together. "What do you think Dad would have to say about you not caring, about how you treat me all the time like some big fat nothing?"

"Sarah, take a look at yourself. You are a big fat nothing." Jared slapped my cheek lightly. He smiled then laughed. "And guess what? I don't give a shit either what Dad would say because maybe he should have said something to you a long time ago. And maybe he should have gotten a job instead of sitting around reading books."

I pushed Jared hard on the chest because he was standing too close to me and because, if I didn't, then that soft, painless slap would nonetheless stay painted on my cheek forever. "Don't you dare say anything about Dad. Don't you dare. You'll never be the man he was."

Jared stumbled backward into the kitchen table. "Well, thank God for that. I guess I lost my chance to get a fifteen-year-old pregnant and then sponge off her parents for the rest of my life. Mrs. Schendel told you that part, too, right? About how Dad was our mother's high school teacher? And these grandparents that you think are going to be such a big help to you? They had him run out of town."

Mrs. Schendel had indeed told me all about the shameful nature of my parents' relationship, casting by extension a dark perspective on my father's own desire to teach me at home, apparently forever. Still, what other choice did I have but to believe that my grandparents couldn't—in fact that no one could—carry a grudge for more than twenty years? "Yes, I knew."

"And still you want to find them, play nice with them? You're just like Dad. You have no pride," Jared said in a quiet, exact way, biting down hard on each word.

I stepped forward again and shoved Jared harder. He fell into the table with enough force that it scraped across the floor. He rebalanced himself and grabbed my arms, digging his fingers deep into my soft, soft flesh, holding me there. There would be bruises, and I didn't want to be marked by him.

"And another thing," he said, "I've just about had it with you slapping at me and pushing me. We're not kids anymore, but you keep it up, and I'll teach you a real lesson." He let go and turned around quickly, his back to me.

I pushed because I had to. Anything else would have been a tacit compliance I would never give him. By putting my shoulder into

it, Jared would have to feel my full force, the enormity of my existence. He fell to the floor, sprawled there for what seemed like only
a second, then he was on his feet again quicker than I realized. He
grabbed a handful of my blouse and hit me hard with the back of his
hand. My ears rang. I tasted blood. He immediately turned away and
held his hands to either side of his head, pounding his fists against
his temples.

"Jesus Christ, Sarah. Why did you do that? Why did you make
me do that? Shit, you're bleeding." He cracked open a tray of ice from
the freezer and put some cubes in the dish towel. "Here, put this on
your eye before it swells. And stop, okay? Just stop."

"Stop what? Getting in the way of your fist?" I never thought he
would actually do it.

"Just stop everything, okay?" Jared started to cry, something I
hadn't seen in years. I held the ice pack to my face, watching him,
much like he had looked at my tears day in and day out, almost daily
in fact, without flinching or caring.

Then I cried as well. Tears, tears, tears. So many tears—a veritable
river of my tears had sluiced through the kitchen, had soaked my
mattress, while I had done nothing more than cover my eyes and my
face, my fat face. I was tired of crying, of how it puffed my eyelids
and trickled down my throat, and of the awful sensation of choking
with my mouth and nose muffled in my pillow, a dish towel, or my
folded apron. Every corner of that house, every flat surface, and every
bit of cloth or softness, and even the food I cooked and ate and ate
seemed tear logged and infected with my sadness—my useless, lum-
bering grief.

"Then help me. Tell me how to contact these people, how to find
them. Help me get the money I need so I can have my own place to
live."

Jared sat down in the recliner, bent forward with his elbows resting on his knees. "I don't want any part of this. You want the infor-

mation, you can have it, but leave me out of it. I don't want to know them, and I don't want them to know about me. And I sure as shit don't want them sitting in the church when Missy and I get married, like a happy bunch of goddamn hypocrites."

His words made me realize that their wedding might happen sooner than I thought. Jared's vehemence surprised me, too, showing me that on some level I had been expecting him to smooth the path for me with our mother's family, to be the good-looking one that grandparents would like to see, to offer them a palatable, conventional life of a pretty fiancée followed by a frothy wedding and irresistible great-grandchildren. He had a job, ordinary though it was, and could walk down the street without people laughing and staring—far more than I could expect to have.

A balance had to be respected. A blow like that to the face had to come with some price attached, some valuable form of recompense. It was Jared's duty now to want to make it up to me for hurting me, but he was violating the principle by refusing to help. "I'll figure it out for myself. You just give me the information I need."

Jared laughed. "You haven't listened to a goddamn word I've said." He went to our father's old bedroom, now his bedroom, and came out with a locked metal box. "Here's where Dad kept all his important papers. Here are his bank statements. When I closed the account, I put that paperwork in here."

I took the documents from his hand without really understanding what I should do with them or where to find the names of my grandparents. "Okay, thanks."

Jared laughed. "That's all I have to give you. I guess you'll have to call the bank and see what else they can tell you."

"Okay," I repeated.

"Your birth certificate is in here too. You might need that for when you're living with your rich family. They probably won't believe you're related to them without some proof."

"Shut up," I said. He sounded just like the voice in my head telling me I didn't know what I was doing and that it wasn't going to work out for me. "Stop being so mean to me all the time. Can you just stop it for once?" I tossed the bowl of potatoes into the sink with Jared's plate and the cooking pots then dropped the chicken platter on top of it. They clattered together in a loud, satisfying way.

"Be careful with those things, and don't waste good food like that." Jared came over to the sink. He placed the potato bowl and chicken platter back on the table then reached up into the cabinet again for the bourbon bottle.

"Why don't you save yourself the trouble of walking back and forth and just drink straight from the bottle?" I dumped the dishes back into the sink.

"For God's sake, Sarah." He half jogged over to the recliner, making a loop around the coffee table. "Why can't I ever get a break from you? You're just always here all over this house. Then all you do is complain about having everything handed to you on a silver platter. Has it ever occurred to you to say 'thank you' for that chicken or for anything, for that matter?"

My face burned with shame, but even I, who didn't know how anything really worked, knew better to thank a man who had just hit me. "Thanks for nothing," I said.

Jared was lean, a young man in the best shape of his life, so he was fast as he rushed toward me. Before he could even reach me, I picked up the small cast iron skillet from the range top where I always left it and held it up. "Back off. Just back off. Or else."

Jared stood directly in front of me, breathing bourbon vapor enough to make my eyes water, so worked up he was almost panting. "Or else what? If you think you're going to threaten me in this house, you've got another think coming." He took the smallest step forward. His hands twitched at his sides.

What had happened between us that night was a scissor, a break, a fault line running between the before and after. We had reached an irrevocable point and gotten down to the brassiest of tacks. It would serve as a gauge, too, for the relationships I had, a yardstick for measuring the intimacy and loyalty of everyone I knew or met.

He'd come at me. I had no time and possibly no inclination to figure out what he was going to do next. Sometimes pausing to analyze a situation was the right thing, and sometimes it was better to follow your heart in complicated situations—but sometimes taking a swing was the only option. That was what I did.

The frying pan was compact and heavy, and I had a good grip on it. My reaction was faster and less flinching than Jared seemed to think it could be. He had always underestimated me. He hit the floor facedown and stopped moving while I stayed frozen in my follow-through position for a few seconds, hearing the echo of the splitting ripe melon sound of his head.

"Oh my God," I said, the pan still in my hand as I stared down at Jared's unmoving body.

"Jared? Are you okay?" I asked even though I knew the answer. "Oh God, please don't let this be happening." I thought about turning him over, but I was afraid to touch him. If I didn't see his face or check his pulse or breathing, maybe some part of my mind would let him still be alive, would give him a good, blessed life better than the one he had really lived. He could go on and marry Missy, who would turn out to be a sweet wife, and they would have some beautiful children and a sprawling, graceful house with a swing on the porch. This parallel alternative I imagined was perhaps the only love I ever showed Jared.

The only sound in the room was my breathing—my huffing, unaccompanied breathing.

I didn't know what to do, standing over Jared's body in the kitchen I knew so well, with my mind unspooling and my chest heaving, and just as I was thinking about raising the dead, my mother appeared to me in an amazing vision. Until that point, I had always pictured her the only way I could imagine—a shadowy, warm face bending over me, a pair of caring arms rocking my infant self. She came to me at that moment as she must have really been in the last year of her life—young, delicate, beautiful. She was a waif, a willow, standing next to me. She rested her tiny hand on my shoulder. Nothing could shake this woman who'd had the willpower to drink drain cleaner.

"Sarah," she had said, leaning close to speak directly into my ear. "You have to get out of here. You better run."

And Then It Was Morning

I stayed in the trailer with Jared's ghost for the rest of the night, never sleeping, never daring to close my eyes for longer than a blink. I was trapped there with him—subject to his whims, like I had always been. A part of me knew I deserved to be haunted and even craved the abject terror because it mirrored the punishment I seemed to have dodged, at least for the time being.

Many times during that long night, I thought about leaving the trailer so I could perhaps be free of this hallucinatory spell by standing in the open and confessing my crime, but I wasn't going to jail, not for Jared. And even if it didn't come down to that, there was no point in going home either.

"Go away," I told him. "I'm not going to be a prisoner again, no matter how much you haunt me."

Maybe I slept at some point. The darkness had become a pale gray, making the familiar shapes in the bedroom discernible once again, and then at last, morning sunlight streamed in from around the edges of the closed curtain. A light breeze made the shade bang against the window.

The trailer door swung open, like a miracle, and Jim stepped inside. My relief at seeing light again and at being in the presence of another living and well person was such that I slid over to him when he came in the bedroom and sat down on the mattress. His body drooped as he leaned forward over his knees. He looked tired for once, whereas usually he crackled with impatient energy.

I threw my arms around his neck, squeezing as hard as I could. "You don't know how happy I am to see you."

"Hey now," Jim said, patting my forearm with an awkward flap of his hand. "No need to carry on like that."

"Okay, okay." My voice was soft, edged with unexpected tears. "I'm sorry. I just... I was just so scared waiting here by myself."

Jim gave a weak smile. "You're gonna be all right, kid. Don't worry about it." He kissed me on the mouth. I couldn't help but notice how old he looked, older than my father even.

"So, you didn't tell the police I was here?"

"What do you think? I'm some kind of rat fink? Is that what you think?" Jim pulled away from me.

"No, no, no. Nothing like that." My elation switched to a sort of panic at the sudden intensity of Jim's tone. "I didn't mean anything by it. I just..."

"Well, be careful what you say, then. There's nothing I hate more than a rat. And I've got no use for the goddamn fuzz either. People are better off settling their own problems." Jim pulled off his boots one by one.

As I watched, it occurred to me that maybe part of the reason Jim kept me close was to prevent me from being an easy target for the police. In his system of measurement, the consequences of aiding a fugitive fell on the light side compared with any action that could lead to another person's imprisonment. "I don't think that about you. In fact, no one I've ever known has helped me as much as you have." I risked placing a hand on the top of Jim's smooth head.

Jim covered my hand with his and brought my fingers to his lips. "You are some sweet kid. A pretty one too. Don't mind me, all right? I can never get any sleep around this place. You know what I mean?"

I kissed Jim's mouth with a hard pressure, the first time I had ever made an initial sexual gesture toward him. Jim gave a muffled laugh.

"Maybe you're not such a kid, after all. This is also very tempting, but I've got to get some rest."

"I could make you some breakfast first. Coffee too."

"You go on ahead. I'm going to get some sleep." Jim took off his pants and stretched out on the bed. "Just so you know, Hinkle doesn't have any idea that the police were here asking about you. He thought it was just the usual bullshit I'm always dealing with, like some townie complaining that a joint is rigged or some shit like that."

"Okay," I said, thinking about the bright new day, about the many days in front of me. "So I don't have to leave?"

Jim's eyes were closed. Maybe he was already asleep, but then he answered. "Yeah, it looks like the coast is clear for now, at least. Besides which I'd get a raft of shit from Hinkle if you was to leave now, owing money."

Jim had brought home some nice big sacks of groceries the day before. I was going to go to the kitchen to cook an outstanding breakfast for myself to celebrate having made it through the night. "All right, you get some sleep, then."

"Hey, hang on a second." Jim reached over to grab my hand. His touch filled me with a warm liveliness, a sensation of being singled out in a good way, of being seen and visible. This affection, which people on television and maybe in real life, too, indulged in with casual indifference, felt unique and special, something intended for others but not for me. "You know, though, there's no way of knowing for sure if everything is really squared away with the police. If you want, I got a buddy who could drive you up to Canada. You'd have to figure it out from there, but the fuzz wouldn't be able to touch you." Jim kept his eyes closed while he spoke.

Being outside the reach of police who may or may not have still being looking for me seemed like meager compensation for being dropped off alone with nothing in a foreign country. "No. No, thanks," I said. "I'd rather stay here."

Jim opened his eyes and smiled at me. "Good," he said, squeezing my fingers. The gesture made me realize that he thought I wanted to stay to be with him. I left myself hold his hand for a moment longer. Maybe he was right.

The Locomotion

W hen we arrived in Beloit, I watched, fascinated, as the carnival world was built up around us in a horseshoe pattern, a sort of open oval with the games and food in front so that the visitors would see them first. The rides were in the center, and then the cootch show was toward the back on one side of the loop, and the sideshow was opposite it on the other. In the early morning, before the sun had even risen, a swarm of workers, like the parts of a ticking clock, moved around and crisscrossed what had been an empty field. They erected the rides and built the booths and set up the frame for and draped the canvas sheets of the tent where the sideshow was going to be. They built a raised platform outside the structure where the talker would give his spiel. Folding chairs were set up, and a stage was made. A world was created from nothing in a remarkable amount of time.

Posters in vibrant color and detail hung from the sides of the tent—one of Gigi, with her painted doll's face and whipped-up hair, elegant neck pointing to the sky as she held the hilt of the sword she was swallowing. One of Ike, his painted body garish and eye-catching, with a caption calling him the tattooed wonder of Polynesia. And one of Freddy, the little magnificent man. Jim had a poster, too, showing him as a glass eater with a jagged broken bottle in one hand, his mouth bright red and bleeding. I asked him about it when I saw him later on the back lot. He told me he didn't do it much anymore but that he had gotten the idea to do the glass eating after Charlie-

Charlene, the man-woman, had gotten angry at Hinkle for not paying him-her enough, and they were left with only three acts.

"It can be a tough racket," Jim admitted. "Sometimes, enough tickets don't get sold, so Hinkle takes the difference out the performers' pay, which ain't exactly right." Jim had a worn red handkerchief that he kept half stuffed in the back pocket of his dungarees. He mopped his bald head and the back of his neck in a distracted, repetitive way.

"But that's not fair," I said, thinking of how Hinkle had thrown his dirty shirt at me.

"That's how it goes. Hinkle and Chuck didn't like each other much, so that was part of it. The sideshow ain't what it used to be anyway. Time was you could sell hundreds of tickets, and people believed in what they saw. If you said it was a crocodile boy, they said it was a crocodile boy. Now, everybody wants to stay home and watch TV."

I thought about the image of Jim as a glass eater, the author of his own misfortune with blood running down his chin. "Those posters are really something," I said and meant it. "Will there be one of me?"

"We'll see," Jim said. I guessed that Jim didn't want to commit to spending any money, to anything really, until he had seen me onstage, until an audience had bought tickets and loved my act enough to stand up from their chairs and nudge up to the stage to get a closer look at me.

"Take a look at yourself," Gigi said, nudging me closer to the full-length mirror on her bedroom wall. Her trailer was cramped and so small that we couldn't both stand in the bedroom without having the sliding divider open. The beautiful magenta dress, sewn with such painstaking care, no longer seemed so wonderful now that it was draped over my body. At Gigi's insistence, I had raised the hem higher so that it fell well above my knee. The mirror was narrow, and my image overflowed the sides, even when I took one step away then another until my back was against the opposite wall of the trailer. Mrs. Schendel would be proud of my sewing, but my giant exposed legs, beaded and rippling with dimples and bumpy slabs of fat, made me want to cry. The dress had no sleeves, just a pair of sequined straps, leaving me astounded at the ham-like solidity of my arms. I couldn't remember ever seeing myself like this in my fullness. Gigi had liked the idea of high heels, but that was too dangerous a walk for me, and so we had settled on frilly ankle socks and a shiny pair of patent leather Mary Janes.

Gigi had also worked a deep henna into my hair, giving my ordinary brown a reddish flair. I focused on that and on the dramatic perfection of my makeup—the deep color on my lips and the sweeping blue under my brows that made my eyes seem more green. The big false lashes clung to each other when I blinked. Gigi had even drawn a beauty mark for me. Such a pretty face, I heard Mrs. Schendel say.

"You look good." Gigi pulled one of the straps closer to my neck. "I'm glad we did that curl in your hair. It's nice."

"Yeah, thanks," I said. "So, um, I don't know. Now what should I do?"

Gigi opened the snaps of her housecoat. "Well, I'm going to be just a few more minutes to put on my dress. You head on over to the tent and go in the back. Jim will introduce me, then when I leave the stage, you're up." Gigi leaned over and hugged me. "Just stay relaxed, and you'll do fine," she said with such conviction that I wanted to believe her.

With precious few ideas for my act, I figured my best bet was to do a little dance. That way people could get a good look at my fat, which was what they were paying to see, while I could stay silent and at least partially hidden behind loud, blaring music. The only problem, of course, was that dancing was another one of those things I knew nothing about. I had listened to the radio quite a bit, though, turning the dial away from the stilted AM stations that my father favored as soon as he left the house, and then later, after his death, abandoning them altogether. I remembered raising the volume on the heart-thumping sound of Grand Funk Railroad belting out the song "Locomotion." The beauty of that song was that its lyrics were a type of instruction in movement, telling me what to do, exhorting me to put my hands in the air and swing my hips before making a train. So I wrote a list of body movements and practiced them.

My plan was to prance out on stage then introduce myself, tell some stories about how much I ate, about how it was that I came to be so hugely fat in the first place. People wanted to know that. Then I figured I could hold my arms over my head and do a few twirls so the crowd could see me from every angle. Jim would start the music on my cue, and then the dancing would begin.

I had wanted to watch Gigi do her act, but once I was inside the dressing room, my panic and sense of disbelief made it impossible for me to do anything other than breathe in and out. In and out. In and out. Moments passed. The heat built in the tent, making me wish for a tall glass of delicious icy water. Time carried on, and at last, I had a dim but growing awareness of hearing applause. Walking up the steps to the back of the stage, I was in time to see Gigi rise to her feet and toss her sword into the air before catching it behind her back. The trickiness of the maneuver, the skill behind it, was astounding. How had she ever managed to practice such a thing? The crowd ate it up, cheering, with some of the men whistling through their teeth.

Gigi walked off the stage, waving to her admirers. She passed by me, her face pink and hot when she pressed her cheek against mine. "Knock 'em dead, kid."

Then Jim stepped to the center of the stage, microphone in hand. "Ladies and gentlemen," he said. "We've got a brand-new act for you this evening. We're about to show you something you've never seen, something no one has ever seen. We have a lovely young lady here with a figure so big and robust—why, you could sew together three of an ordinary wife's dresses, and it still wouldn't cover this girl's big backside. I tell you, I found this girl eating a stack of pancakes, ten high at a church supper social. Because, folks, that's the nice sort of wholesome girl she is and well-mannered, too, with her knife and fork. You'd have thought maybe that she was at the queen's house to dine. And I said that's mighty strange, eating pancakes for supper. Then the deacon told me it was because the lovely Lola Rolls had ate all the ham steaks and potatoes they had fried. She had five ham steaks and another eight pounds of fried potatoes and a dozen ears of corn. So when she was still hungry, there was nothing left to give her but pancakes and syrup. It's all true, her father told me. I can hardly afford to feed her..."

I stuffed my fist into my mouth, shocked and appalled at this mention of my father, even just as some imaginary character in Jim's talker spiel.

"So I told her father I would give her a job here in the carnival where she could meet you kind people and help her aging father to boot."

As soon as I was alone with Jim, I was going to tell him to back off my father, make it straight that Jim had no right or reason to mention him.

"And now it's my distinct pleasure to present to you, ladies and gentlemen, Miss Lola Rolls." Jim half turned toward me, extending his right arm in my direction.

I took his hand and stepped onto the stage—and then I saw them all. The faces looked shiny and globular, like raw poultry. The glare from the lights drenched my body in immediate sweat. All eyes were on me, just like they had been when I sat on the schoolroom floor, when I sang in church. Really, whenever I went anywhere out among people. Jim stepped to the side. My first instinct was to walk right back off the stage, to go back to Jim's trailer to wash my face and take off my beautiful, ridiculous dress. There was a long cotton nightgown I had sewn two years ago and brought from home with me. I wanted to rinse my body in cool water, tucking a fresh towel into my folds to dry my skin, then cover myself from head to floor in that fine white material. Instead, I made up my mind to pretend that I was wearing a costume, by which I didn't simply mean the absurd new dress that was like nothing I had ever owned—rather I viewed my entire body as a cover to hide me. Plucking up the hem of my skirt in a delicate pinch of thumb and forefinger, I experienced something similar to what I imagined was the sensation of being inside a submarine, looking out at the wavering water but not getting wet.

I crossed the stage and took Jim's hand. He held the microphone away from his body. "Make this good," he whispered then handed the microphone to me.

After Jim left the stage, I stared at the crowd and smiled. "Well, thank you, Jim, for that lovely introduction. Now, folks, I would have been here a bit sooner, but I baked these two big old cream pies this afternoon. And well, I had to get a spoon and eat them up right away. You see, I only had one roasted turkey for lunch, and I was so hungry I thought I would die."

The audience gasped and laughed at me, at my fat, at the overt audacity of my imaginary food binge. Gigi was right. These people were nothing but a bunch of goddamn marks. When the noise died down a bit, I apologized again, this time for having a nonexistent blot of whipped cream adhered to my upper lip. I lifted the front hem of my dress to wipe my mouth, giving the people a pretty good look at the upper part of my legs and the frilly undergarment I wore. That really caused a stir, especially among the men. I feigned girlish embarrassment, twisting from side to side. My movements felt outlandish and idiotic, but the crowd appeared to love it.

I cued Jim to blast Grand Funk Railroad and swayed my body to the beat, making a train and moving on.

When the carnival closed for the night, after I had done my act several times, everyone filed over to the G-top. This time I was able to join them. Gigi called me over to a table where she was sitting with Ike and two other women. She introduced me to Ora Ann, the fortune teller, who offered me a tarot-card reading whenever I was so inclined. The other woman was Daisy, one of the cootch dancers, who, it seemed, was friends once again with Gigi. Daisy filled a plastic cup for me with beer from the pitcher on the table. I had never tasted beer before, and to the laughter of the others, declared it not too good but not too bad either.

Some of the people were playing cards or shooting dice. The "G" in "G-top" stood for gambling. Hinkle sat at a big table toward the back, a fan of cards half hiding his face.

Gigi noticed me glancing in that direction. "Gambling is Hinkle's thing. When people play with him, they get cleaned out."

Seeing Hinkle as part of the scene I also inhabited ironed out some of the rough resentment his presence had ignited in me until then. I saw that, in one sense or another, we all had the same way of life. We were all with it.

My performances that night were, to put it plainly, not fabulous or even especially great, but they were good enough to cement my place in the sideshow and to make Jim happy. The full extent of this measured success became apparent the next morning when Jim asked Ike to help him move an extra box spring and mattress from his truck into the trailer.

When I got tired of standing there watching the two of them work, I went to sit down in the truck. Ike saw me struggling to pull myself into the cab, so he ran over to help me by pushing on my backside with his left shoulder, his face pressing against me in an awkward way. Jim laughed so hard he had to bend at the waist to rest the flat of his hands on his thighs. I could imagine what Jim saw—the incongruous image of a painted man with his bald, rainbow-bright head mashed against big, waving buttocks until it seemed his face would get lost in them.

"Stop giggling, Lola. I'm gonna lose my grip on you," Ike said, also laughing. The hilarity of the situation only further decreased my ability to help pull myself into the truck. I couldn't remember when anything had ever been so funny to me or even the last time I had laughed at all. The joy of the sensation created an open lightness in my chest. The sheet of calm blue sky filled my vision when I looked up to try to catch my breath.

Later, when Jim flopped back on the new mattress, pushed up against the existing one to make a sea of bed big enough for me to swim in, I crawled on all fours toward him. Jim held out his hand to steady the mattress. Still on my hands and knees, I pressed my face into Jim's chest, my forehead compressing his heart.

"Home sweet home," he said.

Gulf Town

A lot of the carnies from Midstate Carnival and all the sideshow performers spent the winter on the Florida Gulf Coast in a flyspeck town called Gulf Town, or Gulfy, for short. Back in the 1940s, Gulfy was home to mostly shrimpers and a few fruit growers, but in 1951, a couple of sideshow performers known as Jonah the Skeleton, a thin man, and Sweet Chenille, a bearded lady, traveled through one winter. They liked the look of the town and the rhythm of the Gulf waters so much that they decided to retire there. As the word spread among the carnies, more and more of them poured into the town to spend the winter, with many settling there on a permanent basis.

Little Freddy, in particular, was anxious to get away. "It's a great place, Lo-Lo," he said. "Sideshow folks like you and me can really relax there and get a break from all these normals pointing and laughing. Did you know the post office even has a section of low counter for the dwarf performers, and some of the barstools at the Showstop have steps up the side?" Little Freddy, Ike, Gigi, and I were all sitting together to eat dinner on our second-to-last night in Onalaska, our final gig of the season.

The evening air had the smallest nip of cold to it. I closed my eyes, seeing a big expanse of water like I had never seen and a Christmas without snow. A warm winter, instead of one spent staring at the wall, wrapped in blankets, waiting for something to happen, for my real life to begin. Back then, I had imagined a university education or maybe a glittery literary career or a gentle husband. I understood at last that those dreams had never been plans for the future but rather devices to move me from one day to the next, to keep me steady while I inched my way along the canyon's edge.

Making money also helped. Having grown up with no luxuries other than food, the sensation of cash in my hand was extraordinary. I developed a certain taste for items, like makeup and shoes and slippery lotions and snowflake-light scented powders for my body, items I had never coveted or even considered before then.

The trip down to Gulfy took about four days, with Jim driving the truck and me riding in the trailer for most of the way. We could have made it sooner, I was sure, but traveling south offered a type of interval to switch from the frenetic pace of the carnival circuit to the calmer air of the offseason. When we stopped for the night, parking the truck and trailer at some campground, it seemed there was never a shortage of old or new friends or at least acquaintances with whom we could drink and sit around the campfire, exchanging stories about events that seemed better in the retelling.

On our last day of the trip, I sat next to Jim in the truck cabin so I could see Gulf Town as we approached it. "What's that smell?" I asked, rolling down the window to better catch the complicated scent, a murky saltiness, sharp and fishy, that I had never experienced before.

Jim laughed. "That's the gulf, baby. We're almost there."

When the water finally came into view, Jim pulled to the side of the road so I could stare at its expanse from the window.

"It's amazing," I said in a quiet voice, and Jim kissed the side of my face.

The town itself enthralled me, smallish with two gas stations, if you didn't count the pumps at the docks that the fishing boats used, and a grocery store where I could wheel my cart through aisles where no one would point or stare. There was also a drugstore with a lunch counter, a small diner, a post office, and an eclectic department store that somehow managed to sell everything despite its reduced size. Of the handful of bars, we liked to gather at the Showstop, where Gigi and Jim were good friends with the owner, Lonny. I understood right away what Little Freddy had meant when he described Gulfy as the perfect place for a sideshow freak. In an area populated by carnival folk and human oddities, like the man and his sons whose fingers were fused into claw shapes and who earned their livings as Lobster Man and the Lobster Boys, I had found my place. In that conglomeration of outsiders, I was where I belonged—on the inside.

I assumed that Jim and I would simply park the trailer somewhere in Gulfy, but to my surprise, he rented a nice white house for us close to the gulf, where a lovely slice of water could be seen from the front window. "I have half a mind to go on and buy this place, if I ever get around to retiring," Jim said.

The house was probably only a bit larger than the one I had grown up in. It even had the same division of space—two bedrooms separated by a bathroom down a short hallway, a living room with a big bay window facing toward the gulf, and a largish kitchen. After living with Jim in the trailer for two months, though, the space appeared cavernous, an open area where anything could happen. "I love it. It's perfect."

Jim kissed my lips. "It is nice, isn't it?"

I had set my mind to learning two things that winter—how to drive and how to contact Mrs. Schendel and make her believe that I was in fact living in New York City, with my grandmother, maybe. The first part was a simple matter of getting some lessons from Jim and Gigi in his truck. In fact, the two of them were happy to have me practice my driving on the way home after drinking at the Showstop because they always drank more than I did. My body spread so far out on the driver's seat that Gigi would sit on Jim's lap and play endless stupid jokes, like covering my eyes with her hand or screaming at me to look out and holy shit what was that in the middle of the road. In the mornings, I liked to take the truck down to the parking lot by the dock to look at the water, where I would sit motionless for long stretches, my body swaying with the roll and pull of the soft waves.

Jim told me to cut the tie with Mrs. Schendel, that whatever good she could provide me in terms of information about the events following Jared's death was outweighed by the risk of my revealing too much or of her not being able to keep a secret. I ignored him, though, in part because he didn't know anything about Mrs. Schendel, a hard worker who had carried on a quiet affair with a married man in broad daylight with such discretion and tight-lipped aplomb that I hadn't noticed, even though I lived in the same house where it took place.

As it turned out, getting a letter stamped with a postmark from another place was a pretty easy thing to do. Paul at the Gulf Town Post Office, with its low counter for dwarves just like Little Freddy had described, explained the whole thing to me. You put your sealed letter in a second envelope addressed to General Delivery in whatever city you want—New York, in this case—and the letter goes to the post office, where a postal worker opens it. He discards the outer envelope and processes the sealed and stamped interior letter addressed to an Ursula Schendel with a New York City postmark. The same steps could have been applied in reverse to receive letters from Mrs. Schendel. She could have mailed her letters to General Delivery in New York. I suppose I could have then filled out a form to have my mail forwarded to a post office box in Gulf Town, but that would have created a paper trail. Though I didn't have a tremendous amount of respect for the investigatory prowess of the police from my town, likely I was better off relying on Mrs. Schendel's discretion than on their incompetence. So I told Mrs. Schendel to send the letters to me at a post office box in Gulf Town, under the name of Dolores Barnes—Barnes like the Schendels' dairy barn outside the back window of my old house, and Dolores, a legal, formal version of Lola.

February 6, 1977
Dear Sarah,

Thank God I got a letter from you! I've been worried to death about you ever since you left, not even knowing what to think half the time. I did like you asked and told everyone that you're living in New York City now. I know for a fact that some people, Missy especially, didn't believe me. Truth be told, Missy has been saying a lot of ugly things ever since Jared died. She was the one who found his body. When I saw the rescue squad in your driveway that morning, my first thought was that maybe you had fallen, and Jared had called for help to get you off the floor. When I opened the door, Missy was crying in one of the kitchen chairs with poor Jared lying there on the floor.

I asked where you were, but no one could tell me anything. Missy had this blank look on her face when I mentioned your name, like she had never even stopped to wonder what might have happened to you. I looked around your bedroom, trying to figure out what was going on. Your clothes all looked like they were still in the closet, but when I started flipping through them, I realized that your good skirt, the one with the tiny checks, and the two blouses we had just made were missing. That made me think maybe you had packed those things yourself and left under your own steam. I searched your dresser and bedside table and even under the bed, thinking you must have left me a note to say what was going on.

Right about then, when they were wheeling poor Jared out on the stretcher, Missy jumped to her feet. "Your precious Sarah did this because she hated Jared when he was never anything but good to her," she said.

You could have heard a pin drop. I told her to shut her mouth and that she couldn't say such terrible things, no matter how upset she was.

Rick Wilkins, that nice boy who helps Luther buck hay sometimes in the summer, was one of the rescue volunteers. He told me not to worry because you were sure to turn up soon and that they had already radioed for the sheriff to come check out things. I didn't know what to say, but I thanked Rick anyway.

Missy rode along to the hospital with Jared's body. After everyone had left, I searched every inch of the house for some kind of message from you. Then I set about cleaning and ordering all the rooms because I had no idea who would do that. Just so you know, I made sure the kitchen and stove really sparkled. I scrubbed the dishes and bleached down all the cooking pans and surfaces.

The sheriff came by just as I was closing up. He informed me that Jared should have been left where he was because his death looked suspicious. He also said that I shouldn't have been allowed to be there in the house by myself. He wanted to know where you were, too, and I said I would let him know as soon as I found out anything. Right after you called me, I stopped by to tell him that you had left to live with your grandmother in New York City. I also mentioned, just like you wanted, how you and Jared had parted on good terms and how, even though you were sad about Jared's death, you didn't have the money to travel back home so soon after paying your way to get there.

Your father bought a four-plot parcel over at Maple Lawn, and Jared is buried there with him. We took a collection at First Lutheran to pay for the rest of the funeral expenses. I was there for all the viewing hours and for the burial. All the mourners, even Missy and her family, came to my house afterward for a luncheon.

There was some ugly talk—and not just from Missy either. People wanted to know where you were and why you weren't taking care of things yourself. The important thing, though, is that, in the end, Jared was laid to rest, and he's at peace now.

When I got your letter, I took that to the sheriff also. I especially wanted him to see the New York City postmark on the envelope, but I'm not sure it made much of an impression on him. He says Jared's death is still considered suspicious and that you're a person of interest and that he needs a concrete return address so he can find you. "Of course," I told him. "I'll do my best to get that to you."

Anyway, Missy must have a friend down at the sheriff's office who lets her know if there's any news about the investigation of Jared's death because I took your letter to show the sheriff just the other morning, and by afternoon, Missy had shown up at my house, all dirty from working in the sty, talking like a crazy person. She said that she didn't believe a word about you being in New York City with your grandmother and that she thought you ran off with the carnival.

Honestly, I barely even recognized her at first because every other time I've seen Missy, she's had makeup painted up to her eyebrows and enough lipstick to choke a horse. I told her she had to give up those aw-ful ideas and to move on with her life because that's what Jared would have wanted. You know I don't believe in speaking ill of the dead, but I reminded her of how Jared drank almost every day and how careless and sloppy he could get.

I don't know if she'll take my advice and forget about this or if she'll keep trying to find you. Thank you for sending me your address. I miss you a lot, and a day doesn't go by that I don't wonder how you're doing. To tell the truth, though, I think you're smart to stay away.

I owe you a big apology, Sarah. After your father died, I worried about you and Jared living alone together in that house from the very beginning. I tried to see you every day or get you to try and visit me. At least that's what I did at first. And then maybe it was every other day. I let myself think that things weren't as bad as they were between you and Jared because that's what I wanted to believe. I hope you can forgive me.

Anyway, Luther is laid up sick, so I've got to go make his lunch, a light soup probably that won't be too hard on his stomach. You know I'm not one to complain, but I do wish that he'd get up out of that chair. I've certainly done my fair share of work while I've had aches and pains.

I hope this letter finds you well and that you'll write back soon.
Take care of yourself.
Love,
Ursula (Mrs. Schendel)

Scratchy

Gigi, Jim, and I spent a lot of time at the Showstop, which was located right in the center of Gulf Town, not too far from the water. One afternoon when business was slow, Lonny, the owner, took advantage of the lull in action to sit down at the table with Gigi and me. "How are my two favorite girls?" he asked, tucking the corner of the damp rag he always carried into the waistband of his pants. No matter how much Lonny wiped the tables, polished the long surface of the bar, or shined the mirrored backsplash adorned with license plates from all over the country, the Showstop still retained a complicated smell—a beery yeastiness mixed with old smoke and ammonia—that a person only became accustomed to over time.

"Hey, Lola," he said. "That's Scratchy over there talking to Jim. Remember I was telling you about him?" Lonny jerked his chin toward the table where Jim had been shooting pool and was now engaged in conversation with a small, skinny man who had long black-and-gray hair pulled back in a ponytail. When I had told Lonny that I needed some real, legitimate documents with my actual name, Dolores Barnes, printed on them, he had said I should talk to a guy named Scratchy who lived a few hours inland.

"Gigi, baby," Lonny said. "How many free drinks would it take for you to marry me?" He cupped her elbow, linking his arm through hers.

"You're too good to me, Lonny." Gigi patted his hand and looked away.

Lonny laughed, even as his eyes flashed with sadness.

"You're too good to us all," I told Lonny, slapping his knee to distract him from staring at Gigi.

"Scratchy's a funny little guy. Why you want to talk to him?" Gigi asked, probably only to change the subject.

Missy wouldn't stop. I knew it. Mrs. Schendel knew it too. The best I could do was to be prepared, and Scratchy could help me with that. He could get me identity documents for Dolores Barnes, make me be on paper the person I claimed to be in conversation.

Gigi leaned closer and half whispered, "I hear Scratchy shacks up with a black woman."

"Well, the heart wants what it wants," Lonny said. He stood up and wiped the table with his cleaning rag and then went back behind the bar to wash glasses. Gigi watched Lonny walk away, her eyes following him with such a degree of concentration that she looked as if she had been assigned the task of memorizing his movements.

"He keeps this place spotless ever since he took over for his father," she said. "He fired Alfredo from the kitchen because he didn't wash his hands enough." Gigi glanced at my plate of French fries. "I hear the new guy is better, though."

Jim placed his pool cue on the rack, then he and Scratchy walked over. Pressing his hands into my shoulders, Jim massaged me, working my bulk like bread dough. "Scratchy here's saying we should drive out to his place." Jim took a drink from my beer glass.

I smiled at Scratchy, but his attention was elsewhere, staring at the wall behind me. "Hey, is that you?" he asked, pointing at the photograph of me eating a giant bowl of spaghetti and meatballs. Lonny had asked to have that picture taken, making me feel like a minor celebrity. He had framed it with a sign that read Fat Ladies Love Our Food. I hadn't expected to like the photograph as much as I did. I had even signed it *Lola Rolls XOXO.*

"In the flesh," I told Scratchy.

After I finished my beer and food, Jim and I left for Scratchy's, heading away from the gulf, down a network of smaller and smaller roads with stretching green swampland, part earth and part water, on either side. The sky had turned sunset pink by the time we reached Scratchy's house, a peeling white building with a sagging covered porch extending along the front.

Once we were inside, Scratchy started talking about how to build an entire identity and create a new person. "It's probably easier to do than you think." We were sitting at his chrome-legged kitchen table, the surface of which, at least the parts that weren't cluttered with dirty ashtrays and stacked newspapers, was a soft pearly white. "Most people don't get their Social Security number until they get their first job. You got ladies who get married and never work, or at least not on the books, anyway, and you can get them a number anytime." At this mention of ladies, Scratchy pointed at the back door. "Thelma should be home from the store any minute now, if one of the gators hasn't got her." It was hard to tell if he was serious or making a joke.

Scratchy and Jim went on to talk about the number of people they both knew, while my supposed part in our little party focused on waiting for another woman to show up and entertain me.

"Yeah, I had a good trick too," I said, tired of being left out of the conversation. "I needed it to look like I was sending a letter from New York City, so I figured out how to do that." Scratchy listened with great attention to my description of how I had arranged for Mrs. Schendel to receive a letter with a New York City postmark.

He sucked on his cigarette. "Yeah, that's a good one. Completely aboveboard and hard to trace." This praise from Scratchy, the way he nodded, how he appeared to weigh my words, made me feel like an equal sitting at the table.

Jim, however, scraped the legs of his chair against the linoleum as he shifted in his seat, tossing his cigarettes and Zippo lighter onto the table. The abruptness of his movements and the distinct metal ting of his lighter hitting the hard surface made me realize what I had done. Jim had told me not to contact Mrs. Schendel, and not only had I ignored that command, I had also disclosed my actions to another person. It was a relief, then, when Scratchy's old lady, Thelma, walked in through the back door toting a bulging paper sack, a medium-sized caramel-colored dog with a white bib of fur and lopsided ears by her side.

"Hey, Tellie," Scratchy said. "You know Jim, and this here's Lola."

Thelma stopped in her tracks when she saw me. Only her soft cloud of hair moved under the ceiling fan. She wore high-stacked platform sandals and deep-purple lipstick, an unlikely match to the plain-faced, skinny Scratchy. I struggled to get to my feet because it seemed like the sort of thing one should do. The certain taboo of a white man living with a black woman caused me to forget about my problem with Jim. When I smiled, the skin on my face felt hot and tight.

Thelma sucked in a deep breath. The grocery bag she hugged to her chest slipped a few inches before she recovered her grip on it. "Hey there," she said at last.

The two of us stood frozen in place, studying each other for so long that Jim and Scratchy stopped talking to watch us. Then, in the same precise moment, Thelma and I burst out laughing. She put her paper sack down on the table while the two of us kept on going in that hysterical way that feeds on itself and fills your eyes with good tears.

"I made some pudding," Thelma sputtered. "It's butterscotch."

And then Jim and Scratchy started laughing too. Thelma took a big glass bowl of butterscotch pudding from the refrigerator and put in on the table while I emptied the paper sack of its oversized bottles of beer and orange soda and a carton of unfiltered Camel cigarettes.

"So, you didn't have no trouble then?" Scratchy asked Thelma.

Thelma was pulling down drinking glasses from a high kitchen shelf. She halted in the middle of that task at the sound of Scratchy's voice, her back looking hard and solid, unbendable. "Nah. Just to the store and back. Besides, I had Useless with me." Thelma nodded toward the brown-and-white dog resting his head on Scratchy's knee.

"Some of the people in town where we go grocery shopping and buy gas don't like me very much," Scratchy explained as he rubbed Useless's crooked one-up, one-down ears. "They get pissed off that I can earn money out here in the swamp, and they're so poor they can't even afford to pay attention."

I laughed a little bit at Scratchy's joke.

Thelma sat down across from Jim and me. "They hate us both," she said. "Me for being black and him for shacking up with me. They're going to burn down this damn house one day with us inside it." Thelma's matter-of-fact tone, at odds with the seriousness of her words, made me understand that she and Scratchy had been facing threats of harm for so long that a certain latent danger had become part of their daily lives.

"Hang on. I got something to show you all," Scratchy said, breaking the spell. He left the kitchen and came back holding a mayonnaise jar with a clear liquid inside, which he explained was moonshine made by a second cousin in Tennessee. "This is some good shit," he announced, passing around squatty jelly-jar glasses to all of us.

The first sip of moonshine was painful and horrible, but like so many things, I got used to it. That home-brewed liquor appeared powerful enough even to have rinsed away the hard edges of Jim's anger. His body became more pliant as he drank, sinking down in his chair and then leaning over to kiss my neck. The alcohol blurred my earlier anxiety over Jim's rage as well. Even though I suspected the topic of my contacting Mrs. Schendel would come up again later, it seemed less important than it had before we started drinking. I squeezed Jim's leg under the table, liking the hard, sinewy feel of it.

"I ask you, Lola," Scratchy said, "have you ever tasted anything like this hooch? It's as clean as water. You can drink all you want, and tomorrow morning, you'll wake up with your head as clear as a bell."

Thelma slapped her legs then buried her face in her own lap, her whole back heaving with laughter until she was able to come up for air. "That's a damn lie," she said, wiping the tears from her eyes. "That shit is so strong that Scratchy has to change the tops of the jars because the moonshine eats away the lining. It's a fact."

"Ah, Tellie here don't know what she's talking about. You listen to me, darlin'. You'll see I'm right. You flying yet? Because this shit will give you some wings." Scratchy poured some more of the moonshine into my glass. "You want an ice cube, you can have you an ice cube, but you can't mix something as fine as this with anything else."

The alcohol didn't send me on an upward trajectory like Scratchy suggested. Rather, I experienced a type of spreading, a lateral, encompassing flow that pushed Jim's previous displeasure and Thelma's deadpan fear into some forgotten part of my mind, leaving space for me to be filled with a sense of warmth and well-being. "Jim," I whispered in a loud voice, "come here. I have to tell you something." Wrapping my arm around Jim's neck, I pulled his head close to me. "I love you."

Jim and I spent the night on a makeshift bed of pullout-couch mattress and pillows and made love on the floor in a pawing, jumbled drunken haze. I kept telling Jim that we had to be quiet, shushing him with such hissing vehemence that some drops of spit landed on his face, which only made me laugh more. When we were finished, I noticed that Scratchy and Thelma must have had the same idea, judging by the creaking bedsprings above us and the rhythmic thump of something, probably a headboard, hitting the wall. The pace of the banging increased then ceased with a final slam as Scratchy yelled loud and clear, "Save me, sweet baby Jesus."

I had to press a pillow over my face because I couldn't remember ever having heard anything even half as funny. Jim wiped tears from his eyes and struggled to catch his breath. "Scratchy's daddy was a preacher," he said.

"Poor baby Jesus—getting called upon at a time like this."

When I laughed, a small throbbing kernel of pain, like bright light, pulsated behind my eye. "My head is killing me." I pressed the heels of my hands against my temples and smacked my dry lips together.

Jim walked to the kitchen to wash his face and head in the sink, taking a squirt from the dish soap bottle on the counter and rubbing it on his chest and under his arms. I sifted through the linens and pillows on the floor to retrieve and reassemble my clothes, but bending down like that made my head pound, so I simply wrapped myself in the sheet and went to stand next to Jim. His body looked wet and slippery. The sleek freshness of his skin made my chest constrict.

"I'm sorry I didn't tell you that I sent a letter to Mrs. Schendel," I said because I had hated having that secret between us, and the grimness of my hangover notwithstanding, I was happy with how the party with Thelma and Scratchy appeared to have spurred a new intimacy between Jim and me, giving our relationship an everyday feel. "She's the only mother I ever had." When Jim didn't respond, I tried to think what else I could say to convince him it had been a good idea to contact Mrs. Schendel. "Also, she wrote me with some really good information about what's going on at home."

Jim ceased his ablutions to stare at me. "How's that? She wrote you a letter? Where did she send it?" The tap was still open. The water ran into the sink over the glasses we had drunk from last night. "Jesus Christ, Lola! Did you tell her where you are?"

"No, of course not," I said, turning off the water because the sound of it only increased the feeling of panic rising in my chest. "I mean, not exactly. Paul helped me open a post office box so she could send me stuff."

Jim stood motionless, his face expressionless. The eerie calm of his demeanor scared me a bit. "Do you mean Paul, the one who works at the Gulf Town Post Office? That Paul?" Jim took a deep breath, probably trying to remain calm. He wasn't very successful. "What the fuck is wrong with you, Lola? Do you want the fucking police to find you? Is that what it is? Never mind that it's my goddamn neck on the line too!"

I could feel myself shrinking away from Jim's rage, hating my own fear, how it settled in the bottom of my stomach, stretching down into the backs of my legs to make them weak. "It's not like that. She's helping me by telling the sheriff I'm in New York City, and she even used bleach to clean the kitchen where my brother died. So nothing bad is going to happen because she would never tell anybody anything." I pictured Mrs. Schendel sitting at the sewing bench in our old house, humming as she worked, keeping me company, making my family's life better and more normal than it ever could have been without her. "If you knew her, you'd know she's no rat." The quiet conviction of my words soothed Jim somewhat. "I wish you could meet her," I continued, talking to try to fix the situation. It made me sad as well to think that Mrs. Schendel and Jim would never know each other, never sit together at a table to talk and eat and drink—the before and after of my life joining together somehow.

Jim pulled a strand of paper towels from the roll sitting on the counter and started drying himself. "All right, I get it. I do. It's just that now's not the time for any trouble, you know? Goddamn Hinkle is running Midstate into the ground with his gambling. One season we're running high, and the next we don't even have enough money to pay people. Little Freddy and Ike are pissed off about one thing and another, and you got Gigi crying into her beer because she says she's swallowed too many swords as it is." Jim wrapped his arms around my shoulders. I dropped the thin sheet I'd been holding in front of myself so he could press against me, pushing me into the edge of the table, sliding it across the linoleum and into the wall. His naked body was damp from the water and perfumed from the dish soap.

"Hey, where you all get off to?" Scratchy called from the bottom of the stairs. "Ah, shit," he said when he walked into the kitchen and saw the two of us naked and holding on to each other. "Will you look at that?" he said. "Damn, Jim, you got yourself a whole lotta woman there."

The Next Season

With a new birth certificate in hand, I was far better prepared for the next season with Midstate. I had also bought an old sewing machine to fashion myself some costumes and, more importantly since I'd left home with only two extra outfits, new clothes. They weren't as expert as what Mrs. Schendel might have made, but they were more colorful and comfortable, too, because I allowed myself shirts and dresses without sleeves, skirts above the knee, and cropped pants.

Hinkle appeared to have a renewed good spirit about him that Jim said was the result of some big wins at the Tropicana in Las Vegas. "That's what he does when he's not with Midstate," Jim explained. "He plays poker and some blackjack. He used to bum around the Indian bingo halls in Florida, but that got too small stakes for him."

My ability to handle the audience also improved during my performances. By relying on Gigi's advice to remember that the people in the crowd were only marks and by having a quieter mind and more experience during my second season, I was able not only to inure myself to the audience's unkind comments but also to control the situation and, by extension, the people who had paid to watch me. One night during a stint near Oak Creek, some guy, probably twenty to twenty-five years old, yelled out, "Hey, you big whale. How about I fill you up, do you a favor, and make you a sperm whale?" He laughed so much that his idiotic friends had to slap him on the back. His voice was loud and piercing, with the sharp clarity to carry a good distance. People around him started laughing as well.

I had been doing a few tap dance steps, the bouncing motion of which really made my body jiggle, while singing something like one of the chants that schoolgirls did when they jumped rope. I tip-tapped my way to the front of the stage. "Hey, man!" I yelled. "Yeah, you. Honey, if you want to catch a whale, you're going to need a great big harpoon, not that little fishing pole you've got. You're better off in the shallow end."

The audience drew a deep, collective breath at my outrageous statement, followed by immediate raucous laughter. I would never have had the nerve to say such a thing out loud a year ago. An older man, probably in his sixties or so, clapped his hands in glee at my response and said that he loved me. He was close enough to the stage that I could hear him as plain as day, but still he mimed the words to me by touching his sternum then crossing his arms over his chest and pointing at me to make sure I understood.

That older man became an admirer, of sorts. Over the course of a week or so, he waited for me outside the sideshow tent until the carnival closed down. Every night, he brought me a basket of corn cakes, which I would later take with me to the G-top to share with the girls. Each time he told me a bit more about the course of his life—of how he had been widowed three times, with each wife dying before she had the chance to produce any children, and of how lonely he felt with no woman to warm his bed. He said I looked like a big strong girl, though, and that he was certain he could handle me. Though I joked with the others about Old Man Corn Cake, who had never once thought to tell me his name despite his interest in making me the fourth Mrs. Whatever, his devotion—bumbling, harmless, and just this side of creepy—helped me understand that Jim was not the only man who would want me. After that, the sexual tinge of the way men inventoried my body when I was on stage became more apparent.

The last night I saw Old Man Corn Cake, he was wearing a nice button-down shirt and a tie. He had his usual basket but also a paper grocery sack. "I figured we should spend some time and get to know each other better." He held up the basket. "How about you and me go to one of these trailers? You can take off your dress, and we'll have ourselves a nice snack."

"Mister, that's not going to happen, so you better get on out of here." His unchivalrous approach made him seem less like a besotted admirer and more like a dirty old pervert.

"Now, sweetheart," he said, "I got some bottled beer and sticks of butter in this grocery sack, so you don't have to worry none about having a dry muffin."

Then I started laughing because I couldn't help myself, unable to stop even as tears filled my eyes and ran down my cheeks. Old Man Corn Cake shuffled away without another word, leaving behind his basket and grocery sack, the contents of which I took to the G-top to share with Gigi, Ora Ann, and Daisy.

"You know," Gigi said, buttering one of the corn cakes, "these really do taste a lot better with the butter."

"And they go better with beer than you'd think." Daisy laughed.

"To tell you the truth, girls, I feel a little bad that I laughed at the poor guy, even if he was a bit of a dirty old man," I said. "He seemed so lonely."

Gigi leaned over to put her arm around my neck. "I know," she said in a quiet voice. "And he cared so much about your muffin too."

The three of them laughed again. I joined in, knowing there was likely no way I could ever make them feel sorry for a mark.

"Easy come, easy go, I suppose," I said. "Too bad, though, that he couldn't have waited one more day to see the new show with me and Little Freddy."

Little Freddy and I had concocted the idea of acting out a wedding ceremony. The bridal gown I had made, a time-consuming endeavor, was hot and scratchy with layers of crunchy crinoline underneath. Little Freddy, the incongruous groom, would jump into my arms once we were married, then I would dance, spinning him around and around. We also did a separate performance for some inside money where we acted out the wedding night. Little Freddy would dive under my dress and make obscene noises and movements out of the audience's view. Then he would try to belly crawl, gasping and desperate, out from under my skirt. "That's just too much woman for me." And I would take our prop broom and sweep him back under my gown and tell him he wasn't done yet. The crowd ate it up, cheering and whistling, so we made some good money right from the start.

Jim loved it much less so. "You need to rethink that bit with Little Freddy," he told me when we were back at the trailer after the act debuted. He opened one of the kitchen cabinets then slammed it shut, as if he had no idea what he was looking for.

"Why would I want to do that? Fred and I made some good inside money on that." I filled a glass with water from the kitchen tap, suppressing my smile at the idea that Jim was jealous of Little Freddy. He wouldn't want to admit that, of course, but neither did he seem able to think of any logical way to explain his objection.

"For one thing," Jim said, "it doesn't make any kind of sense for you to spend money to make a wedding dress when you can only use it for one single act."

Jim's line of reasoning would seem to argue in favor of my doing the wedding act with Freddy as much as I could. Rather than engage with Jim in a pointless conversation in which he would likely never cop to feeling threatened by a man half his size, I simply kissed him on the forehead. "Who knows? Maybe I'll get married in it."

"Ha ha. Very funny," Jim said.

"I don't see what's so funny about it."

Jim slammed out the door. He would probably be gone for the rest of the night. As the hours wore on, my hurt and outrage that Jim should find the idea of marrying me a laughable, far-fetched possibility when, in essence, we lived together as husband and wife warred with the knowledge that he held me in enough esteem that he believed I was sufficiently attractive to entice another man.

Jim's absence for an entire night wasn't a particular cause for concern. In fact, he stayed out until dawn about three or four times a month, usually leaving in a good mood with a kiss or an affable wave of his hand. I imagined he spent the time with Weedy or Roscoe or maybe Ike playing cards and getting drunk, or else hitting the bars in whatever town we visited. Sometimes, I went with him, but I also liked to stay home, happy for the extreme privacy of being able to eat with no one watching. Other times, Gigi would talk me into going for a ride, or she would know who had good hooch or pills or even some special delectable food for me, and we would make the rounds that way. The oddities and hardships of carnival life notwithstanding, I had come to realize that I could have fun as well, something that had been in very scant supply at home.

Jim's side of the bed was still empty the next morning. The clock on the night table, the one I had put in the trailer because its endless ticking soothed me, as did its ability to help orient me upon waking, showed that it was past seven. I pulled down the heavy brown blanket I sometimes hung over the window frame at night to keep out the morning light.

Gigi's trailer was visible from the bedroom window. Later on, I would go over to tell her the story about how Jim had laughed at the idea of ever marrying me. She would listen to me and probably tell me not to worry, that I was Jim's old lady anyway even if we weren't married. Thinking about my future conversation with Gigi and her reasoning, my anger at Jim began to dissipate. Then, as I watched, the door to Gigi's trailer opened, and out stepped Jim, wearing his clothes from the day before. He rubbed his hands over his face and started walking back home. A cold lump fell from my throat to my stomach.

Jim looked surprised to see me standing in the kitchen when he opened the trailer door. "You're up early," he said, going over to the kitchen sink. He stripped off his shirt and tossed it onto the counter and splashed water on his face and under his arms then put his whole head under the tap.

"Is there some reason you can't do that in the bathroom?" I snapped, saying the first thing that came to mind.

Jim dried himself with the dish towel. "What's up your ass?" He let the towel fall onto the counter. "You're not still mad, are you, that—"

I placed both hands on Jim's chest and pushed him to rid myself of his galling nonchalance. He lost his balance and stumbled against the counter. Knowing that I had this power to move him fueled my voice with authority, ensured that Jim would hear what I had to say loud and clear. "What's up my ass? Well, let's see, my old man was out sleeping with my best friend."

Jim stood shocked to immobility, as if my anger defied belief. Grabbing two handfuls of my own hair, I squeezed my eyes shut and screamed. "I don't know who to hate more. You or Gigi."

Jim grabbed my wrists and held them tight in front of my face. "Stop it now. Quit acting so goddamned crazy."

I pulled free and turned my back on him to stare at the wall because I feared I might splinter and break if I looked any longer at this man who, flawed and unpredictable though he could sometimes be, had seemed like one of the few trustworthy people in this crazy carnival world. Gigi had been the other one.

The kitchen and back living room walls were covered in beige wallpaper with interlocking circles in pale green, now gone yellow and peeling back in certain places. Staring at that ugly design, seeing it anew after many months of not noticing it, of having forgotten the truth of how unappealing and worn out it really was, showed me the words I'd been holding down somewhere, nestled in a dark corner of my mind, waiting to awaken at just that moment.

"No, you stop it," I said. "You stop running around and lying to me, saying one thing to my face and then doing something else behind my back." I ran my hand along the wallpaper, faced Jim, and waited.

He took a can of beer from the refrigerator, pulled off the tab, and put it in his pocket. "You're too much. Just too fucking much." Taking a long drink of beer, head tilted back, he showed me his bobbing throat. Wiping his mouth with the back of his hand, he studied the beer can for a moment before throwing it into the sink, sending an explosion of foam bursting into the air. "I don't see why the fuck this whole thing with Gigi is such a big deal now when it never bothered you before."

The shame of not knowing was almost as bad, worse even, than the pain of the betrayal—a breach of trust of a promise that had never been made. "Because I didn't know about it before. Okay? I'm that damn stupid. If you weren't here at night, I thought you were drinking or playing cards or something like that." I sat down on the couch and pulled the edge of my housecoat up over my face to hide in the dark space I had made.

Jim sat down beside me. "It's not as bad as all that, Lolly." He pulled on my arm until I unburied my face. "Here, look at me." He touched my face lightly to make me turn my head. "You're my old lady. Not any of these other girls. Not even Gigi."

So it wasn't just Gigi. I had probably talked to a lot of these women, laughing, telling stories, passing the time of day. And what had they thought of me? "I think the best thing would be for me to leave the carnival." I didn't want to rely on Jim for anything ever again. "I'll go home, back to my house." The heat of Jim's stare caused a searing pain in my chest. "I've got money saved. I'll go to the police station and answer their questions. And I bet they'll believe me, you know? They'll see the fat and won't think that I'd be capable enough to kill a man. Even though it's the easiest thing in the world to do." That last statement felt right and close to a full confession. Breathing in, the air felt good and clean in my lungs.

"No," Jim said. "Come on, don't talk like that." He put his arm across my back and moved closer, falling into the side of my body. "You belong here with me, going places and meeting people, not boxed up in a falling-down house with no job and no friends and no nothing." Jim pressed his mouth to the side of my face and wended a trail of feather-light, silky soft kisses from my ear down my neck. Each point of contact with his lips felt like a small starburst of warmth, part tingle and part shiver, making going home and being without Jim seem like death, only worse because there would be no peace to it.

"I don't want to be alone." Tears filled my eyes as my brain struggled to process the desolate sadness of that prospect.

Jim pressed his lips hard against mine and kissed my face, smearing my tears. "You're right here with me." He reached under my housecoat and started to rub me between my legs the way I liked.

Did he do the same things with Gigi? My skin flushed with rage and shame at the thought, but more than that, I didn't want Jim to stop touching me or wanting me or loving me. I closed my eyes and pushed my thoughts, my consciousness even, down to a quieter, more opaque layer of the mind. In that nearly hypnotic realm, it occurred to me that Jim had never once asked if I had actually killed Jared, had never even requested an account of what happened that night. Jim knew I wasn't an inert, incapable blob, but he never asked if I was a killer. He slept soundly beside me night after night, never shocked or appalled at the thought of what I might have done, apparently not caring and not needing any explanation. Maybe he made his choice that day alongside the road when he didn't drive away and leave me.

The realization of such extraordinary tolerance and acceptance deflated my anger, in that moment, at least. We had moved to the bed and taken off our clothes. Jim was on top of me, having sex with me, when at last I opened my eyes.

"Oh," I gasped.

Jim smiled, surprised and pleased, because I had never before uttered a sound when we made love. "Thatta girl," he said, causing me to wrap my arms and legs around him with spine-cracking force to pull him closer and draw him into drowning in my flesh, holding him tighter and harder.

"Oh my God." I pounded his back with my fist as my body tensed and locked into the accelerating track of orgasm. And when it happened, the sensation and the wonder of it, too, because I had never had one with Jim, made me squeeze him with all my strength.

He came after that and collapsed on top of me for a moment before freeing himself from my grip and rolling off me and over onto his back on the other mattress. Jim lay there naked with his chest heaving, holding his heart and gasping for breath. "Jesus," he said. "Sweet Jesus, Lola, you're going to kill me."

I liked the idea of having worn out Jim and the sound of his quiet laughter while he tried to catch his breath. I rolled to my side, ran my hand down Jim's chest, and touched my mouth to his sweaty skin. Raising my head, I could see out the window and noticed Gigi standing in the doorway of her trailer, fists digging into her hips, pressing her spine forward to stretch her back. She looked as she had the hundred other times I'd seen her on a morning after with her melted eye makeup and wearing that ratty, threadbare housecoat that only came down to the middle of her thighs and was missing two snaps on top. She hadn't combed out her stage hair from the night before, and as I watched, she began unraveling its intricate mass.

"There's your whore out there," I said, slapping my open hand down hard on Jim's chest. "Standing around in that short nightgown, hoping someone will come take a look, I guess."

Jim grabbed my wrist to push me away from him. "Jesus Christ," he said, jumping off the bed to stand in front of me, naked, holding his hands stiff with the fingers splayed. "Goddamn it, don't start up again. Enough already."

I grabbed one of the heavy pillows from the bed and threw it at Jim, who batted it to the side with no real effort. "Don't piss me off, Lola," he said, jabbing his finger toward my face. Then he stood up and began to walk away.

"Where are you going?"

"To take a shower," Jim said, shaking his head. "I've got too much pussy on me."

As he was leaving, I grabbed the bedside clock and threw it at him but missed and hit the doorframe instead. Jim closed the bathroom door, and the lock clicked before I even managed to get off the mattress. "You're disgusting," I said, hitting and kicking the door to make Jim hear me. "I hate you."

"Jesus, leave me in peace, woman," he said. I heard the shower tap open and the hissing spray.

"Take all the peace you want," I said. "I'm going over to talk to your alcoholic whore." I put on my clothes and stomped away, slamming the trailer door after me. It didn't close properly and instead bounced back on the doorjamb from the strength of my hand. Jim called something after me, maybe about not making a scene or leaving Gigi alone or being careful with the goddamn door, but I didn't hear, and I didn't care.

Gigi had set up her aluminum lawn chair in front of her trailer with the door propped open. Holding a cigarette between her fingers, she waved her hand over her head when she saw me approach. "Hey there, Lola. Come on, and I'll pull down a chair so you can pass the time with me." Her voice was friendly and normal, like always, her actions ordinary as she disappeared into the trailer and brought out a sturdy, armless, straight-back chair. That was our habit. We liked to sit outside and talk about whatever we wanted to say.

Gigi patted the ladder back of the chair. "So, what's got you up so early?" she asked, plopping back down into her own chair. "I got the door open"—she pointed to the trailer—"so I can air the place out, you know. It gets real stuffy after a long night. You doing okay? You look sort of funny."

I stood in front of Gigi, looking down on her. The casual response first from Jim and now from Gigi made me wonder if maybe I were losing my mind. "You really have no idea why I'd look funny or maybe be upset? I saw Jim coming out of your trailer! That's why. I know he slept with you last night. And it's like you can't fucking figure out why I'd even be mad about it." That was the first time I could recall saying the word "fuck" out loud to another person. This situation seemed like the perfect occasion. When Gigi didn't respond, more words I didn't know I had at my disposal tumbled out of me. "You're a dirty whore for fucking my old man behind my back. That's what you are."

Gigi sprang to her feet directly in front of me so that we were standing almost nose to nose. "What's that you called me?" she yelled. Her breath, hot and outraged, smelling of old cigarettes, fanned my face.

"I'm pretty sure you heard me just fine." My own voice was calm and measured because I wanted her to understand that I meant every word.

"Well, you say something like that again, and I'll slap your face. You've got a nerve coming over here and talking to me like that." Gigi sank back down into her chair. Even with her face turned away from me, I could tell she was crying, the wetness mixing with her old eyeliner and mascara, cutting rivulets down her cheeks that looked like dirty runoff. "Why don't you just get on out of here if you're going to be so mean?"

I had the instant urge to put my arms around her, to comfort her against my own cruelty, an inclination that made no sense. "But... I'm the hurt one here. Why are you crying? You're the one who did me wrong. Not the other way around."

Gigi wiped the entire underside of her forearm across her face, leaving a black smear. "How'd I do you wrong? You never said nothing about me and Jim before, so why come stomping over here now and call me names?"

I banged my fist on the open trailer door. "Because I didn't know! Okay?" Even though I'd learned how to put on a performance and control an audience and how to have friends and make love with a man, it appeared there was still a lot I didn't understand.

"Really?" Gigi asked, as if my gullibility defied human belief. "I'd a thought you were smarter than that."

I grabbed the ladder back of the chair Gigi had brought out and lowered myself into the seat. My knees ached from maintaining my rage-filled posture. "Yeah, me too. I guess I'm the stupidest goddamn person on earth." A feeling of hopelessness and confusion overwhelmed me, leaving me to wonder what else I didn't know.

Gigi squeezed my shoulder. "Come on. No, you're not. It's just... you know, I think there's a lot of things that went on before you even got here. Me and Jimmy always got along real good. He's had my back more than once. Yeah, he's old, but he's an important guy around here and definitely better looking than some of these dirtbags, better than Hinkle, at least. Then you show up, and all of a sudden you're his old lady, but it's like you don't realize how lucky you are. You know how hard I had to work and hustle to buy this trailer or anything else I've got? And there you are, living in the one of the best spots on the back lot without hardly lifting a finger. And did I ever say anything about that or complain and call you names?"

Gigi's words, her description of my unappealing arrogance, filled me with a deep sense of shame when only moments before I had been convinced that it was Gigi who should be embarrassed and remorseful. "No," I whispered, my cheeks flaming hot. "You've always been a good friend to me. I'm sorry I called you names, Geeg." My voice sounded pitiful, the sniveling of a child, someone who, just as Jared used to say, didn't know how things really worked.

"Don't be so sad." Gigi reached over to grasp my hand. "Us girls got to stick together, right?"

We sat there in silence for a few moments, still holding hands. The morning air felt refreshing and the smallest bit damp against my skin.

"Why do you think Jim did want me as his old lady?" I asked. The question had occurred to me before, and it had risen to the front of my mind again as I watched Gigi, whose prettiness and slim perfection were visible even in her haggard state.

"Come on, now," Gigi said with a laugh. "You're lovable enough, aren't you?"

"Right, but like you say, he could be as picky as he wants, and..." In my mind, I pictured cootch dancers, pretty townies, friendly cashiers, and Gigi, especially, walking across a stage, all of them far more thin, perfect, and beautiful than I was. People surely wondered what Jim saw in me, in a way that never would have occurred to them had he been with any of these other women.

"Geez, Lola, don't get down on yourself," Gigi said, as if she could read my thoughts. "He's lucky to have you too. Just so long as there's no hard feelings between us."

She went into her trailer and came back out with a large wadded-up ball of toilet paper and gave me some to wipe my face. "Have some Oreos too," she said, pulling the package from under her arm. She rubbed her half of the paper across her eyes and down her neck. "You know, I was thinking while I was getting this stuff that I'm going to try not to sleep with Jim again if that makes you feel better." Gigi flopped back in her chair and stuck her hand into the cookie package. "If it was me, though, I'd rather know where my old man was dipping his wick than send him out to find some floozy."

Maybe Gigi was right. Maybe bodies didn't matter. The clean simplicity of this philosophy made me wish I could hold similar beliefs. Then again, maybe Gigi drank too much too often to ever know what she was talking about.

The Long Season

S ome part of my mind worried I would never forgive Gigi or be able to adopt the casual perspective she applied to matters, like monogamy and marriage, that were quite serious to me. Over the next winter in Gulfy, though, spending so much time with her and Jim, I had the opportunity to reflect on the ways Gigi had proved herself a stalwart friend and to consider how, at the very least, my relationship with Jim was no more flawed than the one between Mrs. Schendel and her husband or even between my father and mother—the only two marriages of which I had any direct knowledge.

The next season, seeing Hinkle in the G-top after opening night, I had my first inkling that something had changed for him in the off-season. His aspect seemed duller, his presence more lifeless. The gold chain and medallion and the pinky ring with the diamond chip he liked to wear had disappeared. At some point over the winter months, Hinkle must have also decided to grow his hair long, unburnished with pomade, leaving it hanging in a sad, thin ponytail. He resembled a shuffling, older, defeated version of himself. The lateral incisor and canine teeth were also missing from the left side of his mouth, damage that he hadn't taken the time to get repaired. Watching him shell peanuts and poke them between his lips while he played cards in the G-top nearly turned me off my own eating.

When I mentioned to Jim how different Hinkle looked, he told me that Hinkle's luck had turned sour over the winter and that Hinkle had lost a lot of money gambling. In the weeks that followed, Hinkle tried to find consolation in Gigi's company, seeking her out more and more often. Sometimes I would see him in the morning leaving her trailer, shirt hanging open, his bare feet stuffed into his boots, a bundled handful of socks and undershirt clutched in his fist. Other times he would be waiting for her to return home after a long night, a bottle of Jim Beam in his hand. If I were with Gigi in Ora Ann's or Daisy's trailer, he would show up there too. In response to this concentrated, unremitting attention, Gigi's already-robust drinking took a sharp uptick.

Hinkle's constant presence and obvious willingness to flood Gigi's spirit with alcohol exacted a higher and higher price as the season wore on, making it more difficult for her to hit her marks on stage. I watched her act with great care every night, chewing my knuckles, while she slid the sword down her throat with shaking hands.

On one of our last nights in Grafton, Gigi was drinking under the stage before the show. She claimed the secret confinement of that space was comforting, the dust and heat no problem at all, and that downing a shot or two of whiskey before a performance helped steady her nerves and anesthetize her throat. But crunched up beneath the floorboards, sitting on an old cushion, her back against one of the support posts, she looked different—less steady, less like herself, more glassy-eyed. And she had a full bottle with her.

Gigi's ankles wobbled the smallest bit when she walked out on stage in her high-heeled sandals, unnoticeable perhaps if I hadn't been watching her with such a degree of attention. Wearing the white-sequined outfit I had made for her, the one that looked like a shiny one-piece bathing suit with a poof of marabou at each hip, she sashayed and twirled, stepping close to the front of the stage, letting the footlights bounce off the tiny sequins sewn into her clothes. She put the sword down her throat once and then again. The second time, she faced the audience so they had a good view of her pretty swan neck. She stuck one arm out to the side. The tips of her fingers and then her whole hand began to shake. When she pulled the sword from her throat, I thought I could see glistening teardrops in the corners of her eyes. Gigi curtsied to the applause. She walked around the stage and then circled again. She was delaying, hesitating, which as she had often told me, was the worst thing a sword swallower could do. Gigi inhaled, the profound depth of the motion visible to both the audience and me. The crowd grew restless with anticipation. Gigi dropped to her knees, tipped her head back, and swallowed the sword without flinching.

The people, the men especially, went wild with clapping, shouting, and whistling. Heavy, obvious tears flowed from Gigi's eyes now. She pulled the sword from her throat, unable to restrain a sob as she walked back to the front of the stage, swinging her hips, tracing sharp figure eights in the air with the sword.

She went to execute her final move, where she tossed the sword into the air and caught it behind her back. Her reaction time was inexact, though. The sword rose in the air. Gigi took a misstep. The sword fell on a path to slice through the top of Gigi's skull. She screamed and dropped down at the very last second, curling into a ball with her hands over her head as the sword clattered across the stage. Jim rushed out to help Gigi to her feet, making jokes about how the Milwaukee Brewers' catcher Darrell Porter missed a few now and again. Backstage, I pulled Gigi into my arms as she sobbed and vomited down the back of my dress.

Jim walked Gigi back to her trailer and wouldn't let her perform for the rest of the night. I sent Ike on next so I could clean myself up. As the passing minutes stretched on, my concern for Gigi grew, as did my fear that she had suffered a real injury on her last swallow. Jim was back at the microphone, though, by the time my act ended. When I had the chance to ask him if Gigi was okay, he only nodded.

Later that night, able at last to rest in my bed, I tried to ignore the lamplight from the living room and the weary sound of Jim's amphetamine-induced pacing. I consoled myself with the thought that the situation had reached its lowest layer. We had to be in the deepest part of the trough. The wave would crash soon and release its energy.

The next morning, Jim was finally coming off his high. We sat on the couch together, drinking coffee. "Jesus, I need a break, Lola. I been running all over creation, spreading around money that we just don't have. It's getting to be too much, you know? Last night, I could have sworn I could hear little voices having conversations with each other in the walls." Jim cradled his head in his hands.

I knew about those voices as well because sometimes after my father had died and I was alone, especially on long dark winter nights, I imagined I could hear mumbling in the background static of the radio, which might then become distinct as a noise within the house or as an extra voice straining to speak to me. I touched Jim's ear with the tip of my finger to see if he was jumpy enough to flinch.

Then there was a banging on the door that startled both of us. Gigi pushed her way into the trailer before either of us could respond. She had walked over wearing just a pink nylon nightgown. "Hey," she said. "I'm—" Gigi glanced down at her outfit. "I guess maybe I should have changed before I came over." I also noticed that her feet were bare.

Jim stood up to get a closer look at Gigi. "What's with you? You been drinking already?" It was barely nine o'clock.

"Don't start with me, Jim, when you don't know the night I had." She sank down into the couch and smashed her face into her bare legs. "Besides, I came over to tell you both something important."

Jim sat in the chair across from Gigi. "Lola, is there any coffee left for Gigi?"

Gigi grabbed the blanket draped across the back of the sofa and wrapped it around her shoulders, even though it felt like it was already eighty degrees in the trailer. "I don't need no coffee, and Jesus, don't get so mad at me for drinking."

I took Gigi a fresh cup of coffee half filled with warm milk and five teaspoons of sugar because that was how she liked it. "How's that?"

"Thanks, Lo," she said then took a sip. "It's nice and sweet." Gigi squeezed the blanket tighter, wrapping her fingers around the coffee cup, while Jim and I waited.

"Yeah, well. You two saw what happened on stage. So later on, Hinkle comes by. He says it's because he wants to check on me, to make sure I'm all right. I mean, I know that's a lie because when has Hinkle ever been that nice to anybody?" Gigi put her coffee cup down on the table in front of her and extended the ends of the blanket out like a giant pair of wings.

When I sat down next to Gigi on the couch, my weight made it easy, logical even, for her to slide into my side and rest her head on my shoulder.

"We started drinking after that, even though I was already in rough shape. And..." Gigi glanced up at Jim, who had moved over to the other side of the room and was looking out the window with his back to us. "I told Hinkle I didn't know what to do because, after what happened on stage last night, I won't be able to get another sword down my throat without it killing me. And then Hinkle starts to get all funny and jokey, saying shit like he can get a sword down my throat. I'm sorry, Jim. I guess this is a lot to hear."

Jim didn't turn around, but I could see his right hand gripping the windowsill hard, the tendons along the inside of his arm standing out in violent relief.

"When it's all done and over, Hinkle tells me he can see about getting me put back in the cootch show. I tell him I'm not going to do that no more, and he knows it. And then he goes, well, I guess you're too old for that now anyway. He gets me confused—you know like how he does because I don't want to be in no cootch show—but he's got me mad thinking about how no one wants to see me do it anyway. And now I don't know what to do." Gigi began to cry, pressing her tear-wet face against me.

I stroked her hair, a soft gesture, as if she were a light, delicate thing, a special, spoon-fed creature requiring a gentle touch.

"Anyway," she continued, "I came over to tell you that I'm leaving because I don't have an act anymore, and I'm tired of Hinkle being around me all the time. And I don't know what I'm going to do. I'm such a goddamn mess that even if I could get back on stage, the only place that'd take me would be another fucking ragbag like this one."

A piece of the window molding broke off in Jim's hand. He threw it to the side and came to kneel in front of Gigi. He took both her hands in his, making them seem like small white birds in a welcoming nest. Had he ever shown me such exquisite gentleness?

"Listen to me, Geeg," he said. "You steer clear of Hinkle, all right? Don't get caught alone with him, and keep your trailer door locked. Don't open it up for him no matter how sweet and nice he sounds or how sorry he is or if he offers you booze. Okay? You stick with me and Lola. You don't go nowhere without one of us, and if you need a drink that bad, I'll give you one. All right? We'll see if we can't figure out a new act for you."

"Okay, Jimmy. Okay," Gigi whispered. "I don't know what I'd do if I didn't have the two of you as friends."

I kissed Gigi's cheek while Jim pressed his face into the palms of her hands. The intimacy between them made a lump in my throat, but I couldn't fault him for loving her, too, for how his own heart broke for her pain, not when mine did the exact same.

I had learned a lot about sideshows from Jim's stories and from what I had heard and read about freaks during the calm winter days in Gulfy. Some of the pictures I had seen had made me cringe as I imagined those people eating breakfast and doing ordinary things, like licking envelopes or making telephone calls.

One image in particular replayed in mind with some frequency. It was a photograph of a four-legged woman. Dangling between her own walking legs were the foreshortened limbs of her parasitic twin, clinging to her more fortunate sister forever. If the look of it fascinated me, then wouldn't other people feel the same? And what if the legs were backward? Then wouldn't it also make sense that maybe the weak sister's eyes and some other parts of her face would be at the back of the main woman's head, shielded under her hair perhaps?

As far as I knew, there was no exact freak of nature like that, no such creature in existence, but the idea was perfect for a good gaff and a new act for Gigi. She could be as drunk as she pleased to sit in a chair wearing gross backward legs.

After Gigi left that morning to rest in her trailer, I gathered the materials I would need— opaque pantyhose, white cotton batting that I could stain dye with tea, a bit of children's modeling clay, and old wire hangers to be reworked into tiny shoe frames. The eyes in the back of the head would be trickier. As I unpacked the portable sewing machine, I thought about Mrs. Schendel, wondering what she would think of my handiwork.

I was putting the finishing touches on the legs when Jim came back to the trailer. "Are we set for the breakdown?" I asked, biting off the thread from the last bit of hand stitching along the toes. "Are there enough people for it?"

"Um... what the hell have you got there?"

I laughed and waggled the grotesque little appendages at Jim. "It's a surprise for Gigi. I figured she'd be good for a gaff if she can't swallow a sword anymore. How do you like her new legs?" I kicked first one and then the other into the air. "Can, can, can you do the can-can?" I sang. "This is the bottom half of her parasitic twin. I've still got some work to do on the face."

Jim reached over and tweaked one of the little shoes. "Well, I'll be damned," he said. "That looks pretty good. You know there's actual people who have funny shit like that."

"Well, but unfortunately we don't know any of them."

Jim went into the kitchen to get a beer out of the refrigerator. "Hinkle's in a lather, says everything is falling apart and that you and Gigi need to take a cut in pay if we're going to survive."

I stood the little legs straight up on my thighs. "And what did you say?"

"I asked him what goddamn difference it made when he couldn't afford to make payroll as it was."

I pulled a wig I had bought a few months ago from its bag and ran my fingers through the slippery polyester tresses, marveling at this unexpected strange ability of mine to create new beings.

"Well, he better like this act," I said. The wig was a bright platinum blond. I plopped it onto my head and looked at myself in the hand mirror, liking the shining brilliance around my face, the drastic change in my appearance. "God, Hinkle is such an asshole."

Jim tossed the empty beer can into the kitchen sink, a swirling metallic clatter as it circled the drain. "Yeah, well, tell me something I don't know."

When we finally packed up and headed to Gulfy for the off-season, such was my relief and my hope, too, that everything could return to normal that I wept when the town appeared on the horizon.

"What's up with you?" Jim asked, his hands twitching on the steering wheel.

"Nothing. I'm just so happy to be home."

Jim weaned himself off the pills over the next few days. He began to look and act unhurried, happy to be with me, to listen to me talk about my ideas for the sideshow or to tell him the plots of the many novels I had read, as if they were new and exciting stories that only just occurred to me in that moment. I cooked sizzling, elaborate meals for us, and Jim gained back the weight he had lost. His face transformed from ghoulish and hollowed out back to normal.

Gigi's recovery appeared less certain. With nothing as edgy or sharp as sword swallowing to occupy her during the last weeks of the carnival circuit, she had managed to keep drinking at a hard, accelerating pace. Despite being stone drunk for every performance, Gigi had made a very appealing four-legged woman, dressed in a full, flouncy red skirt that fell past her knees when she was standing.

To begin, she would sit down facing the audience, her face impassive, and raise her skirt to show off the stumpy legs I had fashioned. The crowd loved it, the men especially. The grace of Gigi's actions, part tease and part reveal, a holdover from her stripper days in the cootch show, made her seem sexy and repellent at the same time.

For the finale, she would face backward in the chair and part the long hair of the wig where I had secured a pair of beautiful glass eyes with some strands glued to them since they couldn't withstand close-in scrutiny.

My belief that Gigi would revert to her usual self with the same speed as Jim proved to be incorrect. One afternoon when we'd been back in Gulfy for about three weeks, I got a call from Lonny at the Showstop to come pick up Gigi and drive her home. He left Luis to watch the bar and led me up the back stairs to his apartment, where I found Gigi wearing only her bra and panties, asleep on the living room couch.

"Now, don't look at me like that, Lola," Lonny said. "She took her clothes off herself. I brought her up here because she passed out on the pool table, and one of the fellows she was talking to looked like he was going to mess with her."

The sound of our voices woke Gigi. She sat bolt upright on the couch. "Hey, Lola, hey. Let's go on down and have a drink. You and me. Right now, okay?" Gigi tried to stand, but her bare feet got tangled in the bedsheet that Lonny must have given her. She fell back onto the couch. "What the fuck?" Gigi pulled at the sheet and kicked her legs free.

I grabbed the flower-print dress crumpled on the kitchen counter and handed it to Gigi. "Come on and get dressed now. I'm going to drive you home."

"Hey, Lonny," Gigi said, pulling the dress over her head. "I took off my clothes. Did you see that?"

"I saw it," he replied, looking away.

"Hey, Lola, let's have a drink. All three of us. Lonny don't mind. Where the fuck are my shoes?"

"We'll get them later. Let's go," I said.

"No, Lola, it's okay. We'll just have a quick one." Gigi stood swaying in the center of the room. "You know," she loud whispered to me behind her hand, "I think Lonny likes me." She nodded. "No, really," she continued. "I think he really likes me."

I glanced at Lonny then away again when I saw his face start to color. "God only knows why," I said, grabbing Gigi's arm before she fell. The climb up the stairs had made it hard to breathe. The pain in my back and legs wore thin my patience.

"Lola, don't get so pissy. Let's just have one drink, and then we can go."

Lonny shook his head. "Trust me. I know when someone's had enough." He put his hand on Gigi's shoulder. "I don't want to carry you out of here, but I will if I have to."

Gigi grabbed Lonny's neck and pulled his face close to hers. "I'd like to see you try." She kissed him on the lips, putting her tongue in his mouth, and for an instant, Lonny kissed her back.

Lonny pushed Gigi away and flattened her arms against her sides. "Whoopsy daisy," he said, slinging her over his shoulder like a sack of potatoes.

Gigi beat against his back, and her face turned red as the blood rushed into her upside-down head. I walked behind Lonny as he carted Gigi down the stairs, unsure whether to feel jealous that her graceful thinness made such a maneuver possible or relieved that I couldn't be moved around like that against my wishes.

Lonny ignored Gigi's pleas and slaps. "You probably want to ride with the windows open in case she pukes," he said to me.

By nighttime, Gigi felt horrible, hungover and remorseful that she had caused such trouble.

"Shit, I'm sorry," she said. "I'll clean out the truck. I promise." She had come over to the house to apologize and was trying to drink the cup of coffee I'd made for her, but she gagged a little bit every time she took the smallest sip.

"I hosed it out hours ago."

"I'm sorry, Lo. Poor Lonny too. I ought to go apologize to him too. You want to come down to the Showstop with me?"

"You're going to go like that?"

Gigi seemed to have given no thought to how horrible she looked and smelled. She unstuck her blouse from her body and tried to comb her fingers through her hair, but they got snagged on the tangles.

"Come on and take the night off. You got to ease up on the drinking anyway. Even Jim said as much." I nodded to the empty chair where he usually sat at the kitchen table. "Jim drove out to see if he could help Scratchy and Thelma. They've been having more trouble with their neighbors."

Jim's way of helping them would no doubt involve what he sometimes referred to as "cracking skulls," and even as I objected to that approach on some level, it was likewise impossible to imagine how deliberate conversation would be any help at all.

"I get antsy just sitting around. You know?" Gigi scanned the closed kitchen cabinet doors, wondering, I knew, what there was to drink in the house.

I pulled a deck of cards from the silverware drawer and started shuffling, liking the falling click-clack of the cards as they bridged together. I dealt out a hand. "We can play some gin rummy. I won't even keep score."

Gigi put her head down on the table and started to cry, big unexpected sobs that nonetheless didn't surprise me.

I nudged her pile of cards closer to her. "It's your turn."

When she kept crying, I patted her shoulder and rearranged her cards into an organized fan and played her turn for her. Little by little, she began to pay attention to me, to what I was saying, answering when I asked what she wanted to discard and what she wanted to hold.

"I can't do this no more, Lo."

"Yes, you can." I peeled a card from the take pile and pushed it facedown toward her.

We played for a good long while, until finally Gigi fell asleep on the couch. I sat in the recliner next to her, wending my way between dreams and wakefulness, not wanting to leave her unattended for fear she would find the Four Roses above the sink or leave and go home or, worse still, make her way to the Showstop.

My vigilance appeared to have some good effect because Gigi developed and refined an ability to go full days and nights without drinking. Something always came up, of course, to prevent her from giving it up entirely, but the truth of the matter was she wouldn't have had much of a social life or much to do even if she had wanted to attempt such a feat.

March 4, 1979

Dear Sarah,

I haven't written in months, and I surely apologize for that. You remember when I mentioned that Luther was sick and had awful stomach pains? Well, not long after I sent that letter, things went from bad to worse. First, Luther started sitting in his chair every morning and some afternoons, too, staring at the television. There's nothing on that time of day except for soap operas, but he watched them anyway. And this from the same man who used to tell me to get back to work and not to waste daylight if he ever caught me taking a break to look at my stories.

No matter what I said or how often I walked between his chair and the television screen, dusting the furniture, he stayed right there in the recliner. He would get dressed in his barn jacket and muck boots like he was going to go do some work but then would just sit there holding his stomach. I should have known something was wrong sooner than I did, but I got caught up in keeping house and doing all the milking on my own and cleaning the barn and, well, in short, doing the work of two people.

Luther complained so about the burning pain in his stomach that he kept a pillow clutched to his waist. Sometimes he would bend forward with his eyes squeezed shut and rock back and forth, sucking air between his clenched teeth.

Doc Person sent us to Milwaukee to see a specialist. They did exploratory surgery on poor Luther. They no more than took a look inside than they sewed him back up. The cancer had spread all over his body by that point. I cried like a baby when the doctor took me into his office to tell me that. He said that even if I had gotten Luther in to see him sooner, it wouldn't have mattered.

I had a hospital bed set up right in the living room, and I kept the television on from morning to night because I knew Luther liked the sound of it. I hired a few men to do the barn work so I could be in the house to take care of Luther. The morphine made him loopy, but I gave him plenty of it so he wouldn't suffer.

Thankfully, the county paid for a nurse to help me take care of him. One afternoon after she left, I closed my eyes for just a second. When I opened them again the room was pitch dark except for the black-and-white snow on the television screen. I told Luther good night and went to bed without even remembering that I had skipped both his evening and bedtime doses of medicine. I still didn't realize until I heard him moaning in the early morning. I knew it had to be around five o'clock because the men we'd hired had already turned on the lights in the barn.

I ran downstairs. We were in the last days. I knew it, Doc Person knew it, and even the nurse had stopped calling out, "See you next week," every time she left.

I was so angry at myself for letting Luther suffer through the night. I told Luther I was sorry as I got his medicine ready, but he shushed me. "Sully," he whispered. Luther used to call me Sully when we were growing up together and for the first few years we were married. Until that moment, I had almost forgotten about it. "I think I'm dying."

I tried to tell him he was only having a bad spell but that we could pray together as soon as I gave him his medicine. You see, I wanted him to feel happy and hopeful in his last days on Earth, but I had to worry, too, about the state of his soul. He needed the chance to make peace with God, like we all do.

And then he said the most unexpected thing to me. "Sully," he said. "I know something's not going right. So I want to know, right now, once and for all, if there isn't something you want to say to me. Tell me plain. Have you been a faithful wife? Don't let me go to my grave not knowing the truth."

It was on the tip of my tongue to reassure him again that he wasn't dying, but I knew he wouldn't believe me. I think people sense deep down when it's their time, just like animals do. I knew what Luther wanted me to tell him and what he needed to hear on his way to the afterlife. I said that I had always been faithful to him and that I had loved him every moment we had been together.

And you know, Sarah, it was true how much I loved Luther. When I thought about how hard I had worked for him, about how much care I had given him, especially since he got sick, I knew I was saying the right thing. Anyway, he seemed relieved at my words.

He passed a few days after that. Even though we all knew what was coming, it was still a shock. I prayed for an end to his suffering, but then when it happened, I wanted more days with him, even bad ones.

All our friends and neighbors came to the wake and funeral. It pleased me to see such a turnout, and I think it would have made Luther happy too. It got me thinking about your father. I've outlived two men now. Some days, I can't imagine going on or even wanting to go on, but that's no way to think.

Anyway, I keep busy sorting out the house and settling the estate. Everything has passed to me, of course, so now I've a farm to run all on my own. I'll have to make all the decisions, where before I never had much say in the matter. I know some women are left with a lot less. My brother-in-law, Harold, has said he will help, except his way of helping is really to take charge of everything. Honestly, Luther never cared for him that much.

It all just seems like such an awful lot of work. I'm strong enough to do it and to keep this place running and tell Harold to go to hell. I guess I don't see the point, though. We don't have any children to inherit the farm. It will probably go to Harold and Edna's kids when I die, which hardly seems worth it.

I dread the thought of winter coming. The nights are so long, and the cold seeps into my bones. Edna came around to visit with me one day not long after Luther died. She almost fainted when I told her I was thinking of selling the farm. She even clutched a handful of her blouse, like the very suggestion might give her a heart attack. Edna laid on the guilt pretty thick about how I needed to preserve everything that Luther had worked so hard to build. I let her talk and just kept drinking my coffee.

I didn't mention anything more about it, but I haven't stopped thinking about moving away—probably to someplace warm and sunny.

I keep my eye on Missy. In fact, she came with her parents to the viewing hours, and I saw in the paper last week that she's engaged now to marry Steve Johnson. I think his family is from somewhere near Patawaunee, so I don't know too much about him. Even so, I can't imagine he would tolerate his fiancée running around and pining after some other man. It looks as if she has finally moved on now after Jared's death.

I hope this letter finds you and finds you well. Please write to me as soon as you are able.

Love,
Ursula

Punks

For many months after reading Mrs. Schendel's letter, I struggled against the nearly inescapable urge to write and tell her the truth of what had been going on in my life. During that time, I came to view keeping secrets from her as a terrible form of isolation. The thought of unburdening myself, of telling Mrs. Schendel what happened the night Jared died, made me dizzy with imagined relief. If nothing else, though, life in the carnival had taught me the value of being a sensible person, of living as and asserting myself as nobody's fool. There could be no higher form of idiocy than a written confession. I realized, too, that Mrs. Schendel would suffer having to view me in such a way, so I extended her the same self-abnegating grace she had given her husband. I could see, certainly, how some people might have thought we were both putting on a performance or simply liars avoiding the truth to protect ourselves. They didn't understand, though, the relief we were denied by keeping secrets.

The Tuesday before we planned to get back on the road, Gigi and Lonny came over to drink and play cards with Jim and me at our kitchen table. It was the one night of the week that the Showstop was closed, and Lonny said he liked to get out from behind the bar and have someone pour him a beer for a change.

The late-spring heat of the day lingered in the kitchen, filling the corners of the house in a clinging, uncomfortable way, making me unable to draw a deep-enough breath. I reasoned that the hot, edgy unease I felt must be my trepidation about the coming season, a byproduct of wanting to believe that Hinkle had fared better over the winter, acquiring wins and riches enough to underwrite all our satisfaction. The pendulum had swung far out when Gigi had nearly been sliced in two on stage and when Jim had suffered auditory hallucinations because of the extreme number of pills he had popped. It would have to swing back now. That was how pendulums worked.

To be on the safe side, I had been doing a bit here and there with Scratchy to learn how to create plausible identity documents for people who needed them.

Gulfy was the perfect place for that type of business. People reasoned that carnies, travelers, gypsies, and showmen knew about shady undertakings, like pills or false documents, so they would go to the Showstop, and Lonny would figure out what they wanted and point them in the right direction. Scratchy had begun to talk about how he and Thelma would probably be moving on before too long, so he was content to share what he knew with me.

The kitchen table where we sat was strewn with stained, crumpled napkins and used butter knives, some with hardened mustard or mayonnaise on the tips and another one sticky with grape jelly. There were also two dirty ashtrays with speckled ashes ringing them, a loose cigarette butt here and there, a plate with individual cheese slices gone limp in the heat, a plastic mold with two curled pieces of bologna in the bottom next to a sleeve of crackers, and an army of glasses—tall ones with beer and water and squat ones, nearly empty, with the barest brown rind of whiskey in the bottom.

"Are the critters ready to go?" Lonny asked, tipping his head toward the big glass jars lined up along the counter. He appeared cool and sleek, wearing only a sleeveless undershirt on top, his dark-blond hair combed back from his face, looking damp and clean.

Gigi clucked her tongue. "Don't talk about those gross things to me," she said. "It turns my stomach just to think of them." She watched Lonny shuffle, concentrating, it seemed, on how his big hands moved the shiny backs of the cards apart and slid them back together.

"Good." Jim laughed. "That means people will probably pay a fair amount to look at them."

They were talking about the set of pickled punks that I'd made to earn some extra cash, in case Hinkle didn't pay us on time or every time we were due to receive money from him.

Jessup, a retired knife thrower, had told me about pickled punks one night at the Showstop. They were essentially malformed fetuses floating in glass jars. As it turned out, people liked to gawk at that sort of thing, making me certain that I could earn good inside money by displaying them.

My punks weren't actual fetuses, of course. One of them, Veronica, was a tiny plastic baby doll. I had grafted a second doll onto the body then melted them slightly and adhered flesh-colored nylons to take away their fake, plasticized look. It was a good gaff, even though I did have to cook a dozen or so dolls before I got it right, nearly poisoning Jim and me in the process with the toxic fumes.

Gator had started out as a baby alligator that had been stuffed by a taxidermist, an easy-enough item to find in the state of Florida. I had cut off the head and hollowed out part of the torso and replaced it with a clear plastic sack of translucent gelatin, formed into the suggestion of a face—dreamy, ethereal, and smiling—on the surface.

Meaty was the most gruesome, though, and Gigi hated him in particular. He was the baby with no skin, his shape carved from a large roll of liverwurst and preserved with salt and vinegar, like a pickle. He was horrible to see, and I usually kept a towel draped over his jar.

The apparent squishiness of the bologna remnants on the table reminded me of the day I had made Meaty, recalling to my mind the horrible, porous softness of his wretched body. The room was too close and smoky, the memory of eating that derelict food suddenly unbearable. I hardly made it to the bathroom to vomit in the toilet, blaming Hinkle the entire time for my stomach upset, my ponderous discomfort.

"You doing all right in there?" Gigi asked in a quiet voice, tapping her knuckle on the door.

"I'm okay." I opened the door to talk with her while I washed my hands and face and brushed my teeth. "I think it's just worrying about how we're all going to do next season, you know? What if Hinkle loses big again this winter and then there's even less money to pay anybody halfway decent or keep stuff running or looking good?"

Gigi stood in the doorway, watching me as I applied a fresh coat of deep-red lipstick. "You sure that's what it is? I mean, you throw up if you drink too much or you're sick, but from being worried?" She watched me in silence, concentrating hard on my movements. "You're not pregnant, are you?"

My hand stopped, my mouth frozen in its open position. I closed the lipstick and dropped it in the wicker basket on the counter. "No." I rubbed my lips together to spread the lipstick. "I mean, maybe. I suppose."

The idea that I could become pregnant from sleeping with Jim had crossed my mind, especially in our first months together. Even though my cycle had always been erratic, I had wondered every time my period had been late or unpredictable, and every time, I had been wrong.

"I'm... I mean I think I'm too fat. It hasn't happened in all this time, so why now? You know?" Even as I said the words, various unexamined twinges or physical sensations formed an instant pattern, making pregnancy seem a certainty.

"Jesus, Lola." Gigi reached over to rub the top of my arm. "I just figured you were taking care of yourself. I don't know about that whole being-too-fat thing. I'd venture what's kept you safe until now is that Jim's so old." Gigi leaned in to hug me, squeezing hard. "Don't worry, though. There's nothing that says you have to have a baby if you don't want one. It's not like how it used to be. You want to get an abortion, you can get a real doctor to do it and everything."

Gigi's words shocked me, both because of her assumption that my weight might not have been the sole culprit in my failure to get pregnant and because of her casual talk about erasing a possible baby that had been an abandoned fantasy until then.

"I wouldn't want to do that," I said. "I mean, I don't know that I'd get another chance to have a baby."

Gigi held tight to me. "We'll figure it out," she said.

Neither of us wanted to get involved in the tricky logistics of trying to get a pregnancy test done while traveling with the carnival. The simple thought of visiting a doctor, of hearing him gasp at my size or of a tiny-waisted nurse telling me to be ashamed of myself, made me think the better course of action might be to wait and see. Gigi nixed that idea, though. Lonny, whom she had sworn to secrecy after explaining in careful detail that, no, she wasn't the one afraid she might be pregnant, hooked us up with Dr. Arnold, an old guy who had lost his medical license sometime in the early sixties. For many years, he had had a brisk trade in illegal abortions and a solid reputation for clean, infection-free results, but business had long since dwindled. He was happy to blood test me for a reasonable amount of cash, and after bouncing back from his initial disappointment that Gigi wasn't to be his patient, he still evinced a certain game enthusiasm at the prospect of giving me a pelvic exam. I told him no thanks, pressing my clothed knees together as tightly as I could.

Dr. Arnold called the house to deliver the happy news on the same morning we were packing our things to head back out on the road. "Congratulations, I suppose." His words slurred. "I should tell you, though, in all the years I practiced medicine, I've never seen or even heard of someone so fat able to birth a normal baby." He sounded drunk.

"Now, folks," Jim said, "I'm sure you all enjoyed meeting this dear lady here, Lola Rolls." It was opening night in Greendale, our first date of the new season, and the main part of my act had ended with a bopping, fat-jouncing dance to the song "Ease on Down the Road." The people clapped and whistled as I waved to the crowd and walked off the stage down into the dressing room, where I would still be able to hear Jim's voice loud and clear as he talked up the pickled punks. In the usual course of things, I would have made my own pitch for the inside money, but unable to think of any other angle to tie the punks to my act other than to describe them as my own malformed fetuses, I was loath to do so. Even if the punks were all gaffed, speaking words to that effect seemed blasphemous, like the invitation to a curse.

Jim had no such compunction. Maybe this nonchalant indifference of his could be excused because, in the complicated maneuvering of closing up the house in Gulfy, of folding up clothes and sheets and stacking cleaned dishes, no real opportunity had arisen to tell Jim about the actual human fetus I carried.

"Now, folks," Jim intoned, "I know when you look at the lovely Lola Rolls, you see a jolly gal who likes to laugh and doesn't need anything more than a big fried chicken dinner to make her happy. But she has sadness in her life, just like we all do. Like most women, her greatest desire is to be a mother. Now, you might ask yourself how exactly such a big lady could have a baby. And you might even wonder what business an unmarried girl has trying to do that. Who's to say, ladies and gentlemen? Who's to say? All I know is that three times, Lola Rolls has tried to bear a child, and three times, she has failed. Her only consolation, slim though it may be, is to keep these poor misbegotten children who never got to be born with her at all times. With recent advances in science, they have been preserved, and they're here with us today. For the price of one dollar, just one measly dollar, I invite you to step behind this flap here to view them. If you have a weak stomach or a heart condition, though, you'll want to stay away because, I must warn you, they do not look like normal human children. They are aberrations of nature so extreme you might think them God's punishment."

Jim's gruesome pitch made my mouth feel sandy, spurred my heart to hammer in my chest, and caused the ground to appear to rise and fall. Even absent knowledge of the factual child growing inside me, Jim should still have realized and cared that in the alternate scenario he described, he would be the father of these freakish lost souls. There was a good solid bench in the dressing room, a match to the table Chicky, the new Ferris wheel ride boy, had lugged in for the pickled punk display. He had done that favor in large part because he wanted to see for free what would have cost someone else money. Judging by how he slapped his knee and removed his trucker cap to lean in to get a better look, he was impressed by the punks. He said he had never seen anything like them, then he made the sign of the cross over his chest.

A lot of workers, the regulars, the familiar faces around the cook trailer and G-top, already angry about missing or delayed pay from the previous season, had disappeared, driven away at last by the anemic wages Hinkle was offering this season. Hinkle had had to do his hiring on the fly, giving people like Chicky, who, if nothing else, could be talked into a bad deal, a coveted gig, like Ferris wheel operator, despite little or no experience.

Thinking about Chicky distracted me at least from what Jim was telling the audience about the pickled punks, helped to push down my superstitious fear. It was stupid, I told myself, to think that my life's course of events could somehow be altered by allowing this talk of my imagined misfortune. This whole endeavor had been my idea, I reminded myself. Jim was only helping because I had asked him to do exactly that. The bench where I was sitting had been placed in the dressing room by Jim. Except for that first night when there had been nothing but a weak folding chair, the dressing room had always had a sound piece of furniture that could bear my weight. Jim had seen to that, something a solicitous man, conscious of small considerations, would do.

At the end of the night, though, after performing various times and having listened to Jim talk about the monstrous half children I had expelled from my fat body, I felt no more accustomed to the process than when it had begun. I left the sideshow tent and skipped the G-top without a word to Jim or Gigi or anyone else, opting instead to rest in quiet darkness, eyes wide open, wondering if a woman like me could ever have a normal child.

Nothing could quiet my mind—not eating or reading or dreaming—leaving me to wait for a long black stretch until Jim came home. In the smallest hours of the morning, he flopped onto the bed next to me, not bothering to turn on the lamp or change out of his clothes.

"Jim," I whispered, clicking on the light. "We need to fix the pickled punk act."

Jim held his hand across his eyes. "Tell me about it tomorrow."

There would never be a good or correct moment to talk with Jim, so I reasoned there couldn't be much harm in selecting the wrong opportunity. "I'm pregnant." An intense relief surged through me for having said those words at last, for no longer adding to the growing tally of days that Jim didn't know.

Jim sat up to stare at me. "Shit. Are you serious? I mean, you know that for sure?"

I could only nod, averting my gaze from the taut energy of Jim's body, from the straining disbelief that pulled it tight. Most of me hadn't expected that Jim would squeeze and kiss me, pausing only to burrow his head into my abdomen in rapt adoration to be closer to our child—or that he would offer marriage. I was unable to stop myself, however, from wanting more, a grander, happier reaction, a reflection of my own secret joy. Tears dripped down the sides of my face, fresh ones sliding down already wet tracks, as I did nothing to clean them away.

"Come on now, Lolly." He was the only one who called me that. Hearing it made me feel better, but it didn't erase the tired resignation in his voice, conveying maybe better than words ever could that my pregnancy was an obstacle, a sticky complication, the last thing he needed right then. "It's not as bad as all that. I know a guy—"

That was a thing about Jim. He always had a friend somewhere he could contact to help out in any situation. "I'm not getting an abortion," I said to avoid hearing Jim make the suggestion or listen to him expound on the ease with which the matter could be resolved. My idiotic hope, thin though it had been, that Jim would somehow rise to the occasion, had been stupid. I saw that now.

"Besides, you know, we probably won't have to worry about it. Doc Arnold says someone as fat as me can't have a baby anyway." Then I truly was crying in earnest, swiping at my tears with both hands.

"Well, fuck him, all right, Lolly? Arnold's so goddamn old he can't even see straight. And what the hell does he know anyway? I seen midgets and cripples and she-men have babies with no problem. Shit, Sweet Chenille had a beard so long she could braid it on hot days, and she had eight kids." Jim pressed the top half of his body against me and kissed my lips and wet red cheeks. "You're gonna be just fine."

The feel of his mouth and hands comforted me, made me want to believe his words, have faith in his conviction. I found myself thinking of Mrs. Schendel instead, of the children she had wished for but had never had. She had wanted more from life than she had gotten. So had my own mother, for that matter. Why should I succeed where they had faltered? Those grim thoughts, compounded by my suspicion that Jim would view the pregnancy and possible baby as my project, which, much like the pickled punks, he would be content to discuss or assist with but not plan for or make decisions about, kept me from telling him any of my nascent, improbable ideas of how I could have a child and still travel with the carnival. Others had certainly done so before, but the ones I knew about had tended to be with bigger, more stable operations than Midstate.

Hinkle asked to talk with me in his office the next day. I had only seen him in brief spurts and from a distance since we had set up in Greendale, so I wasn't quite prepared for how he looked from a close-in perspective. He had gone another winter without getting his teeth repaired, having changed during that time from looking like a man who had suffered a mouth injury to one who was habitually toothless, a condition highlighted and made worse by the clump of chewing tobacco in his mouth. Hinkle was wearing his usual pair of gabardine trousers, but they had a white, stringy stain on the front and deep wrinkles at the tops of the legs, as if they had been worn many times without being washed. He matched them with a faded navy T-shirt that had a peeling white design of three seven cards and a pair of dice under which the words Lucky Las Vegas appeared in neat cursive script. Even if I hadn't known about the substandard, last-minute hires, Hinkle's appearance would have been enough to let me know that he was still on a losing streak.

I eased my body down into the chair in front of his desk, trying to keep my face expressionless, to betray no reaction to how different the office also appeared since the only other time I had been there. It seemed that, for whatever reason, Marva had given up on helping to keep the place organized. Gone were the wooden trays with the neat stacks of paper, the bulletin board with the map of Wisconsin, and the tidy desk with the green blotter and a stapler and small tub of paper clips lined up along the top. Now the surface of the desk had disappeared under a blanket of paper. A calendar with a topless woman had been taped to the wall, and the trash can overflowed with papers, a banana peel, and a closed Styrofoam container that gave off an unpleasant smell of old onions, which may have also been Hinkle's own odor.

"Well, I would say 'have a seat,' but it looks like you've already made yourself at home, Sarah."

No one had called me Sarah for a very long time. I could feel the tendons in my neck tighten to taut cords at the sound of it, the longing and fear it evoked. Hinkle couldn't know why being called Sarah discomfited me, but he was like a dog in many ways, a smart one who didn't require an explanation to be able to spot a weakness.

"Lola, please."

Hinkle gave a slight smile. He was trying to arouse some strong emotion in me to keep me from thinking and speaking in a logical way. "Okay, Lola, then. Now, my dear, first thing I want you to know is that I am doing my very best to be patient right now. Chicky told me you're running your own show out the back of the sideshow tent without ever paying me a privilege to work on this lot, without ever even asking me about it. I told him there must be some kind of mistake, that you wouldn't cheat me like that." Hinkle's voice was low and cold. He pressed on the edge of the desk and leaned forward toward me so that I could see how the muscles in his shoulders and upper arms bunched together. "That money belongs to the carnival. Not to trouble you with the details, but Midstate sure could use some cash right about now."

No kidding, I almost said but stopped myself in the nick of time. "That's just the blow off after my act. That counts as inside money, so it's mine."

"There you have it, then." Hinkle smiled, a sudden, jarring gesture, as he sat back down, his menace deflated. "A simple misunderstanding. You haven't been with it as many years as I have, so I'm going to bet you haven't walked a lot of different lots. Am I right?"

"Yes," I admitted, even though that sliver of truth felt like a concession I'd rather not give.

"Let me tell you, then," Hinkle continued. "There's plenty of these pickled punk shows. Usually, there's a recorded voice playing, people pay up, walk through, and come out the other side. It can be a good money maker." Hinkle paused to spit into a paper cup sitting on the edge of the desk. "You can see, then, how any person with common sense would consider this type of thing its own show. Now, if you're interested in running a concession, that's something we can talk about—"

"Let me guess. And I have to pay up front whatever outrageous price you want to charge me so that I can do that."

Hinkle looked surprised at having his speech cut short, his antics curtailed before he had the chance to execute them. "Well, yes. That is the way it would work. You're always free to try your luck somewhere else, but you seem so comfortable here with Jim I can't imagine you'd want to do that." He smiled again, not showing his teeth, his lips tinged brown from the tobacco.

"Jim helped me do all this. Did you know that?" Even as I spoke, part of me doubted the wisdom of claiming Jim as my staunch supporter when he was already failing me as a willing and enthusiastic father to our child.

"Jim knows that we're running a business here. And there's no need for you to get hysterical, not when you haven't heard my plan. How about we set up a concession for you, and you don't have to pay me one cent for it? I'll even let you keep the money you made last night. How does that sound?" Hinkle's voice had a happy lilt, his expression pleasant, but something about him, the rigidity of his posture maybe, or perhaps how he seemed to be scanning my face with his eyes in a quick side-to-side motion, belied the image he wanted to project. I knew in that instant that this was a desperate man.

"What's the catch?"

"No catch. You get the concession for free. Just pay me back through the ticket sales. And you'll need to make at least two or three more of the punks."

If I went along with what Hinkle suggested, I wouldn't have to hear Jim talk up the atrociousness of the punks night after night. Maybe I was wrong to be so suspicious of Hinkle. He was a gambler and a scammer, but at his core, he was a businessman. "How much do you want?" I asked.

"See there, that's what I like about you. You get right down to the heart of the matter. Now, let's see. To make it worth my while, I'm going to have to say ninety percent of the ticket sales." Hinkle spit in his cup, leaned back in his chair.

White-hot, milky rage surged through me. "I want at least fifty percent."

Hinkle was trying to get the better of me, to put himself in charge of the punks even though I was the one who had made them. If I were their mother, then Hinkle had somehow made himself their father—overbearing and bossy without consideration for the love and effort that had created those children, ready even to dictate how many of them we would have.

"Get out, then," Hinkle said. "Waddle your fat fucking ass on out of here. And I better not hear anything else about you running a concession on this lot without my say-so."

The bitter rage, the quiet savagery of his words, stopped me cold and extinguished my own anger and made me think the whole punk venture wasn't worth any amount of money. My father had often said that superstition was a type of ignorance, but should I tempt fate by peddling deformed babies or listening to them being described as freaks of nature? I stood from my chair.

"Wait, Lola," Hinkle said, his voice softer. "Sit back down, sweetheart. I don't want there to be any bad blood between us. Tell you what I'm going to do. I'll give you fifteen percent. How about that?" Hinkle drew a deep breath. "Now, before you tell me again that you want more, you just remember that the only reason you're even here at this carnival is because I allow it." Hinkle stood up from his chair and extended his hand toward me. "Do we have a deal?"

"No," I whispered. "No deal."

Hinkle hadn't been expecting that response, and he didn't say another word to me as I left. I had no idea what to do with the punks. Repellent and deformed though they were, I didn't want to destroy them. Even after a full night of hearing Jim describe them as my benighted offspring, I had developed a type of affinity for them, the sort of mother's love that obviated the pain of having horrible children. I could keep them with me for a while in the trailer, but if I continued to cart around those pointless counterfeit fetuses for too long, I feared becoming just as Jim had described me—a sad, childless woman whose only comfort was her wretched jarred babies.

Red River Falls

Midstate Traveling Amusements Carnival arrived in Red River Falls the first weekend of August. The preceding days, weeks, and months had dragged and had included two instances of missed pay that no one, regardless of how outraged they might be, had any real expectation of recovering. Jim had begun to lose weight again, worn down to bone and skin from the uppers he took, the crises he handled. Given Jim's apparent stress and paranoia, I simply told him that I didn't want to do the pickled punk display for inside money anymore rather than recount my meeting with Hinkle. I comforted myself by eating more and more often, becoming fuller and softer, as if to compensate for Jim's diminished figure.

Gigi knocked on the trailer door our first morning there, intent on convincing me to go for a ride around town with her, Ora Ann, and Daisy to have something to do while the carnival setup was being completed. Being out in public like that among normal people, so like the very ones from my childhood, usually wore me down, but the day was already hot and boring. Besides which, the other girls would have badgered me until I said yes. Worse still, maybe they would have gone without me.

Red River Falls was ordinary in every way, with the usual town center surrounded by miles and miles of flat farmland. The height and breadth of Red River Falls emblazoned on the water tower seemed an outlandish exaggeration given the town's size and unremarkable nature. We got lost in the network of county roads and

171

tried, without success, to return to the town center or to circle back to the carnival.

Ora Ann rubbed her arms with her hands. Her teeth chattered as if she was standing in a cold wind.

"What's up with you?" Gigi asked in the rearview mirror. The temperature must have been in the nineties. We had rolled down all the windows on Gigi's old, beat-up station wagon.

"I just got a chill, girls. There's something wrong about this place. I'm telling you that." Ora Ann blew on her fingertips to warm them.

"Jesus Christ, Ora Ann," Daisy said, "I told you not to do that voodoo witchcraft when I'm around."

"I can't help it when I get a feeling."

Gigi stopped the car at a crossroads. Every direction looked the same. A dirt road stretching for miles, bisecting deep green fields of corn and soy. "Well, how about you get a feeling about which way it is back to the setup?" Gigi snapped.

We had to stop at three houses where Gigi and Daisy took turns asking for directions because, even though they didn't blend in precisely, they were the most ordinary looking of the four of us. My fat would have certainly startled them, while Ora Ann always managed to look like a gypsy fortune teller with her knotted headscarf and clinking stack of bracelets. A full two hours later, we made it back to the lot, all of us in bad moods. My body ached from being stuffed into Gigi's car. I wanted time to eat by myself and bathe before Jim came home. With a perfunctory "See you all later," I started limping back to the trailer.

"Wait up, Lola," Gigi called. She came up behind me. We both waved to Ora Ann and Daisy.

"I have to get inside and rest, Geeg," I said. "Being in the car for so long kills me."

"Huh? Oh, yeah. Well..." Gigi hesitated. I wondered if she really believed me about the pain. "So, do you think there's something to what Ora Ann was saying? Sometimes she just creeps me the fuck out."

"Ignore her, then." I put my hand on the trailer door in what I hoped was a meaningful way. "Look, I don't know how it works with her, but she gets a lot of stuff wrong. She told me I'd be reunited with my mother, and I didn't have the heart to tell her my mother has been dead for twenty years."

"Yeah, yeah, right," Gigi replied. She slapped the trailer door, gazing after Ora Ann, who had already disappeared from sight. "You go on and get some rest," she said, walking away without a backward glance.

A chill slid down my own back. I hated this spooky, otherworldly feeling that Ora Ann managed to instill, possibly as much as Daisy did. "Superstitious stupidity," I muttered. That was what my father would have said too.

Without the distraction of the pickled punks, either to earn me money or to make demands on my creative impulse, I had devised a new act, a belly-dance number, complete with bare midriff and gauzy scarves rimmed with reflective sequins. I even had a set of finger cymbals and, with some practice, had gotten quite good at playing them—another regular show, an ordinary town. The crowd was a bit smaller than normal, but then again, the carnival itself was shrinking as unpaid workers left without warning. The scream came after my first set, so loud and piercing that it was able to cut through the usual carnival din as a distinct sound. Only a scream fueled by raw terror and shock could travel like that from the Ferris wheel to the sideshow tent—the scream of a mother for her child.

I dropped the washcloth I had been using to wipe my hot face and went out the back flap of the tent in search of the source of that terrible noise, breaking the tough, iron-clad rule of not letting the public see for free what they should be shelling out money to view. They weren't paying attention to me anyway. A crowd was expanding and thickening at the base of the Ferris wheel. Men craned their heads upward, some holding their hats fast to their heads to keep them from falling off. A boy, maybe only six or seven—it was difficult to tell from my vantage point— was dangling by his shirt from the open door of his Ferris wheel car at the eight o'clock position.

Some people were yelling for Chicky, the ride jockey, to turn the Ferris wheel back on to lower the boy closer to the ground. Someone else said not to do that because starting it up would jar the boy and make him fall. There were suggestions to get a ladder and to call the fire department. Yet no one moved or took any action.

I stood glued to the spot, staring at that helpless child and at the mother underneath him with arms upstretched. The boy cried, "Mommy, Mommy," and flailed his arms in a desperate attempt to get back into the Ferris wheel car.

The whole crowd gasped in a single voice.

"Stay still, Mike! You listen to Mommy right now, and stop moving."

A smaller knot of men moved in closer to try to climb up the Ferris wheel, but that asshole Chicky, having acquired some unshakable authority as the ride operator, told them to stay back when he should have already been doing what those men were suggesting. I grabbed the shoulders of the people in front of me, pulling them to the side as I made my way forward. I certainly couldn't climb the Ferris wheel, but I could slap Chicky's face and tell him to get out of the way if he wasn't going to do anything to help. Jim rushed past me with a nylon rope coiled over his chest and back, not pausing or even recognizing me as he barreled through the crowd, knocking people out of the way.

Chicky at least made room when Jim appeared. Maybe in Chicky's mind, as messed up as it surely was by the booze or pills or whatever else he may have ingested, the situation could be handed over to Jim because Jim was a person of authority at the carnival. Chicky clearly thought he had done the right thing by doing nothing and by not allowing anyone else to take action.

Jim began climbing up the wheel support tower, the stabilizing structure that ran from the ground to the wheel's center. My heart—but not just my heart, my entire internal self—heaved upward into my throat, giving me the crazy thought that I would turn myself inside out if I released my breath with too much force. In that moment, I saw with frank clarity that Jim was going to die trying to save that boy. Tears leaked from my eyes. My mind's voice, the one that tried without success to scream during nightmares, yelled for him to come back without making a sound.

The spokes of the Ferris wheel ran out from the center hub, each of them being two parallel aluminum beams with a tight row of light bulbs along the outer faces. There were mechanical cables in an X pattern between the two beams and cross members at the ends where the drive rim was placed. Once Jim reached the wheel's hub at the top of the support tower, he bear walked out the spoke nearest to where the boy dangled. The woman in the Ferris wheel car above the boy called to Jim to hurry, but Jim ignored her, focused only on getting closer to the boy. I had finally made my way to the front of the crowd and stared up at the dizzying spectacle.

"Don't move, kid," I heard Jim say.

Meanwhile, the boy's mother had positioned herself directly under her son with her arms up in the air as if she meant to catch him when he fell, as if her sheer desire to save him would somehow enable her to do so.

When he reached the end of the spoke, Jim braced himself against the drive rim and tied one end of the nylon rope around the cross member and secured the other around his waist. Controlling the slack with great care, he braced his feet on the bottom side of the girder and pushed away. He was so close to the boy that I saw, with complete certainty, that my earlier fear had been idiotic. Jim wasn't going to die, after all. He was going to save the boy and give the crowd the most spectacular, believable performance they had ever seen.

He only needed a bit of momentum to swing over and grab the boy. Everyone on the ground watched in profound silence and held their collective breath. I had experienced this moment many times in books—the suspenseful, heart-drumming interlude right before the hero saves the day.

The boy had the instant recognition that Jim would rescue him, and he lunged toward Jim. The force of that movement tore the flimsy scrap of shirt that had kept him suspended. He fell toward the ground just beyond Jim's reach.

The crowd gasped in one voice, unable to believe the improbability of the worst outcome when only moments before, a happy ending had seemed inevitable. We all stayed frozen with shock and disbelief, except for the boy's mother. She moved under her falling son, and as unlikely as it was, she caught him. It wasn't a clean catch, and she didn't get a good grip on him and wasn't strong enough anyway to keep them both from hitting the ground.

"I got you, baby! I got you!" the mother screamed and squeezed her unconscious son to her chest. A small thread of blood trickled out of the corner of the boy's mouth. "I caught him. I did it. I can't believe I did it."

Then everything happened at once. A man raced forward and said he was a doctor. He peeled the mother away from her son, saying that the boy's back and neck had to be kept immobile. Hinkle appeared on the scene, or maybe he had been there all along. He told Jim to hang tight and restarted the ride. Once Jim was back on the ground, Hinkle got everyone else off as well, while Weedy and Roscoe, who had made their way through the sea of people, moved back the onlookers, more of them who seemed to want to see the damaged boy.

Sirens approached. Jim knelt down by the boy, across from the boy's mother and the doctor.

"Jesus," he whispered. "Jesus Christ, I thought for sure I had him." He covered his eyes with his hands. Jim was crying, something I had never thought I would see.

"Give the boy room to breathe," the doctor said to no one in particular. I stepped forward anyway to touch Jim's shoulder.

He squeezed my fingers, pressing the back of my hand against his eyes. "I thought I had him," he repeated.

The sound of the sirens grew louder. Soon the police would be swarming all over the carnival.

"You better go lie low," he whispered. "The fuzz is going to be here any second, and they're going to ask a lot of questions."

I shook my head.

"Please," he said.

On my way back to the trailer, I noticed that other people were clearing out too. Game and food joints were closing in anticipation of an order from the police to shut down the entire carnival and to avoid questions about what they might have seen or known beforehand about the status of the Ferris wheel or its operator.

I spent the rest of the night sitting on the couch with only the dim stove light to cut up the darkness. Getting up to change out of my belly-dance costume seemed like too much effort. That boy kept falling to the ground. It was worse when I closed my eyes. Meaty was sitting on the counter in his jar. One of his arms looked like it was disintegrating in the pickling solution. His small meat hand appeared to be waving, beckoning me. A tickling sensation in the pit of my stomach, like the movement of small fingers, unnerved me, made me heave myself up from the couch to vomit in the toilet. As I washed my face and rinsed my mouth in the bathroom sink, the knowledge that deep within my formidable bulk, a small baby was growing and wanting to be born into this unsafe world, shrank the confined space to claustrophobic proportions.

"Dear God," I whispered. "Please let my baby live. If I can have this one thing, I'll do whatever you want."

Someone knocked on the door in the predawn hours. Probably Gigi, I thought, because she hated to be alone. I was surprised then to find Little Freddy waiting for me, wearing the baggy chinos I had hemmed and tailored for him last season and a white T-shirt. He smelled good, as if he had just showered. His hair still looked wet, and I noticed a damp patch on the back of his shirt.

"I thought you'd be Gigi." I glanced over Little Freddy's head but didn't see anyone else around. "Jim's not here."

"Don't worry about that. He's not going to be back for a good long while." Little Freddy put his foot on the first step. "I just need to talk to you. It's important, okay?"

"Sure, sure. Come on in," I said, even though the only thing that could make the situation worse would be for Jim to find me and Little Freddy alone together.

Little Freddy and I sat next to each other on the couch. He touched the tail of the chiffon scarf hanging from my waist, threading it through his fingers. "You're still wearing your costume." He stared at the soft material in his hands. "It looks good, you know. Real good."

"So, you know anything about what's going on out there?" I asked to distract him.

Little Freddy shook his head. "Nah. Not too much. Just that the ambulance finally took the kid away. Nobody knows how bad the fall messed him up. The thing is this never should have happened, you know? If this place was working right, you wouldn't have a kid getting hurt like that or a shithead like Chicky as a ride boy. We're going to get run out of town for sure, and who knows if that bastard

Hinkle will land on his feet this time." Little Freddy stopped fiddling with my scarf to look me full in the face, the first time he had done so since he had entered the trailer. "I'm not going to stick around for it. That's what I came to tell you."

I clutched Little Freddy's arm in disbelief. "What do you mean? You're leaving? Is that what you're saying? You can't do that."

Little Freddy placed his hand on mine. "It's time for me to move on. I got family in Kingston, New York. I could get some work there in dwarf tossing. It's murder on your back, but it's money."

Little Freddy deserved far better than being tossed like an inhuman object for money and laughs. His back and knees troubled him already. What would his body be and feel like after even a month of tossing? A tear streaked down my cheek. Then I cried in earnest at the thought of losing my friend but also for the hurt and damaged boy who had fallen through the sky and for the grasping mother who had managed, against all likely odds, to catch him.

"Come on, don't cry now. Goodbyes are already hard enough." Little Freddy pressed the scarf he had been holding into my hand. "Wipe your eyes."

I swiped my fingers across my cheeks, not wanting to dirty my costume with melted eye makeup. "I'm going to miss you, Fred. This place won't be the same without you."

Little Freddy stood up on the couch, facing me with one foot planted between my legs. He placed a hand on each cheek and tipped my face upward to kiss me with the hard, sweet pressure of a man desperate to have his lips on me. He put his tongue in my mouth. We kissed like that for a moment. I knew Little Freddy wanted this goodbye to end with the two of us in bed, but my terror of Jim coming home and finding us together outshone my desire to have that experience. I pushed back on Little Freddy's chest until he pulled his face away from mine.

"You stay beautiful, Lo-Lo," he whispered. Then he stepped down and went out the door with a small parting wave.

In the kitchen, I pulled the dish towel from its hook on the wall and draped it over Meaty's jar with great care. "Go to sleep," I said.

The sun glimmered on the horizon, the world lit with the spooky gloom of dawn, when Jim returned to the trailer. He sat on the bed, bent forward, holding his face in his hands. His skin looked slack and gray. I pressed my fingertips against the small of his back.

Jim pulled off his boots to lie down next to me, shuffling his body against mine to nuzzle his head into my chest and to stretch his arm across my expansive softness. "I really thought I was going to save him," he whispered. "The kid's back is broken. The mother's a war widow. The father was killed outside of Saigon."

I stroked the top of Jim's bald head in a featherlight, swirling pattern. "What's going to happen now?"

Jim held me in such a close embrace that when he shrugged, it felt like my gesture too. "The crowd just about mauled Chicky. The police said they were going to take him for questioning. Hinkle almost shit himself when he heard that because Chicky was drunk and high and would look for somebody else to blame. The fuzz really just wanted to get some time alone with Chicky to beat on him, since they couldn't come up with a crime to charge him with. I've never seen it as bad as this. We got to get the carnival out of here, but I've been passing around so much money to try to smooth things over I can't see how we're going to have enough left to do it. You know, people smell blood. They start leaving. They figure they'll just cut their losses and try again next season with someplace better maybe."

"Little Fred left for good," I said. "He says he's going to live with his brother in New York State."

"Ah shit." Jim rolled away from me and stood up. "You got to get out of here too. There's a campsite about sixty miles east. A couple other people are already there. I know for sure Ora Ann is on her way. I'm gonna take a quick shower and get a little pick-me-up, then we'll hitch up the trailer and drive over. That way I can come back in the truck."

I didn't like the idea of being stranded at some campsite, but I wanted even less to stay where I was. I could become a target for the fallout, visible to the police, a possible sticking point for the blame that would need to be assigned. "I'll go wake up Gigi," I said.

Gigi took such a long time answering the door that I had nearly made up my mind to try again later. She finally appeared, clutching her housecoat closed as if there hadn't been time even to snap it as she had stumbled toward the door. "Shit, Lola, what are you doing here at this hour?"

"Oh," I said. She smelled like alcohol, and I wondered if it was from the night before or if her night had never really ended. "Jim is going to move the trailer to a campground near here, and I'm going to stay there until this whole mess blows over."

Gigi's face didn't change expression or register any reaction to my words.

"You need to come too," I clarified.

"Yeah, well, Jim's not my old man, so I don't have to do what he says." Gigi leaned back to stare into the shadows. "It's just Lola," she said over her shoulder.

The room behind her still held the sepia tones of dawn. The ordinary objects hadn't yet resolved themselves into their usual shapes. Ike, wearing jeans but no shirt, slid open the divider wall of the bedroom.

"I thought you might be Hinkle," Gigi said to me. I realized she was naked underneath her housecoat.

Ike stood behind Gigi, putting his arm around her shoulder. "You getting out of here? I'm thinking I might go stay with a buddy of mine out in Sacramento that's got a tattoo parlor and maybe see about learning the trade or getting with a new outfit next season."

"Oh, Ike," I said. "Little Freddy took off. What's going to happen to us if everyone leaves?" Our little sideshow family might disappear altogether at this rate.

Gigi's face softened at the distressed sound of my voice, and she reached over to hug me. "Don't worry, okay? I mean, of course I'm going to. Just not right this second."

I nodded and reached over to pat Ike's forearm. "You take care of yourself."

Gigi and I stayed at the Whispering Winds campground outside of Red River Falls for nearly a week. A bunch of us congregated there, even Ike, who failed to make good on his threat to head off to Sacramento, opting instead to spend most of his time with Gigi. Their relationship, such as it was, intense and obvious in close surroundings and ultimately short-lived, sent up a hot flare, something for people to talk about when there was nothing else to do.

Jim showed up to tell us that the carnival was moving on to Patawaunee. I think we were all relieved to be given a plan, a way to move forward—a break from the possible obligation of having to make new arrangements on our own. Later that night when Jim and I were alone in bed together, he talked about the departure from Red River Falls, about how ugly and protracted it had been. When Hinkle didn't have enough money to make payroll, workers had fled like rats from a sinking ship, so Jim hired a bunch of local boys and offered to pay them cash to help break down the carnival. Then he had had to stiff them the money.

"I didn't feel good about it," he said. "I even paid a few of the kids—the ones who really looked like they needed it—out of my own pocket."

As Jim spoke, the word *Patawaunee* echoed in my mind. Why, I didn't know or couldn't remember. The beast, long submerged and slinking its way through the water, raised its back and broke the surface.

Patawaunee

On the second or third night in Patawaunee, I decided to wear the magenta dress with the sequined straps, the first stage outfit I had ever sewn, a sign of a new life for me then and, I hoped, now of a better life to come. I couldn't handle much more of Hinkle's anger and suspicions, his demands for loyalty and hatred of everyone who had left. Jim was popping pills like chocolate drops to stay ahead of the problems and crises he was expected to mend and, I suspected, to blot out the excruciating memory of failing to save that falling boy. As if that wasn't enough, Gigi was too wrapped up in her fizzling relationship with Ike and often too distracted or drunk to offer me any real advice or comfort.

Getting ready in the trailer, I soothed myself with the notion that the season would not last forever. Time, at least, was moving forward, and before too long, we would all be down in Gulfy. Gigi would be over and done with Ike by then and relatively more sober, and Jim would go back to normal. I pressed my hand into the soft fat below my belly button. Then he and I would have time and peace enough to prepare for the baby's birth that December.

With no great ideas about what to do on stage, I figured I would probably just talk to the audience like I had on the previous few nights. People liked that. Outside, the sun beamed big and bright in the cloudless late-afternoon sky as I made my way up to the sideshow tent. I hoped to have a minute or two to chat with Gigi, not about anything in particular but only to calm my nerves. Being around Jim, who appeared to live in a constant state of high alert these days, had begun to make me jumpy as well.

By the time I made it to the tent, however, Gigi was gone, probably having a drink right then in her little hidey hole under the stage, and Jim had already started his bally. He clicked off the wonders that the audience was about to see.

"A woman who, let's just say, is very close to her twin sister."

"A wonder of the South Pacific covered in tattoos—a true colored man." Here he paused for the crowd's laughter.

"A big, enormous gal who can't wait to jiggle her way into your hearts with her common sense and good looks."

I took my cue and walked across the stage, waving to the crowd. I executed a small twirl, lifted the edge of my dress, and bent into a dainty curtsy. The audience loved when I did that because it gave them a good view of my bare thighs and the full tops of my breasts. Many of the men lowered their heads, contorting themselves to see what else I had up my skirt.

"Good evening, ladies and gentlemen, and thank you, Jim, for that lovely introduction." There was a sturdy, straight-back pine chair on the stage for my act. I sat down and crossed one ankle over my thigh, which prompted the men to try looking up my dress again.

"As you might imagine," I simpered in a quiet voice, "I'm a bit of an expert on matters of the heart and feel quite confident on advising the ladies in the audience about how to get and hold on to the man of their dreams and on telling the gentleman with us tonight how they can get beautiful women eating... oh, I don't know... a pork chop... out of their hands."

The audience laughed, and I giggled along with them. The events of Red River Falls, combined with my worry for Jim and the exhaustion of pregnancy, had reduced these performances to rote chores. I relied a lot on audience participation to get through them. I liked to call a man up on stage, a young, handsome one if possible, and embarrass him with a funny stock set of double entendres, racy innuendos, and gestures.

"Let's see," I said, index finger pressed to my chin. "Maybe there's a fine young fellow with us tonight who can come up and help me out."

I scanned the audience, trying to find a good-looking man, an uncommon commodity in Patawaunee, it appeared. The thought depressed me, and I couldn't wait to conclude with my usual double pirouette and then a few of the stomping tap dance steps.

A movement distracted me at the back of the tent. A woman was pushing her way through the crowd, moving people to the left and right, in her determination to plow forward toward the stage. The people around her seemed annoyed at her treatment of them. "Well, excuse you," an old man said to her.

The strangeness of the woman's actions caused me to lose my train of thought. Why would she, or anyone for that matter, want to rush the stage? That sort of thing might happen at the cootch show but not here in the sideshow tent.

Even as I wondered what was going on, an answer was already forming in my mind. This person knew me. She had found me. And then there she was, front and center. Missy. Sections of her dark hair, remnants of the lavish feathered bangs I remembered her wearing, had fallen free from the clip at the back of her head and hung in sweaty waves around her face. With arms crossed over her chest, she looked like a haunted house apparition, ghoulish and impatient.

That was right: Patawaunee was the hometown of Missy's new fiancé. Somehow, somewhere, I had forgotten that a girl like me always needed to watch her back. Seeing Missy was like being awake inside a nightmare.

"I got you," Missy said in apparent disbelief. "I actually got you."

I could feel the crowd growing restless. Side conversations broke out as people murmured to each other, wanting to know what was going on. At that moment, I wished there was a security detail, like at the cootch show, to get rid of Missy.

I walked to the front of the stage and waved my arms over my head to signal to Jim or Ike to come help me. At that same moment, Missy lunged forward, gripping the floorboards.

"Killer! This big, fat slob is a murderer who killed her own brother because she knew that no man would ever want her!"

My head was lowered, putting me in the perfect position, at the exact right angle to spit in her face and make it count, too, but I couldn't depend on the crowd. If I'd learned nothing else in my career as a performer, I knew it was impossible to know how the audience might respond, with whom they would side. Instead, I straightened and took a step back, looking around again for someone to come help me.

Lionel, the ticket seller, elbowed his way to the front and grabbed Missy. He pulled on her arm to try to get her outside. She turned and started slapping him on the face and head with her free hand. Ike ran out from behind the stage to take hold of Missy's other arm. The audience gasped in astonishment at the sight of his multicolored skin, at his sudden appearance, like a demon from hell had materialized. The people were shifting positions and refocusing their attention, forming a horseshoe, as they closed in to circle Ike, Lionel, and Missy.

"You can't make me leave! I paid my ticket. That giant sack of fat is a cold-blooded killer. Grab her! Get her!" Missy kicked her legs in front of her, using Ike and Lionel as leverage to lift her feet in the air, pummeling some of the spectators who had moved in too close.

Jim made his way through the crowd. He latched on to Missy's ankles, pinning one on each of his hips, but still she bucked her torso up and down and flailed her head from side to side. "Let me go, you assholes!"

A collective gasp rippled through the crowd, and one woman covered a little girl's ears with her hands and squeezed.

"I thought this was a decent place!" the woman trumpeted while, even in those extreme circumstances, I had to wonder what could have possibly given her such an idea.

Other people in the crowd took a cue from the woman and started raising their voices too.

"You be careful with that girl now," one man said. "She's wearing a dress, after all." He laughed.

"Will you look at that tattooed man?" another woman asked. "I wonder if he's part of the act."

The audience had come alive, stealing the show and deciding for themselves where they would put their attention. It was quickly becoming a mob scene, with people boxing in Lionel, Ike, and Jim and preventing them from hauling Missy out of the tent.

I stamped my foot as hard as I could on the stage. Then I jumped up and down with both feet, causing some people to turn and look at me.

"My God, she's like a bowl full of Jello. Every part of her jiggles," a man said.

I bounced myself around some more. "Friends, friends!" I yelled. "Please let those men remove that very unfortunate young woman from the tent."

As more people turned toward me, Lionel, Ike, and Jim took advantage of the break to push toward the exit with Missy.

"That poor, poor girl," I said. "She must be very hungry to behave like that." I pointed my finger toward Lionel, Ike, and Jim. "Gentlemen, please take her away and get her a coconut cake immediately. She is far too thin, without even cushion enough to give a little shimmy." I leaned my chest forward and moved my shoulders back and forth to make my cleavage ripple.

There were some hoots and whistles as the audience began to resume its regular configuration.

"I daresay I have never seen such lapses of comportment. I can only hope that those kind, dear men will slather butter for her on a nice, soft..." I turned to the side and slapped my rear end. "Biscuit."

The audience laughed. Even after Ike, Lionel, and Jim had gotten Missy out of the tent, she could still be heard yelling in impotent rage, not even bothering to form words now, but at a greater and greater distance as they carted her away.

I sat back down in the chair onstage. My body shook. My mind shook. If I had been any other act besides the fat lady, I would have made a break for it, would have started running to save my life. At the very least, I had to get out of plain sight. Missy might return with the police the next time. The more I considered that possibility, the more likely it seemed.

"Well, that was something. Wasn't it, folks? Here I wanted to talk all about love, while that woman had murder on her mind. I must admit that this whole incident has left me rather famished. So I'll just be on my way now to make myself a stack of ten butter-and-bacon sandwiches. My good friend Gigi and her sister will be along next."

I glanced back to see Gigi waiting on the stairs leading up to the stage. She swayed a bit while standing in place, making me wonder how much she had heard or knew about what was happening. At least she hadn't missed her cue.

My bow was the same maneuver for every show. I raised both arms straight up with my hands toward the top of the tent and out to the sides and then flung them down and back while I leaned forward, as deeply as I could, at the waist and held that posture for a few seconds before standing back up and dropping my arms again. It sent the blood rushing to my head.

"Thank you very much, ladies and gentlemen."

I went down to the makeshift dressing room to the side. There wasn't much in there—just a sink connected to some piping that ran back out under the tent and emptied into the gully. An old mirror was attached to one of the wooden poles. Sweat stains had formed along the neckline and under the arms of my dress. Someone, probably Gigi, had left a cleanish towel balled up on the bench. I sat down and patted my face and underarms with the towel and spread my legs and fanned myself with my dress to cool down. I dried inside my leg rolls before stuffing the towel into my sopping underwear.

Part of my mind screamed for me to get the hell out of there—not just the dressing room and the sideshow tent but the carnival itself. I wanted to take Jim's truck and not stop driving until I reached Gulfy. Yet the questions and possible pitfalls of an action like that held me immobile. What if I ran into Missy or the police on my way to the truck? What would I pack, and would it make sense to change clothes first? Most importantly, could I just leave Jim and Gigi like that without even saying goodbye?

I dropped the towel where I had found it and stood to splash water on my face again and again, hoping that cool freshness would help me think. Mrs. Schendel once told me that if you stared in the mirror for too long, the devil would appear behind you. The canvas flap opened, and there was Hinkle, materialized from seemingly nowhere, standing in the glass. His sudden appearance startled me even though I had known that he would come and find me, of course.

"You're looking lovely as always, Sarah," he said.

I turned to face him, not liking the sensation of having him behind my back. "Remember I asked you to call me Lola?"

"Oh right, right." Hinkle sat down on the bench. He picked up the damp, used towel and wiped his face with it. "I must say I'm a little surprised to find you here."

My mind's eye pictured the top of a rich vanilla cake covered with stiff white frosting. Mrs. Schendel would use the long spatula to smooth the sides and top of the cake, pausing between each swirl to dip it into a glass of water. I struggled to keep my face unlined, colorless, and soft like that. I made myself smile by thinking of Hinkle wiping his face with the towel I had used to dry my ass. "How's that?"

Hinkle laughed a little bit. "Aw, well. Let's just say I had a very interesting conversation with Lionel. I saw him and Jim and Ike throwing some girl off the lot. And that's odd, you know? Because it's usually men. I mean it's always men. Or if it is a woman, then it's because the guy she's with is being some sort of asshole. Then Lionel tells me she was some crazy person who yelled at you on stage and said you killed your brother, her fiancé. I didn't say it right to Lionel, but that seemed that like a very specific accusation and not the ramblings of some lunatic. Then I remembered that you do in fact have a brother, or maybe you did. That's how we found you, after all. He was at the carnival that time, and some folks were making jokes about him having a fat sister, so Jim and me came to take a look at you. And let me tell you, you did not disappoint."

I didn't want to imagine a cake anymore. "So what are you getting at? I can't help what this woman says or what she thinks she knows."

"Well, aren't you a cool customer, Sarah? If memory serves, your brother... Yes, Jared, that was his name. He looked very embarrassed hearing all those people laugh about you. And you turned us down when we first asked if you wanted to join up. A pretty firm 'no, thank you.' Then a few days later, you change your mind, and you're so anxious to get here that you can't even wait until morning. I'm not saying what might have happened, just that this is a very interesting set of facts. Wouldn't you agree?"

"Not really. People change their minds all the time."

Hinkle had the look of a man settling in, getting comfortable for some significant conversation. It made me realize that he must want to make some sort of deal with me. Somehow, some way, I had something he wanted.

"Is there something I can do for you here?" I asked him.

"All right, then. There could be some serious heat on you. And that would be very bad for the carnival. That's my main concern in all this. It's called harboring a fugitive, and it's a really big deal. You better go on and leave Midstate. I'll tell Jim goodbye for you." Hinkle made no move to stand up.

"Jim doesn't want me to leave," I said and wished I had kept quiet because my words sounded high-pitched, squeaky even.

"Oh, sweetheart," Hinkle said in a soft voice with such tenderness that for a moment I doubted every harsh thing I had ever said or dreamed of saying to him, every unkind thought and every homicidal impulse. "You know, I've seen a lot of old ladies with their men, and I can see you're a real good one. The pretty ones are never that loyal, but a girl like you, who can't just get herself a man every day, that kind of girl has some real staying power. We might not always see eye to eye, but I like you, Sarah—I mean Lola. I truly do, and a part of me is tempted to go out on a limb for you."

A spear of hope rose in me even as my instinct, the lower function of my brain stem, the reptilian impulse, reminded me that Hinkle never offered anything without expecting something in exchange. "I'd sure appreciate that."

"Good, good. Look, you can make up whatever story you want if the police come around, and I'll back you. You want to be from Oregon, I'll tell people I met you in Eugene. And if you never want to perform in Patawaunee again or any other town, that's fine. We'll play cards together instead, and I won't even win all your money from you. If I'm going to take a big risk like that to keep you here, though, and cover for you, maybe you could help me out too—go out on a limb for me, so to speak. It actually has to do with Jim, and you, being so close to him, are in the best position to do it."

Hinkle took a breath that I knew preceded the pitch meant to convince me of something requiring extreme persuasion. It was the same inhalation that Jim drew before starting his bally. "Like I said, Lola, the carnival is the most important thing. I think about that all the time. If the carnival suffers, well, then we all suffer. If the carnival loses money, well, then eventually we all lose money too. And it seems to me like the carnival has been losing money lately. It's like a leak has sprung somewhere." Hinkle paused to wipe his mouth with the towel. "I think Jim's the one who's been siphoning off all that money. You know, I never worried when he was just skimming some off the top because we all do that a little bit. I just figured he was using it to have some fun or maybe to send back home to his wife."

I sat down on the bench next to Hinkle because I didn't have the strength to stand anymore.

"Between you and me, I hear he owes her a shit-ton of money." Hinkle slid farther away on the bench because I was too close to him. "You knew about Jim's wife, right? I mean, I hope I'm not telling you some big secret. Nobody has ever met her, but Jim mentions her once in a while. Last I heard, I think she was living down Paducah way." Hinkle paused, waiting for me to say or do something.

"Oh, I knew about her. It's no big deal." The baby inside me moved, rolling, it felt like, from front to back, agitated, like me, wondering what to do next.

"See? That right there is what I'm talking about when I say you're loyal. There's plenty of women who'd fly off the handle at the thought of their man sending money to another woman. What was her name? Was it Cathy or Debby—something that ends with a y. No matter. You've got a great big old heart, Lola. I admire that. I really do. Like I said, though, Jim is taking a lot more now than just a little nibble here and there."

Hinkle folded his hands in his lap and drew in his lips. We were reaching the last stages of his pitch. "The sideshow is dying out, you know. Not just here but all over the place. I blame television. I think Jim is building himself a nice little nest egg because he means to move on. Part of me thinks I should part ways with him right now because at least that way I could dam up that outflowing stream of money, but I'd rather try to get some of it back. I know Jim, and he's no fool. He's got that money hid somewhere, likely in the trailer." Hinkle glanced back over his shoulder, probably to make sure we were still alone.

"And that's where you come in, my dear. You could find that money easy. You might not be one hundred percent comfortable with doing this. I get that, but really it would only take one phone call from me to get you arrested for murder. You see that, don't you? I can tell one story about you just as easily as I can tell another."

Hinkle reached over and took my hand, though I suspected that the soft feel of any part of me repelled him on a deep level. He very much needed me on his side. His willingness to touch me like a sweet, trusted friend was the best proof of that. "Lola, come on. He never even told you he had a wife. I'm helping you, and now you help me. That's the way it works."

I had to keep participating in the conversation in a rational way. Hinkle held all the cards, and he knew that. "Maybe you're wrong, though. Maybe Jim's not doing any of this."

Hinkle raised his upper lip in some rictus of sneer and grin. "Don't come back to me with that story, or I'll know you're lying. You show up with, let's say, five thousand dollars to start, and we're all square for now." Letting go of my hand, he allowed himself to laugh a little. "Jim won't even think twice that it was you, not when we got all these ride jockeys and halfwits that we don't got the money to pay."

I couldn't very well agree to steal money from Jim to pay Hinkle. That would be like saying that I trusted Hinkle to keep his word. Likewise, I couldn't tell Hinkle no. Maybe the best course was to promise him anything at all, if only to buy myself time to drive away.

Jim pushed aside the tent flap and came into the dressing room. He looked startled to find Hinkle and me together. "Here you are," Jim said.

"Here I am." My voice cracked.

"So, that girl's off the lot, then?" Hinkle asked.

"Yeah, she's gone," Jim said.

Hinkle surprised me and likely Jim, too, by laughing. "We better make sure she stays away. If she gives us too much trouble, I guess I'll have to round up Weedy and Roscoe and a few of the Canucks to run her off. Maybe Ike too. That's work they don't mind doing, at least."

Then he walked out, leaving Jim and me alone together.

I stared at the floor, packs of words running around my mind, chasing each other like slippery animals I couldn't capture or hold. "What exactly did Hinkle mean about running off Missy? Do they just... chase her away and tell her not to come back, or what?" I asked, despite knowing or at least suspecting that they would do something so much worse.

"The problem isn't them chasing her. It's what they do when they catch her." Jim shook his head. "Most of these guys are drunk or cranked up or both, so when you get a group of them together, they're a bunch of wild, mean animals."

"Oh God." I covered my eyes with my hands. "I don't even understand what's going on anymore. Hinkle was in here, saying he would cover for me and make up whatever story I wanted if the police show up. The catch is I have to pay him five thousand dollars." Talking with Jim, I was able to draw a full breath at last.

Jim sat down in the space that Hinkle had just left. "Where the hell does he think you would get money like that? That doesn't make sense."

"From you. He thinks you're skimming money off the top and that you've got all this cash hidden in the trailer, and all I have to do is find it and give it to him. Otherwise, he says he can call the police and tell them... tell them that I killed my brother."

I had never said those words aloud. They echoed in my brain. I wanted to cry or scream or show some emotion or reaction, but I felt trapped, pressed in place by the terrible truth of what I had done.

"Nah, nah, nah. None of that is going to happen. We're gonna get you out of here, Lola. You're gonna walk on over to the trailer right now. You lock the doors and turn out the lights. Don't make a sound, and don't open up for anybody but me. You just sit tight. I got this friend Mickey. I'll call around, and we'll have you a set of wheels by morning. Meanwhile, Gigi can keep her eye on Hinkle over at the G-top. He'll sit tight until tomorrow at least if he thinks he can get some money out of you."

"Okay," I said, even though I didn't like this idea, not any part of it. How had driving alone for hundreds of miles suddenly become the best option for me?

Jim kissed my forehead and held open the back flap of the tent for me. "I need to finish up, but trust me, we'll get you out of here."

A perfect plan, except I didn't want to leave and be alone, especially not now. I knew Hinkle had only told me about Jim's wife to make me doubt myself and question Jim's loyalty and transparency. It had worked too. I couldn't help but wonder if leaving the carnival would be the same as disappearing from Jim's life.

The timing was all wrong, but I had to know. "Wait, hang on. Do you have a wife? Are you married?"

"Ah shit," Jim said with a small laugh. "I see Hinkle has been singing my praises. Come on, Lolly, he wants to put ideas in your head so you'll side with him. You see that, right?"

"Sure. I do. I thought the same thing. But... well, do you? Have a wife, I mean?"

Jim lifted the flap higher and held it up over his head. "Yes. And you never asked, and I never told you different."

And with that, I stepped outside and started walking toward the trailer. Darkness had begun to fall, the western sky bisected with lavish flares of pink. The colorful afterglow of the sunset distracted me with its beauty. One of my feet snagged on a tree root, nearly causing me to fall on my face. My heart bounced around in my chest at the thought of what had almost happened, at what could have happened. I had forgotten to be careful again, to keep track of where I was walking. The hairs on my neck rose with the sensation of being watched, but I couldn't run to safety, so I kept moving with as much care and speed as I could.

"Sarah." It was Missy again. She had been hiding out in the back lot, knowing I would have to return home at some point. I didn't even turn around to look at her. She must have been expecting me to do that because she sounded surprised. "Hey, come here."

I wasn't taking orders from her, though. My mind had to be clear enough to focus on my most important goal. Getting to safety. There wasn't even space enough for me to consider the fact that the man I viewed as my husband was, in fact, married to someone else.

I walked on without a word, determined not to let my panic make me careless, cause me to fall and hurt myself, leaving me trapped. I would be fine, as long as I kept moving.

Missy ran up behind me to grab my shoulder. "I want to talk to you."

I brushed her hand off and kept going. "You better get out of here. They told you to stay away, lady. And if they catch sight of you again, they'll run you off good." Even though Missy and I were alone, my words and tone betrayed nothing.

"What? Quit it." Missy stepped in my path so that I had to stop or plow into her. "Don't pretend like you don't know me." She whispered those last words while looking behind her. My threat of being run off must have scared her at least a little bit. "You're going to rot in jail. You know that, right? And you deserve it, too, because Jared was never anything but good to you."

I could tell she wanted to hit me, but I solved that problem by reaching out and pushing on the bony plates of her chest. There was a lot of force in five hundred pounds, and she felt like a bird under my fingertips. Missy fell to the ground while I kept on walking.

Likely the shock more than the pain of being knocked down kept her stunned in place for a moment. I could have yelled for help. Some lights were on. There were people walking around. Someone would have heard me and come running. For my own sake, however, and for Missy's, even though she was too stupid to appreciate my consideration, I kept my mouth shut.

At last, I reached the trailer. I turned the doorknob, planting my foot on the lower step to grab one of the handlebars that Jim had installed.

Missy caught up to me. "Oh no, you're not going anywhere," she said, patently ignoring the fact that I had already covered quite a bit of ground from where she had first tried to get me to stop.

Opening the trailer door, I turned to squeeze myself inside sideways. If Missy got into the trailer, I'd be trapped in there with her.

"Hey, how about I give you a push?" she said. "Would you like that?"

I was balanced in a precarious position. Hauling myself into the trailer was no easy task and no quick one either. Missy could probably have knocked me down. I couldn't imagine what she thought she would do with me if I were sprawled and broken in the dirt.

She would get some satisfaction from seeing me in that position, I'm sure, but what would she do next? I'd have no option but to call for help. Then she'd have to hightail it out of there. In any scenario, she couldn't drag me away with her, and she also had nowhere to take me. Her dumb lack of planning as well as her full conviction that it was her right, her duty even, to torment me with an endless stream of accusations only made her seem exactly as I had always viewed her—a moronic, entitled bully.

I punched her in the face with my closed fist, hitting her like a man would because that was the surest way to stop her. She staggered backward, clutching her cheek. She never saw it coming. I pushed myself into the trailer with time enough to close the door behind me and lock it.

Missy lunged forward, but she was already too late. "You don't get to hurt me, and you're not going anywhere."

"I'm going to bed." Pain throbbed through my hand. I shook my fingers to soften the pulsating sting. I shouldn't have hit her. For as much as I had always hated Missy, I couldn't fault her for trying to avenge Jared's death—not when I would have done the same and more for Jim.

My breath came fast and deep enough to burn a streak of pain in my chest. Lowering myself onto the couch, I wanted so many things, like cool water and heavy food and soft light. I didn't turn on the lamp, though, sitting in the dark as Jim had instructed. That way, Missy also couldn't see me moving around or have a scene to comment upon. Sweat poured down my body, soaking my dress. Pressing one of the small pillows from the couch against my face, breathing in the stale, dusty scent of the fabric, I waited.

"Hey, I know you're in there." Missy must have been standing right under the window. She slapped her hand on the side of the trailer, the very tips of her fingers visible along the bottom of the screen.

I thought about rolling the window shut, but the trailer was already hot enough. How long would Missy stay out there? She would have to clear off at least when Jim came home. I slapped the pillow on my face a few times, determined to stay silent.

"Hey, hey." Missy thumped the tips of her fingers on the screen. "I'm not finished with you yet. You thought you were so smart, like no one would find you. But I did. What do you think of that?"

Where only moments before I had been willing myself not to respond to Missy in any way, now I wondered if she might have some information that could help me. "I don't know what you're talking about."

"Oh really? I knew right from the start that you were with the carnival, no matter what Mrs. Schendel was saying about how you went to New York City. Like you just got on a train and rode away. As if that could actually happen. Jared and I went to the carnival right before he died. Did you know that? And we ran into Dave and his girlfriend, Stacey, outside the sideshow tent. And Dave says, 'Hey, Jared, you ought to get your sister to come be the fat lady.' And then Dave and Stacey both laugh. You don't know what it was like for Jared, how he had to put up with stuff like that all the time."

"Poor guy." I said this to keep Missy talking. I wanted to ask her, though, why, if she thought that ridicule was so tough for Jared, was she unable or unwilling to consider how horrible it must have been to be the direct target of such derision.

"Yeah, well, at least you admit that—"

"I'm not admitting anything because I don't know you or this Jared. I'm just saying it sounds tough. I don't even know your name."

Missy stayed silent for so long that I was tempted to look down through the window to see if she was still standing there. I hadn't heard her walk away, but she was light on her feet.

"It's Missy. My name is Missy. I know you know who I am, Sarah."

In her quiet voice, I was able to discern the smallest speck of doubt. "I'm not Sarah. Not by a long shot."

"Yes, you are! You have to be. I went and told the police that you were with the carnival. They went looking for you, and then, when I asked, they said you weren't there and treated me like I was some sort of crazy person, grasping at straws. I couldn't believe when they told me that because I was so sure, you know? Then I started to wonder if I was wrong. Maybe you really had gone to New York City. I watched Mrs. Schendel because, if anyone knew something, it had to be her, but she didn't give anything away. She was so tight-lipped, you know, like how she was always so superior even though she was no one to talk."

I had already turned around to tell Missy not to talk that way about Mrs. Schendel before I caught myself. "Lady, I've got no idea what you're talking about." Saying those words felt like a betrayal.

"Yeah, right. Anyway, she did finally mess up, though."

"Who did?" Though I wanted Missy to keep talking and tell me everything she knew, I did wonder why she continued to do so. Maybe she couldn't stand being the only person who knew the string of events that had led her to stand under my window. She wanted to tell her story. That, I understood.

"Mrs. Schendel. You remember Jean, who works down at the post office, right?"

"No." Jean liked to wear very short skirts and grew her fingernails so long that they curled over at the tips.

"Anyway, one day Mrs. Schendel comes into the post office, and she's got this stack of letters with her, and Jean sees the one on top is going out to Florida. So Jean asks Mrs. Schendel who she knows there. It's just to make conversation because it's winter, and the weather is really shitty. And Jean's saying how nice it would be to have some sunshine. Then Mrs. Schendel reaches out quick and pulls the letter back and drops it in her purse. That's the whole reason Jean told me about it. Because Mrs. Schendel acted so weird. Jean didn't get a good-enough look at the envelope to say who it was addressed to or what town it was going to. I knew, though—I just knew it had something to do with you. I asked Jean to keep her eyes open in case Mrs. Schendel dropped off another letter to Florida, but it only happened that one time."

Of course Mrs. Schendel didn't make the same mistake twice, I thought. After that, she must have sent her mail from a different town. That would explain why her letters became more sporadic, especially after her husband had gotten sick, and she wouldn't have wanted to leave the house for long periods of time.

"It confused me more than anything," Missy continued. "What did Florida have to do with you? Did that mean you were living there now, or had you been there all along? I also still couldn't shake the idea that you had left with the carnival. Then I was here visiting Steve. That's my fiancé. And I'm driving down the road, and there's this long line of trucks I can't get past. I'm behind this one, and it has a Florida license plate. That catches my eye, and when I pull out to pass, I see Midstate Traveling Amusements Carnival written on the side. That's when it all came together. See? I remembered the name of the carnival Jared and I went to, and it was the same outfit. It never occurred to me until then that carnivals didn't just travel around. They also sort of had to be from somewhere. Midstate Carnival was from Florida. It all made sense, then, why Mrs. Schendel wouldn't want anyone to know where she was sending letters. Then I come here, and I see this poster of a big fat lady, and I can't tell if it's you. But I buy a ticket to the sideshow anyway, even though that's not my idea of entertainment. And there you were right up on stage, plain as day, strutting around like you had the right."

Missy paused, as if deep in thought. "The only thing I can't figure is why the police didn't find you at the carnival right from the start."

Because, I wanted to tell her, Jim lied for me and probably gave the cops some money, and they were more interested in that than what you had to say.

"It doesn't matter, though," Missy continued. "You need to come on out of there because you're going to pay for what you did."

Now I did turn myself fully around to address Missy directly through the window. "For the love of Christ! Will you just go away? I mean, what exactly are you going to do if I come out there? Pick me up and carry me off? What do you want, then? To beat me up? Make me hurt? I can get any number of these animal men over here in a heartbeat. Do you know what they have planned for you? Do you?"

Missy's fingers were absolutely still, so I knew that she was listening.

"The head guy says if he sees you around here, he's going to get a bunch of the workers and anybody else who wants to join in to run you off good. Do you know what that means? They'll go at you one after the other, and they won't care because you're just another mark to them. I'm trying to warn you, but you're too stupid to listen." Tears clogged my voice, bizarre and unexpected, the runoff of too many events and a stuffed-full basket of emotions.

Missy's hand disappeared as I held my breath. "Please," she said in a feather-quiet voice. It sounded as if she was pressing her face against the side of the trailer. "Please. How about you just let me in, then? I only want to hear you say that you're Sarah and you know what happened to Jared. I need to know I'm not going crazy."

A voice spoke up from the deep water of my subconscious. "It's a trap," the voice said, sounding just like Gigi. "Don't admit anything, and don't trust her just because she sounds sad." I nodded in the dark. Intuition Gigi was right.

"Go away," I told Missy. "I warned you. Now, if you don't listen, then whatever happens is your own fault."

"Sarah. Help me, please."

The forlorn tone of her voice, each word like the sound of a pebble being dropped into water, gave me pause. I had to ignore her, though. Nothing either she or I had to say could change what had happened.

In the windowless bathroom, I peeled off my dress to wash myself in the dark and put on a fresh cotton housecoat. I went into the kitchen to eat, meeting all my needs in the dark-purple cast of images that had replaced the initial impenetrable blackness of when I first entered the trailer.

When I eased onto the bed to sleep, exhausted and overwhelmed, my thoughts vanished in a deep tangle of intertwined dreams with one image threatening to choke another. Threaded through it all was Missy's voice, seeming real and imagined at the same time, outside my bedroom, calling to me, using the name of a trapped, invisible girl who never shimmied or twirled. "Saaaraah..."

A rim of gray light outlined the bedroom window shade. Jim was in the kitchen, closing the refrigerator door and clanking a spoon on the inside of a mug. The sounds were normal, typical of our morning rituals, even though the sun had yet to rise in full. Closing my eyes for a moment longer, I savored the peacefulness, deceptive though it might be, before shuffling to the edge of the mattress and pushing myself to standing.

Jim was at the kitchen counter, his back to me, buttering slices of sandwich bread. He turned at the sound of my approach. "Hey there," he said. Just that and nothing more.

I went to him, and we embraced. Time seemed to stand still for a blessed moment. Neither of us moved or said anything because doing so would mean having to talk about and plan for my leaving.

"Did you get all your stuff packed?" Jim asked at last.

"What? No. It actually totally slipped my mind. That woman Missy followed me back here last night and then stood outside the window for a long while, talking about how she found me. Then finally, by the time she left, or at least when I think she did, I had sort of forgotten about it."

Looking out the window, I noticed it had rained at some point during the night. Maybe the wailing sound of Missy's voice in my dreams had only been water falling from the sky. I poured myself a cup of coffee from the percolator. It tasted burned and old even though Jim had probably only just made it. The oily sheen on the coffee's surface refracted tiny rainbows.

"Well," Jim said. "Why don't you go on and get your stuff together, then? Mickey is going to come around in a bit, and then you can be on your way."

There had to be a better solution than my traveling alone for days with no trailer to sleep in. I also didn't like to think about what might happen in my absence. Jim was like a silver-scaled fish, iridescent and impossible to hold in cupped hands, that might slip free as soon as I was gone. "I actually thought up a pretty decent idea last night of how to buy some time with Hinkle. I have this key to my firebox, and I could say—"

"Forget it, Lola. Hinkle's not even the one we have to worry about. That girl Missy is the real problem. She knows your stage name and who you're working with. She'll find you again, and the next time, you might not be so lucky." Jim kissed my lips in a firm, gentle way. "You've got to take care of yourself now with the baby coming."

His words melted me, making me realize that the pregnancy mattered to Jim more than I knew.

"Jail is the worst goddamn place on earth," he continued. "All boxed in, always looking over your shoulder, having to stay on top.

You get down to Gulfy, where you'll be safe and sound, and I'll tell Hinkle you ran off and that I've got no idea where you went."

"Jim, I—"

"Hang on a second." Jim took my hand in his. "I know I should have mentioned that I'm married. The thing is Becky and I haven't seen each other in so many years that sometimes I forget about it."

The sound of Jim saying her name felt like being stabbed straight through the center of my body. My feelings must have been obvious, because he squeezed my fingers.

"You're my old lady, Lolly. Hinkle was just fucking with your head. I don't have any plans to get with someone else."

Jim's words reminded me of what Hinkle had said the night before about how a fat girl like me was loyal since I couldn't get another man. Maybe that was my appeal to Jim, but that couldn't be the whole truth, either, because Jim had seen the desire or least the sexual curiosity that other men felt for me. Perhaps we had simply been thrust into each other's lives and then had accommodated ourselves in the spaces we had opened.

That line of reasoning didn't take into account the crazy love I felt for Jim, though, or that I saw from him in the considerations he paid me. Both small, like the sturdy bench he placed in the dressing room for every show, and huge, like his willingness to ignore my criminal, homicidal past and to risk his own neck to protect me. Once, Mrs. Schendel had told me that people loved because they wanted to feel love. She might have been answering some question of mine about why Missy, or anyone, for that matter, would choose someone like Jared, but now I realized that she had likely been talking about my father and herself. Either way, I could see she was right.

"You'll come soon, though, right?"

"Yeah, yeah." Jim stood up and started moving around the room. He was so high on uppers all the time that sitting still was difficult. "Trust me. I don't want to be here any longer than I have to. Everything is so far off the goddamn rails there's no telling what Hinkle might do. Shit, I'm not sure I have the heart for another season even if Midstate does manage to survive."

Unexpected hope surged in me, like fresh energy to carry me through what had to be done next. I allowed myself to consider that maybe Jim really wouldn't want another season with Midstate or somewhere else. We could be down in Gulfy all year long. Him, me, and the baby. And Gigi. "I at least have to say goodbye to Gigi."

Jim looked like he wanted to protest, but I had already stood up and had my hand on the door handle.

Outside the trailer, the enormity of leaving nearly made me lose my balance. Jim seemed to think that Midstate was going to crumple under the weight of its own ineptitude, but I wondered if maybe Hinkle could rise again, reverse his fortunes, and get on a winning streak like he had done before—and maybe Jim would come back without me. Not wanting to waste my energy on thoughts like those, I, likewise, couldn't dismiss them as impossibilities.

There was no time to lose. I knew that. Even so, I couldn't resist the temptation of taking one last look around, to brand into my brain images that I might never see again. Since it was still early morning, the carnival wasn't open yet, so it didn't seem worth the time or energy to go up there. I decided to walk one small half loop, well clear of Hinkle's trailer and the cook trailer and bunkhouse, before circling around to knock on Gigi's door.

Trying to keep my shoes clean, I picked my way through the mud and muck between the line of trailers, smiling to think that I might even miss the sometimes-sewage-like smell of the back lot.

A hand touched my back. I screamed and then covered my mouth.

"Hello there, Sarah," Hinkle said. "Out taking a walk, are you, before it gets too hot?"

Hinkle Hates Blood

Hinkle looked like he'd had a long, hard night. The smell of old whiskey tingled, sharp and sweet, in my nostrils. He was only half dressed, wearing a sleeveless undershirt and a pair of dirty old pants. Jim had called my plan to waylay Hinkle a fool's errand, but now it was my only option. Hinkle smelled like he hadn't washed himself since the day before at least. Forcing myself to ignore the outrageous tufts of hair sprouting from his shoulders, I reached inside my pocket to touch the small key and cash money I had put there the night before.

"Hello," I said. "I was just about to come looking for you."

"How lucky, then, that I found you." Hinkle smiled. "You got some money for me? Ike left us. Did you know that?" Hinkle stared at the ground, dropping his shoulders in a pathetic gesture of defeat, to invite my sympathy perhaps. "I never would have taken him for a traitor. Of course, I never thought Jim would be chipping away at me like this—not when I took a chance on an ex-con like him." Hinkle raised his eyes to look at me. "I mean, I'm assuming Jim told you he did hard time, what with you and him being so close and all."

Ignoring this latest attempt to turn me against Jim, I made a show of digging into my pocket and then glancing over first one shoulder and then the other before giving Hinkle the money I had in my hand. "It's a hundred and thirty-eight dollars," I whispered with a nod to punctuate the seriousness of my statement.

Hinkle snatched the money from my hand. "You've got to be fucking kidding me," he said, pocketing the cash. "When I told you

208

to find the missing money, I didn't mean for you to bring me a week's worth of your pay."

"When's the last time you paid anybody?" I scoffed. Like Jim had predicted, my plan was not going well, but with no other choice or new idea, I pressed on. "Anyway, you didn't let me finish, okay?" I drew a long breath before continuing. "So, you said to look around the trailer, and I searched it from top to bottom. That hundred and thirty-eight dollars is all the money I found under Jim's side of the mattress. But see? I also found this key too." I removed a small key, the one that fit into the fireproof lockbox where I kept my papers. "It's a key to a safe-deposit box, like they have in a bank. I've been thinking, and now I see that what Jim does is he saves up some money under the mattress. Then he goes and tucks it away in this safe deposit box at the bank." I was talking too much. I knew that. "The only problem is there's no way to know what bank it goes to. See? They don't mark them. If I watch Jim, I can figure it out and find the money." I dangled the key between my thumb and forefinger right in front of Hinkle's face.

Hinkle lowered his gaze to the ground, his face unreadable, and rocked back and forth on his heels. His stance, the inscrutability of his expression, tightened the uneasy tension knot in my belly.

Hinkle took the key from my hand and interlaced his fingers with mine, maybe not as bothered by touching me as I had thought or maybe liking the discomfort it caused me too much to care. "That's a fine, fine story, Sarah. And well, it looks like you really been trying to keep up your end of the bargain. But I asked for five thousand dollars, so you see how this fucking one hundred thirty-eight and this useless key don't do me much good."

I started to reach for the key then dropped my hand. "I'm going to need the key back and the money, too, I guess, so Jim doesn't get suspicious."

"Ah, well," Hinkle said in a happy, genial voice. "We wouldn't want Jim to be suspicious. Even so, after everything I've had to put up with, I believe I'll keep this money, since I've a mind to treat myself to some luxuries like a nice steak dinner and a backrub from a naked Asian lady. I'll keep the key too. Because why not? And you, my dear, my dearest dear..." Hinkle took my hand and deposited tens of little kisses all over it. "I hope you can understand me when I tell you to get me my goddamn money, get me every goddamn cent of it, or else I'll call the police and report you as a fugitive from the law."

I pulled my hand from Hinkle's grip. "You'd bring the fuzz around here and be a rat fink like that? Reporting me won't get you your money."

"Now, now, I see you've got enough to lose that you'll figure it out. You're in a tough spot, sweetheart. No doubt about that, and you know I really do want to see you get through this." Hinkle smiled, and I nearly gagged looking at the black lines of something old and rotting between his remaining teeth.

"Well, good." My tone was clear and conversational, like talking about a picnic and trying to decide which sandwiches were best—ham or bologna. "I need a little more time. We only just talked about this last night, after all."

"Sure thing, sure thing, my dear. I can understand that perfectly. I'll tell you what." Hinkle glanced at his wristwatch. "I'll give you an hour. And then I'll make my call."

Without another word, I walked away, no other thought, no other plan, no other possibility, except making it back to the trailer and getting away as fast as I could. My soft, overworked heart chuffed like a dying thing, an engine fueled only with terror and regret.

I could hear Gigi talking to Jim as I approached. "Well, then, where the hell is she now?" she asked. Jim must have told her what was happening. When I opened the door, she grabbed my arm to help pull me into the trailer. "Jesus, Lola, thank God. Jim and I thought something happened to you."

"Something did happen to me!" I shouted. "Hinkle says he's going to call the police on me if I don't get him the money he wants in an hour." I looked at the clock over the kitchen sink, but I couldn't figure out how much time had elapsed since Hinkle had delivered his pronouncement.

"Jesus fucking Christ, Lola!" Jim exploded. "I told you I wanted you packed and ready to go half an hour ago, and now look what happened."

I grabbed both of Jim's arms to shake him. "React later and help me now."

"All right, all right, get your hands off me and let me think."

"There's no time to think!" I hollered. "I've been trying to figure my way out of my problems ever since I left home, and look where it's got me."

"Lola, listen to me, okay. Settle down." Jim reached over to hug me but then thought better of it.

I pinched my nose, panicked and overwhelmed at the sensation of time slipping through my fingers. "You know what? Everything I ever said before about being able to get away with murder in broad daylight and being able to outsmart anyone, I take it all back."

Gigi's hair was pulled back in a long ponytail. She slid out the rubber band holding it in place and shook her hair free. "Look," she said. "I personally think Hinkle is bullshitting you about calling the police, but maybe he'd do it out of pure spite. Anyway, there's no time to get a car for you now, Lola, and if you pulled out of here in Jim's truck, Hinkle would sure as shit notice. Things are only going to get worse here, especially if Hinkle thinks you ducked out on him. I'll go with you, Lola, so we can drive day and night. So pack up whatever you think you need for a few weeks, and I'm going to run to my trailer and get my stuff." Gigi pressed the side of her face against mine, her lips so close to my ear that I could feel the words as well as hear them. "We'll be out of here in fifteen minutes. Then we'll drive on down to Gulfy."

Gigi pulled back from me. "Jim, I guess I'm just going to trust you to get my trailer there for me." She finger combed her hair away from her face and twisted it back into the rubber band, her ponytail swinging high on the top of her head. "Let's go."

Gigi disappeared out the door. She looked both ways and then ran at wonderful full speed across the row and into her trailer.

"Come on, Lola," Jim said as he started filling a plastic jug from the tap.

I threw a pile of clothes onto the bed and made a bundle from the top sheet, determined not to get distracted by the desolate familiarity of my actions, at how identical they seemed to what I had done four years ago when I left home. I stuffed a grocery bag full of food.

Jim handed me the full gallon jug of water. "Here, take this. Because I don't want you and Gigi stopping for anything. No food, no water, no nothing. You pee in a jar if you have to. Whatever you do, just keep driving, but don't go too fast. Stay right at the speed limit so you don't attract any attention." Jim opened up the kitchen drawer where he kept small hand tools, like screwdrivers and pliers. He used a flat head to pop out a false bottom. "Here's a thousand dollars," he said, counting out ten one-hundred-dollar bills and stuffing them into an old envelope. "That should hold you tight and help you out if you need to grease any palms."

"Okay." I paused, even though part of me still felt as if I was moving, wanting to be going out the door. Meaty, my gruesome pickled punk, was sitting on the counter, floating, looking so lost and alone that, despite the heft of his jar and the craziness of the impulse, I wanted to carry him off with me. Jim pushed me toward the door, and Meaty stayed behind.

Outside, we stood next to each other, looking at the path to Gi-gi's door. "Looks like the coast is clear. Now, go. I'll head over to Hin-kle's trailer to tie him up for as long as I can so he won't even notice the car drive away."

The rear bumper of Gigi's station wagon was visible from behind her trailer. Moving with as much care and speed as possible, I set my sights on that and only on that, on getting closer to my means of es-cape. The things in my arms grew heavier with each step. I should have had Jim carry them to save me time. "I'm going to make it, though," I whispered to myself. My mouth felt dry and my tongue thick. As soon as we were in the car, I would drink great big glugs of water straight from the jug.

When there was only the smallest bit left to go to reach Gigi's trailer, when I was almost close enough to stretch out my arm to knock, the door swung open by itself, and there stood Hinkle, still not wearing a shirt and baring his mismatched teeth at me. "Well, I guess we've got company, Gigi." The counterfeit cheerfulness of his words was chilling and horrible.

Gigi stood behind him, clasping her hands in front of her, a wor-ried expression on her face. She mouthed something to me that I couldn't understand.

"Why don't you come on in and set down that heavy bundle you're carrying?" Hinkle asked. Then I knew what Gigi had been say-ing. "I'm sorry." Sorry, I guess, for not being able to help me like she wanted. Sorry, too, for coming so close to an escape and then missing the mark.

Without another word, Hinkle began pulling things from my arms and putting them in the trailer behind him. No matter how I reached after the sheet bundle of clothes, my sack of food, and the envelope of money, I couldn't prevent him from taking these things from me.

"Gigi and I were just having a very interesting conversation. Wouldn't you say that's right, Gigi?" Hinkle asked over his shoulder. She gave him a weak smile in return. When he turned back to me, she shook her head again, trying to tell me, I guess, not to let myself get trapped in the trailer with him, like she was, but there was no way, of course, no way at all that I would leave her alone with him.

I smiled. "I guess I could come in and chat for a bit."

I grabbed one side of the doorframe with both hands to pull myself into the trailer sideways. Hinkle cupped one hand under my elbow and put the other on my shoulder to help balance me.

"Umm... it's actually better if you let me just do it by myself."

"All right, then," he said and sat down on the narrow banquette along the trailer's back wall to sort through my things. "Well, that's clothes," he said, patting the sheet sack. "And this here. This looks like some food, and... and... What's this?" Hinkle shuffled his fingers around in the paper bag.

"I'll thank you to leave my things alone," I said, trying to latch on to his arm.

Hinkle pulled himself free from my grip. He opened the money envelope he had in his hands. "Well, will you look at this?" he said, rifling through the bills fast with his thumb and forefinger. "There's a thousand dollars here." He stuffed the wad of cash down the front of his pants. "You know, I have to say I'm surprised—surprised and pleased, too, because here I thought you had all your things packed up so you could skip town with Gigi, when instead you were waddling on over here to bring me some more money. This is much, much better than that pitiful hundred and thirty-eight dollars you gave me before. And see that"—Hinkle took an exaggerated look at his watch—"you still got you a whole twenty—no, eighteen—minutes left on that hour I gave you."

There was no way to wrestle the money back from him. "So I guess you're happy now. You got your money. I came over to help Gigi get ready for her new act. It's about a hundred times—no, a hundred and thirty-eight—times better than the sword swallowing. It'll make us a lot of money."

"Is that so? Well, then maybe I'll stick around to get a preview. And just so you know, my dear, one thousand dollars isn't the same as five. If I were you, I'd make better use of my time."

"Enough already." I slammed my fist into the wall next to Hinkle's head. "That's all the goddamn money Jim would give me. Okay? I can get more. Just not right this second and not in eighteen minutes either." I shook my head at Hinkle. "You can't pretend to me like a thousand dollars is nothing or that you'd rather have the police swarming around here when I bet I can get you the rest before we blow out of this town."

"Hey, hey," Gigi said. "Both of you sit down. I don't know about anybody else, but my nerves are shot with all this talk and running around. You got yourself a good amount of money there, Hinkle. Let's have a drink and relax a little bit." Gigi rummaged under the kitchen sink and brought out a liquor bottle half-full with a clear liquid. "I got this tequila here from Mexican Bobby. He says it's the best shit south of the border, and I guess he ought to know." She carried the bottle and three jelly glass jars over to the coffee table. "Come on, sit, sit."

Hinkle and I eyed each other, unsure enough of how to end our confrontation, our standoff, that we simply did what Gigi said. I sat down in the wooden chair across from Hinkle while Gigi squeezed in next to him on the banquette, the space almost too small to hold the three of us.

"Here you go," she said, filling Hinkle's glass halfway and then her own. She paused when she reached my glass, the bottle hovering over the rim. "I know you ain't much of a drinker like the rest of us, but I'm going to go on and give you some anyway." Gigi poured me some of the tequila and placed the open bottle on the floor next to her.

"No, thanks," I said, pushing the glass to the side. "It's bad for the baby."

"Geez, Lola," Gigi said in a voice too soft for Hinkle to hear. Her shock at my mentioning the pregnancy in front of Hinkle made me fear that I was playing the wrong card with him, but no other idea had occurred to me.

"How's that now?" Hinkle asked, a look of confused suspicion on his face.

"You heard me," I said, keeping my voice steady and leaning in closer to him. "And if you think Jim wouldn't kill you outright for getting me sent to jail while I've got his baby in me, then you've got another think coming."

For the first time in any interaction or conversation with Hinkle, I had managed to catch him off guard and unnerve him. Unclean and scruffy though he appeared that day, he still possessed the same cunning elasticity that allowed him to bounce back from every situation.

His eyes traveled from the top of my head down to the broad, splayed tennis shoes that I never tied, before settling on the middle region of my body. "Is that so?" he asked, his face realigned, his composure regained. "It's mighty hard to tell, I'd say, just from looking at you."

The three of us glanced from one to the other, no one saying anything, frozen in an unescapable moment until Gigi broke the spell.

"Come on, you two. Let's have our drink now. I've got some soda pop in the fridge for you, Lola. It's good that you're so careful like that. My mother used to say that women who drink too much end up with retarded babies." Gigi raised her own glass. Then all at once her face crumpled, and a ragged, wailing sigh escaped from her. "Oh Jesus," she said, "I'm sorry. Sorry to both of you. It's just that having Lola here, pregnant, and talking about my own mother, it gets me to thinking that I'll never have a little baby of my own." Gigi began to rock back and forth. Her sobs had a bit of the overly sharp edge of the theatrical, that stubborn piece that was hard to conceal. Gigi was a decent-enough actress, but it was safe to say not a great one. Her crying seemed to discomfit Hinkle, however.

"And the worst part," Gigi continued, "the worst part is this morning, right after I woke up from this dream about my mother, I got my period all over the place. You know how that is, right, Lola?"

Hinkle's face had changed color, his usual ruddiness washed white with the palest tinge of green.

"Yeah, it can be a real mess, all right," I agreed.

"I'll be right back," Gigi said. She stumbled into the bathroom with her full glass.

Hinkle shifted in his seat, crossing one ankle over his thigh and then letting it drop to the floor. "Maybe you should go and help her," he said.

"Right," I said, struggling to my feet. "Hey, Geeg." I slid open the bathroom door, my body blocking Hinkle's view of Gigi. "You all right in here?"

Gigi had her glass of tequila resting on the small glass shelf over the sink. She used her thumbnails to pull apart the gel coating of a pill capsule then emptied the contents into the glass. She winked at me and smiled. "I'm okay," she said in a pitiful tear-strained voice. "Just give me a minute. I'll be back out."

"She'll be okay," I said, sitting back down. "Sometimes, the bleeding can be too much—what with the clots and all."

Hinkle gagged in a quiet way, making me worry that I had gone too far, pushed too hard.

"No need for such detail, now, is there? You know, in my day..."

Gigi walked out of the bathroom with a roll of toilet paper in one hand and her full glass of tequila in the other. "I'm sorry about all that, Hinkle. I know it's probably nothing you wanted to hear."

She balanced the toilet paper on the back of the banquette directly behind his head and settled down next to him. She shifted her lower body left and right. "Oh geez," she said. "Oops. Oh, I'm sorry, Hinkle, but would you mind handing me that roll of toilet paper behind you?"

Hinkle turned around, and quickly, so quickly it seemed almost like sleight of hand, Gigi switched her glass of tequila with his.

"Thanks," she said, ripping off a sheet to blot her forehead and blow her nose. "Again, sorry about all this. Well, let's drink, then." Gigi raised her drink to Hinkle. Hinkle did the same, his hand shaking just enough to be noticeable. "Mexican Bobby said that Mexicans all yell '*al seco*' to each other, which means you have to drink your glass dry, or else everybody will think you're a big pussy." Gigi smiled. "*Al seco.*"

Hinkle downed the entire contents of his glass in a single gulp while Gigi and I watched. She set her full glass down on the table.

Hinkle wiped his hand over his mustache and then repeated the motion, pulling harder on his whiskers the second time. "It's got a funny taste—almost like it's bitter or something."

He started to cough. Gripping the edge of the banquette, he leaned forward then seemed to get stuck in that position, frozen in place, a leering demon drained of its power. None of us moved. Nothing stirred, not even a breath of air through the window.

"What did you bitches put in my drink?" Hinkle asked.

"Ah, it's nothing to worry about," Gigi whispered, snaking her hand through Hinkle's arm. "Me and Lola just thought you should relax a little bit. You look sort of tired. You need to rest on my bed. You been working awfully hard lately."

With Gigi half lifting him on one side, Hinkle managed to stagger to his feet, bracing his hand on the wall. She shuffled alongside him to steady his balance while I positioned myself behind them. Gigi eased Hinkle onto her unmade bed, and then, standing in front of him, she pushed on his shoulders, a firm gesture that nonetheless held a disturbing degree of gentleness. Hinkle flopped backward with his arms spread out to the sides, eyes closed at last.

Gigi reached over to hold my hand. "You think he's out?" she whispered. "I emptied a whole bunch of goofballs into his glass."

"Let's give it a little while to make sure." It seemed impossible to believe that Gigi and I might still be able to make our escape when only moments before, our situation had been so dire.

Back in the other room, Gigi finished off her glass of tequila. "You know, you and Jim both think you're so darn smart, but how'd you like that trick from old Gigi?"

Something about her stance, the way she held her glass, or maybe just the outrageousness of the situation, struck me as funny, making me laugh until tears came to my eyes. "I think that was the most amazing thing I've ever seen. You really outdid yourself this time."

Gigi smiled. "Nothing throws a man off his guard like talking about your period."

I glanced back into Gigi's bedroom. "I'll get the money so we can get going, and then we can let Jim deal with him." I had to put my hands down Hinkle's pants. He had stuffed the money right into his underwear, the pig, so that I accidentally touched his penis, digging around in there to make sure I got all the bills. "Gross." I reached into his front pocket, too, to get back my one hundred thirty-eight dollars and the lockbox key. "No steak dinner for you tonight and no massage and hand job either." I laughed, letting myself take a moment to savor the elation of having bested a son of a bitch like Hinkle who thought he held all the cards and could stomp all over people like Gigi and me. "Serves you right." I poked him in the chest, and he didn't move. His body was perfectly still. No inhalation, no exhalation, no nothing. "Gigi!"

"Oh my God, what's wrong? Is he waking up?" She reached behind the divider for the bat she kept there. "Club him back down."

I pulled the bat from her hands by the fat end and shook the handle in her face. "No! We don't need a bat. He's not breathing."

"Oh, holy shit," Gigi said, sinking to her knees on the floor. "What should we do?"

"Maybe this isn't as bad as it looks," I said.

Gigi stood up and leaned over Hinkle and slapped him across the face. "Wake up, Hinkle. Come on, and wake up."

I had to grab her hand so she wouldn't hit him again. "Do you think we should do CPR or mouth-to-mouth or something like that?"

We both stood there over Hinkle, watching his lifeless form, but neither of us made a move to put our lips to his. "Oh, Lola, this is bad. This is so bad."

"I know. I know. I know that."

The trailer door slammed open. Gigi and I screamed and grabbed each other at the sudden sound.

"There you are," Jim said. "Hinkle wasn't in his trailer or anywhere else around, and then I saw the station wagon still here, and I was worried, so... Why are you two standing there like that?"

"Oh, Jim," I said. "We got a big problem here. I think Hinkle's dead."

"What do you mean, 'dead'?" Jim strode over. He slapped the side of Hinkle's face, just like Gigi had done. "Wake up, Hinkle." He knelt down and gripped the edge of the bed. "Shit, shit, shit, shit. How did this happen?"

"It's all my fault," Gigi said with a sob. "I was over here packing up my stuff, and he barged his way in without even knocking and told me I wasn't going anywhere. Then Lola showed up, and he took the money you gave her and put it down his pants. We didn't know what he was going to do, so I tried to fake him out, you know? And it worked because I put some pills into a glass of tequila, and I got him to drink it down." Gigi clasped her hand over her mouth. "I swear, I only wanted to make him go to sleep so me and Lola could get out of here. And then when Lola went to get back the money, she noticed he wasn't breathing. Oh my God, we've got to get out of here." Gigi buried her face in Jim's shoulder.

I tugged her off Jim. "Jesus. Don't fall apart now." I took a deep breath. "Running is the worst thing we could do." Gigi and Jim were both watching me because, I supposed, neither of them was going to have a better solution. "Okay, so we've got to get Hinkle back to his trailer somehow and into his own bed. Then we go about our business like nothing happened. Somebody's bound to go looking for him before we open today. Once the body turns up, people will start leaving, and no one could blame us for going too. We won't look any more suspicious than anyone else. You see what I'm saying?"

Gigi and Jim looked at each other. "Sounds like a fair plan to me," Jim said, "but how are we going to get Hinkle's body back into his trailer without anyone seeing? There's always someone roaming around."

The three of us stood in a small circle, staring at the floor and then the ceiling while we tried to think of some solution.

"What about the blade box?" Gigi asked.

"Bingo," Jim said.

Gigi exhaled. "We do this, you can sure as shit forget about my ever getting in there again."

Half an hour later, I left Gigi's trailer and walked to Hinkle's place. Jim and Gigi trailed behind me, Gigi pushing the blade box on its wheeled cart and Jim pulling it from the other end. She was wearing her purple spangled bodysuit and the white slit skirt crusted with rhinestones, claiming it would be easier for her to stay focused if she was wearing her stage clothes. A roughie named Danny was pissing behind the bunkhouse.

"Put it back in your pants, Danny Boy!" Jim yelled.

Danny waved his hand in return. "What are you doing so dressed up at this hour, Gigi?"

"Looking for you," Gigi said.

Danny laughed and, as Jim had suggested, stuffed himself back into his pants before disappearing around the other side of the cook trailer.

As far as I could tell, no one else noticed Jim and Gigi, or if they did, they didn't pay them any particular mind. I waved to show them the coast was clear for the last part of the operation. Jim took Hinkle's trailer key from his pocket, and then he and Gigi lifted the entire contraption inside. Even if someone saw what they were doing, I supposed they had the plausible tale of moving the equipment inside to give Hinkle a preview of what they were rehearsing.

It would be better and certainly simpler, though, if no one noticed anything. I walked around the back, making my way slowly, giving them enough time to do what they needed to do before knocking again to let them know that it was safe to come out. I banged my hand on the window, but they didn't answer or open the door. The sun was making me dizzy, but I was too frightened to leave my post, worried that something had gone wrong.

At last, the door opened. "Everything's fine," Jim said. Then he and Gigi wheeled the blade box up to the sideshow tent, walking too fast for me to catch up, so I went back to our trailer and waited.

Jim came back about fifteen minutes later. "They'll probably find him soon," he said. "I want you to have time to get all your things together so you can go ahead with Gigi. She's home right now, washing down everything, and then I can help hook up Gigi's trailer."

"What? Let's just wait, and we can all go together." My voice sounded panicked and squeaky, even to my own ears. "We need to stick together."

Jim shook his head. "Nah. I got to stay to straighten things out with the fuzz and make sure nobody says the wrong thing, and you need to get to Gulfy where you'll be safe, as soon as you can." Jim must have read the fear on my face. "I'll catch up, though," he said, taking a stack of cash from his top dresser drawer. "Gigi and I decided to search Hinkle's trailer while we were there. That's what took us so long. Gigi didn't want to do it, but I had a feeling Hinkle had some money squirrelled away, even though he was shaking you down. We found bills hidden in all these different little spots. Who knows if we even got it all?" Jim split the pile and gave me half, all different denominations jumbled together, some of them looking crumpled and old, while others were fresh and crisp, newly printed. "Gigi got some too. I'll use some of the rest to pay off the cops and whatever local dick thinks he needs some money. I'll spread it around to the workers, too, so they don't have to end the season empty-handed."

People asked around the back lot if anyone had seen Hinkle. Within the hour, both Weedy and Billy knocked on our door to ask Jim if he knew where Hinkle was.

"If you don't see him around, he must be in his trailer," Jim told them.

He said the same thing to Roscoe, who dropped by not long after Weedy and Billy had left. "The thing is, though," Roscoe said, "there was no answer when I knocked on his trailer."

About half an hour later, Roscoe came running back to say that he had finally worked up the nerve to push open the unlocked door to Hinkle's living trailer. "And that's when I knew there was something funny, Jim, because Hinkle always locks everything up as tight as a drum," he explained, his hand shaking as he fumbled with a matchbook to try to light a cigarette. Jim lit Roscoe's cigarette with his Zippo. "You gotta come and take a look, Jim. Because I seen Hinkle there, covered over in his bed, and he ain't moving."

Jim turned away from Roscoe, hiding his face without appearing to, as he pocketed his lighter. From my post on the couch, I stayed silent, intent on seeming like a background player with no particular part in what was happening. "I'll be back in a bit, Lola," Jim said as he left with Roscoe.

Word about Hinkle's death would soon spread like fire, slicing through the people eating breakfast at the cook trailer, fanning out through the ride jockeys camping on the lot, and making its way to everyone asleep or otherwise engaged in their trailers. The grunt workers in the bunkhouse and the concessionaires who rented rooms in town would find out as well, and eventually, the whole of us would likely gather to learn what would happen next.

I made up my mind to wait inside the trailer for as long as I could, and in that time, first Weedy came by to tell me what had happened, and then Daisy and Ora Ann showed up to supply me with the same information. At last, Gigi let herself into the trailer and sat down beside me on the couch. "Just about everybody knows now, I guess," she said. "There's a big crowd out in front of Hinkle's trailer. We should get out there too."

Jim stood in front of the crowd on the step up into the trailer. "All right," he said. We all turned to listen to him, drawn by the smooth resonance of his words, his showman's voice. "Most of you already heard, but I'll say it anyway. It looks like Hinkle died in his bed. There's no way of knowing what happened, but Roscoe called for the ambulance. That means the police will probably be here, too, and they might have some questions."

I wasn't used to being part of a crowd, an audience member. I noticed Daisy and Ora Ann exchange looks while Mexican Bobby lowered his head and spit a straight line of tobacco juice into the dirt. People seemed to shift around, turning toward each other, bumping shoulders, anxious to say or do something but unsure how to proceed.

"Are we going to get shut down here or what?" Weedy finally asked.

"I think we can safely assume that this is the end of the season for us. After that, I don't know exactly how things will shake out," Jim said. "In the meanwhile, though, no one is to come into this trailer."

"No disrespect for the dead," Roscoe called out. "But does this mean we're not going to get paid again?"

"Trust me. Nobody's gonna leave here empty-handed," Jim said.

An unexpected, tickly pride rolled around in my chest, making me stand up straighter. It pleased me to see Jim this way, looking out for others when he just as easily could have kept Hinkle's money for himself.

"And what about Hinkle's poor mama?" asked Marva. She was wearing a stained apron and still held a wooden spoon in one hand. "Who's gonna call her and let her know what happened?"

"I can assure you it will get taken care of, Marva," Jim said.

A sob escaped Gigi. She stuffed her fist into her mouth as if she wanted to push it down her throat. A few people glanced at her. I reached over and tugged the hem of her shirt to remind her to keep it together because Daisy was staring at Gigi.

Gigi coughed. "It's awful sad to think of someone's mama hearing news like this."

"Yeah, yeah, you're right about that," Daisy said, leaning back to give Gigi a hug.

Once Jim closed Hinkle's trailer door behind him and sat down on the stoop to wait, the crowd became looser, leaving behind its shape and energy. Marva slapped her wooden spoon on her hand and walked away.

"Let's get out of here," I whispered to Gigi.

Leaving

I went back to Jim's trailer to make sure I had everything I needed for the trip to Gulfy, the prospect of which seemed less frightening now that I would be traveling with Gigi. There would be time enough for everything once we were on the road. Maybe she and I could talk on the drive about what had happened to Hinkle. I wondered if she knew or if I could somehow explain to her the relative advantage of not having to bear alone the knowledge of what had happened. We could reassure each other that we weren't irredeemable. Gigi wasn't, at least.

I was about to walk over to Gigi's when I heard the sound of an approaching car. It must have been Mickey, showing up with the promised vehicle. Though I appreciated how quick and able he had been, the prospect of another delay, of having to tell Mickey that we no longer needed his assistance but thanks anyway, was daunting. He would probably want to chat for a bit and speak to Jim as well, and there was no time for any of that.

I stepped outside, trying to think of the fastest and easiest way to get rid of him. I decided I would just tell him we had a situation right then, which was true enough, and that I had to leave.

The car pulled up so close that it sprayed gravel on my ankles. The passenger door opened, and out stepped Missy.

"Oh shit," I said under my breath.

In the distance, a police cruiser drove toward us. It had occurred to me, of course, that Missy would bring the police here, but I hadn't expected her to be able to accomplish that task with such speed.

"Good morning, Sarah. And this is my fiancé, Steve," Missy said, gesturing to the man exiting the driver's side.

He was tall with thick black hair that he wore a bit long, almost touching his collar. Missy seemed to have had little trouble replacing her first fiancé with another good-looking one. Remembering my view of the audience last night, I wondered if he might be the only handsome man in Patawaunee.

"Steve? Is that right?" I asked. "I'm terrible with names. Last night I thought you told me your fiancé was named Jared. I remember you talking a lot about how much you loved him. My mistake, I suppose."

"No, I never said that." Missy reached into the car to try to grab Steve's hand and hold it, but he slipped away from her grasp. "Steve, that's not how I put it," she insisted.

Steve didn't answer and slammed the car door with more force than necessary when he got out to stand next to Missy. He didn't want to be there with Missy. That much was obvious.

"Anyway," Missy continued, turning all her attention back on me. "Guess where Steve's best friend works? For the Patawaunee Police Department." She gestured at the police vehicle now parked alongside Steve's car. "How's that for a piece of luck?"

"Well, good. Maybe that will help you listen to reason, then." I noticed Steve's slight nod of assent, which only reinforced my belief that this was Missy's project, and affable Steve was only along for the ride.

Gigi came around the side of the trailer. "Hey there, Lola. I came to see what was holding you up. I didn't know you had company." She glanced from Steve and Missy to the police officer getting out of his car.

"It was a bit unexpected. Maybe you could get Jim here to help us out." I swiped at the line of perspiration that had formed along my lip.

"Yeah, sure thing." Gigi turned and walked back the way she had come.

I knew that as soon as she was out of sight, she would start running as fast as she could to get to Jim. Then he would have to take a break from dealing with one extraordinary crisis to face another. Thinking of it that way only convinced me further that all of us needed to abandon this crazy way of living.

"Good morning, Officer." My voice was light and cheery as I extended my hand toward the cop.

"Well, good morning." He looked taken aback by my good nature and manners as he shook my hand. "I'd like to have a word with you, if you don't mind."

"Why certainly, Officer," I said in the cute, sugary voice I used onstage sometimes. "I'm happy to offer whatever assistance I can." I glanced up at the cop's face—a fail-safe posture of feminine deference I'd seen Gigi use to great effect.

The cop took off his cap and grinned down me, intrigued, I could tell, by the size of me. He couldn't stop himself from gazing back and forth at my upper arms and looking down at my thighs and knees.

Missy jumped in front of me. "You'll pay now, you fat bitch." She was only inches from my face and stabbed my chest with her accusatory finger. The sad, vulnerable woman who had pleaded with me under my trailer window seemed like a product of my imagination now.

The cop pushed Missy away from me. "Now, now," he said in a stern police voice, "there's no need for that kind of language from a lady."

"Yeah, come on, Missy," Steve said. "Just let him do his job already."

Missy and I locked eyes. She wanted some kind of sign from me, some flicker of recognition, but I kept my face impassive, steely in my determination not to concede any ground to her accusations. She was the first to look away.

"Officer, I want you to arrest this woman for killing my fiancé—I mean my former fiancé, her very own brother!" She spoke those words loud and clear, like someone who had rehearsed them many times in her loneliness.

For a split instant, the unvarnished truth of her statement and the recent events surrounding Hinkle's death made me wonder if, indeed, I had the right to defend myself. I had earned my punishment. A part of me craved it, even. The baby inside me, though, deserved what I had been denied in childhood—a free, happy life alongside her mother.

"Ma'am, like I said before, you have me mistaken for someone else. I don't even have a brother." I turned back to the cop, my face soft and bewildered. "I'm an only child." I shook my head sadly. "In fact, my mother always said having just one child was the greatest tragedy of her life."

Missy pulled on the cop's arm. "She's lying to you. That's what she does! The police in our town are looking for her because she used to live with her brother. And then one day, she's gone, and her brother, my former fiancé, is lying on the floor with the side of his skull smashed in, and no one can say how it happened." Missy paused and drew a deep breath then continued with forced slowness. "She killed her brother and then ran away with the carnival to hide her crime. She is getting away with murder!"

There it was again—the horrible truth of what I had done. The precision and heat of Missy's accusation silenced us and stamped out my thought-making machinery, nearly derailing my performance. Then I saw Jim and Gigi from the corner of my eye, walking toward us, both of them looking unhurried and unworried.

"Hi there," Jim said, reaching over to shake hands with the cop. "Officer, I'm in charge of the sideshow. Is there some way I can be of assistance?"

"Jim, honey, there's a case of mistaken identity here—"

The police officer silenced me by holding the palm of his hand up to my face. I tasted a drop of blood from biting my tongue.

"I wonder, then, if you could tell me," the cop said, "how many siblings this... person here has."

"My name is Lola—" But the cop snapped his hand in front of my face again to keep me from talking. Missy watched back and forth between Jim and the cop, clearly impatient with the cop's delaying, while Steve stood with his arms folded, staring down at the ground.

Jim scratched under his chin, making a show of thinking. "Well," he said in the calm voice of a simple, bemused man, "you know, now that you mention it, I don't think it ever came up in conversation. I guess I don't really know."

The cop dropped his hands to his sides. "Ma'am, do you have some form of identification to verify your actual name? You said your first name was Lola."

Missy stamped her foot on the ground. "Why is this taking so long? I'm telling you it's her. I'm an eyewitness. I've known this person or have known about her my whole life." Missy swiped tears from the sides of her face. "My God, you could parade her through the streets of our town, and anyone could tell you who she was. You're not going to get away with it, you fat fucking slob."

The cop inhaled audibly. "I hope she doesn't swear like that all the time," he said to Steve.

"Be cool, Missy," Steve said, his voice low and mumbling, like a reluctant, forced apology.

Missy couldn't see or didn't care that Steve's friend, the cop, didn't like her or that Steve hated the bad impression she was making on his friend. Neither did she pay any particular heed when Steve walked away to lean against the trunk of the car, his back to them all. She just didn't know her audience.

"Oh," I exclaimed, pressing my hand against my heart, as if Missy's profanity might stop it from beating. "Officer, sir, could I speak to you privately? Really, it might be the best way... I don't want this lady... this person here to get any more upset than she already is."

Missy inserted herself between me and the cop, standing so close to him that their posture had a weirdly romantic feel, as if they were about to kiss. "No. Anything she has to say, I get to hear that too. Otherwise, she's just going to tell you more lies."

"You need to move away from me." He gave Missy a firm, businesslike shove to the side. "Why don't we step over here?" the cop said to me.

The cop and I walked several paces away, far enough for me to be certain that we were out of Missy's earshot. She looked lost and confused, wondering no doubt how the scene had managed to slip away from her.

"Now, Officer, what we have here is a case of mistaken identity. I'm happy to supply you with whatever information you need to clear up this matter. Yes, my name is Lola, but it's short for Dolores."

The cop pulled out a small notebook to write down that bit of information. "And what is your last name?"

"It's Barnes." In my mind's eye, I stared out the back window at the old house, the Schendel dairy barn visible on the far hilltop. "Dolores Barnes."

The cop wrote again on his pad—possibly the word Barnes. He slid the notebook and pencil back into the inside pocket of his uniform jacket. "All right, then. If you could just show me some form of identification attesting to that fact, we can get this matter resolved."

"Jim," I called over my shoulder.

Jim walked over as fast as he could without it seeming like running. He put his hand on my back, and the warmth of his palm across my bare skin was the richest, most soothing experience in the world at that moment.

"Would you mind bringing out my birth certificate to show this officer? I'm sure he has more important things to do than wait for me to go in and get it."

Jim smiled at the police officer, his face open and friendly, eager to please. He was used to dealing with the fuzz, and I let that idea comfort me. I allowed myself to feel a small squirm of pleasure, near to gloating that I had had the foresight and good money for Scratchy to do up a birth certificate for me.

"I'll be back in a jiffy," Jim said with a slight bow to the police officer.

Missy flapped her arms at him, like an ineffectual, confused bird. "Wait, wait. What's he doing? Where's he going?" She started toward me, but the police officer held out his hand.

"Please stay where you are, miss," he said in crisp tone.

It occurred to me that the cop might like nothing more than to be able to tell Missy she was wrong about this whole matter. Maybe all he needed was a helpful explanation of Missy's delusions. Then perhaps, on some future date, he and his friend Steve might drink beer together and laugh about Missy and how certain she had been of possessing some special information.

"Officer, a case of mistaken identity really isn't so hard to explain in this instance. I bet I'm the fattest woman you've ever seen. Isn't that right?"

The cop's face turned an immediate purple. With no one else around now and having been given a reason, permission, to look, he inventoried me from head to toe. I told myself that it was no different from being on stage, except I never had to stand this close to an audience member.

"Please don't be embarrassed, sir. I know I look very different from other women. So I bet the person this woman is looking for was also really large like me. And then what happens is, you know, people just see the size, and they tend to ignore the face and hair and other things. See, she has this idea in her head that no one else could be as fat as this person she's looking for, so when she does find someone who is that fat, she automatically assumes that someone must be the same person."

"Well, miss, I'll admit you might have a point there. But then again, this is a very serious accusation being made against you."

"Yes, yes, I can understand that." I was performing, telling this cop what he wanted to hear, but the desolation in my voice sounded and felt real, nonetheless.

Jim came out of the trailer with a manila folder in his hand, which he gave to me and I passed to the cop. "Here you go"—I squinted to read his name tag—"Officer Pettiman. Here's my birth certificate, and you can see right there that my name is Dolores Barnes, like I said."

Pettiman removed the document with one hand while the fingers on his other hand rifled through the stack of ten- and twenty-dollar bills Jim had tucked into the bottom of the folder. His lips moved slightly while he counted. The sight of his spit-shiny mouth nearly made me gag, but Jim was right about cops—they always expected a little something extra.

"Well, Miss Barnes, it certainly appears like everything is in order." Pettiman pocketed the cash and snapped the folder closed, apparently satisfied with the money he had earned. "And it looks like you've got yourself a nice tidy little career too."

"Yes. I don't know what I'd do if I didn't have this job. I mean, could you imagine me as someone's secretary or a nurse or a teacher?" I drew a deep breath, letting a whistling, authentic sadness fill my voice. "Can you imagine me as a housewife with children and a nice husband to take care of me?"

Pettiman smiled down at me, looking for a moment as if he might chuck me under my chin or call me a good girl. "You'll do just fine yourself, I'm sure."

"So, we're all set then?" Jim asked.

Our small huddle began to break up. Pettiman placed his hat on his head and tugged the brim in my direction. He handed the birth certificate and folder back to Jim while I smiled the entire time. If Missy and Steve hadn't been there, Pettiman would probably have driven away, leaving Jim, Gigi, and me to deal with the fallout from Hinkle's death in peace.

"Wait! What's happening? Nobody can go anywhere." Missy ran over toward us. "You have to arrest her. That's what we're here for. Steve, come here and tell him to arrest her."

Steve walked over to the group with obvious reluctance. Gigi moved closer as well, as if sensing something was happening.

"Man, are you going to arrest this lady or what?" Steve asked.

"This is a case of mistaken identity," I said in a clear, firm voice. "Officer Pettiman, I just showed you my legal birth certificate." *And paid you more money than you're worth,* I thought.

"That's true what she says about the birth certificate," Pettiman explained to Steve. "So probably not, I guess."

"You can't let her get away with this. I don't care what piece of paper she has. I see her with my own eyes. I'm telling you it's her!" Missy yelled.

"Really?" I asked. "Are you sure of that? What if there were a whole lineup of carnival fat ladies? Are you saying you could identify this particular person out of that group with no problem?"

"Yes," she said.

Pettiman crossed his arms. "You don't actually sound one hundred percent convinced, so I think—"

"Well, then, it doesn't have to be just me. There are dozens of people from our town who can tell you who she really is. We can get them to identify her. She can't just get away with murder."

"Actually, I'm from Oregon," I said.

"Yeah," Gigi agreed. "We've talked a lot about that. I'm from Kansas myself."

"Who gives a shit where you're from?" Missy shouted.

"Officer, do you have an actual warrant for Lola's arrest?" Jim asked.

"Her name isn't Lola!"

Pettiman ignored Missy. The more erratic and irrational she seemed, the easier it was to dismiss her. That was the way most people viewed things, especially when it came to women. I understood that, but Missy did not.

"Well, no, not actually," Pettiman admitted.

"Because I could really use your help with a much bigger matter. The carnival owner died in his bed last night, and I've already called for the ambulance, but I sure could use some real police presence to help keep the scene clear. And then later, this afternoon even, if there's something else you'd like to talk about or some other questions you have for Lola, I'll drive her down to the station house myself. Fair enough?" Despite Jim's easygoing exterior, a sort of electric tension radiated from him.

"Sure, that would work, and I'd be happy to help," Pettiman said. He smiled and drew a visible deep breath that puffed out his chest.

"No! You have to take her with you now. She's just going to leave otherwise. She'll get away!" Missy's voice splintered on those last words.

She pressed her hands to her face and began to cry, her narrow back hitching with her sobs. She was a loud crier and not a particularly pretty one, but Steve wrapped his arms around her nonetheless. He rested the side of his face on top of her lowered head.

"Oh, honey, come on. It'll be okay."

Pettiman looked panicked and contrite as well. "Yeah," he agreed. "Everything's under control here."

Whether she intended to or not, Missy was stealing the scene. Whereas Steve and Pettiman might have been annoyed or offended by her angry outbursts and thoughtless profanity, they appeared powerless against her tears.

An old white Buick Skylark came barreling toward us, moving so fast that a cloud of dust surrounded it. We all watched as it pulled to a stop, and a very skinny man wearing navy shorts with white piping and no shirt got out. He had short, curly red hair and looked to be somewhere in his thirties.

"Hi there, Mickey," Jim said.

"You're driving mighty fast there, sir," Pettiman said.

"Well, sorry about that, Officer. I had to gun it to make sure I could get this old girl over the ruts," Mickey said as he pointed back at the car.

"Mickey, it's good to see you," I said. "If you could hang on for just a moment, I'm going to step into the trailer a minute to freshen up. Then I'll just get my purse and list, if you'd be kind enough to drive me to the grocery store."

"It's awful nice of you, Mick," Jim said.

"No problem, man," Mickey said.

Missy lifted her head. "She can't go to the store."

This conversation with her and Steve and Pettiman, who appeared not to understand how bribes worked, had lasted far too long. So unless Pettiman tried to restrain my body, I was going to get moving and keep going. I glanced back to ask Gigi to join me, but she was already on my heels.

I rolled shut the windows as soon as we were in the trailer so that no one would hear us and also so we wouldn't be distracted by the conversation outside. "Gigi, in a minute you need to pull out of here with your trailer and then drive until that truck stop right there before the junction with 12. You know the one I mean?"

"Yeah, yeah."

"I'll meet you there with Mickey and get right in the trailer, and then we'll just keep going. No one will know where or who I'm traveling with. Take Jim off to the side and let him know what's happening. This is the end of Midstate, so if we get out of here, the whole trail goes cold. It's the end of our troubles."

Gigi nodded. "I suppose. That girl isn't going to keep that man of hers too long if she keeps up with this. That's obvious, at least."

"We're going to make it." I hugged Gigi close to me, and she squeezed me back with an almost painful degree of force.

After Gigi left, I sat in the bedroom and looked out the back window until I saw her drive away, pulling her trailer. I filled an old purse with some last-minute items I hadn't had time to pack and waited until I felt certain Gigi had had enough lead time to get to the meeting spot.

Outside, the configuration of people had shifted. Jim and Pettiman were gone, and Missy and Steve were sitting in their car. Missy waved at me when I glanced in their direction. Mickey was lounging against the hood of the Skylark.

"What's going on here?" I asked him.

"Well, let's see, first that girl that was in the trailer with you comes out and talks to Jim for a minute. Then the ambulance shows up, and Jim has to go take care of that. First, though, he tells those two clowns to get out of here, and the cop backs him up. So sugar britches here and the boyfriend drive away, and then Jim and the cop go to meet the ambulance. Except now, the charming couple is back. And I went over to tell them they were supposed to be gone, and she said no carnie with gross, messed-up skin was going to tell her what to do. I'm waiting here, though, to drive you wherever you need to go."

Mickey's freckles were so numerous it was hard to tell where one ended and the next one began. His face and body had flushed even more red when he recounted what Missy had said about him. I wanted to find some words that would offset Missy's collateral meanness, but since Mickey's skin was in fact terrible from any objective view, I couldn't think of any.

Instead, I leaned in close to him. "Man, can you put the pedal to the metal and get us out of here when I say so?"

"Nothing would give me greater pleasure." He got into the driver's seat and gripped the steering wheel, ready to go.

I motioned to Missy, waving her over to talk to me. "Look," I told her when she was standing next to me, "you've got the wrong person, and I think part of you knows that. You don't have to keep track of me, okay? I'm not this Sarah you're looking for. This will all get cleared up. To tell you the truth, I've had it with carnival life, and now with the owner passing, I'll probably go back to Oregon and look after my parents. They're older, you know."

Many times during my recent interactions with her, though I might have wanted to reveal my identity and correct her various misrepresentations of herself and of me and Jared, too, I had stayed silent because I recognized that desire to be visible as the same compulsion that had killed my mother. That wasn't going to happen to me. I opened the passenger door and got into the car. Mickey turned the key in the ignition. Missy didn't say anything, not even when I took her hand in mine through the open window.

"You know, lady," I said, "you've caused me a lot of worry and stress with everything you've been saying. Despite that, I'm sorry for your trouble. You must be very sad and lonely to carry on like this, and I wish you well. I really do."

I would always feel remorse for what I had done to Jared. There was no way I could see of being a decent person without carrying that burden. My conversation with Missy was calculated in some ways. I knew my compassion would confuse her, and calling her over to me meant she would lose time traversing that same ground to get back in the car with Steve if they decided to follow me. There was also truth in my words as well, however. Even though Missy had a new fiancé and appeared to have moved on to the next act of her life, she was still the one who had loved Jared most. She had grieved him and maybe still missed him. I let go of her hand.

"Hit it," I said to Mickey.

Then we drove off. The car bounded over the bumps and ruts, rattling my teeth. I rolled up my window, despite the heat, to keep the dust from getting into the car.

"Yep. It looks like they're following us," Mickey said as he glanced in the rearview mirror. "We can shake 'em, though. Especially since we're going to get to the road before them."

I told Mickey where we were headed, and he opened the engine. It felt like we were flying. As I saw it, the endlessly flat landscape was our biggest problem. Despite the growing distance between the two vehicles, I knew we were still visible to Missy and Steve.

Mickey's only focus seemed to be on the road in front of him. We needed some sort of plan besides driving faster and faster. Missy and Steve couldn't see me get into Gigi's trailer.

"We've got to get out of their line of sight," I said. "We're coming up on Mary's Point here. Once we get over the town line, you think you could find a place to pull off where they wouldn't see us? Or maybe we could lose them if we took enough turns through the side streets."

"Well, yeah, sure. The only problem is that Mary's Point is past where you wanted me to drop you."

"I know. We can double back, and they'll keep right on traveling in the same direction."

"We better get as far ahead as we can now," Mickey said. "We'll do just fine. That guy driving hasn't got the nerve for any real speed."

That was not the case with Mickey as he pushed the car to go even faster. When we crossed the town line into Mary's Point, he slowed so abruptly that I had brace myself to keep from being slammed into the dashboard. He pulled into a gas station with an attached car wash and drove around the back of the cinder block building so we could watch for Missy and Steve.

About ten minutes later, they flew past our spot without stopping. Mickey and I waited. I heard a siren. My first reaction was to panic, but the police went right by us in hot pursuit of someone else.

"I think that cop is after Missy and Steve because he wants to pull them over for speeding," I told Mickey. The hilarity of Missy's reversal of fortune when she had tried so hard to get me arrested made me laugh until it was hard to catch my breath.

Mickey joined in. "Well, I guess them's the breaks, sugar britches," he said.

We went back the way we had come, with Mickey driving at a more judicious speed this time because only sheer luck had kept us from meeting the same fate as Missy and Steve. Gigi's car and trailer were in the exact location just like planned, but Gigi herself seemed jumpy and nervous as she asked a stream of questions.

I stepped into her trailer and held the door open a crack. "Everything's fine, Geeg, but we don't have time to waste. Mickey, I really do thank you from the bottom of my heart." I placed a hand on my chest to emphasize my words.

"Yeah, no problem. Any friend of Jim's, you know? I'll make sure to tell him you two got off okay."

After Mickey left, and I was closed up in the trailer, it seemed like a long wait until Gigi started the engine. It could have been that only a short while had passed and that my anxiety to keep moving and get away had distorted my sense of time. I was worried about Gigi, though. Her center seemed to be failing her in some fundamental way.

When at last we started moving, I hugged my midsection. Despite not knowing what the future held for me, I experienced a profound sensation of relief. Soon we would be down in Gulfy, beyond Missy's reach and knowledge, and we could stay there for as long as we liked.

I patted my stomach. "It's okay, baby. We're going home."

A few hours later, Gigi pulled the car and trailer over to the side of the road. Her hands were shaking so much, her overall movements so disjointed and spastic, that there was no question of her taking us any farther. Once I adjusted the seat and got behind the wheel to drive, she began having some sort of delayed reaction, moaning with her head hanging out the window, a soft, painful howl repeating on an endless loop. The monotony of the sound became like a strange lullaby, causing my eyes to close for a few moments longer than they should have. The crunching of gravel on the road's shoulder jolted me back awake and quieted Gigi for a while, at least.

We had to pull over at least four times for Gigi to vomit, until she was gagging and heaving but had nothing left to expel. On the last such occasion, after getting down on all fours to retch into a cornfield, she sat down with her back to me, apparently mesmerized by the clatter of the cornstalks knocking into each other in the late-evening breeze. A person could get lost in that endless green.

"You go on without me," she said. The moving field nearly swallowed her words.

"Gigi!" I yelled through the passenger door, which she had left hanging open. "You get your ass in this car right now."

She stood up like she wanted to walk into that swaying green ocean. I knew that if she went in too far, I would lose her forever. Normally, I rode in the trailer on these long trips to Florida because sitting stuffed up in the car for long periods was a type of agony for me. As it was, my feet and calves were swollen, and the entire lower half of my body pulsated with warm pain. If I had to get out of the car to grab Gigi, I would never be able to fold myself back into the vehicle.

"Do not crack up on me, and get back here."

When Gigi ignored me still, I grabbed the water jug Jim had filled earlier in the day. I opened the top and tossed it out the passenger door to Gigi. It landed just behind her. The water spilled out, lapping onto the tops of her feet.

"What the hell?" Gigi said. She turned and looked at me, her eyes like blank mirrors, shining with tears.

"Get back in the car," I said. "And bring the jug too."

The spell, it appeared, had been broken.

Gigi was better after that, like herself even, albeit more silent and restless, shifting in her seat and twiddling her fingers in strange manic gestures. We kept driving past sunset and into the dark of night, determined to get across as many state lines as possible. When we stopped at a campground sometime after midnight, Gigi gave me her bed in the trailer. "I'll never sleep anyway," she claimed.

In my dreams, Hinkle, who was really Jared, pressed the length of his body down my back, reaching around to clamp his hand on my throat and squeeze. I jolted awake. Over my thudding heart, I could hear the moist, snuffling sound of Gigi crying on the other side of the divider.

"Are you okay out there?" I asked.

The speed at which Gigi came in and sat on the bed made me realize how lonely she must have felt in the waking world. She pulled a pillow from the mountain I had built as a prop to keep myself from choking while I slept. Gigi smothered her own face into the pillow to sob as I stroked the back of her head.

Outside, some people from another trailer were still awake and drinking around their fire. A woman's disembodied voice carried through the open window. "No, fuck you. You fuck you. You don't get to tell me what to do."

"Lo," Gigi whispered. "I killed a man. I'm going to burn in hell for all eternity because of that."

Her words reminded me of when Jared had come to haunt me. His presence in Jim's trailer that night, impossible though it had been, had seemed so real, as certain as Gigi's conviction that a painful, retaliatory afterlife awaited her.

"It's time for you to go to bed," a man's voice said in response to the outside woman's laughter. There was a sizzling like the sound of water on fire.

In all the time I'd known Gigi, she had never invoked the name of God except to curse someone or something. "There's no hell. You know that," I said, trying to shake the creepy feeling brought on by Gigi's terror and crying. "And even if you did go to hell, you'd sure as shit run into Hinkle there."

"Jesus, Lo, that don't make it right."

Gigi squeezed the pillow closer to her chest and curled her body into a tight ball so we could sleep next to each other. I kissed her cheek, neither of us caring or commenting about how my tears fell on her face, mixing with her own. Gigi might have mixed the poison drink that killed Hinkle, but she only did it to try to help me. I had killed him just as much as she had.

"I know," I whispered. "I know."

Gigi spent the next two days of our trip talking, talking, talking about what had happened that morning with Hinkle. As we headed south down into Illinois, through the western corner of Kentucky and across the middle of Tennessee, she discussed the nuances of every alternative she could envision, any reality that allowed Hinkle to still be alive and me to still be free. We bought food from grocery stores, making endless sandwiches in the car, not wanting to stop long enough even to eat a full meal in a restaurant. At night, we slept at campgrounds.

When we crossed the state line into Georgia, it felt as if we had passed an important marker, a divider after which our destination was closer in front of us than our point of origin was behind us. Light rain fell from the sky. Some water dripped in through the gap where we had left the windows open to keep the car from becoming too stifling in the heat, the windshield too clouded with our breath. Having told me about halfway through Illinois that she would never drink tequila again, not for as long as she lived, Gigi had switched to gin.

"I been thinking, Lo," she said after a long silence broken only by the repetitive thumping of the windshield wipers. "When we get to Gulfy, the first thing we gotta do is find you a real doctor, a good one. Not like that old perv, Arnold." Gigi pulled a small, flat bottle of Beefeaters from her macramé purse on the floor and took a good, long drink.

Not counting the visit with Arnold, I hadn't been to a doctor's office since childhood, back even before being forced to leave school. Even so many years later, the sensation of the doctor poking his long index finger into the fat roll at my waist, maybe to see how far in he could make it go, filled me with a sick dread, made me grip the steering wheel harder.

Gigi must have sensed my discomfort because she touched the top of my hand resting on the gearshift. "Look, we both know he's going to give you a ton of shit about being so fat, but you're going to have to do it anyway. I'll go with you to all the appointments and tell them I'm your sister. We'll make friends with them."

Gulfy felt safe and familiar when we finally arrived. The smell of the salty, fishy air and the sound of the warm, lapping water soothed me, made me feel as if I could finally release the breath I had been holding for days. We went straight to the Showstop to call about the house that Jim and I usually rented.

"We're home," I said as I pulled the car and trailer into the parking lot.

"Thank Jesus," Gigi replied.

"Listen to me," I said in a sharp voice, clutching Gigi's arm as she went to open the car door. "As far as the two of us know, Hinkle died in his bed. That's why we ended our season early. You can't tell anybody what happened. Not even Lonny."

"I'm not stupid, you know," she said, getting out of the car.

"I know that." I also understood, though, the deep allure of confession, the relief of placing the straining weight of the unspoken on the ground, rather than carrying it with you all your life.

Gigi and I settled into the little house. She kept her trailer parked on the lawn with the vague assumption that she would make some other arrangement when Jim showed up and the rest of the winter crowd began arriving. In the meanwhile, we lived together, spending a lot of time at the Showstop.

One afternoon, about a week after we had arrived, when we were there having lunch, Gigi said she wanted to go in the back to talk to Lonny. When I had finished eating and she still hadn't reappeared, I went through the kitchen to see where she had gone. I stopped just outside the storeroom, where I saw Gigi sitting on a section of the low counter and Lonny facing her with his hands planted on either side of her. Lonny leaned in close, like a man taking great care in listening to what was being said. The intimate intensity of their postures made me wonder if Gigi was recounting to Lonny the story about how Hinkle had really died. Lonny never was and never had been any kind of a snitch, though. I knew that much.

Later that night at the house, I waited for Gigi to tell me what she and Lonny had talked about, but when she didn't volunteer any information, I went back to studying the calendar I had taken down from the wall and placed in front of me on the kitchen table.

"What's that you got there, Lola?" Gigi popped open a can of Tab and sat down at the kitchen table next to me. Her hair was mashed up with thick brown dye on top of her head and covered in swirls of plastic wrap.

"Just trying to figure out when to expect Jim." I sounded cheerful to show I wasn't concerned. A small dot was visible each place where I had touched the tip of my pencil as I tried to count how much longer I had to wait until Jim could wrap up business with Midstate and then travel down to Florida.

"Well, I wouldn't expect him anytime too soon," Gigi said. She lit a cigarette and drank her Tab, as if there was nothing more to say about the matter.

"What do you mean? Do you know something I don't?" I asked, unable to believe that Gigi would withhold information like that from me, that she might possess it when I knew nothing.

"Jesus H., calm down, calm down. Oh, oops." Gigi clamped her hand over her mouth. "I been trying to not take the Lord's name in vain, but sometimes it slips out on me." She tapped her fingers on her closed lips. "Come on, you know I would have told you if I'd heard something from Jim. Besides which, my father used to say, 'Bad news always finds you.' So we'd know it if he was dead or something."

"If you don't know anything, then why did you say I shouldn't expect Jim anytime soon?" I slapped my hand on the table to get Gigi's attention. Her comments about Jim were the closest thing I had to any insight about when he would arrive.

"Oh well," she said. "I only meant that Jim's got that wandering bone, and he's in a good spot now. He used to worry himself sick working for Midstate, always running around fixing problems that probably could have been avoided in the first place. Now, he's got him a little time on his hands. He probably figures you're all set up down here, so why not try out some things, maybe see about getting a gig for next season. He'll turn up before you know it, and we're doing okay here, right?" Gigi squeezed my hand.

There were so many things I wanted to talk about with Jim, like what had happened in the immediate days after we left, how much money he had had to pay to the police and had there been any speculation that maybe Hinkle's death wasn't just a pill-popper accident.

More than anything, though, if Jim stayed away until after the baby was born or, worse yet, if he left me to experience alone whatever tragedy might be in the offing, it would be impossible for me to tolerate his presence after that or to hold him in any kind of esteem in the future.

"No. It's not all right," I answered.

Gigi was as good as her word, though, about helping me with the pregnancy, finding the best doctor she could. She went with me to all the appointments, just like she had promised. Everyone at the doctor's office came to love Gigi and, by extension, to tolerate me. She brought them bowls of candy and sometimes homemade treats, cooked by me of course, always asked to see photographs of children, and in short, gave such a good show of being interested in the lives and welfare of the entire staff that ridiculing me would have seemed plain bad manners.

I was sure it helped, too, that Gigi no longer looked like Gigi anymore. After she had dyed her hair back to a nice plain dark brown, she had gone out and bought herself a bunch of Sunday dresses because she said she needed to get to church and, in her words, "make peace with the Lord."

Gigi played the part well, looking decorous, a little shy maybe, prone to easy shock and adopting something of a southern drawl of indeterminate geographic origin. She drove all over the place, trying out the Presbyterians, the Episcopalians, the Lutherans, the Methodists, and even the Catholics but steering clear of the Mormons and the Jehovah's Witnesses as being too batty and restrictive of alcohol, before settling on the Episcopalians. After weeks of continual church attendance, Gigi truly did take on a sort of holy look, and Gigi being Gigi, regardless of how hard she might pray, she got herself a boyfriend through the church before too long. A sharp immigration lawyer named Doug who drove a green Mercedes. Gigi insisted on referring to Doug as her "suitor" with an irritating degree of adamancy.

"What's a 'suitor' anyway?" I asked her one night when we were sitting at the kitchen table as usual. "Is that to make it sound like you're not sleeping with him?" I laughed, thinking that Gigi would also find it funny.

"Well, we are not, in fact, sleeping together, for your information," she said and sniffed.

Then I did burst out laughing in earnest, certain as I was that her pious tone and words had to be a joke. "Oh shit, you're serious," I said when I saw the hurt look on her face.

Around that same time in October, when we'd been gone from Midstate for about three months, Thelma and Scratchy came by to visit for the night. They showed up unannounced, an uncovered mattress and box spring tied to the top of their car and the trunk so jam-packed it had to be held closed with a section of old baling twine.

While I fried hamburgers and sausages for the two of them and for Gigi and myself, Scratchy talked at length about his brother, who lived outside of Macon, Georgia, and grew peaches, and about how he, Scratchy, had begun to realize the importance of getting back to the land. Thelma sat by his side, not saying anything until Scratchy got up to use the bathroom.

"Those people that hated us so much," she said in a soft voice to Gigi and me, "some of them killed Useless. They gutted him and left him where they were sure we'd find him." Tears rolled down Thelma's cheeks.

Gigi moved over to the chair Scratchy had vacated next to Thelma, and I pulled up closer to her.

"Oh, Thelma, no," I whispered. Unable to think of anything to say, I held her hand while Gigi clasped the other, shaking her head in disbelief.

"Don't say anything about it to Scratchy," Thelma said. "He loved that stupid goddamn dog so much he'll just start crying all over again."

When Scratchy came back from the bathroom, we continued on with the party as if nothing had happened, even though Scratchy must have known what we had talked about when he was out of the room. We maintained a casual and pleasant aspect anyway, determined to enjoy our last night together. Though he didn't mention it, I knew Scratchy was disappointed that he hadn't been able to say goodbye to Jim.

I hated Jim then for his blithe assumption that everything would be fine in his absence even as I feared that something awful had befallen him because, as Thelma's story showed, the world was a terrible place.

November 4, 1979
Dear Sarah,

I'll bet you're surprised to get a letter from St. Petersburg, Florida! I'm pretty shocked myself. To tell you the truth, most days, I can't believe I'm really here. I tried to keep the farm going after Luther died because I worried maybe Edna was right and that I would be a fool to squander all of Luther's hard work to sell everything and move away. But we had that hard winter last year. I tired myself out hooking up the plow to the truck and clearing the driveway and the path up to the barn—all those things that Luther used to do.

Then I had some trouble with the pair of morons I hired to help out. I guess they didn't like working for a woman. I came up on the two of them one day when they thought I was still at the house. One of them was holding the front of his shirt pinched between his thumbs and forefingers, making like it was my boobs, skipping around like he was me, saying how I was old and skinny and needed to get my plumbing cleaned out. With all the work they had to do, they still found time to make fun of me.

Right then, I think I stopped caring what Edna or Harold would say and decided I was going to live someplace warm, where I wouldn't have to work every hour of the day like it was some God-sent mission.

Edna reminded me that I needed to be surrounded by family, but honestly, I think she was just worried that if I moved away, I'd spend all my money and come back looking for a handout from her and Harold—as if that would ever happen.

I'm living at this type of residential hotel called the Beachway. It's nothing too fancy, and there are lots of other people my age, all retired. I'm not ready for retirement, of course, even if I could afford it. So I do some shifts as a short-order cook, and I get a fair amount of business as a seamstress.

Here's some other news you'll never believe. I have a boyfriend. I'm sixty years old, and suddenly, I'm going on dates to restaurants and walking on the beach when I've never done anything like that before in my life. His name is Saul. He's a Jew, but so are about half the people I meet down here.

We go everywhere together, and I've told him things about me and my life that I thought I would never mention again out of respect for Luther's memory. We even talked about your father and how I lied to myself that no one knew what was going on, and Saul just shook his head at that, at the sadness of it all.

Maybe you could meet him. Your letters might have a New York City postmark, but since I'm writing to you at a post office box here in Florida, I imagine you're closer by than that. I've been thinking maybe you could visit me here, where no one knows you or even me really. You would love Saul, and I can't tell you how happy I would be to see you again.

I try to keep up with what's going on at home through Edna and Harold. I'm sorry to say that the bank finally sold off your old house for the back taxes. Neil Smoot's daughter and her new husband bought it. They said it was too much work to repair the house, so they tore it down and started from scratch. They dug a good foundation so that the house has a proper basement now. Edna says the new place is nice, but she hasn't seen the inside of it.

Write to me again soon, and tell me your news. I just don't know enough about what's going on with you.

Love,
Ursula

Sweet Emmy

One night in early December, about three weeks before the baby was due to be born, Gigi and I were sitting at the kitchen table, sewing up a batch of pot holders for the Christmas bazaar at the Episcopalian church. One of the bulbs in the overhead lamp had blown, so I had to squint to see what I was doing. A tidy stack of finished pot holders sat near my elbow. Gigi took a break to smoke a cigarette, the sharp snick of her lighter extra loud in the quiet room.

"That pot holder looks like shit, Geeg."

"Language, language," she said. "You be nice to me, or I won't make you my maid of honor when I get married." Gigi held her pot holder, the one she had been working on for more than an hour, up to the light. "Yeah, I guess it doesn't look that great."

I took the pot holder from her hand and used the stitch puller to undo Gigi's shoddy work. "You'd marry this Doug guy?" I had never met him. That fact alone made me wonder how happy he would be to see me standing next to his bride at the altar.

"Well, I don't aim to go back out on the road."

"I know," I said. Nothing on earth could have made me go back to the sideshow either, if I could even land another fat-lady gig—a far-fetched assumption indeed. Gulfy was a safe place, miles away from any repercussions for my past actions. Besides which, the house where Jared had died no longer existed, and Mrs. Schendel, the one person who supposedly kept up with my whereabouts, had also moved away. "I'm just saying maybe you could find something else to do."

Gigi rolled her eyes at me. My document business had expanded in Scratchy's absence, with Thelma telling me in a letter that he was glad to hear it. The two of them seemed to be settling in well with Scratchy's brother, but there was no way to know, of course, how much of their account was fact or fiction. In the meantime, I had a good stream of income, better even than when I had worked the sideshow and certainly more reliable. Feeling as comfortable as I did with my new way of earning a living, meeting with people right there at the Showstop, maybe Gigi found my suggestions about what she should do with her life sanctimonious, and maybe she was right.

"Well," Gigi said, "I think the real problem is that you'd miss me too much." She reached over and poked my finished stack of pot holders with her index finger, making it slip to the side.

"Ha! You'd miss me too much, you mean." I picked up the completed pot holders in my fist and held them up between us. "What does this goddamn church want with so many pot holders?" I laughed.

Gigi joined in, not bothering to correct my bad language for once, which I think I had started to use more of in response to her admonishments. "They're going to sell them, I guess, and give the money to the church."

"They're only made out of fabric and cotton batting. You'll burn your hand if you try to take something out of the oven with these things."

Gigi stubbed out her cigarette. "Just keep sewing. The Lord works in mysterious ways."

As our laughter died down, I reorganized the fabric, cotton, and sewing tools on the table. "I need a break anyway," I said. In the new quiet, we heard a vehicle, a heavy one by the sound of it, like a truck pulling a trailer. Gigi and I exchanged glances, both of us wondering, I thought, if maybe Jim had finally found his way to Gulfy.

The door burst open in such a sudden explosion of sound that Gigi jumped to her feet and ran a circle around the table.

Jim walked into the kitchen, calm and unhurried, a big double bouquet of pink and white carnations in his arms. "I'm home," he said.

"Holy shit, Jim!" Gigi yelled.

"Jim," I said, struggling in near desperation to stand up from the kitchen chair. Getting up and sitting down, never easy for me, had become nearly insurmountable tasks of panic and fear.

Gigi rushed over to pull on my arm. Jim tossed the flowers onto the table to come help her.

When we were all standing, we huddled together in a close knot, holding on to each other in the silence until I said, "You're home."

"I'm home," Jim repeated.

Gigi pulled away from the group then. "It's good to have you back." She picked up her cigarettes and lighter from the table, placing the strap of the purse she had slung over the back of the kitchen chair onto her shoulder. "I guess I'll leave you two alone for a bit. I'll be over in my trailer if you need anything."

Jim waited until the door slammed behind Gigi. "These are for you." He pressed the flowers toward me. "I thought you might be mad at me because, you know, I meant to get here sooner, but I figured... Well, I guess I should have tried to call."

I took the flowers from his hands. Two of the white carnations already had crumpling brown edges. They were all completely odorless when I raised them to my face. Jim kissed my lips twice then pulled me close and tried to put his tongue in my mouth, the dilapidated flowers between us. "Hey, don't be mad."

"I had no idea where you were or if I'd ever even see you again," I said through teeth clenched so hard a jolt of pain, like a snapping spring, shot through my jaw.

"Come on, Lolly. I always turn up. You know that." His arm was still across my shoulders, and he massaged my neck roll in a soft, insistent motion, like water moving over sand.

"Well, let's see you," he said. Jim touched my stomach, giving me an unexpected, involuntary shot of pleasure. Even with a nearly full-term baby inside me, few people would know or guess that I was pregnant. "You look good, Lolly. Really good."

I felt, or imagined I felt, a singing reverence in his fingertips. "Jesus, Jim, where the hell have you been? I'm here, not knowing if you're dead or alive."

Jim put his lips on my forehead to quiet me. He must have stopped off to have a few drinks, with Lonny probably, because I could smell the alcohol on his breath. "I'm here now," he said. "And don't worry, all right? I got Midstate closed up and made sure everybody got some pay. Everything and everybody were cleared out before dark. And that was the end of all that."

Jim sat down at the table. "What's all this shit?" He pushed the pot holders and sewing articles to the side and took some beer out of the paper sack he had brought. He filled a glass from one of the forty-ounce bottles. "Let's have a drink. There's no sense wasting time being pissed off."

"Beer's no good for the baby," I said. Jim was never going to be the faithful, handsome young man I had dreamed of marrying when I was a girl, while I would never be the thin, elegant woman who would be at such a man's side. We were both something else, it seemed. "Do you want to see the baby's room? Gigi and I did it up together."

With the money I was making, I had been able to set up nice things for the baby, like I could only have imagined during my childhood. The slats of the crib were wooden spindles worked on a lathe to make a repeating pattern of bumps and dips that I liked to skim with my fingers. Everything in the baby's room was white, like mounded sugar or the winter snow I saw only in my memory. "Isn't it beautiful?" I asked.

"That baby will be lucky to have such a soft, sweet mama like you." When Jim kissed me again, I saw that I had a choice. I could cling to my impotent rage, which would only delay our reconciliation, or I could love Jim as he was rather than how I wished him to be.

"I hope so," I whispered. "The doctor says there's a lot that could go wrong."

Jim stretched his arms around me as far as they would go, squeezed me in a tight embrace. "You're going to be just fine. Trust me."

I wanted to believe Jim, to think that his unabashed optimism held some sway in the grand order of things, but I couldn't shake the fear that a woman who had taken two lives was more likely to get divine retribution rather than reward.

Later, stretched out next to each other on the bed, I leaned back on a stack of pillows while Jim pressed his face to my naked chest. The room was dark and still, with only the ticking of the bedside clock to break up the silence.

"So, you're sure everything worked out okay with Hinkle, then?"

Jim paused before answering. "Yeah, nobody asked too many questions. Some carnie dies, these townspeople don't exactly give a shit." He rubbed his nose back and forth across my breasts. There might have been a wetness near his eyes, a drip from his nose. "Hinkle got a nice burial down with his people near Evansville. I helped his mama arrange to get the body over there. I didn't want to say nothing while Gigi was here because I wasn't sure she could take it."

"Right." I wondered if I really was that much stronger than her, unable to stop myself from suspecting that my actual physical bulk made it impossible for anyone to perceive in me the requisite delicacy needed for suffering.

"He wasn't all bad, you know. I ever tell you how I met him?"

I shook my head, not because I wanted to know but because I wanted him to stop talking. I dreaded hearing him praise a man it was easier and more expedient to hate.

"You know I done hard time, right? So, back when I first met Hinkle, I'd just finished with a ten-year stint for manslaughter. It was one of those things, you know. A bar fight got out of hand, and the other guy pulled a knife. He cut me first." Jim paused and traced his finger down the scar on the side of his face. "But I was the one who stabbed him. Anyway, I couldn't get a job nowhere, and my wife, Becky, wouldn't take me back either. Not that there was much to go back to. Her family hated me. The only jobs were coal mining, and I sure as shit wasn't about to go underground. She also took up with somebody else and had a kid with him, pretended like the new guy was her husband. I gave him a pretty bad beating. When Becky called the police, I ran. Fuck, I was sleeping on benches in Chicago and eating mission soup when I met Hinkle. He told me what a great life it was traveling with the carnival and how most of these truck shows, especially the small ones, wouldn't even notice or care that I had a record. It was a good life, but then when Hinkle took over Midstate, I guess it wasn't as easy as he thought it was going to be, but he worked hard until he didn't want to anymore. And then there was the gambling, so he would try to save money and cut corners, but he still couldn't make a good go of it. He kept skimming off the top, which only made it worse. And then I started doing the same thing because any idiot could see that the whole operation was going to hell in a handbasket. Still, he got me out of a lot of jams when I thought for sure I was going to be thrown back in the clink."

Jim sat up and rubbed both hands over his face. "Yeah, old Hinkle. I guess he got his."

I pressed my hand against the flat muscles of Jim's back. "I'm sorry. I wish all the time that Gigi and I could have just gotten in the car and driven away or that he really did only have enough pills to fall asleep and that... God, I don't know, half the time I can't sleep at night, thinking about all the things that could be different. It's like there's this animal that lives in my skull, and it gnaws at my brain. And then it breaks my heart, you know? Because I can't fix things. I can't take back any of it."

Jim leaned over to kiss my forehead. "Don't do it to yourself, Lola. That's what prison was like—long nights wondering how you ended up there, thinking about all the things you wanted to change, about everything you should have done. You worry too much, and it'll keep you from the good thing you got going here."

I tried to smile in the dark. "Sometimes, I wonder if I'm not still back in the house where I grew up, imagining all this." The person that I had been, alone and confined, waiting and hoping for my real life to begin, seemed almost like a stranger now. "I guess that sounds a little crazy."

Jim squeezed my fingertips then put my hand on his penis. "See that? It's all real. What sweet young girl like you were would imagine something so nasty?"

I yanked my hand free and started laughing until I had to bury my face in the pillow to blot the tears running down my face. "My God, you really are a dirty old man."

Jim, Gigi, and I went to the Showstop for dinner the next day. The place was mostly empty, the windows and back door open to air out the smell of old cigarette smoke and to dry the floor, which smelled like it had just been washed with a strong pine cleaner.

"Well, look who's here," Lonny said. He came out from behind the bar to shake Jim's hand and kiss both Gigi and me on the cheek. "Luis, get Big Mama her chair!"

Luis also did us up a good fish fry made with a rich, fluffy batter and slathered in mayonnaise-thick tartar sauce. Between Gigi's religious conversion and my pregnancy, the two of us hadn't been going out at night like we used to. As the Showstop filled with customers, being part of a crowd, sitting in the center of it because people wanted to cluster around Jim, made me feel wonderful in the literal sense. I was filled with wonder at being among people, eating a big meal in front of them with no shame, and being a part of their group.

I learned a lot about where Jim had been and what he had been doing from the stories he told that night. He had spent some time in Arizona. The searing desert heat nearly killed him when his truck radiator sprang a leak and he had to walk long, high-sun miles on a stretching lonely road until a Navajo couple, so old that their mouths collapsed in equal toothlessness, gave him a ride to the next town. In Louisiana, Jim met a man named Sammy Winestone, who had forgotten more about the carnival business than most of us would ever know.

Jim talked, too, about driving Highway 1 the entire length of the California coast, about how much bigger and frothier the Pacific seemed in comparison to the Gulf. People loved his stories, leaned forward into his pauses, breathless to know what he would say next. A squirm of exhaustion snaked through me, but still I tried to match Jim's energy to keep pace with the singing newness of his vitality and presence, ignoring the constrained restlessness that seemed to lurk right below his jovial demeanor. He had crisscrossed the entire country, traveling from one place to the next, succumbing to a continual attraction to the next thing.

Our daughter was born on December 18, 1979. None of the dire predictions of what could happen if a woman my size gave birth proved true. She was healthy and strong, able to raise her little fists in the air, crying in a way that required an immediate response. Once she had been cleaned up from the birth and wrapped in a featherlight blanket, I held her in my arms, awestruck to realize that she was a beautiful child.

I had prayed for my baby to be born alive and healthy, and I had received this additional gift as well. I decided to name her Emma after my own mother, that pretty woman who had had so little in life and had given me so much in the delicate perfection of this breathtaking child that Jim and I had managed to produce.

As I stroked Emmy's flower-petal cheek, I found myself thinking about my father as well. I remembered how, after I had been forced to leave school, he had knelt before me and said that I had a wonderful, glorious mind and that no one could take that away from me. Maybe he could have loved Emmy in a fierce, protective, uncomplicated way.

My little family, the feeling of being a part of it, at times seemed like a dream—something I would have imagined in the solitude of my own childhood and adolescence. I remained resolutely and irrevocably fat, however, and in my fantasies, I had always been some other thin woman. For the first time in my life, I begrudged that fantasy woman my happiness. Instead, I kept it all for my fat self, the actual me.

Fatherhood seemed to have changed Jim. He demonstrated a natural proclivity for it that I had not expected, toting Emmy with him wherever he went, exercising limitless patience, content as well to walk the length of the house with Emmy pressed against his shoulder while he engaged in an endless stream of nonsensical conversation with her. "Is that so?" he would ask. "Well, I have to agree with you there."

Then, one fine morning in May, hot but not too hot, a salty breeze blowing, after Jim had played ickle tickle on Emmy's fingers and toes and she had drifted off into the soft pastel of her morning nap, I found him in the bedroom, arranging his clothes in tidy piles on the bedspread.

"Hey," he said. "I'm packing up my things here if you want to help me."

The beating of the ceiling fan blades was the only sound in the room. "What? Where are you going?"

Jim, backlit by the sunlight streaming in from the window behind him, wouldn't meet my eyes as he pulled a stack of clean undershirts from the dresser drawer.

"What? You're going to work with Sammy Winestone, aren't you?"

Until that moment, Sammy, who ran Bright Star Southern Extravaganza, had seemed like just another character in Jim's endless trove of stories, a human series of actions and mannerisms meant to entertain me, Gigi, and the drinkers down at the Showstop. All of us, really.

"Jesus, Jim, you need to be here with me and Emmy. Do you have any idea how much she'll change when you're running around out on the road? You won't even recognize her come winter." The idea that Jim could know and love Emmy and still be willing to absent himself from her for months at a time had never even occurred to me.

Jim stared at the mounds of clean, fresh clothes on the bedspread. "I've got to go, Lola. You don't need me here. You and Emmy will be fine. I wouldn't leave if I thought any different."

"No, we won't be fine!" I shouted. "You don't have to go anywhere, goddammit." I went to the bed and swept all the stacks of clothes together. I held the whole mess of them in front of me, like a shield. "You don't get to leave us again with me waiting around, not knowing if you're dead or alive. You're too damn old to be doing this. It's time for you to retire already."

Jim tried to tug the clothes from arms, but I held on tighter.

"Goddammit," he said. "I just got that stuff organized. You need to stop acting so crazy all the time. And listen to reason for a change."

The realization that Jim somehow viewed himself as more balanced and mentally stable or competent than I was hit me like icy water thrown in my face. Maybe he had always felt that way, going way back to when he had first given me a place to sleep and food to eat.

"Really? I'm the crazy one?" My voice was cold and steady as I took a small step forward.

Jim wouldn't want five hundred pounds of force smashing down on his delicate foot bones. So when I advanced, he had no choice but to retreat.

"Who are you to tell me that I'm not reasonable? Like I don't how anything works? You're the one who's being stupid and irresponsible." I moved again. Jim backed farther away until his body almost touched the wall.

He grabbed my forearms hard, each finger of his digging down in a painful way. "Knock it off, Lola. You keep trying to back me into a corner, then we're going to have a real problem."

I pulled away from him and threw the clothes in his face. "Fine, take all this shit, then."

I turned to walk out of the room as Jim bent down to pick up his shirts and socks. Looking back at him on the floor like that, it reminded me of the time my father had cried on his knees in front of me, desperate to have me understand and agree that there had been nothing wrong in his relationship with my mother. I saw Jared, too, calling me fat and worthless, hitting my face because he could.

To hell with all that, I thought. I had my own work, my own money, my own life. "You were right about one thing. We don't need you."

I went into the kitchen and started spraying the counters with cleaning solution because I didn't want to look at Jim anymore or watch him get ready to leave us. I focused instead on making everything tidy and well-ordered. Jim came out of the bedroom as I was sprinkling scouring powder into the sink.

"You know, I could have left without telling you anything."

I found an old sponge and started scrubbing. Such an idiotic and ill-timed assertion as that didn't deserve a response. The fact that Jim had deigned to inform me of his plans meant nothing.

Jim down on the couch and watched me. "All right, come and leave that and sit down next to me. Please."

I did as he asked, but I wouldn't touch him. I kept my hands stuffed between my knees so he could see that and turned my face to look out the window, watching the calm waters, hearing the occasional seagull call.

"Look, Lola. I've got to go, okay? You don't want to be on the road. I get that, but I can't stay all cooped up here. I don't want to go away with you mad like this. I'll be back when the season's over, and I'll do better this time, okay? I'll call. You can take lots of pictures of everything Emmy's doing. All right?"

Jim hated confinement of any kind. I knew that. It could have been the time he spent in prison, or maybe that stalk of his personality had been imprinted on him all his life. I had allowed myself to believe, however, that being a father, especially to sweet Emmy, would make a difference. Somehow, though, it wasn't enough. I wasn't enough. Nothing was.

"I just... I think of all the crazy shit out on the road. You've been with it for so many years I can't understand why you want more of it." Here, I started crying because I knew that Jim wouldn't change his mind and that his luck couldn't last forever. "I'm worried that something bad will happen to you when it would be the easiest thing in the world to avoid it."

Jim grabbed my chin. "Don't you curse me, Lola," he whispered.

"You don't need me to curse you."

Gigi the Great

The house had a quiet, deserted feel after Jim left. Eventually, as many of the other carnies—like Ike, who hadn't fared too well in Sacramento, and Ora Ann, who couldn't see into her own future—packed up and left for the season, the town of Gulfy began to seem the same way. The retirees were still around, and Lonny opened the Showstop every day. Gigi and I went there for lunch with Emmy four or five times a week.

It was hard to know what precisely Lonny thought of Gigi's religious conversion, but he sat by her side whenever business was slow. The quiet piety she hoped to achieve looked remarkably similar to a type of prolonged boredom as weeks and then months passed without her finding work or any useful activity beyond Bible study group. Gigi hated to be inactive, and the relative sobriety, which she viewed as necessary, integral even, to godliness only made the problem worse. I worried that she would marry churchy Doug to break up the monotony, to have something to do besides playing with Emmy and drinking iced tea at lunch.

I often wasted my precious nighttime hours thinking about Gigi and her future when I should have been sleeping through the exhaustion of caring for a baby. Staring at the dark ceiling one night, I considered her situation and how much she had changed in such depth that, when I heard the front door open and the sound of Gigi whispering my name, I felt certain she had come to haunt me as a living apparition.

Gigi flipped on the hallway light, a black silhouette that leaned its head forward to peer at me. "Hey, Lola, hey. You awake in there?"

"Gigi... is that you? For real?"

Gigi laughed. "Who the fuck did you think it was? My ghost?"

I followed her out into the kitchen, shocked and wondering what had happened to make her say the word "fuck" again after working so hard to excise it from her vocabulary. Gigi was wearing one of her church outfits, a green rayon dress with miniature cream polka dots. Her hair was pulled back and shaped into a tight curled bun, but thick sections of strands had escaped the net mold she used to hold it in place. When she turned to face me, I could see that the front of her dress was rumpled and buttoned incorrectly. A dab of purple-blue, like a sleeping iridescent mouse, had appeared under her left eye and would probably darken still as the hours passed.

"What the hell happened to your face? Who hit you?" I motioned for Gigi to sit down in the kitchen chair while I dug around in the freezer. The trays of ice cubes had evaporated long ago. "Shit. We're out of ice. But here, take this." I handed a wrapped grape popsicle to her. "Put it against your eye to take down the swelling at least."

"Good thing you told me, or else I might have ate it." She tipped her head back and pressed the popsicle to her eye like I told her. When she did, the overhead light caught the ring on her hand and glinted off the enormous square-cut diamond in the center.

"Oh my God," I whispered. "Look at that goddamn thing."

Gigi extended her fingers. I didn't know much of anything about jewels or settings, but the perfection of the stone and the fineness of the platinum band were obvious. "It must have cost a fortune. Where'd you get it?"

She leaned back in her chair and repositioned the popsicle on her eye. "Are you sure you want to know?"

I swatted her forearm. "Tell me already."

Gigi laughed. "All right," she said, chucking the popsicle into the sink. "Well, I got this ring here from Doug. I guess that part's no surprise. Not that he gave it to me but that it's no secret he has lots of money. So, anyway, we went to dinner at the Fairhaven Country Club, where everyone in his family has been a member since forever, and he's ordering really big stuff, like this expensive steak and red wine. He wants me to drink some, but I tell him no, and I guess he thinks it's because I'm all prim and proper. That's part of it, but the other thing is that red wine tastes like piss and vinegar to me. I'd go for a beer or the hard stuff, but I don't tell Doug all that. Then right before dessert, he gets down on one knee to ask me to marry him. Right there in the middle of the crowded restaurant, he pulls out this big fucking ring. I say yes because it's like something out of a movie, you know? The whole place is cheering, and everybody is congratulating us. I even cried a little bit. Some old lady gave me a hanky to wipe my eyes. I got real caught up in the moment. We went for a walk after that out on the golf course. I knew Doug was thinking he was going to get something out of me now that we were going to be married. I mean Doug's a good-looking guy, so that wasn't a problem really." Gigi paused and laughed. "He would always joke, though, about me being too young and pretty for him because he's thirty-three. I shaved ten years off so he would think I was twenty-five instead of thirty-five. I got this idea in my head that I should tell him my real age, especially when he started talking about wanting kids but that we could wait a year or two. Then he says we could have the wedding reception right there at Fairhaven. 'I already got a place in mind,' I told him. I was thinking of the Showstop. You should have seen Doug's face when I suggested it. He said only dirty carnies and people looking to do shady business hung around there. Part of me thought about keeping my mouth shut, but then I wondered what he'd say about you as my maid of honor or Ike showing up as a guest with all his tattoos."

Gigi got up and filled a glass with water from the tap. "I wasn't about to turn my back on my friends. You know that." She sat back down at the table. "The other thing, though, was I realized if I didn't say something, I'd be stuck in the role of churchgoing lady for the rest of my life. It's like I'd be invisible. Maybe that sounds strange."

"No, not at all." I covered Gigi's hand with my own, taking the opportunity to smear my fingertip on the surface of the perfect diamond. "So, finish the story."

"Well, anyway, I told Doug I used to work for a traveling carnival. He wanted to think like I was just some local who sold tickets or something, but I told him no, that I moved from town to town with them in the Midwest and that I still lived in a travel trailer parked on someone else's lawn. I thought he might die from the shock. He couldn't even open his mouth to say anything, so I just kept on talking. It felt good to get it all out. I told him about the sword swallowing and doing the blade box and even how, before that, I was in the cootch show for a few years."

"Huh. I bet he never even heard of it."

Gigi laughed. "Are you shitting me? He knew exactly what it was because he's one of those upstanding men around town and church that wants you to squat right next to their face. He said something like 'Are you telling me that you danced naked in front of strange men, that you exposed your...' He stopped midsentence like he was at a total loss for words, so I said, 'Pussy.' That's when he hit me across the face, and I got this shiner. He called me all kinds of names, horrible insults like nobody should ever say to another person. 'Where's all your Christian forgiveness now?' I asked him. Instead of answering, he pushed me down to the ground and started kicking me. I'll probably have bruises up and down my legs and back by morning. He might have killed me, except this other couple that was out on the golf course saw what was going on, and the man stopped him. Doug yelled at me to give him back his ring, so I threw it into his face. The couple took me to use a pay phone because there was no way I'd go back into the country club looking like this and worrying that I'd run into Doug or that he'd told people all kinds of shit about me. I called Lonny because I figured he could get there the fastest. He was pissed like you wouldn't believe. So, anyway, he showed up with Luis. The three of us drove around until we found Doug's nice green Mercedes parked outside some bar. We drank in Lonny's truck for an hour or so, waiting for Doug to come out. Then when he does, the three of us jump out, and Lonny and Luis start beating on him. It was sort of awful, but at the same time, you know, that shit had it coming to him. The whole thing happened fast because we were worried that someone might come out of the bar or call the fuzz. They took Doug's keys to open the car door to put him inside it. Doug's nose was bloody, and his eye was all puffy. He was still trying to swing a little bit here and there. Lonny halfway lowered himself into the car so he could press his knee against Doug's chest. 'Hey, asshole,' he said. 'You owe this lady an apology.' 'She's no lady,' Doug said. Lonny punched him good in the face again. 'I'm sorry, I'm sorry, I'm sorry.' Then it was like he couldn't apologize enough, you know? 'And give her back her ring,' Lonny said. Doug started blubbering because he was near to breaking, but he shut up and handed it over when Luis flicked open his switchblade. Then we headed back to the Showstop to have a few more drinks, and Luis cooked us some breakfast."

Gigi reached her arms up to the ceiling to stretch her back. "I brought you some shrimp salad sandwiches." She pointed at a brown paper bag with a rolled top and a splotch of grease on the side that I hadn't even noticed.

I started eating while Gigi poured herself some vodka with a splash of Tab. That mixture was her morning drink, the one she liked to have at the end of a long night that lasted until sunrise, sometimes even beyond.

"It's good to have you back, Geeg."

"Don't you want to hear the rest of the story?"

Some of the filling had dripped from my sandwich. I pinched up the globs that had fallen onto the table. "There's more?"

Gigi nodded. "This is the best part. So, we're back at the Showstop. Luis is in the kitchen, frying bacon, and Lonny and I are sitting at one of the tables, drinking a little seven and seven. I thank him for everything he did, you know, because he helped me out of a tough spot. I can't help thinking about how Lonny has always been there when I needed him and how I never had to put on some act for him. I told him the ring was pretty, but I wasn't sure if I even wanted to look at it. 'Well, then give it to me,' Lonny said. So I did. Then do you know what he did? He got right down on one knee, just like Doug, except he wasn't doing it in some crowded restaurant to get attention. 'Will you marry me?' he asked. 'I know we could be happy together.' And I said, 'Yes, I know it too.' So that's what we're aiming to do."

I laughed then, a big, wide-mouthed noise. For a split second, Gigi blinked in surprise at the suddenness, the hugeness of the sound, then she joined in with me until neither of us could stop, gasping for breath, gripping our stomachs.

"Not a bad story, huh?"

"Not bad at all."

June 8, 1980
Dear Sarah,

Saul and I got married and only just returned from our honeymoon last night. Did you get our wedding invitation? I sent it not knowing if you'd come.

The ceremony had to be at the courthouse, of course, because we couldn't find a minister or a rabbi willing to marry us. The one rabbi we talked to actually called Saul a traitor to his people. My sister, Edna, wasn't much better. "I can't believe you're marrying a Jew!" she yelled at me when I called to tell her the good news.

In the end, though, she and Harold drove all the way down with the kids, which I know must have cost them a pretty penny. "Well, he's certainly not a handsome man," she told me, "but he really loves you, Ursula. I can see that plain as day."

Saul's two grown daughters, Rachel and Samantha, were there too. Rachel told Edna that her driving all the way down with the whole family was the sweetest thing. Edna likes to get credit for the stuff she does, so that certainly made her happy.

The reception was out on the patio of our beach club. We did all the decorating ourselves and spent hours stringing strands and strands of white lights. Our families were there. We invited all our friends, too, and we drank Chablis and ate shrimp and crab legs. I wish you could have been there with us.

Edna and Harold were here with the girls for almost two weeks, so we had plenty of time to visit. She told me that every once in a great while, someone might mention Jared or how you disappeared but that even in a town as small as ours, that's old news now. The house where you lived is gone, and the sheriff retired last year to go live in Arizona. Edna says, too, that Missy got married in the spring to that Johnson boy, then the two of them moved to Minnesota. They got a nice big place near his uncle, where they grow corn. I was never a big fan of Missy's, but I sure don't envy her becoming a farmer's wife.

Come visit us, Sarah. Saul would love to meet you. I don't rest easy at night wondering if I'll ever see you again.

Love,
Ursula

The Wedding

L onny and Gigi planned their wedding for the weekend before Thanksgiving, when everyone was sure to be done for the season and back in Gulfy. Gigi even managed to get word to Little Freddy living in Upstate New York, and to Chuck, who had worked the Charlie/Charlene act before I joined up with Midstate.

"I'm telling you this is some guest list," Gigi said as she jiggled Emmy on her lap. She had a green spiral notebook open in front of her at the kitchen table, next to her coffee cup from breakfast. I turned off the sewing machine to hear Gigi better.

She leaned closer to read me what was written on the paper. "So, that's Little Freddy and Chuck, and Freddy's got a woman he lives with, and it's hard to say who or what Chuck will bring. And there's Daisy and Ora Ann, who will probably come with her mama, and Ike, and then you got Lonny's parents and my dad—"

"What?" I spit a pair of straight pins from my mouth. "Your father?" As far as I knew, Gigi hadn't spoken to him since the day she'd left home at fifteen. "How did you even know how to find him?"

"Huh? Oh, that part was easy. He's still living right there in that same house, exact same phone number, so alls I had to do was call. I thought about having Jim give me away, and I felt bad, you know? I mean, me and my father never had much to say to each other, but I still never meant to go so many years without talking to him. It's just, you know, whenever I would think to call him for his birthday or Christmas, I didn't know what to tell him about what I was doing or how I was getting by. And by then, so much time had passed that it seemed too strange. So, I call him, and he answers, and he says, 'Well, hello, Jenny. How are you?' like he only just talked to me yesterday. 'Dad,' I told him, 'everybody calls me Gigi now.' Then he says, 'Is that so? I'll stick with Jenny, thanks.' Anyway, I told him I was living in Florida and that I was going to get married. He's going to drive here for the wedding to give me away."

"From Kansas?" I smoothed the hem of the white fabric on the sewing table. Gigi told me that she had dreamed of being married in a flowing gown with a beautiful lace veil that touched the floor—so I was making exactly that for her.

"Yup."

"Just like that?" Maybe long-standing, thorny issues like that got resolved with understated ease all the time.

"Yup. I told him plain that I traveled a good long while with the carnival. After all that horseshit with Doug, I'm through lying and acting like I done something wrong by earning a living and making my own way. I didn't want him to be shocked or nothing or waste his time driving, so I said, too, that there'd be a tattooed man and a fat lady and some cootch dancers, and then he interrupts to say he's going to buy himself a new jacket if that's the case."

We both laughed at that. Gigi snarfed the side of Emmy's neck to make her giggle too. "Do you think that's funny, little girl?" Gigi asked.

The two of them came over to look at what I was doing. "Your mama's making me a pretty dress." Gigi shifted Emmy to the other hip and leaned closer to touch the slippery satin material. "You know, Lo, I been thinking. You ought to do up your maid-of-honor dress in this same fabric but purple instead."

"So I can look like a giant shiny grape?"

Gigi jiggled Emmy with the rapid-fire bounces she loved. "Your mama's a grape," she sang over and over again, dancing around the room with Emmy.

"Do you really want purple?" I asked.

"Oh, come on, Lo. If I said yellow, you'd complain about looking like a giant lemon. If said red, you'd complain about looking like a giant apple. If I—"

"All right, all right, I get the picture." Of course, I ended up doing just what she wanted and even made an identical little dress for Emmy.

As it turned out, the tricky part was finding someone to marry Lonny and Gigi. She didn't want a justice of the peace because she thought that didn't have the "right feel to it," but she refused to have the ceremony performed in a church, partly because she claimed to hate all those goddamn hypocrites who had no right to look down on her and who reminded her of Doug besides, but mostly because she wouldn't entertain the thought of getting married any place other than the Showstop. Few clergymen were willing to perform a wedding ceremony in a bar, especially one with such a rough reputation.

In the end, Lonny was able to scrounge up a preacher in Tampa, a Pastor Kindheart, who had been ordained by the New Life Church and didn't give two shits about performing the ceremony in a bar. He smelled like reefer and had a beard and long, wavy hair with streaks of gray in it, bound into a ponytail at the base of his neck. He seemed like a bit of an odd choice to me, more like someone who would get beat up at the Showstop, but Gigi was plenty pleased with him.

"He changed his name to Kindheart because he says he wants his identity to send a good vibration out into the universe." Gigi shook her head at that. "He's an old hippie, and you don't see too much of that around here, but he's willing to do it for pretty cheap. Also, you know, he sort of looks like Jesus, in a way."

Jim came home a full two weeks before the ceremony. On the day of the wedding, I watched him standing in front of the full-length mirror on the back of our bedroom door. He wore a powder-blue tuxedo and bow tie with a paler blue ruffled shirt underneath because he couldn't find a purple one to match my dress. The blue was better anyway because it made the color of his eyes shimmer, brought a magnetic light to him that drew my attention again and again.

"What do you think, Lolly?" he asked, half turning from his reflection to face me where I sat on the bed. He looked clean and shiny, with the overhead light bouncing off his bald head.

I could smell the Aqua Velva aftershave from across the room and held my breath at the sudden sensation of soft wings beating inside my chest. "I think I forgot that you could look so good."

Jim came to stand in front of me and leaned down to kiss me. The feel of his lips on mine lit up my nerve endings, an effervescent yet intense tingling, the feeling of being amazed at his presence, which I hadn't experienced in a good long while and had almost forgotten.

"You look pretty nice yourself."

"I think I look like a grape."

Jim laughed. "A nice big juicy one," he said, pressing me back onto the mattress. He deposited tiny kisses along my chest above the neckline of my dress. Then he stood and helped raise me to sitting. He knelt on the floor, holding my hands in his. "You know, seeing all this wedding stuff has really got me thinking. I mean, you and me can't be married for real because I don't think I could ever get a divorce, but I was wondering if maybe you could use my last name anyway. You know, use it for real, like legally change your name. I'd like that, and it might be nice for Emmy too."

"Okay," I said, ready to be Dolores Stanton from that day forward.

Leaving Emmy with Jim, I went to help Gigi finish getting ready before the ceremony. The inside of the Showstop sparkled with a cleanliness I had never seen or even imagined possible. There were linens cloths on the tables, and sheets of pressboard had been placed across the pool table and then covered with a long tablecloth and empty chafing dishes for serving food later. The back door was propped open with a big stone. A large canopy had been set up outside with rows of folding chairs underneath it. At the end of the center aisle was a raised dais under a bulging white balloon arch that Jim and I had helped build.

I stared out the back door, marveling that Lonny had somehow managed to make the grass look impeccable and respectable when I had only ever seen it matted and strewn with old trash, vomit, and used prophylactics. Passing out back there after a night of drinking was one of the more unpleasant experiences a person could have.

"Looks nice, doesn't it?" came a voice behind me, startling me so much that I screamed and grabbed my chest. "Sorry about that. I didn't mean to scare you."

A man stood up from one of the shadowed back tables near the window. "I'm Jenny's father, Isaac," he said, holding out his hand to shake. "I'd say you must be Lola. Jenny's told me all about you."

"Hi. I guess I didn't see you sitting there."

Isaac was slight, only a few inches taller than me, and thin in the hard-worn, bony way of a man who has done manual labor for most of his life. The skin on his hand was as rough as sandpaper. He had a red, scrubbed aspect about him, dressed in what looked like a new brown polyester suit and a bolo tie with a large turquoise stone that I wouldn't have expected him to wear.

"I suppose I'm easy enough to overlook," Isaac said.

His words, innocuous though he probably meant them to be, caused a prickling sensation in my eyes. "Well, here you are now," I said. "That's the important thing. I know that Gigi—I mean Jenny—is happy to have you."

Isaac nodded in his pleasant way. His tie looked too tight, causing uncomfortable-looking pleats in the loose skin of his neck. "Jenny's upstairs. I reckon you're here to help her get ready."

Gigi met me at the upstairs door. "Dad, you sure you don't want to come up to watch TV or something?" she called down.

"No, no, you two just go on about your girl business," he answered.

"Okay." Gigi rolled her eyes. "So, did you talk to my dad?" She closed the door behind me. "Yeah," she continued without waiting for an answer, "he's a nice old guy. A little funny maybe but nice."

Gigi was wearing her ratty housecoat over her stockings and slip. "I figured I'd wait to put on the dress," she explained as she sat down next to me at the kitchen table, where I was trying to catch my breath from walking up the stairs. "Will you do my rollers for me?"

Helping Gigi set and curl her hair reminded me of how we used to help each other get ready before a show. After I combed her out, I made a small topknot and fastened the veil on it, leaving rows of long curls to hang loose down her back and around the sides of her face. "There you go," I said, staring at our reflection in the bedroom mirror. "Shit, you look really beautiful."

Gigi waved her hand at me, both of us a little surprised, I thought, at how stunning she truly was. "You know," she said in a quiet voice, "when I was a little girl, I used to dream about this day, like how you do. I always sort of thought my mother would find out somehow that I was getting married and that she'd be sitting out there in one of the pews, right at the end, so I could see her when I walked down the aisle. I can't stop thinking about it even now." Gigi stared up at the ceiling to keep her tears from dropping and ruining the lovely precision of her eyeliner and mascara. "But that's not going to happen, right? I mean, I know that's not going to happen. I'm never going to figure out why she left or where she went."

"No, I don't think that part's going to work out. You'll still be happy, though." I reached behind Gigi to pull the veil over her face.

"Yeah, you're right. You know, I tried to tell my dad I was sorry for never calling or writing him a letter, and he told me not to worry about it."

I picked up Gigi's bouquet of white and pink daisies from the dresser. The flowers were cut to size and stuck in a damp block of florist's foam inside a round plastic holder. Strands of lace dangled from the ends. "We should probably get down there."

Lonny had spaced out the two sections of chairs wide enough for me and Jim to walk side by side down the aisle. Jessup, the retired knife thrower who also played the violin by ear and never went anywhere without what he referred to as his "fiddle," played his instrument softly, the bow skimming the strings, hardly touching them, it seemed. Lonny and Reverend Kindheart, who had chosen to wear his hair loose for the occasion, actually looking quite a bit like an aging Jesus in his white robe and Birkenstock sandals, were already on the dais. Jim and I smiled as we made our way to the front, walking slowly and nodding here and there at the people we knew, which, with the exception of a few of Lonny's relatives and some of Gigi's former church friends, was everyone. Jim stood next to Lonny, while I sat on the bench that Gigi had insisted be placed next to where she would stand.

Everyone rose to their feet when Gigi and her father walked down the aisle. Jessup struck up the wedding march, and his wife, Rose, who had successfully dodged knives for some twenty-odd years, accompanied him on the trombone. A collective gasp and sigh made its way through the crowd.

Reverend Kindheart raised his hands above his head. Gigi and her father stopped before the dais. Gigi's father lifted her veil and kissed the side of her face. People patted their hearts, smiling at the sweetness of the gesture. Ora Ann, who was holding Emmy with one arm, dabbed her eyes with her free hand, crying already.

Gigi walked up to join Lonny, and Reverend Kindheart lowered his hands. It occurred to me that I had never attended a wedding, but I had seen them on television, so many of them that I could have probably recited parts of the ceremony script from memory.

"Hey, everybody, all you people, we're here to see this man and this chick get married today. Can I get a 'right on'?" Reverend Kindheart raised his fist into the air. "Right on!" he yelled.

Jim and I glanced at each other while some people shifted in their seats, confused. Gigi drew in her lips, tipping her head to the side like maybe she was going to say something. I had told her that we should do a run-through of the ceremony beforehand, but as someone who had performed cold and usually half out of her mind with booze, Gigi hadn't seen the need.

"Come on. Can you dig it, people? Can I get a 'right on'?" Reverend Kindheart raised his fist again.

Suddenly, Isaac, Gigi's father, stood up from his chair in the front row. "Right on," he said in a loud, clear voice, waving his fist in the air.

"Right on!" shouted Reverend Kindheart.

Then everyone punched the air. "Right on!" they cried with real passion.

"That's what I'm talking about here today, people. We are all here to witness a great and beautiful thing. And that's love. That's two souls telling each other, 'Hey, I could groove with you for the rest of my life.' I look around this room, and I see people who've maybe had some hard times, some bad times when life or other people didn't treat them so kindly. Or maybe someone told them, 'Hey, you don't belong' or 'You don't matter,' like you might as well be invisible."

I looked out at the assembled congregation of people, some of them freaks like Lobster Boy and Stumpy, who had no lower half. Others had unusual bodies, like Ike, Freddy, and me. Still others might have looked normal but nonetheless were unable or unwilling to make a go of it in regular society. It was indeed a hard life—being a spectacle on the one hand but being shunned and disdained on the other, with people willing to interact only under certain circumstances. A lot of the guests were nodding in agreement.

"Life can be rough, my friends. I'll tell you what, though. Maybe nobody does get a big, happy ending, but when you have love, like I see here between Lonny and Gigi and between the other lovers, friends, and family gathered here, then no matter how it all turns out, you've got a good thing going."

More nodding heads. Little Freddy whispered what looked like the word *yes*, and Jessup leaned over and kissed Rose's forehead. I glanced at Jim. He winked at me and smiled.

"So, Lonny, my man, I want to ask you straight up. Do you want to marry Gigi and be her husband? Will you give her all your love and share your whole life with her through good times and bad, when there's plenty of dough and when you're flat busted? In sickness and in health? For the rest of your lives?"

"I do," Lonny replied in a loud, strong voice.

"And what about you, Gigi? Are you ready to love Lonny the very same way?"

"Yes, yes, I am," Gigi said, her voice breaking with tears.

I felt my own eyes fill up and noticed a bunch of the other guests raise tissues and handkerchiefs to their faces.

"Far out. Let's get the rings, then."

Jim reached into the inside pocket of his tuxedo to hand them to Reverend Kindheart.

"Thanks, man," he said. He held Gigi's tiny gold band between the thumb and forefinger of one hand and Lonny's much larger one the same way with his other hand. "These rings are circles, with no beginning and no end. A symbol of love and timelessness. Lonny, give this ring to Gigi and say... You know what? Just say whatever's in your heart, man."

Lonny looked panicked at the thought of expressing his feelings in front of a crowd. "Um, well..."

Reverend Kindheart gave him the ring. "Just go ahead, man," he said.

Lonny slid the ring onto Gigi's finger. "I'm not... I'm not sure what to say here, but I've loved you for a long time, Gigi, and I love you just the way you are."

"Oh." Gigi sighed, tears running down her cheeks. For once, she didn't appear to care how they washed away her makeup. She put Lonny's ring on his finger. "Lonny, I..." she began and then choked back a sob. "I'm sorry, I don't know..."

Reverend Kindheart put his hand on her shoulder. "Take your time," he said.

Gigi nodded. "I love you, too, Lonny," she blurted in a single breath. "And... and... and..."

"Say what's in your heart."

Gigi's chest heaved with the deep breath she took. "This is the best damn day of my life."

"Right on, sister," Reverend Kindheart said, and with no prompting at all, we all put our fists in the air and yelled, "Right on!"

Reverend Kindheart raised his arms. "By the power vested in me by the State of Florida, I now pronounce you husband and wife." It was the only part of the traditional wedding script that I recognized, making me wonder if some law or rule compelled him to utter those exact words to make the marriage legal and binding.

"You may kiss the bride," he concluded.

The kiss lasted longer and went deeper than was usual at a wedding. We laughed and cheered at the sight of Lonny's restless hand sliding down Gigi's back to press her pelvis against him.

Then the two of them slowly, reluctantly separated to face the congregation. We were waiting, it seemed, for some sort of dismissal from Reverend Kindheart, a punctuation to the end of the ceremony. Gigi and Lonny exchanged glances when none was forthcoming.

"We want to thank you for coming," Gigi said. She smiled at her father. "I know it was a long trip for some of you, and we're glad to have you here."

"Well," Lonny said. "Let's get this party started. Drinks are on the house." That announcement broke the spell of uncertainty as we all filed into the Showstop. Lonny vaulted over the bar to start serving guests. Then Jim and Luis joined in to help out. Jessup stood up on a chair and struck up "Cotton-Eyed Joe" on his violin.

The party lasted until the small hours of the morning and then continued on past full daybreak, although by that point, only Lonny, Gigi, Isaac, Jim, Ora Ann, Little Freddy, and I were still drinking at the bar. Isaac seemed to have taken a particular shine to Ora Ann.

"I see a whole different life for you, Isaac," Ora Ann told him.

We danced all night while Jessup sawed on his violin. At one point, Ike played "Staying Alive" on the jukebox and danced the hustle with Daisy. We all gathered around them in a horseshoe shape and clapped. Ike, wearing a brilliant white suit and black shirt unbuttoned to his waist, dropped and did an enthralling Cossack dance, crouching impossibly close to the ground and flinging his legs to unlikely heights, while Daisy twirled around him, doing high kicks.

Little Freddy and I did a slow number. At the end of the song, I hoisted him up, and he leaned his head back so I could swing him in a graceful circle. His old lady, Norma, who had traveled with him to the wedding and was nearly three feet taller than he was, didn't care for that too much, but at some point in the evening, to my relief and probably Little Freddy's, too, she disappeared or left, and Little Freddy stayed behind.

Isaac found an old big band song on the jukebox and grabbed Gigi's hand. His bemused red-faced shyness dropped away as he propelled Gigi through one swing dance step and spin after another. At that moment, I finally saw a resemblance between the two of them in their light-footed grace and precision. Seeing them together made me miss my own father and all that he would never know about me or my life or his beautiful granddaughter, who, impossible though it seemed, managed to sleep, safe and snug, in the kitchen storeroom despite all the noise.

Isaac asked Ora Ann to dance after that. They were a less graceful pair, but they kept at it anyway until they moved together like two people who knew each other well, the type who would spend a long time together.

Jim was his most charming self the night of the wedding. He stayed close by my side the entire time, holding my hand. Jim had a certain something, a stage presence that never deserted him, a subdued liveliness that drew people's attention. He looked so handsome and decent and respectable in his wedding clothes that I felt like a quadruple-size Cinderella, and I laughed at the idea.

"Come dance with me, Lola." Jim held out his hand, and time froze for a moment on that image of him, dashing and exuberant, reaching out for me—generating the sudden sensation of being caught in a dream. I knew that I was seeing Jim at his best.

James Stanton #459621
Louisiana State Penitentiary
17544 Tunica Trace
Angola, LA 70712
June 4, 1981

Dear Lola,

I'm on the inside again.

    It's hard to explain how it all happened. One day I'm running with Sammy, and the next I'm being put in the slammer. We were in Centerville, outside of Baton Rouge. This mark, a young guy in his twenties, got in a beef with Randy, who runs the duck-pin joint, saying it was rigged and nobody could win it. Things got out of hand fast. I threw that kid off the lot. Turns out it was the sheriff's nephew. Too bad we didn't know that then, or else we would have left it alone.

    Anyway, when we were shutting down at around two a.m., the kid shows back up with a friend of his, both of them shit drunk. The two of them jump over Randy's counter to start pounding on him. I yelled for them to stop what they were doing. They ran. One of them got away, but the other guy, the one who started all the trouble, was pretty slow and pudgy. I had no trouble catching up with him to beat him down into the ground. He was a real mess. Then Randy ran over and took a few swipes at him too.

    We put him in the truck to drive him back into town. He was doing all right, I guess, still awake enough that we could hear him mumbling something. Randy kept taking these cheap shots until I told him to knock it off.

    It was a warm night, so we left him on the lawn of the Baptist church, figuring he'd either sober up and make his own way home, or since the next day was Sunday, one of the good church folks would find him and help him out in the morning.

    He died, though. I don't know why or how. We got raided the next morning. The fat kid's friend fingered me and Randy. Then Randy turned on me to save his own punk ass. Because it was the sheriff's nephew, the arrest, the trial, and Randy's bullshit confession—the whole thing was over in about two weeks. With my record, they gave me twenty years. That prick, Randy, only got five. If that snitch moth-

erfucker ever shows up around Gulfy or crosses your path, you do me a favor and make him pay for what he did to me and to you and Emmy too.

I should have listened to you, Lolly, and not gone back out on the road. I'm fifty-two. Chances are that I'll die in prison just like my father.

No matter what happens, promise me you'll never bring Emmy here to visit. No kid should ever have to see their father in a place like this. If you want, you can forget about me too. I wouldn't blame you for it or think you're a bad person.

The only thing that keeps me going from day to day is to think of you and Emmy in that pretty little house, living the sweet life with good food on the table. I'm just sorry I won't be there to see it.

Stay safe, and take good care of Emmy and of yourself too. I love you more than you know.

Jim

Mrs. Schendel

A fter Jim got locked up, I spent the next two years writing letters
and making telephone calls, doing everything I could think of
to secure his freedom, to release him from suffering the worst thing
he could have imagined. It was a long drive to Angola, but I visited
Jim as often as I could. I brought cookies and brownies and bright,
color photographs of Emmy—walking, talking, laughing, growing
up without a father.

Jim had been sent to prison so quickly that part of me thought
there had to be some rapid way to reverse the process. I was convinced, at least in the beginning, that I had only to find the right angle, and then Jim could be free again.

As it turned out, all the phone calls and letters in the world from
someone like me weren't going to make some judge or prosecutor
change their minds about someone like Jim. Living in Gulfy, having friends like I did, running my business, living what I considered
a normal life, I had forgotten or had allowed myself to forget that
we were invisible to people like that. The way the outside world, the
marks, viewed us was one part of the story I couldn't change.

As I struggled to adjust to my new circumstances, my mind
turned to the many tasks I had left unattended in my single-minded
obsession to get Jim out of prison. I thought of the letters I had let
go unanswered and began to crave the one piece of my life that it was
in my power to have. I wanted my mother.

Mrs. Schendel's voice when she answered the telephone was exactly as I remembered it. I was twenty-five years old and hadn't writ-

ten to her in two years or spoken to her in almost eight, so there was a great deal for me to apologize for, but I was determined not to let the time lapse compound, like Gigi had with her father.

"I'm sorry I didn't call sooner. I'm really, really sorry," I blubbered. She forgave me, of course, cutting short my apologies to ask me questions about what was really happening in my life. I confessed that the whole story of living in New York City had been a lie, an invention to distract people from my actual whereabouts with the carnival, working in the sideshow, just as Missy had suspected. I told her that people knew me as Lola Stanton now, part stage and part married name. I described Jim as my husband and our marriage as an informal sort of arrangement. We even talked about my document business, the profitability of it and the independence of having money with no boss looking over your shoulder.

My worst regret, of course, the hardest one to mention, was that Emmy had been alive for nearly three years before Mrs. Schendel even knew of her existence.

"You have a daughter?" Mrs. Schendel asked. The surprise and delight in her voice mixed with a crisp edge of anger that I would keep such information from her.

I promised to bring stacks of pictures, hundreds of them, of every moment of Emmy's life from the moment she was born. I babbled on, desperate to wipe away her disapproval, to have my new enthusiasm erase my former reticence.

"Okay, okay," Mrs. Schendel relented. "I can't wait to see them all. Oh, and I'll have to get her a little present. What do you think her favorite color is?"

"Purple."

The air-conditioned interior of the Breeze Palm Restaurant felt shady and cool after trudging across the shimmering parking lot, holding Emmy's hand. Indigo spots, remnants of St. Pete's everlasting sunshine, flashed behind my eyes when I blinked. I suppose I was easy enough to identify—certainly no amount of clothes or makeup or hair changes could obscure a five-hundred-pound body, which was a lucky thing, too, because I would never have recognized Mrs. Schendel if she hadn't spotted me first.

She had been sitting out on the restaurant's back patio with a hunched, white-haired man. She waved her hand high above her head when she saw us step inside the restaurant and walked toward us, gaining speed as she got closer until she was almost jogging. The man, who must have been Saul, stood up after her, taking the time to push her chair back under the table.

The dark, stringy hair Mrs. Schendel had always worn woven into a lank bun at the nape of her neck had been replaced with a short, springy haircut and frosty highlights. She had on blue eye shadow and coral lipstick, too, and wore orange Bermuda shorts and a sleeveless cotton blouse with tiny oranges and green leaves on an ivory background. Many of the other patrons eating their lunches were around the same age as Mrs. Schendel, but most of them seemed old and dumpy compared to her. She had retained her slim figure and good posture. Her movements were freer, her body somehow more elastic and graceful, and finally, she was the best-looking woman in the room.

"Sarah, my God, is that you?" Mrs. Schendel squeezed me with such strength that I couldn't keep myself from crying. While her appearance might have changed, her scent remained the same. Shalimar and cigarette smoke lined with something plainer, more basic and less easy to detect, a wholesome goodness reminiscent of baked bread. Even in the land of red-and-orange dappled sunshine, she smelled like a warm kitchen on a cold day. Her embrace was the same relief and rush of heat you felt stepping inside from bitter winter weather, your cheeks staining with blood at the suddenness of the sensation.

I pulled back from her. "You look wonderful," I said.

Mrs. Schendel gripped the tops of my arms to study my face. "I look old," she said. "You're beautiful, though." Hearing those words when I had many memories of Mrs. Schendel nagging me to lose weight and think of the future or of her praising the inner me she divorced from my big body was like a cool, healing balm on a wound I didn't know I still possessed.

I did in fact look very different from when she had last seen me. My hair had caramel streaks. I did my makeup every day, not as heavy as when I was onstage with the floodlights washing out my skin, but the overall effect was certainly more dramatic than subtle. I drew dark wings around my eyes and used wine-colored lipstick. In fact, if I compared the image of Mrs. Schendel and me before I left for the carnival against what we looked like on that day at the Breeze Palm, it was as if we had burst free from a drab sepia photograph and were now living in full color.

Saul reached his hand over Mrs. Schendel to tap me on the shoulder. "I'm Saul, and you must be Sarah." He bent down to look at Emmy, who had remained glued to my leg in all the confusion and noise. "And who do we have here?" he asked, leaning his face close to Emmy's until she laughed.

I picked up Emmy and kissed the soft skin of her cheek. "This is Emmy."

"Well," Mrs. Schendel said, "if you aren't just the cutest thing, then I don't know what." She smoothed Emmy's silky blond curls.

"Emmy, say 'hi' to Grandma."

My use of the word *Grandma* caused Mrs. Schendel to burst into sudden tears. Emmy, who normally wouldn't accept being held by a stranger, went without complaint into her arms.

"Hello there, precious plum," Mrs. Schendel whispered into Emmy's hair.

Some of the other diners had stopped eating to watch our reunion. One woman in particular made no pretense of doing anything other than staring outright at my bulk, so I looked straight back at her.

Mrs. Schendel turned her head to see what had caught my attention. "Hey, you," she said. "Mind your own business, and eat your lunch."

We sat at a table out on the back patio under the shade of an umbrella. Mrs. Schendel took a pair of big round sunglasses with bright-white plastic frames from her straw purse. "This place has the best boiled shrimp."

"They get them right out of the Gulf," Saul said.

He was holding Mrs. Schendel's hand, their interlaced fingers resting on the glass tabletop—something that she and my father would have never dared do in public, something that she would not have done with her first husband either. Never in any of the many times Mrs. Schendel had convinced me to attend church with her and Mr. Schendel or when I'd seen them together at her house had I ever noticed any gesture of affection between them, certainly nothing as visible and casual as the way she and Saul touched each other. I smiled, happy that she had this love, that she didn't have to hide herself, to be invisible, any longer.

Mrs. Schendel drew her chair closer to mine so we could look together at the thick stack of photographs I had brought.

"I had two sets made so you could keep one," I said. As promised, there were dozens of pictures of Emmy, who sat on my lap, holding the new purple teddy bear Mrs. Schendel had given her.

"See that, Ursula? Now, you'll have something to show the old biddies," Saul said.

Mrs. Schendel pushed his arm. "You go on, you. It's true, though. All anybody ever talks about around here is their grandchildren."

There were photographs of other people too. "This is my best friend, Gigi," I said. "She used to work as a sword swallower. And here's one of Gigi's father, Isaac, and our other friend, Ora Ann. She's a fortune teller." I smiled at the image of the two of them. "They met at Gigi's wedding and then ended up getting married themselves. He used to be a farmer, but now he takes people out on a fishing charter, and Ora Ann runs Miss Oracle's Parlor out on Highway 41."

"Well, I don't think I've ever met anyone like that," Mrs. Schendel said.

"You can meet all of them when you come visit," I said. "And this is my house."

Mrs. Schendel held the photograph of my neat little white house closer to her face. "Is that hibiscus you've got growing in the back there?"

I nodded. "And here's Jim and Emmy." It was one of the last shots I had of Jim as a free man. He was standing in the living room, holding baby Emmy high up in the air, the two of them laughing. Tears fell from my eyes, dropped onto Emmy's head. She slapped her scalp, twisting on my lap to see what was the matter. I half expected Mrs. Schendel to tell me not to worry, that Jim would somehow be home in no time. Her silence devoured the childlike hope that I hadn't even known I had retained that my mother, Mrs. Schendel, could show up and make everything better.

"Emmy," she said. "This picture belongs to you, honey. Maybe your mommy can get you a pretty frame to hang it in your bedroom."

Saul cleared his throat. "You know, Sarah, if you don't like shrimp, they also do a very nice chicken salad here."

The shrimp were delicious, big pink ones cooked to perfection. While we ate, Saul talked about the dry-cleaning business he had owned for many years in Philadelphia before retiring to Florida. One of his adult daughters lived in Seattle and the other in Boston. "It's hard sometimes because they're so busy. I just wish they lived closer."

Mrs. Schendel nodded. "Edna visits every winter. Harold doesn't like making the trip, so she comes by herself. We go out to restaurants and sit on the beach. I bet it's the most fun we've ever had with each other." She reached over to examine the line of stitches along the sleeve of my blouse. "Did you make this?"

"I did."

"Not too bad," Mrs. Schendel said. "The stuff you find on a store rack is all junk anyway. Maybe I should get you to come work for me."

We all laughed while Emmy slid from her chair down under the table. "Sit up here, Emmy." I waved one of the coloring books I had brought and felt around the tabletop to gather up her crayons.

"Ah, we're too boring for her," Saul said. "Emmy, why don't we go look for shells and leave your mommy and grandma here to talk?"

"You're sure you don't mind?" I asked Saul, who was already reaching down to grab Emmy's hand.

Emmy looked up at me from under the table and then at Saul as if to assess his suitability as a playmate. She smiled as if to say she found him acceptable.

The back patio of the restaurant was directly on the beach, so I took off Emmy's shoes. She accepted Saul's hand and ran with him to the sand. As I watched them go, I wondered if Mrs. Schendel would take advantage of their absence to ask me at last any questions she might have kept preserved in the cellar of her mind about Jared and how he'd died. She turned in her chair to watch Saul and Emmy, saying nothing, though.

The day was hot. Saul shucked his pale-blue polo shirt, showing off the astounding tufts of white hair on his upper body. Emmy picked up something from the ground and gave it to him. He nodded solemnly at the object in his hand while Emmy laughed.

Mrs. Schendel smiled. "He's a good man. The best I've ever known. I mean... not that your father..."

"No, don't worry. I can see how this is different. I'm happy for you. I really am."

Mrs. Schendel patted my hand. "Remember how we used to sit around the kitchen table at your old house after your father died? You would drink tea, and I would have coffee. We'd have to keep our eye on the clock to keep track of when Jared would get home. I don't even remember what exactly we talked about. I was probably telling you to scrub the floors and stop eating cookies and whatever else I always nagged you about."

Mrs. Schendel's incidental mention of Jared felt like a sudden opening, the only opportunity I might have to tell her about the night he died. The moment, brief and unstable, was a doorway that might vanish in an instant.

I began talking, building speed with each word. "Yeah. About Jared. That night, you know? It all happened so fast, and the thing is..."

Mrs. Schendel squeezed my hand rather hard. "Listen to me, honey. Jared is dead. And that is really very sad. It's tragic, actually, because he was a young man who could have lived for a long time yet. And he could have had many experiences that might have changed him, maybe for better, maybe for worse. We'll never know. His opportunities are gone. Don't you waste any of yours, though, on regret. You know, I used to be afraid for you, scared that you'd never get to experience anything in your life. I even told your father at the time that he was wrong to pull you out of school, but I wasn't your mother, so I couldn't stop him. And here you are, so confident and independent. You've got a nice house, friends, a husband, a good business so you can support your family, and that beautiful, beautiful little girl."

Mrs. Schendel's advice sounded remarkably similar to Jim telling me that sleepless nights worrying about the past would keep me from enjoying the life I had built. Jared's death was tragic. She was right about that, and I could mourn him as my brother and as the friend he might have become.

Mrs. Schendel kissed my forehead. "I'm so proud of you."

Mrs. Schendel's praise and her conviction that I had a right to move forward no matter what had happened in the past were like the diaphanous blue of the sky, instilling a sense of perfect symmetry in me. As if after so many years apart, the two of us had completed a cycle, and now we could spend the next part of our lives together.

We were both quiet for a moment as we watched Saul and Emmy playing on the beach and, beyond them, the tide washing onto the shore. Emmy stood in front of Saul, swished her hips, and turned in a circle.

"She's quite the little dancer." Mrs. Schendel laughed when Saul tried to imitate Emmy's dance steps.

"I used to do a similar sort of move when I was on the stage," I said. "Toward the end of my act, I'd do a half spin and then a shuffle hop."

"Is that right?" Mrs. Schendel took off her sunglasses. She leaned her head back for the light to shine fully on her face. "It's so nice and sunny here."

"It sure is," I said, thinking of the graceful moves Emmy had learned from me and remembering the hot glow of the footlights.

I twirl. I step. I raise my arms over my head, reaching as high as I can, and then bend forward to the crowd as I take my bow.

Epilogue

M any things stayed the same in my life. Gigi and I remained friends, and she and Lonny continued to be fixtures at the Showstop, even after their second-oldest son took over the business. The look of the place changed, though, as Gulf Town became less a haven for carnies and more a stop for tourists. My picture, however, hangs on the wall to this day.

Mrs. Schendel also developed a fondness for the Showstop. Blessed with indefatigable good health, she lived until just past her one hundredth birthday. In that time, she became more of what she had always been. A good mother and a giver of love and guidance. Her marriage to Saul, that late-to-the-game surrogate grandfather and father even, provided Emmy all she could ever need in the form of role models for love and devotion.

Despite the setbacks and glacial pace of my progress, I continued my efforts to get Jim out of prison. At one point, I estimated that I had read his trial transcript and case file from start to finish more than sixty times. Thirteen years after he was incarcerated, Jim was granted a new trial on the basis that he had had inadequate assistance of counsel the first time. His new lawyer, a smart man and a good friend, was able to get him acquitted on the argument that no one had ever pinpointed the victim's exact cause of death.

Though I had lovers and even some great loves in Jim's absence, few things have brought me such joy as seeing him set free. After his release, Jim worked with Isaac, running fishing charters. Jim talked often about how he liked being out on the water, away from the sight of land, nothing but sea and sky. He was able to breathe out there, he told me.

Jim remained a free man for the rest of his life.

I think that watching me research Jim's case inspired Emmy to go to law school. She was the best of both Jim and me, and she grew into a beautiful, smart, ambitious woman. Despite being normal-looking and -acting enough to blend in anywhere, she nonetheless found her niche working with the poor, the inept, the crazies, and the type of sharp tricksters she had known all her life.

For a long time, Gigi and I joked about how nice it would be for Emmy to marry Gigi's oldest son. A month before Emmy graduated from law school, however, she introduced us to Diane, the woman who would eventually become her wife and who was like a second daughter to Jim and me.

My own career also changed many times over the years as well. When the risks became too high, I moved on from the document business. I tried my hand in various ventures like disability and insurance claims and in roles such as show promoter, advice columnist, and most recently, memoirist. Though I do still find it hard to sleep at night sometimes, I have done what I could to follow Mrs. Schendel's advice and not waste my opportunities.

The names of the people and places have been changed, but the story remains the same, allowing me at last the satisfaction of setting down the burden of unshared secrets that I have carried for so long.

Acknowledgments

First and foremost, thanks to my husband, Bill, for believing in me and helping to create the time and space I needed to write this novel. Thank you as well to my daughters, Audrey and Julia, for being equal parts inspiration and distraction and for never letting me forget the importance of living in the present.

I am forever grateful to Christina Keller, Emmy Nicklin, Julia Rocchi, and Jennifer Ryan, the members of my writing group. These fabulous writers and friends read and reread many versions of this manuscript, and each time, they offered fresh insights and encouragement. Without them, this work truly would not have been possible.

I had the encouragement of many other friends and family members, who shared their excitement about this book and kept me enthusiastic and hopeful about the work I was doing. Thank you, in particular, to Amy Dacey for being an early reader and to Mary Kubisch for being the last reader before I submitted this manuscript for publication.

The characters in this book first came to life during the MA program I attended at Johns Hopkins University, where the support and guidance of my fellow students and professors helped me become a better and more prolific writer.

I would also like to thank Lynn McNamee at Red Adept Publishing for taking a chance on this book and the wonderful editors there who helped me shape it into a better and stronger story.

Last but never least, thanks to the readers of this published novel. I very much appreciate the opportunity to share these characters and their world with you.

About the Author

Barbara Boehm Miller likes to write about secret societies and marginalized people and to create desperate and unsavory characters who, nonetheless, appeal to readers. She earned a Master of Arts in writing from Johns Hopkins University and has had several short fiction pieces published in literary journals.

Barbara has also worked for many years as a translator of Romance languages into English and has published a series of translations, primarily in the field of children's rights. She has lived in Costa Rica, France, Mexico, and Spain and, at present, serves as a senior diplomatic translator for the U.S. Department of State.

When not writing, reading, or working, Barbara likes to spend time with her inspiring husband and twin daughters, and her sweet brown dog.

Read more at barbaraboehmmiller.com.

Unlocking New Worlds

About the Publisher

Dear Reader,

We hope you enjoyed this book. Please consider leaving a review on your favorite book site.

Visit https://RedAdeptPublishing.com to see our entire catalogue.

Check out our app for short stories, articles, and interviews. You'll also be notified of future releases and special sales.

Made in the USA
Columbia, SC
10 February 2025

53645528R00186